PRAISE FOR
APHOTIC LOVE

"Blurring the lines between dark fantasy and the dark reality of love and loss and life in between, *Aphotic Love* truly takes the reader to the depths of romance with raw short stories and vulnerable poetry that will invite you into the angst and keep you asking: how will the Ever After end? Will it be ephemeral or eternal? And who—or what—will fill that metaphorical Jar of Hearts?"

—Brittany Eden
(Author of *Hearts* and *Wishes*)

"This book had such a gorgeous variety of fantasy worlds! Dragon's lairs, underworlds, ice countries, anything your heart could wish for! It's such a beautiful collection, sure to make you fall in love."

—Bethany Meyer
(Author of *Robbing Centaurs and Other Bad Ideas*)

APHOTIC LOVE

compiled by effie joe stock

an anthology on the depths of romance

DRAGON BONE
PUBLISHING™

To all those who've loved and lost,
And to those who loved most deeply.

TRIGGER WARNINGS:

Some of the stories or poetry in this collection may contain sensitive topics such as suicide, necromancy, fantasy magic and violence, stalking, murder, child/infant death, emotional/psychological abuse, some psychological horror.

Suicide/Suicidal Tendencies:
My Life is Yours
Where Rain May Fall
Only Yours
Nothing More Than Death

CONTENTS

Never Meant to Be....................*173*

A Crime to Love *263*

Anthology on the Depths of Romance

APHOTIC LOVE

Featuring Works By

Adella Quick / AJ Skelly / Annie Kay. / Anna Augustine / Anne J. Hill / Ariel Choate / Beka Gremikova / Betsy Smith / Cassandra Hamm / Cerynn McCain / D.A. Randall / Effie Joe Stock / Emily Anne / Everly Haywood / H.A Pruitt / Hannah Carter / Jessica Smith / Jessika Glover / Joanna White / Julia Skinner / Kaitlyn Emery / Katie Marie / Katrina Nappi / Levi Mitchell / Lorelei Jensen / Mariella Taylor / Moriah Jestus / Nathaniel Luscombe / Nobel Shut Chan / Piper L. White / Sarah Elliott / Savannah Jezowski / Sera Amoroso / Zimri A.Z. Zoran

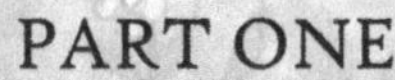

PART ONE

A Love More Than Love

THE PRICE TO TRULY LIVE
Effie Joe Stock

Immortality—the feat no human could achieve, though many would die for—a privilege reserved for the gods.

"And you would give it away as if it were a shell for a child's necklace?" A man with eyes more golden than the sun and bones painted on skin blacker than night stared disbelieving at the man and woman standing before him.

The woman's piercing blue gaze met the black of her husband's. Together, they nodded. "There is nothing left for us to do but live ... truly live." The man spoke softly as if his words would shatter some sort of glass workmanship that hung in the air. His grip on his wife's hand tightened, their fingers entwining.

"And this ..."—the dark-skinned man extended his hand out to the heavens where a million stars twinkled back—"this existence is not living?"

The woman shook her head, and her white hair spilled over her shoulders like liquid moonlight. A laugh clear as starlight left her lips. "No, Death. It is not. You cannot live if you cannot die."

Her husband nodded, his dark eyes sparkling with devotion as he gazed at his wife. "She is right. Since the dawn of time, we have kept watch over the earth. We have pulled the expanse of the heavens over its surface in the night and drawn it back in the morning. And every day I rise to chase after her across the sky, never reaching, never touching, just wishing, and chasing, and wondering."

"What of the humans?" The man's hand tightened on the scythe in his hand as he turned to face the planet called Earth.

The smile faded off the woman's face, replaced with a sad frown. "They no longer have need of us. They worship the new sky gods—Gravity, and Light, and Time. Their suns and stars and moons no longer need us to drive their fiery chariots across the sky. Our time has passed."

"If you give this away, you cannot take it back."

"We don't want it back," they spoke in unison.

"And I cannot make you happy or beautiful."

"We do not need those either. We will make them for ourselves, just as the humans do." The woman's smile returned, shining like a waning moon.

"We will have each other,"—the golden man nodded—"and that will be enough."

"There cannot be true happiness without pain. We have existed outside of suffering, and therefore outside of true joy."

Death clutched his scythe closer to him, a crease furrowing his brow as he hesitated. "Many would die for what you freely give."

"Then let us die for it as well."

With one last breath, one last plea in his eyes, Death nodded and extended his skeletal hand. "Take the other's hand in yours."

The man and woman's eyes sparkled as they clasped their fingers. Her dark skin met his golden hands, and somewhere between shone all the stars of the universe. Their eyes gazed deeply into each other as if they were really seeing each other for the first time ... and the last.

"I will watch you." Tears formed a lump in Death's throat. "I will watch you grow, learn, cry, suffer, fear, dream, live, and die. And I swear by my scythe you will not see me until you have given your last bit of life freely. Now go, and live."

They didn't spare him a second glance as his blade tore through their ethereal bodies.

Their glory, beauty, and immortality shattered before him like glass, and, just like wind through the clouds, they were gone.

And so he watched and waited like he promised.

He heard the screaming cries of babies, the laughter of children, the calling of parents and their tears and shouts, and he watched and waited.

And then, when the fog drifted off the land and the sun shone through the clouds, he saw them.

They were so young, still only babes of children, and their striking characteristics were gone, replaced with common, uninteresting skin and hair colors, but he would recognize his golden hair and her blue eyes across all ages and lives. Nothing could replace what shone deep inside them. They were children, yes, but their love burned brighter than the sun, moon, and stars they had once commanded ever radiated. There was no mistaking them.

The little boy's eyes shining like the sun he had once been, he placed a small kiss to the little girl's cheek, and she squealed with delight. They were too young to truly remember anything they had shared before they were born, but, deep down, they felt that burning love which could never be quenched. They would never forget it.

The slightest smile graced Death's lips, and he settled back to watch and wait.

Together, the boy and girl grew and changed. One of their families moved away. They attended different schools and made different friends. But every night they stayed up late into the early morning sunrise, whispering secret things to the starry sky.

The winds of time shifted, and they met again at college. The moment their eyes met, it was as if they had never been away. The man swooped her up into his arms and kissed her cheek again, her clear laughter ringing as bright as the noonday bells around them, and before Death knew it, the bells were wedding bells celebrating their earthly union.

Never had he seen such bright and joyful faces. It was then he began to learn what they had been chasing after all that time.

Many times throughout their lives brought Death dangerously close to them. All he had to do was extend his hand and take one away, but he refused, remembering his promise. Each time that he did, each time he had breathed on one, his hand tight around his scythe, the man and woman's love for each other had only grown, as if somehow, the inevitability and the closeness of Death could make each other all the dearer to the other.

So time turned and passed. They struggled and lived through a war. Together, they had children, and they in turn, had children of their own, and the light of the love of gods burned brightly in all of them. The man and woman fought, feared, cried, loved, laughed, and lived.

And, one day, when they sat in each other's arms on a couch in their small home, it was time for them to die.

Quietly, softly, Death slipped through the door, making sure to shut it behind him. He cloaked himself in a human form and hid his scythe under his cloak.

It took a moment for their old, dim eyes to see the man standing before them, but when they did, they were not afraid. Their faces lit up as if seeing an old friend.

"So, you have finally come. Welcome," the man said, and the woman greeted the same.

"Yes, I have come. I watched and I waited, and I learned many things. Did you find what you were chasing after?"

The man pushed the grey hair out of his wife's star-blue eyes; she wrapped her dark arms around his shrunken, old body and stared into the sparkling golden eyes that looked down at her with nothing but pure love.

"Yes," they said together and then laughed, "I believe we did."

Death smiled sadly, but this time as he pulled out his scythe, he felt no sorrow nor regret.

"Then I will take what you give freely." He raised his blade, and just before he brought it down, the man planted a firm kiss to his wife's cheek one last time, and one last time, her moonlit smile lit her face.

The blade pierced the air and tore through them, taking their lives and leaving them silent and still in each other's arms, smiles across their faces and all the light of the sun, moon, and stars shining in the memories and love they left behind.

THE SEA'S BELOVED
Mariella Taylor

Rikkana is born, as all creatures are—formed of light and breath and earth. And, as all young maidens do, she grows in grace and beauty in a village by the sea. Each day, she bows her body and places her offerings before the statues of the Four Brothers.

She leaves the small flame of her candle to die out among the others at the feet of the golden statue of Light. She leaves the kiss of her lips against the white alabaster fingers of Brother Breath. For Brother Earth, she brings the fruit of her labor, small leaves or fruits or odds and ends from her garden and prays beneath his bronze shadow the prayer she was taught from birth— "may the Brothers grant her a long and happy life beneath the blessing of their gaze"—before they will deliver her to the fourth.

It has been said that Brother Sea knows all and holds all. He consumes the living and drives out their breath, drags them down into unfathomable depths and empty oblivion to Rest. Nothing may appease him; no one may forgo his choosing.

Wives and mothers leave their fearful offerings at the stone feet of Brother Sea. Gifts of hope and penance, that while their men sail upon his waters, the fourth Brother will leave them in peace. They offer him anything, everything—food, cloth, riches, even bones or bits of fish and shells they have hunted from his shores—for no one knows the gift that will kindle the heart of the sea.

No one but Rikkana.

Rikkana recalls days as a child, sitting in the sand, watching the village women dig for clams along the beach. Their sticks dug deep gouges in the sand on Brother Earth's surface, Brother Light kissing them away when Brother Sea's tides wash ashore. She recalls her mother's stooped body beneath the weight of the basket strapped to her back, the musky scent of death rising from its contents.

Her hands were small then, her tiny limbs too weak to hold a basket of her own—though that time would come soon enough. But most of all, when Rikkana is wrapped in the warm embrace of those memories, she remembers the ripples on the surface of the water, the ones that no one else could see.

Like glass they were—fractured images of light and dark, forming a watery, grim face—a face that has watched over her from the moment her parents brought her to the sea, six days after her birth to sprinkle her with the salt of sea and set sail their pyres of offerings, praying their protections and charms over her tiny soul. Grim features at first, wary and halting. Sharp edges that no man nor child can fathom. But when her mother calls to her to return home, Rikkana smiles at that face and waves. And in the days that come, she finds that Brother Sea cracks open his maw and smiles back, his slippery waves kissing her ankles as he rushes in to mark the evening.

Now, she is older, and she holds a basket of her own. Brother Sea's fingers trace the lines of her legs, and his salty touch presses like stinging kisses along the length of them. The other women dare not voice their jealousy when his gifts wash up at her feet, but they are appeased when she digs for the clams alongside them, digs until her hands split raw and shaking. And at the day's end, when her work is done, they watch with sharp, cold eyes and whisper behind their bleeding, bandaged hands. "What kind of magic is this?" they ask each other. "That the sea has become enraptured by a woman."

"They call me a witch," Rikkana tells him, her voice low, vanishing beneath the crashing of his waves. She seats herself on the edge of that cliff, on the stone they cut his statue from. The jagged edges smoothed by time and salt curve in to hold her as she sinks her feet into the sand. When she closes her eyes and feels the spray of him against her flesh, Rikkana wonders if her prayers and offerings are for naught. She wonders some days if she truly desires the long life for which they all ask.

She opens her eyes to see him come, as Brother Light sinks into his horizons. The man-like shape of him builds in the foaming waters. His face cracks with easy smiles, and she imagines the ache in his arms and his breast is the same as hers when he cannot hold her.

Rikkana has never left offerings at the feet at that stone statue, that single-tailed likeness of the Fourth Brother. But here, in this place, amidst the stone from which he was carved, at the heart of the shrine which they have built together, she leaves him her offerings. She cannot feel his arms around her, cannot feel his kiss on her lips or place her own over his heart, but when she opens her mouth to pour her secrets out into his waiting ears, she imagines the beat of his salt-infested heart.

The Fourth Brother has courted her the way the men have courted for centuries, traditions tried and ageless. Four gifts, four offerings, four choices. He courts her with gifts and music and all the love he knows how to give her. He washes food up at her feet—in the form of small fishes with their glittering scales, crabs with their twisted shells, and oysters with their secret treasures. He grants her freedom, in his own way—in the form of his ear, in the form of his patience, in the form of stolen touches. And when she turns her face into the stinging fingers that brush her cheeks, turns her eyes upon him to give him all the warmth she feels in her heart, Rikkana can feel the dark longing in him.

He bequeaths her rings, thousands upon thousands of them, gathered upon his long walks along the ocean floor. Simple bands, rusted with time, encrusted with the ocean's life, bejeweled with his love. One to mark each count his heart beats while he waits there for her. He places them in her hands, at her feet, marking each one with more kisses on her cheeks, her neck, her ankles. Though she has never felt the warm grip of him around her, she begins to leave her prayers at the feet of the other Brothers in her mornings— prayers in the shape of him.

He has courted her, the way the men have courted for centuries, and yet—there is one thing even the feared Fourth Brother cannot give her. It is the way of man, to give a woman the love of his heart and the pillow of it beneath her head. To give her the strength of his body and the hope of love and long life for many future generations. A long life together—

before their bodies will be fed at death into the grip of Brother Sea.

But this gift, this fourth one, is a gift her beloved cannot give her—for he cannot leave the water, and beneath it she will not breathe.

Instead, he whispers in her ear a secret, a name. The name laid upon him by his own father millennia ago. The name she offers when her mother asks after the man she wishes to be her husband.

Anapos.

He may not give her his heart, and he may not give her his shelter, his strength, but Brother Sea will give her his tenderness and his secrets if only she will grant him her patience and her faithfulness.

He waits, he tells her, beneath the water for the day she will come to him. He waits, he tells her, and he builds her a monument of stone—a memorial for her death that even the gods themselves would envy. He waits, he promises, kissing her ankles as Rikkana trudges back to the village with tears on her face and screaming in her chest. She loves him, the sea, her Anapos, so deeply—so why can she not have him? Why must she be born a human, born of light and breath and earth, unable to even hold his hand?

As she sinks into her bed and weeps, she pretends not to hear her mother's anxious murmuring. Fervent prayers for her protection certainly—from the sea, from the village, from herself. All these prayers Rikkana watches her lips murmur as her father cocoons his wife against his chest. Her mother falls asleep to the beat of a strong heart beneath her ear, while her daughter strains her ears for the labored pounding of the seas on the cliff walls. Oh, to be so lucky. Oh, to have such hope.

Days and weeks and months have passed when she leaves the idol's courtyard with sea-cracked lips and a heavy heart. The Four Brothers have not heard her prayers, she thinks. They have not felt the love, the desperate hopes and whispered dreams she pours out at their feet, though her tears have stained their statues.

She stumbles out from the courtyard into a wasteland of angry faces. And she knows, dear gods, she *knows*. When the men come up those steps for her, she sinks to her knees, Brother Breath drying the tears that stain their tracks upon her face. Laughter comes then, bright and brilliant as Brother Light when he breaks over the morning horizons. She looks up into her father's face as he pityingly binds her hands, while others bind her feet.

When her father carries her down the path, followed by that mob of hissing villains, angry whispers of "witchling," she rests her head on his shoulder and smiles when Brother Earth catches his sandy essence in her curls. And she has hope, so much hope. So much faith that maybe, perhaps, there is life somewhere beyond this.

They take her there—to the shrine Anapos built for her, to the place she sat and whispered all her secrets, to that place where all his gifts to her are buried—waiting faithfully. Her father stands with her, on that precipice, while another man adds the millstone to her feet. The weight of it sinking to the sand, holding her there in that moment, sets her heart free, free, free. Simple, fool, witch, they'll call her, returned to the depths and the devil, they'll say. But gods, she can't stop— she can't stop smiling, tearful dripping thing that it is.

"I am sorry," her father whispers, pressing a rough kiss

against the top of her head. Rikkana gazes over the cliff edge, into the fractured, seething gaze of her beloved. Watches him rage beneath the surface of the water, all snarling foam and cracking waves against the cliffside.

"Don't be," she whispers back to her father. "They cannot hurt me any longer."

Then, she is falling. Brother Breath's arms skim along her body, slowing her descent. Brother Light and Brother Earth whispering their goodbyes into her ears, and then, then the cold. Icy, shocking cold wrapping tight around her lungs. Brother Breath's essence pulling bubbles from her body as she sinks so, so fast into blackness.

And then it separates, gathers into a face—his face—and strong, supportive arms, skin colored in deep blues and greys and rage. There is no smile when he greets her; she gives up her last breaths to lay her fingers against his cheek, feel the solid plains of him beneath her hand, and whisper his name: "Anapos."

She feels them.

She feels them around her, in her, with her—even in death. She feels Brother Breath through the gills ruffling against her neck, feels his resurrecting kiss upon her forehead. She feels Brother Light gazing down at her through the murky waters, gifting her his smile. She feels Brother Earth's hands upon her legs, cocooning them in silt and mud, murmuring his charms until all that remains are smooth fins and glittering scales. And she feels the cut of a knife against her chest, as her beloved rips out her broken, dying heart and replaces it with his own. A heart that is finally, *finally* hers.

When she opens her eyes, it is to a new dawn, a new age. An age where Brother Sea spares none but his own and snaps all men in his teeth. Her village has been washed away, her people's bodies buried in mounds of earth as far as the eye can see, and she rests there in her beloved's arms, her cheek against his chest. She smiles at the Four Brothers and thanks them in her heart of hearts for their gifts.

Brother Sea sits on his throne, a throne built of stone and salt and bone, his darling queen held in his arms, her head against the empty place in his chest. When she raises her head to look up at him with those emerald eyes that he has so deeply missed, he places his kiss upon her lips and revels in the feel of her—awake and alive and *his*.

He smiles then, threading his fingers through her hair and whispers, "Welcome, my queen."

THE PRICE OF ASHES
Zimri A.Z. Zoran

"**You are sure** about this, young man?"

"I wouldn't have come if I wasn't."

"What will you relinquish in return?"

He rolled the sack off his shoulder, hefting it onto the desk. The woman laughed. "Centuries of wealthy kings lived and died in their halls of jewels, and you think gold will buy you eternal life?"

"What do you want, then?"

The woman folded her fingers: knotted, scarred, and wrapped in fabric. "To be mortal is to be human. To be immortal is to forsake your humanity. Are you prepared for such a sacrifice?"

His gaze hardened. "What would I have to do?"

The woman's sooty eyes crinkled. She opened a rusty chest and retrieved a bottle containing dust, or maybe ash. "You are familiar with the Mount that Burns in the West?"

He nodded.

The woman smiled. "Jump into the heart of its flame."

Something inside him choked, but the rest was too far gone. Still, caution clung to the fringes of his tenacity. "How will that not destroy me?"

The woman shook the bottle of ash. "Mix it with oil and paint it on your eyes, nose, and heart. The rest you will drink."

"You are swindling me."

"Such is why immortality is a legend to the world of men. Many have come, but few have nerve enough to try."

Something inside him burned. "I require power to rule this land forever, no matter the cost! Do not compare me to the spineless!"

The woman waggled the bottle in front of him, but when he reached for it, she yanked it away. "Many have said the same, and their desires are insufficient. Now, young man, you are certain this is what you want?"

He lunged for the bottle again, and again she tore it from his grasp. The woman held up a gnarled finger and clicked at him. "Patience, now. Your humanity you give for this power that you seek, but the bottle ..." She licked her crooked teeth as she eyeballed his sack of gold. "It has its own price."

With a snarl, he let her haul the riches behind her desk. He snatched the bottle, but the woman clutched his wrist before he could pocket it.

Her eyes were dark, her grip so tight that his fingers started going numb. "Remember. Once you do this, there is only one way to return your mortality. True love alone can break this covenant. And in that, there's—"

"I know, I know, there's a price, right?"

The woman released him, wagging a knobby finger as he left her hut. "Mostly correct, young man, but true love is—"

But he never heard the rest, not that he cared to.

A droning sigh filtered into the silent library like a fog settling around Xanthe's feet, making the spacious room even colder.

She was bored. Thousands of texts and tomes, and the only thing she could think about was how she'd run out of vermilion paint. Again.

She'd have read the library's contents, but frankly she was afraid they'd fall apart if she touched them. Painting was more relaxing anyway.

Her host once offered to read with her, but he seemed to have forgotten how. She wasn't surprised; it was probably difficult for him to grab books, turn pages, and remember to breathe properly to keep from ruining them. After the dust she'd encountered the first time in the library, he explained that his last tenants weren't interested, and it had been many years since he'd been in the room himself. Probably decades. Maybe a century. She could only guess. He was so ancient they had legends about him back home.

Staring at her half-finished work, she knew she shouldn't bother him. But it was an emergency.

"Canicus?" she whispered. Her voice carried on the invisible wings of mute spirits, echoing off the castle walls and assuring that she felt smaller and more alone than before. He would hear her though. He always did.

The castle rumbled and groaned like a woman in labor. It trembled periodically, more and more intense in the throes of its contractions. Xanthe knew when he reached the doorway. The trembling stopped, and the creature the castle birthed into the library was greater and more terrible than all his legends suggested.

His head entered: the tapered snout, square jaw rippling with savage muscle, and the orange reptilian eyes, each the size of a carriage wheel. His long, scaled neck wove in after it, and the claw of his wing clacked on the floor to keep his balance.

The great silver beast of the mountain.

When he spoke, the scent of ash and smoke billowed into the library, and his voice, even speaking softly, sounded like thunder. "Princess?"

His massive eyes burrowed into her like a vortex of flames. Whenever she saw him, she couldn't help shrinking into herself and wringing her paint-stained hands together. "Um, I'm out of vermilion. I can't get a rose's luster without it."

Canicus's head swung away and he left wordlessly. The faint shuddering of the castle with his steps was the only reminder that any living thing resided on these desolate mountains.

Xanthe sighed again, her fingers caressing her canvas. Her heart full of longing, she allowed her solitude to swallow her.

Xanthe read the latest letter repeatedly until twilight, when she hid it beneath her pillow with the others. She had sent off her reply with the dove a few days prior. She still felt so lonely. She stared at the ceiling, unable to sleep for fear of the beasts that always laid in wait to prey on her dreams.

Wind rattled the windows of her tower chamber, signaling Canicus's return. She hopped up and scurried down the spiraling stairs, still in her dressing gown. Who cared? He was a giant silver reptile who'd been around since before the common folk had cutlery.

Xanthe was never sure how he fetched the things she asked of him. Some agreement with the locals, perhaps, since he always arrived with a bag slung across his mighty chest.

Canicus dipped his great head at her approach into the entry hall, then crouched to let her dig through his bag.

Xanthe withdrew the paints, along with some fresh bread he'd picked up for her. She clutched the items to her chest and scampered to fetch her canvas. Midway, she stopped and turned to her scaled warden. "I can't sleep. Will I see you in the solar room?"

Canicus nodded, and Xanthe continued on her new quest.

Xanthe leaned against Canicus's shoulder while she worked. The hearth was warm, but heat also radiated between Canicus's scales, and it felt nice on her back. She knew he watched her paint, but the company was welcome nonetheless.

Even when he chuckled about it. Deep rumbling, like the distant threat of a storm.

She pouted. "You promised you wouldn't laugh anymore ..."

Canicus lifted his wing awkwardly. "Apologies. You're just such an awful painter."

"Then why do you keep bringing me paint?"

"Because you love it so much."

Xanthe blinked at him, clueless how to respond to his steadfast amber eyes. After a pause, she glanced away and Canicus spoke again. "I ran into your father on my way back."

Xanthe's paintbrush halted, and she glared holes into her canvas. "I don't wish to see him."

"He misses you."

"I don't care." She didn't have much courage, but she allowed herself one outlet for her anger. It was his fault. Now she wasted away in a castle older than her kingdom with a monstrous warden probably just as ancient.

Canicus noticed her souring mood. "Apologies. I did not mean to upset you."

At least her jailer was a good companion. She resumed painting, her paintbrush seeking the shape of the face she loved most until the weight of her eyelids overcame her inspiration.

Canicus missed hands. More than anything, he missed having hands. A claw attached to each colossal wing wasn't the best appendage to pluck a tiny canvas out of a sleeping girl's grasp without rupturing it. The idea of using his teeth was worse. He was excellent at controlling his flames, but using teeth for such delicate actions was still beyond him, and paint tasted disgusting.

To say nothing of carrying her to a sleeping area. He

could've done it if she was wearing something ... heavier. A dressing gown was not substantial enough to get a good grip without hurting her or ripping anything.

Xanthe had a habit of painting in her dressing gowns, claiming she didn't want paint on her good dresses, even when he brought aprons home to protect those very dresses.

He wasn't sure if he was thankful for his reptilian form or frustrated. She was comfortable because she didn't see him as a man, and she was right. He was a beast—a form which offered him sanctuary from any physical reactions his body may have had in human flesh. And no matter how many times he said it was improper, she would shyly apologize, saying it was only him.

Canicus never had the heart to argue, so he eventually dropped the issue entirely.

Her falling asleep like that, though, was a problem. Xanthe would be sore, he couldn't take her anywhere, and he couldn't bring himself to disturb her. So he flushed heat through his scales, curled his head and wing around her, and offered her comfort in dreams.

Another nightmare. They always started the same, a desolate wasteland filled with decay and monuments of the fallen from eons ago. Sometimes someone would come and the nightmare would cease, but others ended in all forms of torturous death Xanthe's brain could concoct.

Tonight, that someone came for her again. She never got his name, but he always felt familiar. He'd show up through a doorway of flames, as if the fire curled at the edges of her dream like kindled parchment. Usually all he did was sit with her, and eventually the wasteland turned into something else vaguely familiar—a place she knew, but not that place at the same time—as dreams often do.

"You're here."

"Another nightmare?"

She rolled her lips under her teeth. "Sorry."

"It's not your fault. It's probably more mine than anything."

"What?"

He shook his head. "Nothing."

He was handsome, yet undeniably chilling. His jaw was always set and his brows drawn, so ferocity dominated his face. But she was never afraid. Her nightmares were far more terrifying than long silver hair and orange eyes.

Xanthe slumped on the rocky ground and her guest sat nearby. It almost made her lonely, how he would never cross that invisible threshold. Like a ghost, he was always present, never close enough to stop her loneliness, but never far enough away to make her forget he was there.

A gilded cage even in her dreams.

"Want to talk about it?" he asked.

"You ever feel trapped?"

His fierce brow furrowed in time with his deepening frown. "Are you all right? Do you need help?"

Xanthe sighed. "Not like that. It's ... complicated. My living situation could be worse, but, inside, I feel ... like I'm still dancing to someone else's strings."

He paused, likely gathering up thoughts derived from her subconscious. After all, he was just a dream.

"To answer your question, I've felt trapped before, yes. Even now. But my prison is my home. My body. My life. So I do empathize to some extent." He glared at his hands then shook his head. "I'm sorry. I wish there was more I could do for you."

Xanthe folded her hands together. "This is enough. Thank you, friend—can I call you friend? It's been so long and you've never told me your name ..."

A stray breeze intruded on their conversation, whipping his hair around his face and lifting his bangs so she could see his eyes. They were wide, blinking like the flickering of a candle in the breeze. His toughened, unreadable expression resurfaced, accompanied by the clearing of his throat.

"If you wish."

And that was that. Her nightmare faded, and the tide rolled in. The wasteland became a beach, and they listened to the waves until reality returned to claim its due.

For the first time in decades, Canicus opened the doors to the ballroom. There was only so much cleaning he could do, but the princess was intent on picking up the slack. Or so it seemed.

Xanthe wore a gown this time, so she clearly wasn't worried about soiling it. She twirled around the ballroom, humming, a broom serving as her dance partner.

How cute.

"What are you doing?"

The girl squealed, dropping her broom and gripping her

heart to keep it from spiriting off without her.

Canicus rumbled. "My apologies. I thought you'd hear my approach."

Xanthe smoothed her golden hair as though calming a startled cat. "I was distracted. This room is beautiful."

"I thought you'd like it."

"Why'd you keep it hidden all this time?"

His wings ruffled. "I sometimes forget it exists. But I thought it might make your world a little bigger ..."

She studied him, and his skin shifted uncomfortably, as if she'd seen too much. The girl broke the silence, pointing to a massive hearth at the end of the ballroom. "Why don't we use this? It's much bigger than the one in the solar room!"

Canicus shook his head. "It is, but its purpose is different. I only light this when it's time to return wards to their people. My fire alone burns red in this hearth, and red smoke plumes into the sky—a call to retrieve the ward."

She considered this and sought his eyes. "Then, will you someday light this for me?"

Canicus wasn't sure how to respond, and something in his chest clenched. "Yes. Until then, you are under my protection."

"I see."

Another indecipherable statement.

The threat of awkward silence loomed, and Canicus warded it off. "I shouldn't impose on you any longer."

As he turned to exit, she blurted out, "Wait!"

Canicus stopped.

"You can stay, if you want ..."

He smiled. "Very well, Princess."

It'd been days since he informed Xanthe about an appointment with her father, and she was still angry. It was obvious by how she walked. Her footsteps, usually feathers against the ground, plodded down the mountain like those of a prisoner to the gallows. Her father insisted on speaking alone, but Canicus refused to leave them undefended. So he flew to the edge of his territory to let the princess and the king converse outside it—a solution he wasn't happy with, but he could stand guard.

It made Canicus uneasy, being unable to hear or smell anything beyond his territory. What happened within those borders were the only things he could control. But they deserved to talk. And he could still keep her safe. It was his job, after all.

Canicus felt the peel of the tether splitting like wet leather. From the way Xanthe tensed when she left his territory, he guessed she could feel it too. He could sense danger afoot from anywhere, but once she left his boundaries, his heightened senses concerning his ward dissolved.

Canicus watched, unable to hear their conversation beyond his invisible fence. It looked like an argument. She was upset. He didn't need the tether to sense that.

When their confrontation ended, they both stepped into his realm, and the tether latched to his ward again. Xanthe thundered past him while her father approached, bearing a satchel.

"Thank you, again, Great Canicus of the Mountains, for guarding my daughter during these trying times."

"It's what you pay me for, Your Majesty."

The king frowned. "My health is failing, Canicus. My kingdom is threatened. They set their sights on the heir to the throne. They will come for her."

Canicus straightened to his full height and flared his wings. "Your Majesty, I've done this for many generations, and I've been master of these lands even longer. This mountain is painted in the blood of armies."

The king handed over the satchel and left. Canicus wasn't about to tell him that his duties weren't something he was proud of anymore. But they were the only things he still knew how to do. Protect. Defend. Scatter the ashes of some unsuspecting pompous fools across the mountainside.

But he was concerned. The second the king had entered the territory, a waft of darkness had tickled Canicus's nostrils. It was mild, clinging vaguely to the king's clothing like the perfume of a mistress. It fizzled out entirely when the king descended the mountain.

No sooner had they landed at the castle entrance than Xanthe stormed through the doors and up to her tower. He had seen family issues in his wards before, but with her, it was such a shame.

Canicus skulked into his dungeon lair and dumped the satchel onto his rolling hills of treasure. He lay on his bed of riches and rubbed his face against the coins. The jewels echoed beautiful melodic notes, and the smell soothed him, though not enough to keep his thoughts at bay. The charred skeleton in the corner made sure of that. He kept it as a reminder every time he was foolish enough to remember his humanity. He was a beast, for defense and devastation.

He had power to rule his land forever, just as he wished.

And it was dreadfully boring.

His only excitement was his status as a glorified bodyguard. Canicus hid their loved ones, important figures, and prisoners away until the clients deemed it safe to retrieve them. He had liked some wards well enough, but never was he close to whatever "true love" nonsense the old, scarred woman had said.

However, somewhere along the line, something had shifted. They weren't just wards anymore. Xanthe wasn't just his ward. It wasn't that she was more special than the others that came before.

No, something in him had changed. He wasn't the same anymore.

The scent and sound of treasure no longer made him feel rich, the scars he could inflict upon the landscape no longer made him feel powerful, and tales of his might no longer made him proud. It was all old and meaningless.

He paid everything for this prison.

"Canicus?"

Xanthe's whisper came through the thrum of their tether, and he reached out his cognizance to feel along its strands. He was always vaguely aware of her whereabouts, but he only intruded upon necessity.

She was in the solar room with her paints, and she'd want him to light the hearth, at least.

His instincts objected to abandoning his hoard when he slid his jaw off the jeweled bed. Despite the protests of his monster shell, Canicus deserted the hollowed dungeons of gold for the company of a princess.

Canicus didn't know why he lay behind Xanthe every night while she painted. He'd felt protective over wards before, but this feeling was different.

He didn't love her, did he?

He couldn't feel any desire toward her in this state. But she smelled like light: cool and clean, almost the way he thought the beach might smell. She was so small, so fragile. Gentle and soft spoken, always afraid of asking for anything, as though she were a burden. She only showed her steel in regards to her family.

Canicus certainly felt endeared to her, but more than that, he wanted this skittish, lonely young woman to be happy.

Was that love?

If any of these things did border on love, would allowing himself to walk that path free him from his scaly prison? Was that something he wanted? He'd lost everything for this life, and he'd probably have to pay with this life to have it all back.

His territory, his hoard, his livelihood. He'd been a monster so long; the world hurtled by without him. He'd forgotten how to be human.

Even if he were ready for such a thing, he didn't know the requirements for breaking the covenant. He hadn't stayed to find out from the old woman. Did "true love" need to be reciprocated? Or could he become human again on his own?

Canicus leaned over to peek at her canvas. It was outlined in what was supposed to be roses, probably, and she worked on a human face in the middle.

Whomever Xanthe was painting, it wasn't him.

He wasn't sure why that revelation made his chest knot up. It was silly. It wasn't as though she knew what his human form looked like. Even if she recalled her dreams, she wouldn't know who he was.

Something about the whole situation unnerved him. "What are you painting?"

Xanthe glanced at the gargantuan burning eye beside her, then stared at her work, her finger tracing the person's face. "Someone I haven't seen in a long time ... I miss him so much."

Canicus felt a prick of guilt for being the lock on her birdcage. "Apologies. I wish there was something I could do."

Something must have cracked then, like winding a music box all the way only to keep turning. Xanthe set the painting aside and rested her head on her knees. He smelled the salt of her tears before he saw them, and settled his head beside her. She clung to his lip and leaned on his jaw.

"Rest, Princess. You are not alone. You are not alone."

"You are not alone."

His warmth must have followed her in dreams, for when she opened her eyes, an arm wrapped around her shoulders and a structured jaw leaned against her head, ruffling her golden hair.

Strands of a feathered silver mane danced across her sightline, and she knew her dream friend had returned. But when she turned to look, he was standing a few meters away in his sleek black coat.

"I'm sorry, miss." He pursed his lips, darting his face away as he dipped his head in an awkward bow. When he rose, his forehead creased and his eyes swam around in his sockets, drowning in some attempt at resolve.

"You're usually so distant. Why not today?"

His whisper was quiet but firm. "You seemed sad."

She rolled her lips under her teeth. He was only a dream, so speaking her mind couldn't hurt, right? "Then, will you hold me?"

He gave her that bewildered stare again.

"Please?"

Her dream-guest approached, and she closed the gap, wrapping her arms around his middle.

"Please don't leave me," she whispered into his coat. "You're all I have left. Without you, I'm alone in my nightmares."

He tentatively embraced her and leaned his chin on her head. "I told you. You're not alone. Here or on the other side."

"I know, but I'm so afraid. I've lost my freedom, my love, my family ... one day you'll disappear, and the nightmares will come back."

The man stroked her hair gently. He didn't answer, but his warmth was comforting. Xanthe curled into the man's black coat and absorbed every bit of solace he was willing to give.

Canicus's eyes shot open like igniting flames. The palace was dark, and his tether stretched thin.

She wasn't in the castle. He'd had countless runaway attempts before, but Xanthe had never tried.

Something was wrong.

He didn't sense intruders, but he felt a crawling tension, a tingle of claustrophobia, like a cell with no windows or doors—only the knowledge that something crept about in the dark.

Canicus lumbered through the castle, bursting through the doors and taking to the sky the second he had room enough to spread his wings. He trailed his cognizance along the thin line of their tether, and felt worms of dread picking at his stomach.

He had to find her.

Xanthe shivered. The mountain was much slower on foot and her stolen pair of boots, likely from a previous ward with much bigger feet, slid in the snow. Guilt gnawed at her gooseflesh, the shame a devoted companion to the chill of the wind.

She would've said goodbye, but he'd have tried to stop her. This was her only chance. Spurred by her longing, she brushed off the nagging notion to return to the castle.

He'd be at the end of this empty mountain. He'd promised.

Xanthe found the edge of Canicus's territory, as she could feel his tether hanging by a few threads. She stared at the invisible gate to the wilderness beyond. The mountainside was peppered in young evergreens sprouting amidst the carbon-ized corpses of their predecessors. A prominent boulder over-looking a ridge made this place the perfect rendezvous point. The ridge even had a mountain path tracing its contour. She had made sure to mention it in her letters. To anyone else, it was a scenic route. To her, this was the edge of her enclosure. Once she walked through, she'd be free, but she wouldn't be safe anymore.

Terror shot up her spine.

Her hands shook, and her swallow felt heavy in her throat.

Why was she so afraid?

Xanthe dusted the snow from the boulder and sat in its grooves, arranging her stolen cloak to keep warm and cam-ouflage against prying orange eyes. The pull of the tether should alert her if Canicus was close, but she couldn't help scanning the skies and scouring the hem of the forest.

The sun breached the horizon, and she still waited, quea-siness shaking her stomach. She was almost out of time, and nothing had crested the mountain path.

Just as her faith failed, a voice hailed her from beyond.

"Ho! My love!"

Her heart leapt in time with her body. A silhouette rose with the dawn from the horizon, traipsing fearlessly along the ridge and straight toward her. Joy overcame whatev-er fear Xanthe had about crossing the barrier, and she leapt from the boulder and bolted down the mountain. She slid to a stop in the snow and gripped her hands tightly together to stop herself from jumping into the arms of her beloved right in the middle of the path.

The last warning of the splitting tether barely registered

in her mind.

Her man stood before her, his wild dark hair and clean beard in stark contrast to his blinding smile. He wore a dashing cloak and a crossbow slung across his back. His armor gleamed in the remaining light.

"Sir Werther! I thought I'd never see you again! You got my letters!"

He ran his hand through his hair. "When your father's soldiers divulged your location, nothing could keep me away. Not him, not some fiery beast! You and I are destined, my love. When you summon me, I come."

A sigh bubbled over her jubilant heart. Xanthe stepped into his embrace, just in time to hear an ear-splitting screech from the sky.

The Great Beast of the Mountain descended upon them.

Canicus landed like an earthquake, eyeing the pretentious rat holding his ward. His voice rose with warning. "Return to the castle. It isn't safe."

Xanthe wouldn't look at him, but she clenched her dress in her fists and twisted the fabric. She bit her lip and scrunched her face so hard Canicus was sure she would start bleeding. Her body shook, and her feet stayed rooted in the snow, unwilling to move. Her companion looked familiar, though Canicus had never seen him before. The man took her chin and sought her gaze. He said something, but the barrier blocked Canicus's hearing, so he could only guess the words.

Canicus itched to roast the man's entrails and knock them

off the mountainside, but Xanthe's affection for the cocky brute stayed his flames. The burning urge to drag her back inside the territory, to hold her and keep her safe, devoured him.

When they both entered his domain, unease crept up Canicus's spine, made worse by how Xanthe smiled in the man's arms. The man held up a peaceful hand, his other arm wrapped around Xanthe's shoulders. "I believe we have a grave misunderstanding. Let's sit and talk."

A distinct scent assaulted Canicus's nostrils, and his instincts flared. He roared, "Your Highness, get behind me! That boy reeks of darkness!"

Xanthe jolted, her gaze shooting to her companion's face. A vicious smile broke the man's pleasant façade. He whipped out a dagger and roughly jerked her into a tight hold in front of him. He pressed it to Xanthe's neck and used her as a shield. If it weren't for her, Canicus would've incinerated the boy where he stood.

She froze, barely breathing. "W-Werther? W-what are you doing?"

The fragility in her voice shot tingles of rage through Canicus's bones. Anyone who made her voice tremble like that deserved to be charcoal.

"Are you really that dim? You honestly thought I went through all the motions to court an unavailable princess only for the old codger to panic and hire a monster to keep the throne out of reach?"

"I don't understand. What's going on, my love?"

If she did not love the pest, he would have been ash the moment his foul stench traipsed into range. Canicus felt the glands at the back of his throat leaking the flammable gas. All he'd have to do would be inhale and exhale deeply and Xanthe would be standing before a pile of soot. But he couldn't bring himself to do it while she trembled in her oversized boots.

"It's a miracle you haven't figured it out," he laughed.

Canicus snarled, "How will killing the princess grant you her kingdom?"

"So it's the beast that has the brains! Allow me to enlighten you, big white brute." The man's face turned predatory. "I'm not the one that's going to kill her. You are." He paused long enough to drink in Xanthe's horrified expression. The deplorable swine. "Or, that's how it's going to look, anyway. Your reputation will fall to ruin, beast, and the continent will demand your death. In the wake, a single hero will arise to slay the menace and be richly rewarded for avenging the death of the king's only child."

Canicus watched his shy, spirited ward's face flood with fury and betrayal. She stomped on her captor's toes, jamming her elbow into Werther's stomach the second the knife dropped from his hand.

Xanthe grabbed her skirts and ran toward Canicus. She slipped and fell face first into the snow the same moment that Werther grabbed his crossbow and aimed ... right at Xanthe's back.

She wouldn't be able to stand up in time.

Werther sneered, "You see, monster, I know your weakness."

The time to think had passed.

Canicus's wings tore across the space between them. He launched himself over Xanthe's head and landed above her, spraying snow over the ridge and casting a great shadow on his ward. He crouched, digging his claws into the earth and spreading the membranes of his wings like great ramparts. His head swung down, his posture aligning to fry Werther on his level. Canicus shielded the woman's body with his own and heard her whimper as the gas for his flames poured into his mouth.

Werther fired.

Something burning bore into Canicus's eye as half his vision violently ceased. It was over.

His last passing thought was the worry that his corpse would crush Xanthe.

Canicus was dead before he hit the ground.

His tether viciously shredded itself from Xanthe's spirit, and she screamed.

He crashed to one side, his wing still sheltering her. His body stretched across the path, his head curled in an unnatural position and his monstrous tail draped down the ridge. His fall had displaced the snow, and loose drifts scattered around him. Xanthe fumbled to get to her feet and maneuver over the drifts to kneel beside his snout, her hands shaking with the fear of touching him.

So long as she didn't touch him, it wasn't real.

A click and the crunching of snow startled her. Sir Werther stepped closer, his crossbow locked with another bolt aimed at her heart. Instinctively, she turned and hugged Canicus's fallen jaw.

It was over.

There was nothing left.

Heat coursed through the scales under her fingertips. Xanthe's eyes shot open.

Could it be?

No, it wasn't the same as the gentle heat that kept her warm in front of the hearth every night. This heat was fierce and unrelenting.

She scooted backwards on the frozen ground as Canicus's scales glowed white hot. One by one, they peeled off and disintegrated into skybound fireflies, their remnants shimmering in the abyss above until they twinkled out of sight.

His skin began to burn, fanning into an inferno that forced Xanthe to shield her face. She struggled to stretch towards him, desperately grasping to reclaim her routine monotony. She could accept all of it, if her only real friend were still alive.

Canicus's body burst in a shockwave of light and heat. It blew Sir Werther back with such force, it was impossible to tell if it sent him flying across the hills or vaporized him completely.

When the explosion subsided, Xanthe blinked rapidly and shook her head, her bleary sight warping with a myriad of woozy colors.

The dragon's carcass was gone.

What lay in its place seized her chest with rapid breaths. The beast's gargantuan, charred pelt, empty like a hunter's keepsake, sprawled across the land like a blackened scar on the mountainside. Amidst the angry sea of onyx and charcoal was a single snow drift.

What was that?

Xanthe tried crawling over to the drift, but the feeling of

the scorched leather beneath her fingers shot uncontrollable chills up her arms.

Shriveling dead skin—

The horror rose in her belly and the substance of her nausea launched into her throat. Her hands flew to her mouth as she swallowed it down.

Xanthe stood and took small steps on shaking feet toward what she had assumed was snow.

It was a human body.

Her ribs ached with the banging of her heart, a defiant maiden behind a locked door. Against all reason, her feet still moved toward the figure that was buried beneath the shreds of Canicus's burnt hide. She couldn't recall a single thought until she saw the person's face.

It was him.

The man from her dreams.

Her friend.

Except ...

He wasn't a dream.

His body was pale, and likely bare, save for Canicus's husk that draped over him and shielded half his form from her gaze. His eyes were closed, but it was definitely him. Strong jaw. Silver hair. Even the bangs that obscured his face. Her heart ached for this inexplicable, tangible fantasy.

Now that she knew, why wouldn't her feet move?

A breath shuddered through the man's lungs. The sound unlocked her legs, but sucked her strength out with it as they collapsed under her. She crawled toward him, too undone to feel the coat beneath her fingertips anymore.

When Xanthe reached him, she shakily brushed the hair

from his eyes. Upon seeing his face, she froze and instantly tore her gaze away from the bloody mess where one eye should've been. The same injury that Canicus had just endured to save her.

She shook away the possible ramifications. Somehow, he still lived. She felt no link, no tether, but this man was alive. For now. Each weak breath inched him closer to the edge. She carefully gathered his head in her arms, gently peeling the rest of the hair from his face. The man drifted back to consciousness and he wheezed a groan, his remaining eyelid opening groggily to reveal an eye like fire. The truth was undeniable.

"C–Canicus?"

The eye darted to her, his brows knitted in that severe expression she had never seen in the waking world but was so familiar she could have painted it blind. Then his face shifted to add pain and confusion. "Princess? Why do you look so sad? I don't feel the—Am I ... dreaming? Why does it—?"

He winced, cutting himself off.

Xanthe stroked his bangs back as they fell over his face again. Her voice croaked. "You're not dreaming, Canicus. I can't feel the tether either. It's gone. You're ... human?"

Canicus's eye widened as he lifted his hand and flexed his fingers, his visage painted in awe. "I'm human again ..."

Xanthe broke. Tears poured unhindered from her eyes. Her frantic, faulty inhales warred against her need to talk to him. "All this time? It was you, all this time?"

"Are you disappointed, Princess?"

She violently shook her head, no longer able to speak.

"That's a relief."

"Can—" she choked. "Canicus?"

He wiped the tears from her cheeks with his thumb, and blinked when the motion smeared blood across her face. He drew his hand away. "My apologies."

She grabbed his wrist and brought his palm back to her cheek as she cried. "Canicus, does it hurt?"

His eyelid drooped, and she saw a trace of something she didn't want to see. Resignation. He recovered and stroked her cheekbone. "Don't worry about that, all right?"

She cried harder.

He was slipping away.

He whispered to himself, seemingly amused. "So the condition for breaking it is the price, huh? How ironic and fitting."

Xanthe swallowed. "We have to go. Come, I'll help you."

His eye sought hers. "Princess."

She started wrapping her arm around him.

"Princess," he protested.

She violently shook her head and scrunched her eyes shut, for she was afraid of what he would say.

He gripped her arm with attempted firmness. "Xanthe!"

Her heart seized, and she finally looked at him. His severe expression returned, forced and weak though it was, his lone eye daring her to avert her gaze. "You're free now. It sounds unsettling, but you need to tear some of this skin. Wrap it around you. It should keep you warm. Go back to the castle. Light the hearth in the ballroom and throw the pelt into the fire. The smoke will turn red. There should be enough food in the pantries until the townspeople come for you."

Fury and sorrow burst from her throat in a strangled, guttural yelp. "No!"

She couldn't lose her only friend a second time in less than an hour. It was unbearable.

"Don't—" he began, his voice filled with compassion.

"Don't, Canicus! I'm going to cry and you cannot stop me!" she sobbed. She clutched his hand, and he wrapped his fingers through hers.

"Why? Why did you do it? This goes beyond your duty ..."

Canicus shook his head. "If you had been my ward alone, I would have died a dragon."

He lifted their entwined hands and brushed the back of his against her face. "Yet, I've been gifted a few extra moments. It would be ungrateful to wish for more."

"Then call me ungrateful! Call me greedy, I don't care!"

"I would sooner call you kind, and gentle, too pure for this place. I would sooner watch you paint again and see you smile. But I am thankful, that I could see you, hear you, and feel your touch, as myself, just this once." His breathing grew weaker, as if he was trying to say everything he needed to before ... "Be happy, my friend," he finished.

And all too suddenly, he was gone.

The breath of life left him, and he dissolved into bits of light. Frigid, lonesome air rushed into the spaces between her fingers. The weight of his head and softness of his hair in her other hand vanished, and her hand jumped in the unwelcome shock of emptiness.

Xanthe was so cold. She lifted the gargantuan, blackened hide and bundled it around herself to pretend her warmth hadn't just floated into the clouds. Then she doubled over and wept, huddling in it. Disgusting or not, the pelt was warm, like he said. And it still smelled like smoke and cinders, just like Canicus.

Soon she'd have to return to the castle and face the notion of throwing the pelt into the flames. That once-beautiful skin—the suit worn by a man trapped inside a monster—would shrivel and crumble into ash. And that would be all that was left of him.

But she couldn't bear the thought of the future at the moment. So she curled herself up in the past for as long as she could.

A thought made her soul ache. He said she was free.

She was free. But she was also, well and truly, alone.

The colossal doors screeched on their hinges. The queen paid them no mind. This creaky old castle couldn't scare her away. She thought raiders would've come, but clearly a deep magic still held over this place, warding off unwelcome darkness.

The queen's guard stood outside, as ordered. Despite their protests, she alone would enter this fortress. Dust stirred and peeled before her, paving a path for her presence. She marched through the halls with grace, her feet like feathers against worn woven carpets, even while she brandished her massive offering. A bottle of ash clinked around her neck.

Every turn she took with purpose, until she came to a mammoth entryway. A ballroom lay beyond, immense and untouched—at its end, a hearth so large a carriage could fit within it. The queen approached, each step echoing endlessly throughout the room like the whispers of forgotten spirits.

Delicately climbing the hearth's stepped stone, she nestled her offering in a crook on its mantle.

When she'd finished, she picked her way down and admired her work. The painting she'd placed boasted a flying silver beast and a handsome man with long silver hair and orange eyes.

"What I wouldn't give for you to tell me how bad this painting is, my friend. My subjects only cast awe and admiration at my feet because of my station, not my talent. But it took me years to finish this one." She gave a wry chuckle. "It's probably awful, but it's the best I've got."

The queen stared forlornly up at the painting. Her hand clutched the bottle at her neck. "I miss you so much, Canicus. I'm so sorry. If I hadn't been such a fool, you'd still be alive."

"Wrong, my dear!" a high voice cackled.

The queen jumped to find an old woman with gnarled hands standing behind her. The old woman wore patchwork rags that matched the strips of fabric wrapping her fingers. She was diminutive and hunched, but in a deliberate way that made it unclear if her posture was by age or by choice. Her curly gray hair rebelled against the headscarves and braids that attempted to tame it. The woman would have been entirely overlooked in a poor village, but in this derelict castle, she simultaneously looked entirely out of place and every bit at home.

"How did you—how did you get in here?" the queen stammered.

The old woman waved her off. "I have my ways, dear. Not important. What I am interested in, though, is that bottle around your neck."

When the old woman pointed to it, the queen held the bottle tightly, her expression hardening. "Who are you? And what did you mean, I'm wrong?"

"Again, not important, dearie. But I know who you are. And you're wrong if you think your behavior could've saved him."

"What do you mean?"

"It wasn't the crossbow that killed him," The woman explained flippantly, meandering aimlessly around the ballroom. "He traded his humanity for immortality. That wound wouldn't have been fatal. Lost an eye perhaps, but ..."

"I don't understand ..."

The old woman stopped wandering and crossed the room to stand before the queen. She pointed a gnarled finger at the queen's chest. "The only way to break that covenant was true love. True love is sacrifice, my dear." The woman's gaze burned into the queen's eyes. "Protecting you at that moment, at the expense of his life, was no act of duty ..."

Once more, Queen Xanthe was reduced to a tragic young girl, suffering the onslaught of grief and revelations she wasn't sure she wanted. She fell to her knees, even as the old woman adjusted her patchwork scarves and continued.

"Now that you know, I'm sure it's too much of a burden to haul those ashes around. Let me take all that pain off your hands."

Through her tears, Xanthe snarled, glaring as if looks were a means of execution. "This is all I have left of him. You won't take it."

The woman rubbed her temple. "Come, dear. I have a business to run. Just give me the ashes, and we can leave this behind you."

Xanthe stood and straightened, radiating a queen's dignity. "Take your offer and leave, permanently. I do not wish to forget, and I will not relinquish his ashes."

A cackle. "Why, would you look at that, my boy! You actually found a good one!"

"Who are you?"

The woman waved her hand dismissively and turned towards the exit. But when Xanthe swung her head, the woman was gone. Had any of their exchange even happened? But as she looked on the painting above the hearth, she knew.

She felt the weight of his sacrifice so keenly that she could hear his voice and feel his hands on her face. She still sensed the ghostly tingles of his tether by memory—or rather, the chilled pain of absence where his tether had once been, somewhere deep in her chest.

Canicus proclaimed her freedom, and yet, her heart had been dungeoned since his goodbye.

Years passed and the ache never left.

"I'm free and yet I suffer!" Her voice cracked as the tears caught in her throat. "I can't bring you back. The only thing I can do ... is live out my life until one day I can fulfill your final wish for my happiness."

The painting stared back in silence, and the castle echoed her mournful exclamation.

But somewhere deep inside her, painful warmth bloomed. Xanthe would carry his death wherever she went, but the cloak of his sacrifice had slipped, and she saw it now for what it was.

She would hold onto that forever.

And for the first time in years, she didn't feel so alone anymore.

CASTLES IN THE SKY
Everly Haywood

I hang your castle in the clouds
high above canyons where dragons
sleep in dark crevices.
Sunlight gleams on the white stone walls
and illuminates the ramparts
where the valiant keep watch
always.

Then your towers begin to crumble—
there's tarnish there beneath the glitter.
I see you're broken too.
Walls collide in broken promises,
expectations too high for this—
when castles fall to earth
like this.

Shattered dreams, blackened palisades,
the fires rage from deep within us.
Do we fight? Walk away?

Broken towers can be rebuilt,
and timber can be hewn once more—
souls can be knit back together,
like a phoenix from ashes
reborn.

POMEGRANATE EYES
Beka Gremikova

Fresh-cut hay, upturned soil—signs of
harvest and hope to end the hunger.
But the earth's stomach still rumbles,
while Kore, with bright pomegranate eyes,
lies
in a field of wildflowers. Nymphs pilfer sweet hay
strands from her mother's cupboards.
Demeter works in far-off fields,
cleaving, tying, tossing, forgetting
that all seeds sown grow into harvest—
and there are Seeds planted in her own child.
Kore blinks back tears—

> *her eyes plucked from the Underworld pomegranate*
> *by the mysterious shaper of lives and cosmos*
> *unbeknownst to the roaming, restless gods*
> *while Persephone slept alone in Demeter's womb,*
> *her life slowly, surely, threading*
> *into the very claws of death—*

Red juice flows from those eyes, the seeds yearning

to return to Hades, to the Underworld, to their roots.

So when the rumbling earth finally erupts,

a jagged seam splitting the harvest fields,

and a strong hand grasps Kore's ankle—

she does not scream.

Her pomegranate eyes return the rich-brown

gaze of the under-earth king they remember

so well, so dearly.

Her soul snags with their same soft

yearning—

she must follow her eyes, those masters

of the heart. So with a dreamy sigh

she slides her arms

around the neck of Hades and

returns

        to

             the

                  dark

THE BATTLE OF DOLOR
H. A. Pruitt

His light is fading.

I refocus on his eyes, and they show it as well. Before the battle began, his eyes always danced with blazing joy. Meeting his gaze had been breathing in fresh, golden air.

Now, though, the fire in his eyes has faded. His light—the orb of anima that floats behind his head—has dwindled to an exhausted flicker. No one can see their own anima. We each can feel our own, but it is so tied to who we are, that we notice it much like we can sense our own subtle, hidden heartbeat. Only those who know the person well can view an anima, read it, and understand what the luminosity or lack of it indicates.

My husband's anima had always shown like the summer sun. Reflecting his power over fire, it had consistently glowed vibrant orange and amber.

In our poorly lit hut, I try to focus my gaze on his face or hands. Darkness has settled into our home, though, and all I can see is his shadowed face in the glow of his anima, which shudders like a pale moon trying to penetrate storm clouds.

It is so dim, and I know I can do nothing. My husband would never diminish my words. He would never refuse to let me speak. He is kind, and his care for those he loves pulses as his greatest strength. However, it is also his most glaring weakness. His heart burns to such an extent for others that it retains no energy to even compose a thought for himself. He is just like the fire God put in his veins: once he determines his course, no one can deter him. Just as a wildfire, an end to his passion comes only when he burns himself out. My words will do nothing because until he extinguishes his determination to save everyone else in this battle, he simply will not turn his eyes to look at his own need to be saved.

During this battle, he is striving to love more ardently than ever yet at the cost of dismissing himself more desperately than ever.

I long to say any words to help him see his fading anima, but I know he is the only one who can choose to open his eyes to what so obviously hangs in and around him. Only he can change his course.

He tilts his head to catch my gaze. "We'll get through this."

I nod and try but fail to smile.

"Tell me what you're thinking. I know you're full of thoughts. I see it in your eyes." He also attempts to give me his calm, assured expression, but his eyes remain dull.

I place my hand on his chest and watch my fingers run down the scars in his armor. My ice leaves temporary hairlines of frost. I notice how much time passes before my power melts against his. My husband doesn't see. All his focus is on my hesitation.

He doesn't rush me because he knows me too well. My fault is paralyzing fear. Just as my ice that God placed inside me, I need the warmth of genuine love to move me from stillness or silence. My husband knows I need time to open. Perhaps that's our downfall—we so well understand how the other works that we believe we are helpless against it. Maybe we have forgotten what our powers can be if they reach out to the other.

I shake my head and opt to voice the worry that constantly hovers at the back of my mind. "It feels like we've already lost."

He takes my fingers that hang between us. Wrapping them in his warm hands, he kisses my knuckles but then simply stares.

I know he wants to say the words. He yearns to assure me we haven't lost, but he feels the loss too acutely to lie.

Since the first surprise attack besieged our home and all of Luctus, we have not lived a day in the village without loss. We lost our security, our light in the sky, our closeness, and so many beloved lives. The enemy knew how to deplete us. He came like a tornado—sporadically, quickly, and promising no chance of survival for those hit. He swept down upon the members of our village—all friends and family—one by one and never in the same way. Some fell from attacks on the battlefield just outside of Luctus. Others faded in their own homes with no explanation except the signs of the enemy's depressing influence hidden in their huts for any caring eye to recognize. I know the belief that he could have done something to stop their deaths haunts my husband, but I contain neither the courage nor belief to assure him he could have changed the outcome of the attacks.

No one could have stopped or even expected the enemy. He timed his assaults in a way that stunned Luctus and drained it of hope. Just as we finished clearing the battlefield or home, just as we believed it safe to remove our armor, just as we regained strength to move forward, the enemy struck again. Each assault stole more of our shaken hope that we could return to life without unbroken darkness. Eventually, we stopped removing the armor. We stopped gazing upward to see if the morning would bring light. We stopped believing we could win and retain life. The enemy backed us into this inescapable valley of eternal darkness and taught us to believe no escape existed.

My eyes fall to my husband's armor that never leaves his chest as he finally answers, "We haven't lost each other."

I stifle my instinctive retort. I feel as if I have lost him. His anima still emits light, but he is lost in the grief and pain. Like his anima, the darkness clouds him so much that all he can see is what he has lost and not what he still holds. His glow has dulled so much that I wonder if he can even read the pain on my face in our dark hut. My anima alone has never been enough. We need both of our lights to see in the darkness.

My gaze darts to our hands, still yet so limply joined.

He loves me—I *know* he does—but I also know his love for anything is choking in the thick darkness right now. Fear of losing everything he loves is persuading him to lock himself so tightly that even while he strives to care for all he has left, it seeps out as only cold, distant effort. Remaining in this hut, stuck in such strained shadows, exacerbates my feeling of helplessness against it all.

I slide my hand from his. "Let's go."

"I wish you didn't have to fight—no, you don't have to. I could do it; you don't have to go out into all that."

"I want to. I ... I want to help. I know I can't do much,

but—"

"No, you do so much. You've *done* so much. That's why I don't want you to feel like you have to keep going out."

"If I don't, who will?" My voice quivers, but I lock eyes with him. He is right. My husband knows I'm sick of dragging dead bodies into graves, trying so hard and failing to mend wounds, and most of all sifting through all the possessions full of memories left behind. He knows my anima is faltering, but I know his is also, and I refuse to let him flicker into nothingness alone.

"I want to," I insist. "I didn't want all the … all the strife that we never asked for, but I–I want *you*. I want to go with you." Hoping he grasps the depths of all my teary words, I place my left hand on his chest and tap my ring against his armor. "I'm with *you*."

Desperation seizes me to tell him that his anima is nearly gone, but he pulls me into his embrace, and I know he won't listen. Still—after he has lost so much—he wants to be strong for me. He wants to pour the little warmth he still retains into me. If I tell him he has lost his strength, that he is the one who needs rekindling, he won't listen.

After the comfort of his closeness calms me, I nod and squeeze him one last time.

We slip apart, and the sound of gathering supplies ensues. The dark interior of our hut hides his actions, but I prepare for what we last left undone: honoring those left dead on the battlefield. I hesitate at my ice-resistant arrows. The enemy never returns before we clear the dead, but a whisper urges me to be prepared. I snatch my quiver as I hear my husband unlatch the door. Together, yet separately, we step out of our hut.

Dread grips my intestines as we head in the familiar direction. I hope for my husband's fire, but he does not ignite a flame in his palm. My fear insists that he no longer can. I force my eyes from his dim outline to the furthest sight I can see.

The encircling mountains only remind me just how completely trapped we are. Although the towers of rock have always surrounded Luctus, I never saw them as a cage until the enemy threw his darkness over the valley. Now, everything around me echoes the loss that has transpired.

My eyes fall to the shadows covering the village of Luctus. We pass the empty huts, but we don't speak among them. Too many memories linger here. The structures stand as empty shells, but they remind me of long hours that we solemnly dug through deceased villagers' unwillingly abandoned treasures and sorted what could be kept from what had to be burned. My husband loathed to sacrifice anything. The enemy had forced so much loss upon him that losing anything more—even an ordinary pitcher or pan—seared his aching heart. Many homes empty of anima still contain those boxes of snuffed out lives he refuses to release.

I peer at his face. The dark surroundings cloak his features in heavy shadows, aging him to a man who has retained far too much grief. I know he clings to them all, and I wish I could tell him to let go, but at the same moment I know I will never urge him to stop loving even those who are gone.

Instead of wrestling with his greatest weakness and strength, I plead with God to help my husband. *Lord, please, please help him. Help him ...*

Our feet slow at the edge of Dolor. I reach for my husband's hand.

He doesn't notice.

Watching him creep forward with an arm held back to ask me to wait, sorrow and gratefulness twist my stomach. He doesn't want me to see more death, but he also wants to clear it away alone. He wants to be strong, but his anima so clearly yet so faintly glowing behind him proves isolation weakens him.

Dolor, this battlefield where we face the enemy, has weakened all in Luctus. It has drank the blood of so many we love, but it has drained my compassionate, ardently loving husband more than any other. Every death has sapped his own soul. I hardly understand how he is still living. He is and we are still alive, though, but we are the only ones.

I wrap my arms around my torso and follow him. He snatches a glance back, and I take his hand that still pleads with me to stay back.

"I want to be with you," I whisper.

His thumb rubs my skin. He *does* want me to be here. My husband is brave and would never ask me to, but he appreciates me coming with him to this battle.

My sight catches movement in the dark sky. "No."

"What?" He halts and tucks me close to his side.

"We haven't even—there's still—" My legs weaken. Never before has the enemy returned while bodies still sprawled unhonored on the field of Dolor. "It's not fair." I want to scream the words, but I barely breathe them.

"You can go home. You have time."

"I brought my bow."

As he loads his own heavy compound crossbow, he shakes his head. "You don't have to. I don't—"

Although he cuts off his words, I know them. "I'm not going to die. And I'm not leaving you. You're—"

"I know." His eyes meet mine. I see his conflict. The pain of being left alone in this moment is fighting with his desire to not lose me permanently.

"I won't die." As the scream of the enemy shatters the sky, I strain up on my tiptoes, pour my love into the deep yet quick kiss, then unsheathe my metal longbow. "Ice and fire?"

"Fire and ice," he assents then adds, "You can do this, wife."

Before I can correct him that *we* can, he runs ahead and releases the first blow. The dangerous clicks and shrieks of his thick, barbed arrows racing to their target send me fleeing to the perimeter of Dolor. My husband excels in bold attacks, but my patient accuracy reigns as my deadly weapon. If my fear doesn't shove aside my wits, we can at least push this final battle to another day. At best, we vanquish the enemy who has stripped us of nearly everything. At worst, though, my husband or I lose our anima and take the sanity of the other into the dirt of Dolor.

No, I internally insist. My husband would tell me we will win. He *had* told me he believes in me.

Despite my terror, my anima's luminosity swells. The renewed glow of cool blue vibrates in me even though I can't see it behind me.

He does love me, I remind my heart. *He's just hurting.*

A bellow yanks me out of my thoughts. I start to scan the sky, but firelight alerts me of the enemy's location. Blacker than the eternal darkness he brings, the enemy snaps his flaming mouth shut and digs his enormous claws into the barren ground. My husband stands unharmed in the flickering circle of the enemy's fire. My eyes crinkle in relief and pride. The enemy did not expect him to still retain any power against fire.

Truthfully, that haunting worry in the back of my mind had believed it as well. So much time had dragged by with no sign that his God-given power still burned; I thought the enemy and the grief he created had squelched it. I had thought we already lost, and I had feared that I had already lost him. Watching him now engage in a deadly dance with our enemy, though, I feel that fear struggle to control me.

The enemy's head dips, and his teeth flash, but the glint comes from my husband's flaming arrows sailing by. As my husband dashes past his distracted eyes and under his hulking yet slender catlike body, the enemy roars in frustration. A fiery arrow shoots into its chest, and the enemy spreads its wings, kicks a leg, and dislodges the shallow blow. Then he clips his wings shut, twists, and drops so a hind paw barely misses my husband. I squint, pleading with God to let this favorable battle bolster his anima just as it is renewing my lost hope, but the orb behind his head has not brightened at all. My shoulders slump but instantly tense again as the enemy strikes.

Fearlessly, my husband darts away from his tail's wild swipe and looses a blazing arrow into the inky eye that looks nearly as big as him. The enemy thrashes, but even the power of his long neck can't dislodge the arrow.

Triumph starts to swell in me, but a voice freezes it.

From everywhere and nowhere, the enemy's voice echoes across Dolor. "You seem so capable, little warrior. Why did you do nothing? You could have stopped so many deaths."

I stifle my compulsion to scream a denial. Our victory

depends on my secrecy.

"You could have carried their loads, lightened their burdens. You have such broad shoulders; why didn't you use them sooner so they could carry life instead of the dead?"

My husband's anima dims to nearly nothing.

Angst courses through me. Eliminating the enemy depends on my quiet patience, but I can't let it cost my husband's soul.

God, what do I do? I beg in my mind.

The enemy strikes with his bearlike paw. It barely catches my husband's arm, but he stumbles. His knees thud onto the dirt.

Impulsively, I load my bow and sprint toward the pair. Fear has drowned in the desperate love gripping my whole being. Halfway to the enemy, he swings his dragon head then rotates his leopard body to me.

I halt and stretch my bow.

Wait, that trusted whisper urges.

One calming breath eases into then out of my lungs.

The enemy tilts his unharmed eye to me, and his laughter shivers through the dark air. "Oh, you fearful little—"

Noiselessly, my ice-coated arrow flies and speeds to its mark. The enemy does not know love can dispel fear. He does not understand that the fire of my husband's love that melted my fear before this war began still pulses in my veins. The enemy does not comprehend what God gave us.

He roars, outraged by the unforeseen attack. I cringe at the awful force of the enemy, but in my crouch, I dash to my husband. As the enemy retreats into the sky, trails of fire and ice leaking from his waving head, fear does intertwine with my love.

His light is fading.

I drop on all fours to be near him.

Gingerly, as if drained of life, he props himself up on his elbow. His other hand caresses mine. "You did it, wife."

"No, I didn't. He'll be back."

He doesn't reply, but his downcast eyes speak.

"Husband, listen to me, please," I beg and move my hand from his fingers to his neck. "I know you don't like it when I—or anybody—tells you anything like this, but your anima is almost gone, and I have to say something."

"I'm fine."

"No, you're not!" Frustrated tears mix with the terrified ones. "You're not okay, but you're trying to act like you are so you can take care of everyone else, and it's—it's killing you. It really is killing you. You're going to kill yourself trying to save everyone who doesn't need saving."

His expression hardens.

"I'm not trying to be holier-than-thou or dramatic or something!" I cry. "I just ... I—husband, I want you back." Now I wrap both arms around his neck and pull his head to my chest like a treasure. Unable to look at him in my swirling irritation and grief, I howl at the overhead darkness. "I want *you* back! Since this whole battle started, I feel like I've lost you more and more. Every time someone dies, it's like a part of you—part of your heart and your fire—went with them to death, and now ..." I force out the words. "And now you're almost extinguished."

The sensation of his fingers sliding through the hair at the nape of my neck sends welcome chills through my body. Following the gentle urge of his action, I look down.

His eyes find mine. "I didn't want you to know. I didn't want you to hurt because of me."

A broken laugh puffs out of me. "I can see your anima. I can see you. Every day. Hurting. How could I not see that half of who I am is fading?"

Sitting up, he huffs out a sigh. "I'm ..." Apologies don't fall from his mouth often. For once, I wait for him to find words. "I haven't been loving you like I should. I want that to change. I'm angry, and I believe what the enemy said, but I want to ... find a way out of this darkness."

"I'll be with you," I tell him, gripping his wrists. "I will be with you however you need, and we'll bring back your anima."

He nods and rests his forehead against mine.

"Fire and ice," I whisper.

His comprehending, ironic chuckle shakes me as well. Then he mumbles the words I hope he never forgets again. "Alone, fire burns out and ice freezes up."

The hint of a hopeful smile eases onto my face. "But together they make water, and water can find a way through anything."

My husband wraps his warm hands around my chilly fingers. "Eventually."

TO LOVE A PHOENIX
Hannah Carter

"I want to go with you," Thomas declared softly. He huddled close in the moonlight and shuddered, a chill settling into his bones. It seemed to magnify the fear in his heart, the fear that he couldn't conquer, despite knowing what he had chosen to love. His brain rationalized that he had to trust in the Sacred Texts, but his heart ... his heart trembled, which only amplified the effects of the autumnal wind.

Suffice to say, Thomas was miserable in all facets.

Aerin tied the knot that secured her invisibility cloak around his shoulders. She reached up to twist his long, dark curls around her finger while the mist swarmed around them both. The forest's curved trees seemed to protect them from the outside world, though it could not hold back the monsters for much longer.

"I know, love," she whispered in her thick Faelic accent, "but you cannot."

Thomas reached out and grasped her waist, but she slipped from him and turned to face the incoming darkness.

Thomas chased after her. "If we fight them together—"

"Then they'll kill us both." She shook him off. "No one is braver than you, but there are too many of them."

A howl pierced the night. Thomas shuddered, and this time,

when he moved closer to Aerin, she didn't protest. He seized her hand and squeezed it. That should have steadied him, but he couldn't silence the niggling doubts that swirled inside of him, taunting him with the fact that this could be the last time he did so.

The words spilled out of him a bit quicker as he continued, urged on by panic. "But you're the Phoenix. You have immeasurable power! Surely we can defeat them together." He brought her fingers to his lips to kiss them. Despite the cold, they were warm, a testament to the fire inside her veins, the power that flowed through her.

Aerin's red hair twisted in the wind, and she tucked it behind her pointed ear. Though she was not pure fae—not many people in Faeland could still boast pureblood—she was more fae than Thomas, who came from second-generation immigrants from Dyfed.

"Thomas." Aerin tugged him down with her one free hand to press her nose to his—a fae sign of affection. "Please don't make this harder than it has to be. I don't want to leave you either, but this is my job. Ever since the Phoenix Revelation of the Sacred Texts, I've known my lot in life. I shouldn't have fallen in love, but you had to be so persistent. And so persistently underfoot whenever I tried to do anything."

They both chuckled, though it was a weary sound, filled with bittersweet nostalgia. "I knew if I kept putting myself into perilous situations, you'd come around eventually."

Aerin closed her eyes as she rested her face against his. "You must have been right, although you didn't have to put yourself into peril in such endearing circumstances. How was I supposed to ignore a boy who crawled down onto the cliffs to rescue a waterlogged pixie who couldn't fly to safety?"

"See?" He wriggled his nose against hers and then captured her lips once, briefly. "It was all part of my devious plan."

"Ach, somehow I imagine there wasn't enough thought in your actions to call anything a *plan*." She returned his kiss, though she didn't linger.

For some reason, the thought of deepening such a pure peck offered more anxiety than pleasure for Thomas.

Another bay interrupted the moment. Long, loud, and more chilling than the weather could ever be.

"They're here." Aerin cupped his cheek. Her eyes flickered across every feature of his face, as a soldier would memorize their creed before marching into battle.

And indeed, they were marching. The magic-users of Kingland had somehow organized their own werewolves and the wulvers of Faeland. Through a form of dark sorcery, they'd compelled or ensorcelled the beasts to turn against the people of Faeland.

Thomas's breath hitched in his throat. He could feel her pull away, and his grip tightened.

"Aerin! No. *Please*. Don't go. Let's run. Please." His voice broke, and he felt like he might vomit.

"Remember the Sacred Text." Her own voice trembled. "Even if I die here, I am the first Phoenix. I will be reborn infinitely."

"But I don't know *where*! The Sacred Text says it could be in any world, at any time—you won't be *my* Aerin!" Thomas brought her closer so that the invisible cloak covered both of them somewhat, but neither of them completely. "We can hide," he whispered in her ear, his grip tightening on her shoulders. "We'll go. To Dyfed. They're not involved in this blasted war."

"I cannot let others suffer. If we leave, if I do not fight here, then all of Faeland will die." Aerin shoved him away. He staggered backward.

His eyes widened, but when their gazes met, he saw no betrayal in her forest-green eyes.

Only tears.

"Stay. Here." She held up her hands like he was an animal. "Hide. I refuse to let you sacrifice yourself here. I have to know you will live on."

Thomas took a step anyway. "How can I live on if I know *you* sacrificed yourself and I did nothing? It will be hard enough without you, but to know I did *nothing* ..."

"Thomas, *please!*"

Red eyes flickered to life in the trees behind Aerin. Their arrival was heralded by a symphony of howls. "Use the cloak. Go invisible! Now!"

"But—"

"*Thomas!*" Wings of flames unfurled from behind Aerin. "Please, love! *Please!*"

He backed away a few more paces as flames enveloped her skin. He winced and held up his hands to protect himself as the heat forced him farther back still.

She rose into the air and faced her enemies. Behind her, he stood—and all of Faeland.

"Demons," Aerin growled, "my death will be your death. But my rebirth will be victory. Faeland will endure!"

Fire exploded from her skin, and the inferno tripled in size. Even with his eyes shut, Thomas could still see the imprint of the flames on the back of his eyelids.

The Sacred Text also spoke of Hell; he imagined this was the closest man could get to such a conflagration without facing the second death itself. He cowered on the ground, ashamed of himself even then.

He had to help. There had to be *something* he could do.

Yes, the Sacred Text said she would be reincarnated, and he

believed that. But knowing her spirit would continue meant nothing to him if he couldn't save the one he loved.

The werewolves and wulvers snarled and growled. The smell of burning flesh made Thomas gag, and he brought the invisibility cloak up over his nose. Tears and smoke stung at his eyes until he heard something that spurred him to action:

Aerin's scream.

He flung the cloak away from his eyes. She wailed again as more flames poured out of her body—but this was not her normal power. It almost looked as if the Phoenix essence was *peeling* away from her.

The giant werewolves snapped at her feet, her legs—anything they could get ahold of. But each of them only got a few tries before they were devoured by Aerin's blaze.

"Aerin!" Thomas bellowed.

"*Stay back!*" Aerin cried. "Thomas!"

He bolted ahead.

The heat made him lightheaded; the smoke clogged his throat. He had no weapons to speak of and not an ounce of magic in him. Thoroughly unremarkable in every way, save one: his desire to save his love.

He tackled the first wulver.

Somehow, I imagine there wasn't enough thought in your actions to call anything a plan, Aerin had said. And, as always, she was right.

The beast snapped at him. Its teeth dug into his shoulder and ripped a chunk of flesh and fabric away. Sweat dripped down his face as he slammed his fist into the creature's maw and shoved it upwards. It clawed at him, and, if it made impact, he hadn't yet felt it nor the shoulder injury.

A werewolf tackled him from the side.

They tumbled off the wulver and kept rolling until they were nearly underneath Aerin. Thomas shoved the beast upwards and into the path of the fire before crawling away.

Three ... four ... *five* more came his way.

Aerin flew up higher as the perimeter of her massacre grew.

Blood poured down Thomas' arm. He clutched at it as his mind slowly started to recognize the agonizing pain he was in. He buckled, and their enemies began to circle him.

"I'm so sorry," his voice broke, his whole body and spirit ragged. The ground rose up to meet his face as the world began to swirl.

And, though it could have been delirium, he could have sworn the Phoenix severed itself completely from Aerin.

But it must have been true. Her wings disappeared, and she plummeted. He reached out to catch her, but he was too far away. She collided with the grass a few feet away from him, but before a wulver could devour her, the Phoenix glided past the monsters nearest Aerin and Thomas. The beasts reversed their course and began to flee, but the Phoenix swooped throughout their ranks. One moment, an enemy soldier ran towards the tree line, the next, the Phoenix swooped down and enveloped it, cutting off their cries. Thomas could see the outlines of the monsters as they were incinerated, dissolving away to nothing but ashes.

Thomas pulled himself over to Aerin's body with his one good arm.

He tried to choke out her name, but the word clogged in his throat.

He coughed and wheezed until he could finally prop himself up, surrounded by the charred remains of the monsters.

He reached for her cheek.

She was so cold.

Sobs ripped from somewhere deep inside his chest, as painful as if someone had ripped his beating heart from there instead. He gathered Aerin up into his arms and rocked her. His tears dripped onto her cheeks and slid down, as if she shared his emotion.

"Please, Aerin. Please come back." He could barely move his lips. "You promised. The Sacred Text promised. Why does it have to be another world? You're the Phoenix; come back to me in this one!"

But Aerin remained limp in his arms.

Meanwhile, her Phoenix power only grew in ferocity as it swept through the forest and burned through the mist and every threat that had come to the shores of Faeland.

Though he wasn't psychic, he knew in his heart, as heavy as it was, that Aerin's sacrifice had won the day today. No adversary could withstand its potency.

He rested his lips on her clammy forehead and rocked her lifeless body.

"You did it," he whispered, though it took all his effort.

But somehow, knowing she'd accomplished her mission didn't give him any comfort. All of Faeland couldn't stop the wound inside him that bled far worse than his arm.

I have to know you will live on, she had said. But a life without Aerin was not one that was worth living.

A silence hung in the broken forest, only broken by the soft beat of flapping wings.

The Phoenix returned and hovered over them. Most of the inferno had calmed down until it was just warmth upon his face. It enveloped him like a hug, made him remember what it was like to be caught in Aerin's embrace. Its blazing, colorful feathers were just close enough to him that he could touch it.

"Please," he murmured.

And its dark eyes, though inscrutable, seemed to whisper to him. *What is it that you want of me?*

His heart thudded, and he coughed once before he could find his voice. "Bring her back. Please. Take anything. Take *everything* from me. Bring Aerin back."

Her time as the Phoenix is over. She will be reborn in the next life, in the next world. There are dangers that we must stop there.

"She needs her life here!" Thomas' arm ached as Aerin grew too heavy for him to bear. He gently placed her on the ground and settled next to her. He groaned as his shoulder protested even that. "Please. I need her. She needs me. You saw. You *were* her." He stared at the bird, searched for any sign that it retained the briefest of Aerin's memories.

The Phoenix dipped its head. *I grieve with you, but we cannot stay here. Aerin's time as the first Phoenix has concluded.*

Thomas started to tremble. Whether the main contributor was blood loss, adrenaline, or raw emotions, he couldn't say. He curled over and wrapped his arm around Aerin and pulled her corpse next to him.

"Then take me with her."

He thought of her words again. *Somehow, I imagine there wasn't enough thought in your actions to call anything a plan.* This time, it brought a smile to his face.

Perhaps he didn't really *plan* or think anything through, necessarily. But his makeshift thoughts and cobbled together schemes had served him right thus far.

The Phoenix's wings glided back and forth. *What?*

"Take me with her. Wherever she goes, I want to go." Thomas closed his eyes and pressed his nose against hers. "If you have enough power to send her to wherever she has to go, then I know there's enough for me."

You would really abandon this world? All that you know? For her?

"My world is wherever she is."

The Phoenix shook itself and unfurled its brilliant feathers. They seemed to grow and shine brighter, as if the sun itself had descended upon the face of the earth.

I have seen no greater dedication in all the worlds. Pluck one feather, and we shall see if you are worthy enough to follow.

The Phoenix hung in midair right above Thomas. He groaned as he adjusted himself. Exertion threatened to split his body apart from his injuries, but he ignored the agony as he strained to grasp the lowest feather on the Phoenix's tail.

And then—

Pain.

Power.

Purification.

Thomas' mouth opened in a wordless scream as holy flames traveled across his body and set him ablaze. He understood how the wulvers and werewolves must have felt in their final moments.

He extracted the singular feather from the Phoenix's plumage; it flew off into the sky.

Blackness encroached his vision, and he slumped forward, all senses gone as the blaze consumed his body.

A scorched husk collapsed beside Aerin as the flames from the Phoenix smoldered in Thomas' burnt hands. His eyes, lifeless and black, peered out from a disfigured face. Later, that would be how they were found: her, untouched, an angelic expression even in death, and him—mutilated to the point that he was only identified by process of elimination.

But if someone had searched the skies that night, they would have seen a sight far more spectacular and beautiful: two stars bursting into a great shower of colors and meteors right at twilight, during the magical time when the veil between the worlds is at its thinnest. The beacons heralded the birth of two new babes in a neighboring dimension, born of sacrifice and desire, yet unaware of the future:

The next Phoenix ...

And her lover.

WHERE THE LAND MEETS THE OCEAN

Effie Joe Stock

She didn't think she could ever tire of visiting the ocean. Not because of the sunsets or the salty air, though. Because of the way the waves would gently kiss her feet as her toes sank into the sand. Because though the waves would leave, they would always, always come back again, never leaving for long.

She saw those same waves in *his* eyes, in his eyes of swirling blue. The darkness and light they held as she felt his gaze kiss her softly and sweetly was the same warmth in her chest as a loved one coming home—someone who left but always came back.

The ocean itself is in that gaze, she thought. *The wonders of the deep, the beautiful thoughts, and the thoughts hidden in the depths.* No matter how much she discovered in the ocean or his heart, she always uncovered something new, something more, that held her constantly enraptured.

Such beauty and complexity was almost impossible to comprehend. What could stand against it?

Nothing, of course. Her heart sank as she slid her hands into her pockets, not wishing to turn away from the ocean's spray. For when she walked away from the ocean, all she could see was the inevitable stretch of land, of the brown, bland earth—the desiccate, boring dirt.

The same bland dirt rested in her eyes—a stretch of boring nothingness in the gaze that always frowned sadly back at her in the mirror.

Mindlessly, her fingers played with her hair. It too was brown like the dirt, brown like the earth where nothing new or exciting ever seemed to happen.

A flash of gold in the thick clouds against the setting sun caught her eye, and a smile bloomed on her face. *His* hair was golden like the sand under the waters or the sun smiling back at itself from the glassy, blue waves.

The smile fell from her face as she stared down at her hands. *Why would he want to look at me? At my dirt brown hair and eyes which hold nothing but dry dust and hard rocks? Why,* she thought, *would he want to look back at me?*

The ocean spray mixed with her tears as she cried, rivers of water streaming down her face after swirling in her dark eyes and then dripping into her hair. Warm, rough hands brushed the salty tears and ocean from her face; when she looked up, her eyes met the waves of his moving gaze.

Gently, he ran his fingers over her face. Gently, he brushed away her tears and caressed her cheeks and lips. His gaze moved across her face, down her neck, to her hair, but he always looked back at her eyes. A smile grew across his face.

"Why?" she asked in pain, unable to share the peace he held while looking at her. "Why do you smile when you are faced with something so bland, so common, so boring? Why would something so beautiful want to come back to something so dull?"

His grin only widened as he spoke not a word, and took her hand, leading her to the edge of the land where it met the drifting water of the ocean.

With her feet sinking in the sand, the water kissing her toes, she turned her face to his before following his gaze to the horizon.

"Oh, my dear, you are far from dull, but if you must know why I return, it is because the ocean needs the earth." His hands tightened around her own. "The land holds the water in. It controls the path of the streams, making sure they arrive safely at the ocean and that they reach their dreams. Under the waters, the land holds up the ocean, though the crushing depths may hurt the earth. At the highest peaks, the earth holds up the sky and towers into the stars, reminding us that we can reach our dreams and soar in the clouds."

Her brows furrowed as she tried to understand, tried to see what he saw, hear what he heard, and feel what he felt.

"The earth does not fear the turmoil of the water," he continued softly, "and never flinches when the water rages against it. While the ocean rages and plummets and turns, the earth stays grounded and stable. The land never moves and never leaves."

His gaze returned to hers. She watched him unfailingly before he turned his wandering attention to the fire the sun left dancing on the water.

The tears slowly stopped trickling down her skin. With wide eyes, she gazed at the land she stood on, seeing how it sloped under the waves while still peaking to the stars behind her.

His hand brushed her soft brown hair out of her face, and

he let the darkness of her eyes consume him.

"I may not be able to drown in your eyes, but I don't want to. They are the color of warmth, of comfort, of home. They are the color of mystical caves and hidden secrets, and they hold the life of the dirt that flowers grow in. They steady the storm within me. They are the rock on which I rest."

New tears streamed down her face, but they were tears of joy. *Perhaps,* her heart skipped a beat, *I finally understand.*

"I love coming to the ocean," he whispered into her ear, a strange smile crossing his face. "But not for the sunsets or the salty air. Because no matter how many times the waves wash away, the earth is always here when they return."

He took her hand in his and turned her to the horizon, stepping out into the water. Together, they felt the earth between their toes while the water washed over them.

They were one with the ocean and earth, just as they were one with each other. Neither could exist without the other, and where the land meets the ocean is where their love grew.

PURPLE WATER
Savannah Jezowski

Baby, kiss me in the rain;
Kiss me underneath the purple water.
Kiss me in the grey dawn,
And as the sun rises, hold me tighter.

You are always waiting,
Waiting for me with a glow on your face.
And when I see you waiting,
I understand about amazing grace.

Darlin', kiss me in the rain;
Dance with me in the purple water.
Dance until the grey dawn,
And as the sun rises, hold me tighter.

I am always running—
I never thought it would come to this—
That in all the glittering world—
All I would want is one more kiss.

Just one more kiss in the rain,
One more kiss under the purple water.
One more kiss in the grey dawn.
While the gold sun rises, hold me tighter.

Baby, kiss me in the rain.

BLACKHEART
Joanna White

Syrath stood in front of the wall inside his room, glaring at his clenched fists in concentration to force them to stop trembling. *Stop,* he commanded, but his body wouldn't listen. In Syrath's mind's eye, he could only see the man with the scarred lip and hear the cries of the man's wife and children as Syrath robbed him of life.

"Syrath?" a soft voice murmured. That voice was like velvet, so soft and innocent in a world so dark and cruel. Syrath's muscles relaxed.

"You're trembling. What happened?" Syrath flinched as Jineza touched his arm. She moved to stand in front of him and, even now, it amused him how small her frame was compared to his. He had the body of a killer: toned, with enough muscle and power to overcome his opponents, yet lean enough to slip inside places others could not.

"Killed a man. Your father's orders. But the man's wife and kids were there. They saw—" A lump formed in Syrath's throat, and he couldn't force the words out.

Jineza's eyes glistened with tears, but she wrapped her arms around his waist and pressed against his chest. Why was she embracing him? He was a monster; they both were, thanks to the cult that had forced them into this life.

Images appeared in Syrath's mind, memories that he didn't want to see ...

Syrath's ten-year-old form trembled before the Sorcerer King who cast a High Magicka Pain spell upon his young body.

"We serve Nemesis. Nemesis leads us. We will bring order to this world." The Sorcerer King towered over the young boy's trembling figure.

Syrath closed his eyes and clung to the image of his mother, of his siblings, of their beliefs. *No,* he thought. *I serve no one.*

As the years went by, the pain became too much and he gave in to what the cult wanted, what Nemesis wanted. It wasn't order, as they proclaimed. They wanted pure chaos—a world under their strict rule, to kill anyone who stood in their way.

And they had turned Syrath, Jineza, and others like them, into monsters to cut down their enemies and bring about the so-called order that the cult desired.

"Oh, Syrath ..." Jineza's voice snapped him out of the memories. Her words were a cry, a plea of agony that flashed in her eyes.

The pain in her eyes, the guilt and agony etched on her expression, tore at his heart. Syrath finally forced his fists to unclench and he gripped her cheeks in his hands. "Jin ... the man was a soldier, a warrior. He had a scar over the left side of his lip ... and so many others. He—he fought so hard to live, for his wife, for his children." Guilt welled up inside him and ate away at him until he could no longer stand upright.

Syrath collapsed, but Jineza was there. She clung to him as if he was her lifeline. He *was* her lifeline, as much as she was his. How many times had he comforted her after the Sorcerer Kings or the Overseers tortured her? How many times had she stayed by his side, despite the terrible things he had done?

Another memory welled up.

Fifteen-year-old Syrath gazed down at the poor girl about his age. Her back was covered with blood that oozed from several lashes. He swallowed deeply at the sight. A quick glance around told him they were alone, so he reached down toward her.

"Father, please don't hurt me," she begged.

"I will not hurt you." Syrath lowered his voice as he gently picked her up in his arms.

The girl's eyelids fluttered open to look at him. "Who are you? Why are you helping me?"

Syrath winced as he shoved open the door to an empty room in the barracks. "Because I remember what it felt like to help others." By now, those memories had faded, but he clung desperately to them each and every day, afraid of losing them to the doctrine the cult wanted him to believe.

Gently, Syrath lay her on a bed. "What is your name?" he asked.

"Jineza. Yours?"

"Syrath. Y—you mentioned your father ..." His voice trailed off.

Jineza's eyes filled with tears. "One of the Thirteen Sorcerer Kings is my father ... I—I was born here."

At least Syrath had the gift of knowing life outside the cult; Jineza never had, not until they had met and Syrath used every free moment they had to tell her of the outside world, of compassion and kindness, of many things she had never known before.

"Syrath, one day we will be free." For a moment, Syrath had no idea whether Jineza had said that to him in the past, or the present, not until he felt her tears against his cheek, where she cuddled with him.

Syrath shook his head. "No." He could never hope for it. Hope, in a dark place such as this, was a dangerous thing. It held power to break him apart, and he did not have much left to break. Everything else had already been taken from him. Everything, except Jineza.

He placed a hand on her stomach. "Is the Low Magicka spell still in place?"

Jineza nodded and interlocked her fingers with his. Such a precious life she carried inside her—their child. "Yes. No one knows how big I am since the illusion spell hides my baby bump. I—I am getting to the point where I should be resting, but they won't allow it. Not without an explanation and you know love is forbidden here. If I am caught, if *we* are caught—" She choked, gasping for air as if she were drowning.

Syrath pressed his lips to her forehead but said nothing. They would be torn apart, if they were caught, and their child killed. In a place such as this, there were worse punishments to endure than death.

"Would it have been better to ... to ..." Jineza choked, and her hands tightened on his. "To end it before now?"

Syrath shook his head, glaring down at her, but his anger was not toward her. "No. Never, Jin. This child deserves a life. I will request that you accompany me on a mission when you are close to labor, and we will have the child and give the baby away. Please, just—just trust me."

"I do." Jineza swallowed deeply, and her eyes flicked to the door. "I have to go. We can't be caught." As she headed to the door and Syrath watched her leave, he felt his heart leave with her.

What if her father, the Sorcerer King who led their unit, did not allow Syrath and Jineza to go on a mission together? How would Syrath excuse such a thing? Would he truly be able to pay off a healer to help her give labor, and give away the child to an orphanage, all without word spreading back to the cult somehow?

The cult worked in the shadows—most of the world of Alrika did not even know they existed. They influenced everything—from starting wars between kingdoms, to assassinating any king or council who stood in the way of their goal. One day, Nemesis and his cult would rule all of Alrika; of that, Syrath had no doubt.

How could the outside world stop a threat they could not even see?

Would their child escape this life? Or would the baby be discovered? Worse, what would happen to their son or daughter in a world where the Cult of Nemesis gained complete domination?

Syrath leaned against the wall as tears fell from his eyes. All he had was Jeniza. She was the only good he had ever been given in his life, and even the mere thought of anything happening to her, or their unborn child, nearly drove him to the brink of insanity. His stomach tightened, and he tried to slow his breath to stay calm.

Yet, his sins were many. The man with the scarred left

lip appeared in his mind, and he could not stop staring at the man's wife and children, sobbing and crying for their dying father—demanding justice to his murderer.

What gave Syrath the right to have love, to have a child, to have even a brief moment of happiness?

"Why do you want to go on a job with my daughter?" the Sorcerer King eyed Syrath closely. He was a bulky man, with a stern gaze that made every man before him tremble. He was one of the most powerful Spellwrites in the land, able to wield not just Low Magicka, but High Magicka as well. All members of the cult were Spellwrites, called Sorcerers, but only the strongest members, like Jineza's father, became Sorcerer Kings who controlled the various units of Sorcerers within the cult.

Yet even a Sorcerer King answered to the cult leader: Nemesis.

Syrath met his gaze and held it. "I believe we can learn from each other. She is far better at stealth than I, and there is much I could teach her about using her strength properly in combat."

The Sorcerer King crossed his arms with a curt nod. "Very well. I will send you to East Lavaste to assassinate a nobleman who is rallying the people to his cause. We cannot have them getting strong enough to overthrow Western Lavaste." The Sorcerer King waved his hand, and a scroll appeared in the air.

Syrath inclined his head and snatched the scroll. On it, the details of the mission were written down. He quickly read them over and then inclined his head once more. "It will be done."

On their way to Lavaste, they could stop by an infirmary. Hopefully, the healer could use a Low Magicka spell to induce Jineza's labor and would take the child. Then, they could complete the mission and succeed without the Sorcerer King or the Cult of Nemesis finding out.

Syrath gritted his teeth as he paced in front of the door. From inside, Jineza screamed in pain, and he flinched. They had endured much worse, but not being able to see exactly what was going on made his heart hammer in his chest, and he could not force his body to still. She had been in labor for over eight hours, and stopping for much longer would be difficult to explain to the cult. Then, there was the concern of whether Jineza's body would recover well enough without the cult noticing, even with the healer giving her Low Magicka spells to aid in her recovery.

Jineza's cries silenced.

Syrath held his breath and stared at the door.

It opened, and the healer smiled at him. In her arms, a tiny baby screamed and reached out a hand for him.

"You have a beautiful baby girl!" The healer held the baby out to him.

Syrath gazed upon his daughter's beautiful face and felt his heart expand. His baby girl was so tiny and innocent, knowing nothing of the world or its cruelty. With a deep breath, he reached out for her and the healer gently passed her to him. "How do I ...?" he choked.

"Just support her head. Like this." The healer smiled at him.

His daughter's cries stilled, and she peeked open her eyes at him. "So precious," he whispered, and tears fell down his face.

"Yes, precious indeed," a deep voice rumbled from behind him.

Chills skittered up Syrath's spine, and he whirled around, gaping at the door to the infirmary. The Sorcerer King towered there, along with other Sorcerers from the cult—at least six of them. One of them had cast a death spell onto another healer and dropped her body onto the floor.

The healer behind him screamed and backed up into the room.

"Father!" Jineza cried from where she lay on the bed. "Wait, please, I beg of you! Forgive me. Forgive me, but let our child go! She has nothing to do with this!"

Syrath backed up into the room as quickly as his body could move. By that time, Jineza had stumbled out of bed, so he handed his daughter to her. "Go! Out the window, now! I'll hold them off!"

As Jineza opened the window with one hand and slipped through it, Syrath called energy to his hands. Ten fireballs shot out from his palms as he cast the spell, and the fireballs grouped together like a wolf pack. They surrounded two of the Sorcerers, who focused on countering them with their own spells.

The Sorcerer King formed a greatsword entirely out of ice. The temperature in the room dropped, and as he slashed the sword toward Syrath's chest, a burst of ice magic erupted from the blade.

Syrath called wildfire to his hands and combined it with vines—another one of his classic spells—before hurling them at the Sorcerer King who easily cleaved through them with his sword.

In those few seconds, the other Spellwrites had worked together to cast a High Magicka Spell by channeling the Sorcerer King's power. Strands of energy formed chains that clamped around Syrath's wrists and ankles, forcing him to the ground.

He glared up at the Sorcerer King, who held the ice blade to his throat.

From the door to the room, an Overseer shoved Jineza onto the floor and tossed the baby at the Sorcerer King.

Jinza screamed, and an explosion of raw power erupted from her body. Three of the Sorcerers fell to the ground dead as she charged toward her father

Syrath closed his eyes and poured magicka into the chains, to try to shatter their spell, but to no avail. It was fueled by the Sorcerer King, so only his death would break it. Still, he channeled as much mental Ether energy into the Sorcerer King's mind as he could.

The Sorcerer King stabbed his ice blade into the ground, and an inferno of ice burst all around them. It pinned Jineza to the wall across from him and coated the walls, the floor, everything. "Father, I beg of you ..." Jineza sobbed, thrashing, but it was no use. Ice coated her entire body, forming a prison around her. Their precious little girl wailed and thrashed in the Sorcerer King's arms. He drew a dagger out of his belt and held it in front of the baby.

Syrath glared at him. "Leave our child out of this! Punish us; kill us, instead!"

The Sorcerer King grinned, and the sight twisted Syrath's stomach. "I am." With that, he brought his blade down and ended the precious little life in his arms.

Jineza's cries tore at him.

Syrath met her gaze, thrashing and roaring in fury and anger and pain. Agony twisted his stomach and heart as he pleaded and begged, but the words and pleas were lost.

Syrath watched as the Sorcerer King killed Jineza, the only light in his life, the only woman he had ever loved. He watched as everything good in his life was ripped away from him, watched helplessly as death consumed everything he loved.

His daughter. His wife. Everything.

Syrath's world shattered around him, and he could not see beyond the tears that fell from his eyes and his heart.

The Sorcerer King walked toward him. Hope fluttered in Syrath's chest, hope that he would die and be reunited with his daughter and wife.

But that twisted grin returned to the Sorcerer King's face. "Oh, no. No, no, no. I will not give you the relief of death. Instead, I am going to punish you the only way I can: letting you live."

ETERNAL LOVE
Moriah Jestus

What if you were you,
And I were me,
But our souls connected for eternity?

Would you love me as much as the day we met,
If you never got a break from me?

Or would our love grow dim like the dying stars?
A spectacle in the eyes of others,
But a tragedy in our hearts?

TILL DEATH
Julia Skinner

Jace limped into the outskirts of his hometown right as the pain in his injured leg became nearly unbearable. He'd been walking for miles, ever since the coward he'd hired to transport him had refused to come any closer.

"Don't you know?" the man had said. *"That's where the monsters live!"*

Clenching his trembling hands into fists, Jace stumbled down the single dirt road. It had been eleven years since his team killed the last monsters prowling around these parts. *But they're coming back.* Claws of fear clenched around his stomach at the thought.

On both sides of him, blocky cottage homes rose up like burial stones. If he looked closely, he would see memory upon memory etched across their worn walls. Lanterns hung from the posts of each house, in hope that the weak light within them would be enough to keep the monsters away.

It wouldn't be enough.

It was *never* enough.

But maybe ... maybe he would be able to keep his promise. If he got there in time. He glanced over his shoulder, and a chill prickled the back of his neck. The barren land stretched on for miles—empty, save for the gathering darkness on the horizon.

They're coming. The words were a sickening mantra in the back of his mind. *They're coming. They're coming.*

Jace could *feel* them clawing across the land as they hunted for the ones who had imprisoned them for so long—could almost *see* their eyes, red and murderous. *The Kalaik.* The monsters he and his best friends had sworn to protect the world from. A sharp pang shot down his left leg, and he gritted his teeth. It had never fully healed from being mangled years ago.

He risked a glance up at one of the curtained windows, and thought he caught some movement inside. A heartbeat later, the door to his right cracked open, and a woman peeked out. Shadows bled from her eyes, streaming into hooked fangs.

Jace slipped his trembling hand to the hilt of his sword and forced himself to blink. The shadows on the woman's pale face vanished. *Stupid brain.* He gritted his teeth. "Does Aerie still live in the last house?" The woman nodded nervously, then clicked the door shut again.

Sucking in a shuddering breath, he struggled down the road. Something as simple as walking seemed to be getting more difficult with every passing day. Years back, when he was young and sane, this walk had been a joyful event. He and his friends would gather at Aerie's house to dream of the future—a future in which they saved the world from the monsters cursed to destroy it.

They'd succeeded. But they'd also failed.

And now, once the monsters consume Aerie just as they did the others—his mind hissed—*you will be left alone to fight the dark-*

ness.

His throat grew tight.

Alone.

It was a word that had plagued him his whole life. A *curse,* he'd often thought. Until he … until he met Aerie. She'd fit in the cracks of his shattered soul. And for a time, she had *filled* it.

But nothing good ever lasted.

That was one bleak fact he'd learned over the years.

Jace paused as he came to the edge of Aerie's yard. Her house's worn trim had been replaced, and on each side of the door was a flower bed with foreign yellow plants. Everything was so vibrant. So *alive.* His eyes stung. A few steps from the front door, a little boy sat building a miniature house out of sticks.

"Hey kid?" Jace said. his heart squeezing in his chest

The boy jumped, and looked up, revealing green eyes identical to Aerie's. "Who are you?"

"Nobody," Jace grunted. "I'm looking for Aerie." He glanced over his shoulder. The darkness had grown as the sun sank lower, stretching long, obsidian fingers toward the town.

"Your sword looks like my ma's." The boy said, as if he hadn't heard Jace.

Jace's throat tightened. "Yeah? Where's your … your ma?"

"She says hers is to help her fight monsters," the boy continued. "Do you fight monsters too?"

Jace's brother's face bled through his memory, screaming as the monsters devoured him. Suddenly, the boy's long, dark hair morphed into jagged claws. Jace dug the edge of his hilt into his palm, struggling not to let his broken mind take control. "Just get your ma."

The boy rolled his eyes. "Ma! There's a weird man out here!"

Jace cast another quick glance behind him. *They're coming.*

"Weird man?" an achingly familiar voice asked from inside. His heartbeat quickened as *Aerie* stepped out of the house. She was wearing a plain wood-brown dress instead of the bulky armor he always remembered her in, and there were more lines etched across her face, but it was ... it was *her.*

And suddenly, after eleven long years, Jace felt as if he could finally *breathe* again.

Aerie froze as she caught sight of him. "Bren, go inside," she whispered. The boy—Bren—frowned but scurried in without a word. "*Jace?*" her eyebrows arched incredulously.

"In the flesh." He tried to straighten his shoulders, to put on an air of strength, like he always used to. But even his sword felt so much *heavier* than it used to.

"Are you ... alright?" She asked. When he didn't answer, she reached inside the door and pulled out her sheathed sword. "Why are you ... I mean, it's been ..."

It's been too long, he thought, letting his hand drop from his sword's hilt. A thousand words inside him ached to be set free. Words he'd stuffed down deep inside for every day they'd been apart. Words he could *never* say, now.

"They're back," Aerie guessed, a slight tremble to her voice, "the monsters. They're free, aren't they?"

He forced his eyes away from Aerie, sweeping his gaze across the yard. They'd been standing right here the day his older brother first introduced them. "Aerie?" Jace had mocked. *"That sounds like a character in some stupid, old legend."*

He'd been young, and *stupid*, and so wrong. The old legends were *extraordinary*. And she had lived up to every single one.

"You okay?" Aerie repeated, cautiously walking forward. Of course, she would be afraid of him. She'd seen him at his worst. She knew just how badly his mind had been broken—how little he was in control.

I'm here to keep my promise. He wanted to say. But the words stuck in his throat. Behind her, the door swung open again, and Jace stiffened by reflex. A tall man stepped out, with hair the same dark shade as the boy's, a short-cropped beard trickling down his jawline. The lamplight behind him cast a long, jagged shadow against the ground. A shadow that ... *contorted* into a sickeningly familiar shape with dripping black claws.

Jace panicked. For a moment, his mind slipped back into the past, and he jerked his sword free, stumbling away from the monster.

"It's not real!" Aerie snapped.

Cold sweat trickled down his back. He forced his eyes away from the hulking monster, and toward Aerie. She had her own sword drawn, but instead of facing the nightmarish shadow, she pointed it towards him, lips drawn in a thin line. Eyes that had once softened whenever they looked at him now hardened to stone. "Put the sword *away*, Jace."

But ... But ... the Kalaik were ... He forced himself to blink, once, then again. The monster vanished, leaving behind a normal shadow, cast by a normal man.

"Jace." Aerie raised her voice warningly.

Jace tightened his grip on his sword, clinging to the cool, metal hilt. Logically he knew he should put the sword away, but ... *what if they are here? What if he just hadn't seen them yet? They could be sneaking up right now, about to pounce, about to ...* his thoughts tumbled over each other, a chaotic, dangerous mess. *STOP IT!* Jace shook his head, trying to clear it. *I can't lose control. Not now. Not here.*

Please.

"What is going on?" The man stepped beside Aerie, peering at Jace worriedly.

Monsters, Jace cursed silently, stepping back a few more steps. They weren't just hunting him out there beyond the edge of town. They were in his head, crawling and scraping and *howling.*

Aerie sighed. "This is Largon. My ... husband. And this, is Jace."

"Jace?" Largon said. There was a note of recognition in his tone. "It's good to finally meet you! What brings you this way?"

Jace tried to focus on Aerie and ignore the haunting shadows flickering around Largon. *It's just in my head. It's not real.* "You're in danger."

"Danger?" Largon asked, smiling good-naturedly. "We live out here in the Graves, *everything's* dangerous here. You're going to have to be a bit more specific."

Black splotches flickered across Jace's vision. He could feel his mind slipping into the crimson-stained shadows of his memories. *Don't lose control. Don't lose control.*

"What happened?" Aerie stepped closer.

I ran. He thought. *When I could have stood and fought, I ran.* Images of the gate he guarded all these years rose in his mind.

It had been the only thing keeping the monsters locked away. Cracks had appeared, splintering as the monsters' dug their long black claws through, ripping it apart from the inside out. He hadn't been able to face them alone. Fear and shame burned holes in the pit of his stomach.

"The seal broke," Jace whispered, throat raw. "They're … free, Aerie"

And they're coming.

"Who—" Largon began.

"The Kalaik," Aerie answered before he could finish. Largon stilled, a look of horror creeping across his face. "We have to go." Aerie glanced toward the mass of shadows just outside town. "Maybe we can make it to Westhar? It should have some guards."

"I'll get the wagon ready." Largon spun, running for the back of the house.

"I'm sorry," Jace muttered. He'd gone his separate way so that she would be safe—so that she would have a good life. And now, here he was, tearing it all away from her, dragging her back into the darkness with him.

She will die, and you will be left alone.

"It's not your fault," Aerie said. "This was bound to happen."

He squeezed his eyes closed. They were the same words she'd said the day she left. The day they … they finally admitted they weren't supposed to *be.*

This was bound to happen.

It's not your fault.

Some people aren't meant to be together forever.

Jace clenched his hands into fists. "It's always been my

fault, and you know it."

"*That*," she said, "is not true."

"It *is*." he muttered.

"Oh, so you don't trust me now?"

Jace clenched his jaw.

"*Maybe*," she said, an edge to her tone, "if you would just listen to me more, you wouldn't—"

A cackling howl shattered the still night. Jace whirled around, heart pounding. Thick shadows crept down the street, looming alongside the houses, and dousing the flickering lamps in pitch black. Only those who'd spent years watching for the creatures could catch the subtle way the darkness shifted and slunk.

They're here. They're here. They're here—

Jace struggled to breathe. Scarlet suddenly dripped from his blade, matching the blood-red eyes that peered at him through the shadows. *No ...*

Tinasy, the youngest member of their team, appeared to the side, writhing on the ground. Blood seeped from the slits in her armor.

Please, no.

Gir—his best friend—reached out a desperate hand before plunging into darkness.

No!

His brother collapsed in front of him, face contorted in pain.

Jace fell to his knees, left leg searing with pain, as if it were being ripped open by the Kalaik's claws all over again. All around him, his friends screamed as they fell to the monsters they swore to defeat.

Someone grabbed his arm. "Jace!" Aerie's voice sounded so *far* away. "Jace, please, just focus on my voice. We can get out of this. But I need your help."

Jace blinked, trying to push through the black swimming around him, pummeling him, *drowning* him. But he was so ... weak.

"You're safe, Jace, you're at my house. We can still get away, but we have to go now. Do you hear me?"

Jace blinked, and the darkness of his mind receded slightly. *This isn't real. I'm at Aerie's home.* Not in the middle of battle. He sucked in a deep breath. *We don't have to fight them.* The memory of his friends blinked away into the shadows, and Jace shoved himself to his feet. Aerie was next to him, and she grabbed his arm, helping him stand.

When had he started shaking?

"We will get through this together, just like always." Aerie said. She sounded so *sure*. The words stacked themselves in his mind as he stumbled toward the back of the house, creating a soft wall against the onslaught of shattered memories threatening to overcome him.

Largon and Bren sat in the wagon. As soon as Jace and Aerie hauled themselves into the back, they lurched into motion.

"Ma?" Bren asked, "what's going on?"

Aerie settled down beside him, face pale. "Monsters, hon."

Bren let out a squeak. "Are they coming for me?"

Aerie somehow managed to *smile*.

She was ... she was *so beautiful*.

"You don't have to be afraid." she said. "Didn't I tell you?

I'll protect you. They can't get to you."

Red eyes—not just a memory anymore—burned from the shadows around the fading house. Jace's stomach flipped nauseatingly.

"Largon, we need to go faster." Aerie said, voice forcibly calm.

We won't make it.

Jace inhaled. His sword suddenly felt *so much* heavier.

They're going to catch up.

"Mamma," Bren whispered behind him. "Who is that?"

"Oh," Aerie hesitated. "Just ... someone I used to work with."

He'd been so much more than that. *They'd* been so much more. But none of it mattered, now, did it?

You don't have to be afraid. I'll protect you.

Jace looked back at her and Bren. Aerie would die to protect her family. If the monsters reached them ...

"I have to go." The words came out without him meaning them too, and for once, the darkness in his mind quieted.

Aerie vaulted to her feet. "*What?*"

I promised.

The Kalaik skimmed across the ground in great slinking strides. "Someone has to hold them off."

"You can't do that!"

"I have to."

Desperate anger flashed across Aerie's face. "Jace, you are *not* going to go face them alone! I'll—I'll come with you; we'll face them together."

He looked at her, and memories flickered through his mind. *Good* memories, from a time when the world wasn't so dark. Of them arguing over the last slice of pie or challenging each other to duals to prove once and for all who was the better fighter. Sitting up at night to count the stars whenever the nightmares kept one of them awake. *I guess that's why we like legends,* Aerie had said one such night. *They're like little stars we can take out whenever we like, and they make us feel less alone.*

"You need to stay with your family, Aerie. And I ..." The words snagged in his throat, as if they'd grown claws. "I made a promise." *To protect you.* "Remember?"

Tears brimmed in her leaf-green eyes, making them glimmer like stars. After a long moment, she nodded and held out a shaky fist.

I love you. Jace thought, an ache rising in his chest, washing over the fear, *filling* the cracks in his chest. He rested his fist against hers and met her eyes. "Forever," he said, voice hoarse.

"Till death," she whispered.

It was their promise. Their oath. And he was going to keep it, even if it meant going their separate ways. *Again.*

Blinking his burning eyes, Jace turned toward the darkness—toward the monsters—and jumped.

MY LIFE IS YOURS
Katie Marie

The streets were filled to near bursting with milling people, the buzz of hundreds of conversations overlapping each other. Robots beeped and dinged as they assisted their masters to make purchases. Hovercrafts zoomed recklessly through the crowd surrounding her. Lizzie was just another thing taking up space, wasting the precious air she breathed.

Unseen.

Unwanted.

Useless.

The three 'U' words were used to describe Lizzie and other cyborgs daily, interchangeable with: barbaric, mere property, thing, and animal.

Not human.

Lizzie was on her way home that night, keeping to the edge of the night crowd so as not to get in anyone's way and cause a scene. She kept her head down, her brown hair pulled back into a sloppy ponytail, hands tucked into her pockets.

Her left leg was heavier than her right, making her steps uneven, but it'd been seven years since the accident that'd changed her life forever, plenty long enough for her to be used to it. Even so, she'd never be able to understand how one unfortunate instance could make her different and disgusting. Change her from a normal girl to something not worthy of life.

What's the point? Lizzie gazed at the world around her, always flowing and changing, never stopping for a second to notice one particular cyborg out of the rest of them. *What's the purpose of life if everyone around me says I'm unnatural? That I'm nothing more than the robots they make and break at whim, with no soul or heart?*

She sighed, her steps never pausing as they traversed the packed sidewalk. Lizzie dodged Normals on their way home, jumping over destroyed robot parts, blending in seamlessly with the noise and bustle of the city.

Stopping at an intersection, Lizzie looked left and right, searching for an opening in the busy street, hovercrafts and cars flying past.

Lit-up buildings lined the streets, neon signs and screens blaring advertisements for cyborgs for sale, the new ultra-hovercraft, and many other new and exciting inventions.

The light turned green, and she stepped into the road behind the others who'd been waiting with her. She trailed several feet behind them—the proper distance for a cyborg and Normal.

Lizzie focused on the white stripes stark against the black road, tuning out the never-ending noise. As she reached the middle line—the others far ahead of her now—her ears picked up one particular roar out of the nighttime hubbub.

Lizzie's head shot up, her eyes widening as a car charged straight toward her, not caring that she'd be run over.

Lizzie screamed and tried to jump out of the way, but her metal leg tripped her up and she fell, bashing her head on the concrete.

The car flew past her, but before she could move her human foot out of the way, the tires drove over it.

A strangled scream tore from her throat as unbearable pain flared up her foot. She rolled to her stomach, stars dancing before her eyes as tears streamed down her face.

Besides a few startled glances back, no one paid any heed to her, sprawled out in the middle of the road, her one human foot crushed beyond fixing.

Lizzie sobbed, holding herself up on shaking arms, the immense pain muddling her brain. She knew she needed to get off the road before the light turned red, but even the thought of moving left her mind reeling with dizziness.

The ding of the light changing signaled her doom.

This is it. I'm going to die. Her breaths came out in shuddering gasps.

Vehicles revved as they started moving again, the asphalt beneath her hands vibrating as they came at her from the front and back.

Unseen.

Unwanted.

Useless.

She lowered her head in resignation, tears leaking out of her eyes. Her arms shook so hard she didn't think she'd be able to hold herself up much longer. *Let it be swift.*

Headlights blinded her as a car roared closer and Lizzie braced herself for impact. Instead of feeling tons of metal slam into her, Lizzie felt heat radiating from the vehicle's engine as it screeched to a stop inches from her face.

Lizzie slowly raised her head

What ... the heck?

The driver's side door opened, jarring her out of her trance. Lizzie eased back into a sitting position to put distance between herself and the vehicle, groaning when she moved her crushed foot.

A young man slid out of the car, his face furrowed. He jogged around the door and squatted next to her. "Are you all right?"

He must not realize I'm a cyborg. His empathy would disappear as soon as he saw her fake foot.

"Miss? Are you hurt?" The man stared into her eyes, and Lizzie suddenly didn't know how to act. She wasn't used to people respecting her enough to look her in the eyes, much less hold her gaze with such care like he did.

"Miss?"

Lizzie realized she'd been openly staring at him for a long time now and still hadn't answered him.

She coughed, her face flaming, and jerked her eyes to the road. "Forgive me, sir. I—I am fine." Her fingers curled at the obvious lie, but she wasn't allowed to ask a Normal for help.

He made an unconvinced sound in the back of his throat. "If you're fine, then why are you lying in the middle of the road? Here, let me help you up."

He reached for her, his gaze roving over her for signs of injuries.

Lizzie tried to push her pant leg down but wasn't quick enough. She knew the moment he spotted her prosthetic leg.

His eyes widened and he gasped, his hand flinching back. Disgust and uncertainty clouded his blue eyes.

Despite this being exactly how she'd expected him to react, hurt still squeezed her heart at his obvious contempt for cyborgs—for her.

She should bow her head and stay quiet, but something about him made her want to try to get him to help her. Or maybe it was just that she didn't want to die, crushed by the inhumanity of her city.

Pushing past the pain threatening to send her into unconsciousness, Lizzie looked him in the eye. "Please, sir, help me. I can't walk on my own. I—I can pay you for your troubles." She implored him with her eyes.

He opened his mouth and licked his lips, no longer meeting her gaze. "Um, I don't ..." He looked about to bolt, his legs braced to run, arms flexing.

Lizzie's heart sank. *He's not going to help me.*

Tears stinging her eyes, Lizzie drooped to the ground, too tired and in too much pain to care anymore.

Vehicles continued to pass them, honking as they swerved to avoid

"What's the point of life?" she muttered, not expecting an answer from the boy still crouched next to her. She was shocked when he spoke.

"The point?"

Lizzie lifted her head, hesitant hope stirring at his determined expression.

"That, I don't know, but how can you find out if you die here?" He offered her his hand, his gaze steady. The city lights glinted in his blue eyes, something almost ... sad and regretful swirling in his irises. "Come, I'll help you."

Lizzie placed her hand in his.

He flinched when her cool metal hand touched his warm

skin, but he didn't back away. He pulled her to her feet, catching her when she cried out and fell into him.

"We better hurry," he said, guiding her into the passenger seat of the car before jogging to the other side and sliding in. The car still running, he put it into drive and merged with the traffic, speeding up to match the high speeds of the highway. "Do you have someone who can help you? I don't think hospitals take um, you know, your kind." He swallowed, refusing to look at her as his face flushed.

Lizzie nodded. "Take me to the western side of town. Please," she hurriedly added.

She knew a guy who specialized in cyborg injuries. She had her whole left side to thank him for, having gone to him after her accident.

Using a shirt she found in the car, she tied a makeshift tourniquet around her leg. Releasing a sigh, Lizzie leaned back against the leather seat. The adrenaline drained from her body, leaving her tired, shaky, and in so much pain she wanted to scream.

The guy kept shooting furtive glances at her. He'd probably never seen a cyborg this close before.

It took every ounce of strength Lizzie had not to pass out, her boot slowly filling with warm, sticky blood. Her eyes fluttered closed.

Silas gripped the steering wheel so tight his knuckles turned white, fingers aching, but he didn't loosen them.

What've I done?

He couldn't believe a *cyborg* was sitting in his car, not even a foot away. His skin crawled at the thought, but Silas forced himself to keep driving and not demand she get out.

Silent minutes passed as he drove to the western side of town until he couldn't stand the silence anymore. Silas cleared his throat and glanced at her, noticing her skin was pale as a sheet. "My name's Silas Hunter, by the way."

She slowly opened her eyes, their brown depths clouded with pain. "Lizzie Axiom."

He blinked. *Lizzie* ... Such a normal name. Silas shook his head at his ignorance. If there was something he didn't know anything about, it was cyborgs. His mom grew faint whenever one was near, claiming their unnaturalness sent bad energy into her, so he'd never had the chance to talk to one before.

So far this one seemed ... well, *normal*, if you excluded the metal contraptions she had for an arm and leg. Silas didn't know what to do with that. His whole life he'd been taught they weren't human, they were things to be bought, sold, and made to work, nothing else.

He slowed the car down and took a left, entering the western part of the city.

Just dump her and run, a little voice inside of him whispered. *You have no obligation to this abomination.*

Yet a small, morbid part of him was curious about her. He eyed her. Why did she become a cyborg? Was she born missing limbs, or was she injured and forced to make the change? Hundreds of questions swirled inside of his head, begging to be answered, and he knew he couldn't leave until his curiosity was satisfied. *Which means I'm stuck helping her for now.*

Lizzie gave him directions and they soon arrived at an apartment. He made his way to her side, not wanting to touch her again but knowing she couldn't walk on her own.

He wrapped her right arm around his shoulders and walked toward the entrance, letting her lean her weight against him. He thought she'd be light since she barely reached his chin, but her cyborg parts made her heavy, causing Silas to stumble.

With her guidance, Silas led her to a door at the very end of the hall, a plaque next to it reading "Dr. Garn," and knocked. A minute later, a middle-aged man opened the door, peering at Silas and Lizzie.

Silas blanched when he realized the man's eyes were bionic. They were an unnaturally bright blue with little computer grids in them. On further notice, he realized almost every part of his body was metal.

Silas gulped, everything inside of him yelling at him to run, but he stood his ground. He shifted the girl to the front. "She's hurt and said to bring her here."

He inwardly groaned at how his voice shook. *These are cyborgs, Silas! They're beneath you and therefore should be the ones afraid.*

Dr. Garn beckoned them inside, closing the door behind them. "Come, come." He had Silas place her on a small white bed lined up against the wall, medicinal cabinets, surgical tools, and other equipment taking up the rest of the space. A door to the right led to his bedroom.

At least Silas assumed so. *Cyborgs have to sleep too, right?*

A groan brought his attention to Lizzie as Dr. Garn pulled off her boot, exposing a mess of bones, flesh, and blood—so much blood.

With a hurried, "Excuse me," Silas ran out the door and slid down the wall, where he sat for the next hour, listening to the girl scream and cry as the doctor worked on her.

It was past midnight by the time Lizzie was allowed to go home. Dr. Garn wanted to make sure her prosthetic foot had enough time to correctly wire into her flesh, but it seemed her body, already used to the metal and wires, accepted the new limb quicker than usual.

She stared at her bare cyborg feet, the left one skin-toned, the right one a tarnished metal. Lizzie had hoped Dr. Garn would have another real-looking foot, so she'd at least look like she belonged, but she hadn't been so fortunate.

Not like I ever am.

"Are you ready?"

Lizzie looked at Silas, who stood in the doorway. He was handsome and looked to be around her age.

"Why are you helping me?"

Now that she wasn't in immense pain—though her leg burned where the metal had been fused into it—her mind was clearing and she realized he was still here, despite having seen her humiliation of losing another human part.

Silas stuttered for a moment before blurting, "I was hoping you can answer some questions for me." His face flushed and he winced, covering his face with his hand.

"So, you're saying you used me to get answers to your questions about cyborgs? Cold." Lizzie shook her head at him, not knowing where her boldness came from but liking it.

I'd be beaten bloody if I dared say such things to anyone else, but for some reason, he doesn't seem as righteous as the rest.

"N—no!" His eyes grew wide, and he dropped his hand from his face. "It's not like that. I just ..."

It's almost as if he sees me as a human, which is ridiculous. No one has since I became a cyborg.

Using the small bedframe for support, Lizzie stood, testing the weight and feel of her new foot. "Hey, it's okay. It's only natural for you to have questions about us, seeing as cyborgs take up thirty percent of the population."

Satisfied she could walk and not fall flat on her face, Lizzie thanked Dr. Garn for his service, promising to pay him back soon, before turning to Silas and crossing her arms. "Tell you what. It's late, so why don't you stay at my place for the night, and I'll answer all of your questions in the morning?"

Silas hesitated, indecision clear in his blue eyes, before nodding. "Deal."

Lizzie eyed him, surprised, despite having made the offer. Why would a Normal willingly consent to stay the night at a cyborg's house? Surely he felt some reservation at the thought, but if so, he hid it well.

I have questions of my own about you.

Silas stared at the stained ceiling above him, wondering how he'd found himself here. He laid on a hard, uncomfortable couch while Lizzie—a *cyborg*—slept in the bedroom.

I'm sleeping in a cyborg's apartment.

It was unheard of, yet here he was. He forced himself to fall into a restless sleep, imagining bugs crawling on him all night.

The next morning, they convened in her tiny living room, sitting a comfortable distance from each other.

Silas could feel her eyes on him while she waited for him to speak. But now that he was here, about to get all of his questions answered, Silas didn't know what to ask. *Start simple, then go from there.*

Clearing his throat, he spoke. "How long have you been a cyborg?"

"Seven years."

So, she wasn't born deficient.

"What, you know, happened?" *Why are words so hard?* He scratched the back of his hot neck.

Lizzie was silent for a moment. "I was in a car accident when I was eleven. Some idiot hadn't engineered his hovercraft correctly and it suddenly malfunctioned and sailed forward, ramming into the front of my car. The bottom of it smashed my entire left side, rendering my left arm and leg useless and my ribs completely shattered, puncturing vital organs. The fumes from the hovercraft burned my left side, the skin on my chest and stomach disintegrating."

Silas stared at her, his stomach churning at the horror of what'd happened to her. How painful that had to have been, and at such a young age.

"He left, not even bothering to check on me. The safe-tracking installed in my car alerted my parents about the wreck. They came, but my injuries were too severe for a hospital. My parents were desperate, every second costing me my life, and knew the only way to save me was to make me a cyborg." Lizzie's voice was monotone as she relayed her past, as if she was numb to the events that'd taken place years ago.

"Against their better judgment, they took me to Dr. Garn, who amputated my arm and leg and put in prosthetics. He fixed my damaged organs with different gadgets before fusing metal to my right side, making half my torso cyborg."

Bile rose in his throat. Were all cyborg's stories so horrible? She'd been a normal girl, just like him, until the wreck changed her life forever.

An uncomfortable inkling floated at the back of his thoughts, that maybe, *just maybe*, cyborgs shouldn't be shunned.

"That's ..." Silas shook his head, cleared his throat, and tried again, looking at her prosthetics. "I'm sorry."

She looked at him with wide, questioning eyes. "Why are you sorry? My troubles are far beneath you."

Silas laughed it off, hoping she didn't ask more about his words. *Trust me, I wish I knew. Something about you compels me to sit and listen, to know more.*

They continued back-and-forth like that for the next hour, him asking and her answering until all of his questions had been answered. His head hurt trying to work all of this new information into what he'd thought he'd known.

As he left her apartment and made his way home, one thought stayed at the forefront of his mind the entire time.

The world has it all wrong.

They met up many times over the next several months, finding random excuses to satisfy their curiosity about each other, mostly meeting in empty parks or at her apartment.

As they talked, sharing things they'd never told another soul, a bond started to form. It was strange and completely unorthodox, yet it worked. They were cautious and guarded at first, quick to judge and hate, but slowly, through conversations on rooftops, goofing off in abandoned parks, and laughter over delicious food, they opened up, letting themselves be free in the presence of someone who no longer cared if you were rich or poor, normal or cyborg.

Silas had his moments where he judged, but he was getting better, little by little.

Lizzie shared how she struggled with what her purpose was and how she wanted more for herself. Silas understood, said he often battled the same thoughts, though he never said why, and she never pushed.

She'd discovered that Silas was smart and tinkered with inventing things in his spare time. Silas mentioned he'd be interested in making cyborg parts to see if he could improve them, to which she was ecstatic. He was shy about his passion, claiming his parents found it foolish, but Lizzie thought it was incredible.

He was incredible. He made her smile and laugh more than she'd ever done in her lifetime and listened to her like no other.

As time went on and they met with each other more frequently, their bond grew stronger, morphing into something more. Something sweet and wholesome, something that was forbidden between Normals and cyborgs. They fought it at first, pretending like the feelings weren't there, but nothing they did could stop it from growing until they could no longer deny it.

They were in love.

Lizzie felt like she was living in a happy daze. Life meant so much more than it used to. Yet, she felt suspended in time, as if her true purpose still hadn't arrived. As if there was still something she was supposed to do, but what, she didn't know.

One night, eight months later, they sat on the roof of her four-story apartment, their legs dangling off the side as they took in the city lights as far as the eye could see. They were both quiet that night, content to simply be together.

The night was chilly, but Lizzie didn't notice, flush against Silas.

Lizzie looked at the dazzling lights, thinking about how far they'd come and how Silas accepted all of her now. She glanced at him beside her, her insides warm.

I didn't realize what I was missing until I met you. Didn't realize how nice it felt to have someone by my side, who treated me like a regular human. Now that I have you, I never want to leave you.

A small smile formed on her lips as she stared at him, his handsome features outlined by the lights below. Purple light reflected in his blue eyes, bounced off his mussed blond hair, falling over his snug shirt. He had dark circles under his eyes, probably from the late nights they spent together.

He caught her staring and crooked a grin. "What?"

"Nothing." Lizzie shook her head, her brown hair falling over her shoulders, and looked out again.

"Come on, tell me." Silas tickled her. "What were you thinking?"

She laughed and swatted him. "I was just thinking about

how you're going to change the world one day."

A laugh startled from his lips. "Me? Change the world? I don't think so." He shook his head as if she was crazy.

"No, I'm serious." Lizzie pulled her legs up and crossed them beneath her, facing him, unable to contain the excitement on her face.

He copied her, their knees brushing, one metal, the other flesh.

"Think about it. The world needs someone who's smart, inventive, and thinks for themselves. Your words and inventions could change the world and its opinions on cyborgs." Lizzie's hands flew as she talked, her words tumbling one after the other.

He opened his mouth to protest but Lizzie grabbed his hands in hers, holding them to her chest. "Listen to me! I've thought about this for a long time, Silas. No other Normal is willing to take a chance on cyborgs, so we need you to open the way for us. How we're treated isn't right and it's about time that changed. Don't you think?"

He stared at her, his mouth open, but no words formed. Different expressions flitted across his face.

She knew he loved her with his whole heart. But even now, even dating her, the fear that he didn't fully accept her grew like a dark cloud.

Silas fumbled for something to say, but his mind drew a blank. Normally, he wouldn't hesitate to say yes, but his life wasn't normal anymore. But Lizzie didn't know that.

He racked his brain, all too aware of the uncertainty and hurt growing on Lizzie's face.

Say something, you idiot!

"I-I, um ..."

Lizzie's countenance fell. She dropped his hands and stood, her face guarded. "You still think cyborgs are beneath you." Her voice warbled and her enchanting, dark brown eyes glistened with tears.

"No, wait!" Silas scrambled to his feet and stopped her from turning away with a hand to her arm. "That's not why I hesitated." He cupped her face in his hands, leaning down so she could see the truth in his eyes. "I promise, Lizzie, you're as far from beneath me as the sky."

A tear slipped down her cheek. "Then why?"

He licked his lips, torn. He wanted to tell her, desperately, but didn't know how. How did you tell the person you loved more than the whole world you're dying?

Silas drove home, dejected. He'd ended up unable to give her a good reason and she'd run off, her metal foot clanking on the brick rooftop, the bright lights outside mocking him.

Silas's chest ached so bad he could hardly breathe. His hands trembled on the wheel, his blurry eyes making it hard to drive.

I can't lose her.

But hadn't he already? The moment he'd become ill he'd lost her. *We were never meant to be.* But Silas refused to believe that. He couldn't bear the thought of leaving her, especially through death.

There *had* to be a cure for his illness. The doctors said there wasn't one. That it was incurable and led to death in every single case. They'd given Silas one year.

It'd been nine months since then.

Already, Silas was weakening, his body tearing itself up from the inside out. He couldn't move as fast, had a hard time breathing, and his body ached nonstop. So far, he'd kept it hidden from Lizzie, telling her it was the cool weather, but he wasn't sure how much longer he could keep it up.

He gritted his teeth. *I'm going to find the cure, and when I do, I'll return. I promise, Lizzie, I'm not leaving you.*

He parked in his family's wide garage and bound into the house, his insides burning with desperation.

"Mom! Dad!" Silas ran through their grand, two-story house, past robot servants cleaning the windows or dusting the fixtures, past wall-sized screens showing exotic scenery in place of windows, ignoring how his breath caught with every step until he found his parents in the living room.

"Dad, Mom!" He panted, his pounding heart feeling bruised, and dropped onto the couch across from them.

"Son! Whatever is the matter with you?" Dad looked at him sharply. "You shouldn't be running around like a fool in your condition." His voice was stern and demanding, but Silas knew it was out of concern.

"You have to help me find a cure for my illness. I—I don't want to die." The tears finally spilled over, burning trails down his cheeks. "I *can't* die."

"Silas ..." Mom walked over to him, wrapping her arms around him. "There's nothing we can do, baby. You know that." She sniffled.

He fixed his gaze on Dad—one of the richest and most knowledgeable people in the world. "If anyone can save me, it's you, Dad. I'm not asking. You have to find a cure."

Two weeks passed before his dad came back from looking.

Silas hadn't seen Lizzie at all in that time, despite how it killed him, but he knew he couldn't face her until he could tell her the truth, and that he wouldn't die.

He currently sat across from his dad in his office. His dad stared at him, his gaze hard.

Silas cleared his dry throat, anxious as he waited for the verdict. He clenched his hands together in his lap to keep them from fidgeting.

"There's a cure, despite what those foolish doctors told us."

Silas released his breath, weak with relief.

"Though, the way to the cure is a little ... underhanded, to say the least. I know you have a soft heart, so do you think you can do what must be done to live?"

He shifted in his seat, not sure what all 'underhanded' entailed, but knowing he had to try. "Whatever it is, I'm willing." *For Lizzie, I'll do anything.*

Dad nodded his approval. "Good. In my research on your illness and symptoms, I discovered there's a rare blood type that has certain properties that, when injected into your bloodstream, can heal you. Only a handful of people in the world have it. But luck's on our side. On further digging, I found there's someone who has the blood type in this very city—a cyborg."

Silas's heart renewed its racing at Dad's words. *I'm not going to die.*

But his new elation quickly turned to horror as Dad continued speaking.

"To make sure you are fully healed, you must inject as much of the cyborg's blood as you can."

"What are you saying?"

Dad looked Silas dead in the eye, unflinching. "You must kill them."

"Are you out of your *mind?*" Silas jumped up, his blood boiling. "I can't kill a human being!"

"Calm down, son. It's a cyborg, hardly worth the energy of getting upset over."

Silas wanted to scream. He couldn't kill anyone, much less a cyborg like Lizzie. *Lizzie ...*

He dropped his head into his hands, remembering why he was doing this. If he wasn't healed, he'd die and leave Lizzie alone in this cold world. *I can't do that to her.* But he also couldn't take someone else's life ... could he?

Bile rose at the thought, but Silas forced himself to think it through.

Whoever it was, they probably led a miserable life, just like his precious Lizzie had before she'd met him, alone and shunned. *They probably don't want to live anyway, so I'd be helping them, right?*

He couldn't believe he was even contemplating the idea but love and desperation made you crazy.

For Lizzie.

Silas hardened his heart and looked at his dad. "I'll do it."

For Lizzie.

Lizzie approached a dark alley at the edge of town, a paper clenched in her hand. Warning bells went off in her head, telling her this was crazy and to turn back before someone kidnapped her and scrapped her body for parts, but she forced herself to keep walking until she stood at the corner, peering into the darkness.

Earlier today, she'd found a note on her doorstep saying if she wanted to be liberated from her life as a cyborg, to meet them at this alley at night. Who knew what 'liberated' meant, but despite having no idea who this person was, Lizzie had decided to hear them out, her heart still hurting after the incident with Silas.

Maybe they'll make me human again, so he'll accept me, her heart whispered. Pathetic, yes, but she couldn't help it. Her need to see Silas again was driving her mad.

If meeting some stranger in a dark, creepy alleyway will help me, I'm at least going to try.

Taking a deep breath, Lizzie strode deep into the alley until the city lights had all but disappeared, leaving a faint purple hue behind her.

"Hello?" She squinted, trying to make out any shapes in the dark.

"You came." A voice, obviously deepened on purpose, came from her left. It sounded somewhat familiar.

"Y-yes. Who are you? What do you want?" Lizzie backed up as a form grew closer, swathed in black clothes.

"I'm here to liberate you from your cyborg life. You'd wish that, yes?"

Hands trembling, Lizzie nodded before remembering he couldn't see her. "Yes, I—I don't want to be a cyborg anymore." Tears pricked her eyes, her emotions rising. "But how can you possibly make me human?"

The man was silent for a minute before whispering, "I'm sorry."

"Wha--"

He lunged out of the darkness at her, the little bit of light glinting off of the needle of a syringe.

A silent scream rose in her throat as Silas's face appeared before her, his brown hair tucked into a black beanie. The syringe—filled with a dark green liquid—was poised to strike as he halted, his eyes widening.

"*Lizzie?* What are you doing here?" His voice shook, his face frozen in horror. He shakily slid the syringe into his front pocket as he stared at her.

What's going on?

Lizzie backed up, shaking her head dumbly. "Tell me you weren't just about to hurt me. Tell me, Silas!" Tears streamed down her face unbidden as the weight of his betrayal crashed over her.

"No! I would never hurt you!" He reached out but paused when she flinched, his face crumpling. "I promise, I had no idea it was you. My dad set this up and is the one who delivered the note. He never told me who!"

"What are you talking about?" Lizzie yelled, hurt and rage flaring.

"I ..." His hands fell to his side, his face lost. "I'm dying, Lizzie."

What ...?

"What do you mean you're dying?" she rasped, her insides sinking.

"I'm sick." Silas edged closer, keeping his hands raised. "I've been sick for nine months and only have three left to live. That's why I couldn't respond when you said you wanted me to be a spokesperson for cyborgs. I'm not going to live long enough to do so." His eyes pleaded with her to understand.

Lizzie gasped, more tears leaking out as the knowledge that he was dying sunk in. The grief that came with it threatened to send her into hysterics.

"If that's the case th-then what's this?" She motioned between them and the syringe. "Why were you going to kill me?" Her voice broke.

Shame sent his gaze skittering. "Dad found out that a rare blood type—*yours*—could heal me if all of it was injected into my bloodstream."

Her pulse pounded in her ears. *He needs my blood to live.*

He grabbed her hands and peered earnestly into her eyes, his own anguished. "But I realize now how mistaken I was. I could never kill anyone. I love you, Lizzie. I'll find another cure and we'll marry, grow old together."

Lizzie's heart lifted at his words, truly knowing now that he accepted her as a cyborg, but at the same time hurting worse than ever before. Because as he was talking, it was like she opened her eyes and suddenly knew.

Knew the answer to the question that'd haunted her ever since she became a cyborg—why was she here?

Unseen.

Unwanted.

Useless.

But she wasn't any of those things anymore. Silas saw her, the *real* her, loved and wanted her just as she was, and now, he needed her.

Clarity cleared her emotions, and she straightened, all of the hurt, fear, and self-loathing falling away, leaving her with a peace that told her this was what she'd been born for.

"Silas."

He looked at her, his beautiful blue eyes focused on her only.

She lifted their intertwined hands to her lips and kissed them. "Thank you for entering my life all those months ago. You saved me, literally and figuratively, and I can't possibly say in any amount of words or languages how much it means to me that you took a chance and found worth in me."

"Of course, Lizzie." He leaned forward and kissed her, his lips inviting. "I love you and am so sorry for all of this."

"I love you, too," she whispered, grazing his jaw with her fingers. "No matter what your dad or anyone else says, you're amazing, and your inventions and open mindedness will take you far in life. I believe that wholeheartedly. You're going to change the world, Silas." She smiled at him, knowing he didn't understand what she was saying and that she had to act before he did.

She kissed him, soft and lingering, gathering her courage. "Forgive me, my love."

Lizzie snatched the syringe from his pocket and, with one last look into his confused eyes, plunged the needle into her neck.

"No!"

It was as if Silas caught her in slow motion, sliding to the ground as the syringe emptied its lethal injection inside of her. "What have you done?" he cried, his voice strangled.

Tears streamed down his face, dropping onto her cheeks wet with her own.

Lizzie fumbled for his hand and squeezed it, her face twisted in pain. "I know my purpose now, Silas. It's to die, so you may live."

"No, no, no. You're not making any sense, Lizzie!" He looked around, his thoughts running rampant. "We have to get you to Dr. Garn, now!"

He tried to scoop her up, but she groaned.

"You can't save me, not this time." She coughed and cupped his cheek, gazing at him with such love it tore his heart in two. "You'll be okay without me."

He sobbed, pulling her close to his chest. "Why, Lizzie? Why would you do this?"

"Because I love you, Silas." Her voice was weak. "In another place and time, you would be mine. But, for now, my life is yours."

He smoothed back the hair stuck to her wet face and pressed a kiss to her forehead. "I love you, Lizzie. So, so much."

She smiled at him, her brown eyes whispering her love, and breathed her last, her chest stilling.

Silas bent over her and screamed into the night until his throat was raw. His insides felt like they were ripping apart. All he could do was hold her, begging her to come back, knowing she wouldn't, her skin cooling beneath his.

Eventually, Silas forced his tears to subside and looked at her, grief suffocating him. "You were wrong, Lizzie. I can't live without you. But I will try, for you, to live every day to its fullest, never forgetting for a moment your sacrifice."

For Lizzie.

The rest of his life would be dedicated to Lizzie, for because of her, he had a life to live. And he would do his best to change the world, so that in a different life, Lizzie might be his again.

ONLY YOURS
Lorelei Jensen

My maids readied me for the day. Every strand of my golden hair was tucked into an elaborate arrangement. A dress made of the finest silver silk laid softly against my skin. Jewels from deep within our kingdom's treasury adorned my neck, ears, and wrists. I was being prettied up, but I had no idea why.

Unlike most mornings, the maids spoke the bare minimum, asking only how I slept and if I was uncomfortable. Unlike most mornings, my dearest knight had not greeted me. My heart ached at the thought of him being caught up in something besides me.

The moment my father, the king, entered my bedroom, I knew something was wrong. Our green eyes reflected into each other. He grinned with a strange ecstasy. Worry knotted in my stomach. Father never visited me, never breathed the same air as me, but here he was, offering to escort me. Reluctantly, I placed my hand in the crook of his arm. Sweat ran down my back. My maids were sniffling as I left the room.

The sun warmed the hallway as we walked through. We passed precious portraits depicting the kingdom's history—

paintings of brave knights and beautiful nobles plastered all over the wall. Suits of armor lined the right-hand side while stained glass windows adorned the left. Their colors bled onto the marble floor. Riches graced the walls in a way that only the royal family could truly experience.

I never saw my knight. It was odd. He stood out and would never abandon his duty. I imagined his beautiful chestnut curls and warm brown eyes. The facial hair he was growing for a bet was not my favorite, but I had to admit, he looked much more mature with the stubble. He usually appeared by my side as soon as I exited my room if he couldn't give me a morning greeting.

Father led me into the courtyard as I reminisced. My knight and I met the summer I turned fourteen. He had just been appointed squire and was following around his lord at my day of birth celebration. My father had used the opportunity to search for a suitor, but I was enamored by that lanky boy. He grew into his height what seemed months later and now at twenty-three, he was a full-fledged knight, a member of my personal guard. It hadn't been hard to fall in love with him.

A large crowd gathered around a ginormous wooden platform. My reverie broke and so did my heart. I knew what this was. My punishment. It was a crime I'd commit over and over again.

My father dragged me up the dais. I couldn't even fight if I wanted to. His loyal minions were glued to my side. Before me, kneeling on the ground was my love, my dearest, my heart. Every second drove me mad, but it came hardly as a surprise—Father had warned me.

Father turned to the people. Knights, servants, and nobles

murmured together, wondering what special occasion called for an execution. Father smiled but looked at me with contempt.

Just like my mother, I ruined his plans. Though, he never expected Mother's betrayal like mine. She ruined his reign, but she died before all of it came to light. The people only knew of his bribery to the Church.

I stomped on the foot of a minion. He released me and I ran to my love. Bruises spotted on his cheek and bare arms. His left eye was swollen shut. Blood dribbled down his lip. Tears streamed down my face as I hugged him.

"I'm so sorry, Al," I whispered in his ear. He rested his head on my shoulder as we both wondered when we would be forced to separate.

"Don't be, my Princess." I couldn't fathom his calmness when a war of emotions raged inside me. "We knew this would not work out. I am a mere commoner, and you are the only princess."

"See here, a knight dares to seduce my daughter who has been recently betrothed to Duke Wellton," her father announced. Duke Wellton was older than the king and had been married thrice. They all died mysteriously, and Wellton was violent when drunk.

Hands grabbed onto my shoulders and tried to wrench me from Al. I shook them off, just for a moment, but it was long enough. I kissed my knight with all the living passion I had in me. My heart was breaking in two. I couldn't let him die. My hands wrapped around his neck one last time as I deepened our kiss. If all our other kisses had been sweet, this one was fire. It burned every inch of my soul. This heart would belong only to him, and Al knew that.

"I love you!" His words caused the burning in my body to increase. I tried to run back to him, but strong hands kept me locked in place.

Before I knew it, his head came falling down.

It rolled off the dais and into the crowd. Besides the initial screams, the courtyard was silent. An innocent man had died, and I did too.

The minions let me go, which was their mistake. I ran to Al's body, sobbing. I was dying.

My heart tried to rip out of my chest until I felt nothing. It was a smooth transition in all reality, as the storm inside me quieted, and numbness ran from my core to the very tips of my fingers.

I grabbed the dagger Al always had strapped in his boot. He was too loyal to this kingdom to ever pull it out on another guard, let alone the king. However, I did not have the same qualms.

"Now, let us celebrate the princess's new engagement with a feast," Father said so jovially. "Let us go, Elaine—"

My blade sank into his fatty flesh. Birds chirped around us. The wind brought the sweet smell of spring. Life would continue normally for everyone else even if Al was gone. Everyone else but me. But not anymore.

"You took my everything," I whispered.

Gasps rippled through the crowd below us. The situation hadn't caught up to everyone.

"Now I will take the only thing that matters from you."

I shoved him off my blade, pushing him off the dais. His blood dripped onto my fingers, sticky and warm.

I stared into the sky. The sun blinded my eyes. Life really

wasn't worth living without him—my knight.

A soldier grabbed me, preparing to take me in for treason. Execute me for murdering the king.

A smile lit up my face. "I'm coming, my Darling."

I plunged the knife into my heart. As the world dimmed around me, I knew only peace. *After all, I was truly only ever going to be yours, my Darling, heart, body, and soul. So, let's hope I find you in the sky.*

DEAD MEADOWS
Zimri A.Z. Zoran

"Do you not have to leave soon, Thales?"

Thales leaned against the rock behind him. The pool was fresh and cool, and his veins tingled at the sensation. He extended the vines on his wrist to snake around the nymph's shoulder. "Ah, but who would make your lilies bloom after I depart?"

The water nymph on his left snuggled into his side, and the one on his right traced the ivy leaves growing from his chest, cooing, "But Ília is about to retreat, and take her heat with her, you shouldn't tarry too long."

Thales chuckled. "My friend knows what I fancy." He squeezed the nymphs' arms and let his vines snake down their backs. "She'll wait 'till I finish."

The nymphs giggled and squirmed under his touch until another nymph poked her head above water. She ran her fingers gingerly along the corded vines and sturdy stalk of his shin. "As much as we'd like you to stay, Thales, the waters downstream have already chilled. The touch of Death will soon be upon us."

The atmosphere darkened and the other nymphs groaned and tried to shoo the newcomer away. Alas, she was right.

Thales hesitantly withdrew his touch from them. They whined, but he shook his head. "It seems Ília finally tired of my antics. I best move on."

He stepped from the pool, the root fibers on his feet absorbing the water that dripped down his body. Then he blew them all a kiss full of sparkling pollen and sauntered off, sprouts flowering up in his wake.

If Kataiyída wasn't comprised of clouds and hot air, Nekri would have certainly struck her by now, though killing Kataiyída likely wasn't the best idea. Vexing or not, the world needed her. But the Stormbringer insisted on following Nekri around and blathering her ear off about all her mortal conquests while Nekri tried to work. It wasn't like Kataiyída's storms were helping anything grow with Nekri around. The only thing Kataiyída did was use her illusive storms to block the Ceding Point: the entrance Nekri had used to get topside from the depths of Fthorá below.

Nekri brushed her fingertips against the nearest tree and watched as the tree's greenery wilted. It started dropping off and fluttering around her like brown, wilted snow.

She breathed a deep sigh, and with it, she expected the familiar stench of death. But her nose caught the scent of something else. Something fresh and floral.

"I tell you, that mortal nearly blew me away!" Kataiyída prattled. "He was unbelievable."

Nekri held up her hand. "Shh. I smell something."

Kataiyída's arm misted into position beneath her chin. "And maybe you can explain to me how me being quiet affects your sense of smell."

Nekri ignored her and followed the strange scent, the grass shriveling with her every step.

When she heard humming, she ducked behind the foliage, careful not to touch it lest her cover crumple to the ground. The man she saw, the hummer and certainly the culprit emanating the beautiful scent, was the most captivating creature she'd ever beheld.

Lush, green and full of life, his body consisted of winding vines and ferns, with the fullest leaves and foliage she'd ever seen sprouting from his head. A forest spirit, surely. He had a beautiful voice, if his humming was anything to go by.

He was gorgeous.

The light wind of Kataiyída's movement accompanied her suggestive squeal. "Oh my. You certainly found some worthy prey."

Nekri coughed. "Pardon me?"

Kataiyída motioned towards the handsome forest spirit. "Come now, look at him!"

"Truly." Nekri sighed. "Did you forget I kill everything I touch?"

Kataiyída's mist imitated a shoulder shrug. "You don't know. Have you ever tried with something sentient? No animals in the plants you touch die, correct? And what about that magic azfiddle plant of yours?"

Nekri shook her head, the blackened leaves of her hair swishing with the movement. "Asphodel, and never mind that. What is he doing here? All life spirits should've moved on with Ília."

"All the better for you, though."

Sparing one last glance toward the handsome spirit, Nekri turned and stalked off. "No, I'll do the rest of the forest, maybe he'll leave before I return."

When Kataiyída was silent, Nekri looked back, but the Stormbringer was gone.

Thales tarried, following Ília's path at his leisure. She wouldn't move on without him, of course, but she would be angry. Still, he could relish the warm weather and greenery in this beautiful landscape one more time.

A gentle breeze wafted towards him, and he inhaled. With it, a strange scent tickled his nostrils. A plant that he'd never smelled before? How was that possible? He stoked the growth of all of them.

He had to know.

The wind picked up but changed direction, urging him towards the mysterious scent. His nose led him down a path carpeted in dead leaves, its canopy skeletal and bare, to a massive asphodel, blossoming a stunning black in the midst of ruin.

Thales approached, squinting at the black velvet petals. "What are you doing here, beautiful?"

When he stepped before it, he reached his roots into the earth to find the roots of this unearthly blossom. Before he could make contact, the plant's roots lurched out of the ground and wrapped around Thales's legs.

"Wha—" He didn't even finish his question before thorns jabbed into his legs and the browns of the forest around him started swirling. His legs gave out, and all went black.

Nekri sighed. She'd cleared the forest of its greenery too quickly.

She was supposed to give the green man time to spirit himself away!

Did she secretly wish to see him? He was a lovely sight, indeed, but the chill hovered about her like a mist of death. The forest had cooled already, the frost that spread from her footsteps would freeze his feet before she even approached.

She likely couldn't even get close enough to talk to him.

Nekri brushed her hand through her shriveled hair. She checked the clearing where she'd seen the forest spirit. He was gone, and the chill had caused the flowers from his wake to begin to wilt. She followed the trail, stepping in his footsteps and putting to death everything that he'd given life.

Something felt strange. She stood at the crossroads where the path of Ília split from the direction where Nekri had breached the earth, and where she'd return when she was finished. Her Ceding Point. The forest spirit's trail lingered at the crossroads, then strayed from Ília's path. Down the path of Nekri's portal.

Nekri's breath hitched. Nay. It could not be.

She bolted down the path of death, following the spirit's wilted wake. Dead leaves flurried from her dress at the motion like dust shaken from an old rug.

She never should have lost sight of Kataiyída.

Nekri halted when she returned to the Ceding Point, where the Stormbringer's illusive winds were supposed to conceal the giant asphodel. Her asphodel split the barrier be-tween the wastes of Fthorá and the thriving lands of Zoí.

There, at the roots of the flowering black plant lay a prone heap of decaying greenery.

Oh freezing flora, no.

Please.

Nekri panicked, her breath releasing in pants that sprayed chilled puffs of smoke into the air. She hadn't made a mis-take like this in centuries. And every other time, someone was with her to dispel the poison. Her head swiveled in every direction.

Someone.

Anyone!

Anyone but her.

"Kataiyída!" she screamed.

Nothing.

"Ília!"

Still nothing.

She didn't have time to wait. If the asphodel's thorns had gotten to him already, theoretically, she might be able to touch him without him dying immediately. After all, he was already on borrowed time.

If he was still alive at all.

Nekri knelt beside the tangled pile. It was still recogniz-able as the male forest spirit, but his foliage already had the telltale blackened veins of the asphodel poison trailing up the leaves. His feet had already blackened and shriveled. She could sense the weak pulse of life, the klorosphyllon in his leaves struggling to absorb sunshine.

That would not work anymore.

The bite of her asphodel prevented life, so those kloros-phyllon were useless to him now. Nekri reached for him. One wrong move and she might kill him instantly. She clenched her teeth and held her breath. Nekri tilted his head to the sky and leaned close to listen. When she heard and felt his shuddering breath, she immediately stood and looked around again.

She'd killed the whole forest for the season. The soil had hardened with frost.

He'd die either way if she left him here.

Nekri cracked her neck like the snapping of branches and approached her massive floral portal of death. She glared at its petals.

"Witless windbag. You needed only to maintain the illu-tion! Why meddle in deadly impossibilities?" she snarled.

Nekri glanced down at the prone forest spirit and extend-ed her hand, the dead branches of her body snaking from her wrist like gnarled rope and encircling him as she hauled him upwards. Using one arm and all its snags to keep him aloft, she returned her attention to the perpetrator of his poisoning.

Her flower, her own portal.

Nekri grabbed it and violently wrenched it from its roots. The roots came loose and tore from the turf. A yawning abysm opened beneath it, howling with the freezing wind of the depths. Her snags tugged him close as she plunged into the ruptured void beneath the earth.

Thales groaned, which emerged in a strangled wheeze. What happened? He opened his mouth, but his body rejected the air. His limbs stiffened as the struggle to breathe devoured his mind.

"Calm. Panic not. Breathing doesn't work here. Relax."

The voice fluttered in, the sound of crackling dead leaves in the wind. It sent a shudder through his foliage. It sounded like the death he knew by heart every season when he returned to bring life back to the forests. But this time, the warmth of growth and sunshine that always burgeoned inside him ...

It was gone.

His fronds rustled, and the distinct crackling sounded closer. As if it came from ...

Thales seized, unable to breathe as his brain fought the realization that his body was dying.

He felt a chilled hand against his chest, pressing him back. He couldn't tell if he was laying on rotting detritus or if that was the crunch of his own dying body.

"Relax. Cease thoughts on breathing. There is no need for air here. You will not die yet, unless you insist on functioning in the same manner with which you are accustomed."

Thales tried to focus on the words instead of the sound of its voice. He scrunched his eyes shut and tried to turn his thoughts elsewhere.

How could he when his entire existence was life?

"You wake, that is a good sign. Had you not, you'd have been unable to return to the living world above."

Thales slowly forced his eyes open. His blurry vision focused on a pair of frosted white eyes, held in black sockets by intertwining black vines that formed eyelids.

His eyes shot open, and his disturbing companion leaned

back.

Dried leaves and vines framed the face of a woman; at least he thought it a woman. Knolls of dried moss rested on her chest, immediately interrupted by the exposed jutting ribcage of a small deer beneath it, the white bones caked in blackened clay and still clinging to dangling strips of dried skin. The ribs stopped at her waist, but as she turned around to retrieve something from a stone table, Thales choked at the view of the protruding skeletal spine down her back, the enlarged ridge of each vertebra shifting with her movements. Soil, thorns, and dead foliage wedged within the gaps in bone to resemble a fleshed shape.

He was going to be ill.

As though she sensed his discomfort, she turned quickly, a clay bowl in her hands.

"I am sorry. I realize this will be much to process. My name is Nekri."

Thales swallowed the lump in his throat. "You mean, you are—"

"I am the Deathbearer, yes."

"Am I ...?" he croaked.

"Not yet. Though due to my foolishness, you were poisoned by my asphodel's thorns. Your body functions differently now. I will not withhold the truth from you. I do not know if I can save you, but I will try."

Thales lifted his head to glance around. He lay on a bed of dry moss in an elaborately chiseled stone chamber. Gnarled, crooked roots snaked down from the void above. Glowing stones of blue and green rested in sockets along the walls. "Where are we?"

Nekri stooped at his feet and began to brush a strange

gloopy soil from the clay bowl on the roots at the soles of his feet. "In Fthorá, my realm. As my asphodel's toxin courses through your veins, you would not have survived had I left you. That toxin may kill you, but currently, it is the only thing keeping you alive in this place."

"You were correct." He laughed bitterly. "It is much to process."

Nekri massaged soil into his heels and stood, the withered palms and willows of her skirt swishing limply. "Take your time. Think not of breathing nor sunlight, you cannot use them anymore."

Thales dropped his head back to the moss bedding. How did this happen? His stiff limbs ached as he covered his face with his hands.

Nekri wasn't sure what she could have said to him that day. Ill and exhausted as he looked, he was still so handsome. Watching his expression sputter in confusion and devastation broke her heart. He distinctly averted his eyes from her after that, and avoided speech entirely, answering with nods or shakes of his head when necessary. No one ever came to look for him. With each passing day, even using fresh soil from her asphodel meadows on his roots, she could see the death in his eyes, though she couldn't tell if it was death of body or spirit.

"Thales," he mumbled as she put her clay bowl away.

"Pardon?" She looked at him, even as his eyes were glued to the hewn stone wall.

"My name. You deserve that much."

Nekri was unsure what to make of the conversation, but she smiled to herself nonetheless.

"May I use it?"

"I wouldn't have told you otherwise."

"Very well, Thales. Do stay where you are. I have matters to attend, but I shall be close if you need me."

As she left the chamber, an ache in her chest soured her giddiness, alongside a nagging nibbling at her mind. Like she was forgetting something.

Thales was so thirsty. He could hear the crackling whistle of his throat when he left his mouth open.

The crackling of his own body faded from thought when he heard the worst sounds he'd ever heard in his life. A grating rumbling sound echoed through his chamber, followed by cracks, clacks, and scraping. Then, the disturbing sound of a thud and a horrible crunch.

If Thales didn't think he was going to die before, whatever was outside was going to kill him.

But instead of impending doom, he heard the gentle crackles of Nekri speaking, followed by a rumble like a mudslide. The longer the strange interchange continued, the more curious he became.

Thales sat up and tested the movement of his legs. He might just have the strength to find water and slip by whatever was outside ...

Thales slowly limped for the doorway, glancing out to see an enormous tail waving out of view in time with more terrible crunching noises. The tail of the creature, like Nekri, boasted an entirely exposed spine. Its "flesh" was made from compost, dripping tar, and bones. Bones of other creatures, all sizes great and small, half-buried in the mire of the rest of the beast's body.

And that was only the tail.

Thales could only imagine the sound of this gargantuan creature's footsteps included the crunching of the bones that made up its flesh.

He shuddered.

"Quickly, dearest," Nekri said to the beast, "while he lives."

Thales gritted his teeth. If he could just find water, he might be able to free himself from this place. Somehow.

Nekri walked down a separate hall, and Thales studied the world outside his chamber. There was no roof, only black roots curling down from the blackness. Thales wasn't even sure if this was inside or outside, or if either even existed. Glowing trees, too geometrical and smooth to be biological, lined the halls like leafless sentries. A massive gaping gateway stood opposite of the direction Nekri and the beast had traveled. Would that be considered outside? There had to be some kind of water somewhere. It shouldn't take long to grab enough to satisfy and form a plan from there.

Thales slipped from his chamber and down the hallowed hall towards the open gateway. His shoulders tensed under the gaze of the lifeless trees' haunting glow as he passed beneath them.

The feeling fled once he'd crossed the threshold of the arched stone gateway.

Another sound filtered into his ears.

Water.

He heard water.

Glowing stones lined paths through the darkness. In the distance, Thales could see a pier and a hunched cloaked figure, looking more like a hulking vulture than anything else, perched on the beastly skeletal figurehead of a skiff. The waters the skiff floated in shimmered silver and moved like oil.

Thales chose the other direction.

He followed only the sound of flowing water. He used to be able to sense it and smell it, but those things were beyond him now. So he followed the trickling of water off the path and into the darkness.

It was a large stream, from the sound of it. When he reached the shore, he ached to step into it, but his roots likely would not absorb water anymore. Thales placed his hand in the liquid and focused on how it felt in his hands. It felt normal.

He couldn't smell it nor see it in the darkness, but he could wait no longer.

Thales cupped his hands and lifted the liquid to his lips. It was cool, refreshing his dried tongue and soothing his parched throat.

His sight turned bleary. As his ears started ringing, he felt like he heard his name from somewhere. His body swayed and his head started swimming as he plummeted into the water.

Thales woke to suffocation.

The fear of being unable to breathe came flooding back. Something dry pressed against his lips as dirt and clay poured into his throat. The earth crawled deeper. Thales felt it permeating every fiber, certain he'd burst if he were to take any more. He wanted so badly to cough, choke, anything!

He was going to die.

When his eyes started to reel, the pressure on his mouth lifted and he immediately gagged, spewing wet clay to the shore.

An angry shaking of dry leaves rustled in his ears. "What did you think you were doing?"

Thales choked, unable to voice his recognition.

Nekri.

She took a deep breath and calmed her voice. "Regurgitate it, Thales. All of it."

His stomach lurched as another round of wet earth launched from his mouth. He heaved and spat a few times, too overwhelmed to worry about decorum.

"I warned you to stay. If you'd absorbed water from this stream, you would have forgotten all things and remained behind a brainless husk," Nekri explained.

Thales couldn't bring himself to talk. His companion hummed. "Well, are you well enough? Do you remember my name?"

"Nekri," he rasped.

He must have imagined the squeaking sound afterwards.

"Come, can you walk?" she asked, clearing her throat.

T'wasn't a kiss.

Spewing soil from her mouth down his throat to absorb the noxious water could not be considered a kiss.

Nekri tempered her frenzy with her shame.

"There is water I can bring you. Asphodel dew is safe, but it will take time to gather. Can you wait for me?" She glanced at him lounging once again in his moss cot.

At his nod, her chest clenched. "Forgive me, Thales. I forget what things need to survive. Please, tell me when you thirst?"

He chuckled bitterly. "I didn't think of it. I've never had to ask for water before."

Nekri knelt beside him. "This is my fault."

Thales glanced between her face and her folded hands before touching her fingers. Nekri wrenched her hand away.

"Apologies. I am unaccustomed to touch. It is safer to keep your distance."

A crooked grin crossed his face. "So. That was your first kiss, then?"

Nekri halted with a squeak. He raised his eyebrows as she fumbled for words. "What of the boatman? Seems like you do have company ..."

She pursed her lips. "Varkáris is a husk, and most of my company have no lips or interest."

Thales chuckled. "What a delightful gift you've bestowed upon me."

When he followed his jest with silence, the Deathbearer glanced at her patient. He stared at his wilting fingers, and admitted, "Pity I cannot gift you the same."

She shook her head. "My purpose was to save you, but I

am aware. Worry not, I have always known the love of another to be beyond my reach."

Thales lifted his arms and legs, blackened with poison. "Well, you are no longer alone, then. Even if I could go back, naught a soul would give me favor now."

Nekri chewed on her lip before she responded. "That is my fault."

Thales watched her, but she couldn't bear to return his gaze. Her hands bunched into fists in her lap. "Kataiyída conceals my asphodel when I surface every season. She beheld my fancy for you and likely lifted the veil to give me a chance to court you. Thus, if I'd concealed myself better—"

"You fancy me?"

"I kill everything I touch, Thales!"

An awkward silence ensued, and she hurriedly retreated once she finished tending him.

"You may look now!"

Thales opened his eyes to a sprawling meadow of asphodel blooms. "Oh m—"

"Nay, not those. Here!" Nekri stood down an embankment, pointing to a small glowing pool that collected in a cove below.

He followed, leaning on a stone cane she'd lent him. Much of his body had wilted and blackened with asphodel toxin, but he still had the strength to walk with her. A smile hit her strange face as she knelt beside the water.

"This is all asphodel dew. It is safe. Drink, stand, bathe to your heart's content."

The grin on her face hit him off kilter.

Before he could formulate a response, a rumbling and crunching sound signaled the arrival of that strange beast he'd barely seen once. As the beast crested the hill, Thales wasn't ready for the sight. The behemoth's body consisted of the same clay, rot, and bones as its tail had, but it boasted three enormous skulls attached to its necks. Each skull had the teeth of a lion and deadly antlers; one of an ibex, one of a stag, and the last of a ram. Only much larger.

Nekri ran to it, leaving him behind with nary a thought. She greeted it as a treasured friend, and the monster leaned down as its heads fought for her affections.

The grin on her face as she talked to the beast made his chest warm, and he couldn't restrain his smile as he watched the woman stroke the animal's skeletal snout.

"Woman ... huh."

"Thales!" Nekri called, waving to him, "would you like to meet Ptómaskýlos?"

His crooked smile wouldn't leave his face even as he limped up the hill to meet her.

Thales leaned on the doorway, watching Nekri pace before the stone arch entrance. She hadn't told him what she was waiting for, but his curiosity consumed him.

Surely over the centuries a single soul must have looked her way. Her gentleness and warmth belied her cold exterior. Her looks mattered not to him anymore.

Him on the other hand ...

He glanced at his blackened body, sure that his face looked even worse. Now that his appeal and powers were gone, what was left?

Did he have any personality at all beyond selfish rake?

Thales winced as his leg gave out. That leg wouldn't last much longer.

A shining portal appeared in the archway, and a tall, shimmering man emerged. Thales crept closer to hear their words.

"Stav," Nekri said, "Thank you for coming. Did you discover something?"

Stav. Stavrodrómi. The Wayfinder. He handed a satchel to Nekri. "Only this. A ródi fruit from Ília's court."

Nekri cradled the bag to her chest.

"Apologies for arriving this late. I started hunting a cure the moment Ptóma arrived in my courtyard."

Ptómaskýlos. Nekri's three-headed beast. So that's where he'd been.

"I cannot thank you enough, Stav."

The man shook his head. "Nay, you need to hurry. The fruit won't survive here long. He needs to swallow the seeds before they rot. Even then, the cure is imperfect."

"I-imperfect?"

Stavrodrómi shooed her away. "Hurry! We speak later!"

Nekri scurried straight towards Thales. She grabbed his arm in passing and dragged him back to his chamber. She plunked him on the moss cot and grabbed his pitcher of asphodel dew they'd been keeping on the table.

Nekri shoved the satchel in his face. "Take it!"

"Wait ... cure?" Thales's head spun. Had she sent Ptóma out that long ago to send for a cure for him?

"Hurry! Open it, please!" Nekri's urgency startled him, and he reached into the satchel to find an already rotting thick-skinned fruit.

Nekri shoved the pitcher in his face. "Please, you must eat every healthy seed capsule you can! It will die if I touch it!"

"You did this, for me?"

"Eat!"

Thales focused his decaying fingers on the fruit and used all his strength to press it open. Nekri fell back to the floor, nearly spilling the pitcher.

"It's already dead ..." she yelped softly.

Nekri curled into herself, the branches of her limbs extending to entrap her within her own grip.

Thales glanced back at the fruit, carefully fishing through the seed pods.

One. Two. Three. Four. Five.

He plucked five healthy ones from the fruit and cast its rotting shell away. He put the seed capsules in his mouth, tasting the sweet juice on his tongue, and downed a sip from the pitcher to wash them down his dried throat.

Nekri's branches started to retreat from her as she watched.

Thales's head started spinning. He heard Nekri calling his name as he fell.

Thales's color wasn't right. Nekri hadn't left his side, and his color had definitely changed, but it wasn't exactly healed either. His leaves were weak and purple.

He groaned, and Nekri leaned over to watch him closely.

"So you see, the cure isn't perfect."

Stavrodrómi's voice nearly sent her into her skyroots. She swiveled to look at him.

Stav leaned on the doorway. "I wish I could do more, but I only create portals, Nekri. Ília said he may regain his powers on a seasonal basis. The poison has been with him for a long time. He will not be as he was."

Nekri shrunk, the sticks of her brows knitting together. "Why didn't she search for him earlier? Why did no one answer? I sent Ptóma for help the second I thought Thales was stable enough to travel ..."

"You care for him," Stav stated.

Nekri looked at the floor. "I do."

"Rather slow in admitting so, are we not?" a croak came from the cot.

Nekri squealed, "Thales!"

Her hands flittered in the air as though she were unsure what to do with them. Thales sat up slowly and took her wrists. "See? You cannot hurt me anymore."

Nekri threw her arms around his neck and knocked him back to the cot.

"How many seeds did you eat, forest spirit?" Stavrodrómi asked.

"Five." Thales sat up on his elbow, his other arm wrapped around the Deathbearer clinging to his neck.

The Wayfinder thumbed his chin. "Then you should see

your powers return for five moons, so you can walk Zoí in Ília's time every season. The rest you must spend here, or you will wither immediately. The asphodel holds deep, and you must now feed the nature of death within you, as well as the nature of life."

Nekri searched his face. "Will you be well, Thales?"

A crooked smile stretched his mouth. "I believe I can cope. The color may take some adjustment."

She watched him as he studied the purple leaves on his hand. "Perhaps," she said, "though I would say it looks rather fetching."

He raised his eyebrows as Nekri slapped her hands over her mouth. Then a thought crossed her mind she didn't wish to acknowledge. Thales's eyebrows fell into a furrow, and he lifted her chin.

"What ails you?"

"Nothing." She swallowed. "I'm sure you will enjoy yourself to the fullest when you return!"

She tried smiling, but any movement would shatter it.

Thales's gaze pierced her. "Nekri," he said, "What woman's touch would satisfy me once I've been the first to taste Death herself, then lived to tell the tale?"

As Nekri fumbled for words, Thales brushed the wilted vines from her face. "I shall sprout the lands of Zoí in flourishing verdure and hurry home to your arms before you recognize my absence. Now, that first salutation was rather muddy, care to reprise?"

When Thales tapped his lips to accentuate his point, Nekri's branches flared, and her ribcage rattled as she buried her face in her arms. Stav groaned from the doorway and stalked back towards the entrance. "Why did I not leave, that was revolting."

Nekri rubbed her lips together, then hazarded a glance at him. He pressed his palm against her cheek and gave her a gentle crooked smile. Her darting gaze slowed, and she relaxed into his touch, finally closing her eyes.

She was sure the dry vines of her lips were dreadfully unpleasant to the touch, but her worries receded when his mouth reached her. Slow and gentle, he didn't overstay his welcome, bestowing her with a small endearment before retreating.

Nekri felt shame bubble within her when he plucked something out of the tender greenery of his lips. "Oh, Thales, I'm so sorry! I never should have—"

Thales gave her his crooked grin, sparkling with mischief. "A splinter, love, nothing more."

He grasped her face with both hands and descended hungrily upon her mouth the moment she licked her lips. Nekri's arms flew around his neck as she lost herself in a warmth immune to death.

That time was indubitably a kiss.

GHOSTLY AFFECTIONS
Emily Anne

Friday

Ian **started awake** at the sound of the phone ringing. Glancing over at Katie, who was blissfully unaware of the obnoxious noise, he grabbed his cell and pushed "answer"; his feet hit the cold floor.

"Hello," he whispered, going into the bathroom connected to their bedroom, closing the door quietly behind him.

"Good morning, sunshine, do you plan on being late every day this week or just Monday through ... what day is this? Oh yeah, Friday."

Ian rolled his eyes at his partner's chipper attitude.

"Listen Grimes, just cover for me and I'll mad dash it there."

"Ian, my man, just a friendly reminder that you don't have to be back at work yet, we all understand I mean with the loss ..."

Grimes didn't get to finish his sentence.

"ETA thirty minutes." With that, Ian hung up. He washed his face, pausing to look in the mirror. Running his hand across his jaw made him want to shave; he turned away quickly. No time today. He grabbed his uniform off the floor, not caring if he wore the same one two days in a row. He just needed to get through another day and come back home. Slipping back into the bedroom, he gave Katie a kiss on the forehead and grabbed his EMT jacket before heading to the kitchen. He flipped the coffee pot on, then snatched a piece of cold pizza from the box on the stove, eating it in four bites even though it tasted like the cardboard it was delivered in. He filled a thermos with coffee and headed off to work.

When Ian pulled into fire station eleven, Grimes was outside the building waiting for him.

Ian got out of his pickup truck and slammed the door, knowing it wouldn't completely close otherwise.

"Grimes."

"Ian. About this morning, I just want you to know I care and will help in any way possible."

Ian flinched and closed his eyes. "I'm good Grimes. Let's just make it through the next twelve hours."

"Ok, but the offer from my cousin for counseling still stands."

Twelve hours later, Ian waved goodbye to Grimes and headed to the local supermarket. He picked up some flowers for Katie and some frozen dinners, even though the fridge was full of casseroles he never intended to eat.

Ian pulled into the driveway too quickly, causing him to bump the trash can, knocking it over. After cleaning up the mess he made, he trudged towards the front door, managing to unlock it with his hands full of groceries.

"Katie, I'm home."

Silence welcomed him. This made Ian panic for a moment, but he found his wife sitting in a chair on the back porch basking in the setting sun, the colors playing in her blonde hair.

"I grabbed some dinner and got you a surprise."

She looked up, smiling. "Those frozen dinners aren't actual meals, my love."

"Maybe flowers will make up for it?" Ian grinned and kissed his wife gently on the lips. She pulled away and looked at the bouquet of daisies, her favorite.

"Ooo, I love it. Can you put them in a vase for me? You're so much better at arranging them than I am."

"Next time, just say you're comfy and enjoying the sunset, would ya?"

She laughed and leaned back into the lounge chair, closing her eyes to the warmth once more.

In the kitchen, Ian found everything untouched. The coffee pot was full except for what he had drunk that morning. The take-out was still on the counter and the fridge full of covered casserole dishes. With a heavy sigh, he set the oven to preheat and started cleaning up his mess.

Later in the evening, the couple was curled up on the couch, watching reruns of their favorite show, *Mad About You.*

"What should we do tomorrow?" Katie whispered.

"Let's go to the park."

"I've been thinking, love, how much more we would enjoy the park if you got a dog."

"Your allergies pose a problem, Katie."

She rolled her eyes. "I don't think it's a problem anymore. Why don't we go look at the shelters tomorrow?"

"Hmmm, fine you win," he replied with a mock frown before smiling.

Saturday

Katie, dressed in the same outfit from yesterday, sat on the kitchen counter waiting for Ian to finish his morning routine.

"I'm thinking of finding a new job," Ian announced before drinking the last of his coffee. He rinsed the mug and stood at the sink, staring out the window. The fall leaves were piling up in the front yard.

"You love that job."

Ian shook his head. "Not anymore, Katie. It's too much pressure having everyone looking at me, monitoring my grief."

Katie sighed before jumping off the counter and coming to stand behind her husband. Wrapping her arms around him, she laid her head against his back.

"I truly am sorry, Ian. Maybe things would be better if I left."

He turned around and put his hands on her shoulders "Katie dear, you're the one thing in life I care about. Without you, everything is pointless. I think maybe a change of pace ... maybe in a new place, would make everything better."

"Did you just call me Deer?" she asked with a laugh.

He frowned and then chuckled as well. "I suppose that pet name is off the list now."

"Quite removed. Speaking of pets, let's go find one!"

Ian entered the animal shelter, followed closely by Katie.

The man at the counter looked up from his phone. "How can I help you today, sir?"

"I'm interested in adopting a dog for my wife and I."

"The kennels are down the hall to the left. If you're interested in meeting a certain dog, we can take them to the dog walk outside. Or, if you have any questions, I'll be right here." With that, he went back to his phone.

Ian and Katie made their way down the hall. The concrete echoed all the dogs barking, making the damp room seem louder than it was.

"What exactly are we looking for?" Ian asked.

"I'm not sure. I think it's like picking a spouse. When you know, you know." Katie smiled and took hold of Ian's hand.

Walking down the row of kennels was heartbreaking. Each dog seemed like a gem, but they couldn't take them all home.

Katie came to an abrupt stop, pulling Ian with her. Staring back was the shaggiest dog he had ever seen. But what held his attention was the animal's eyes, one blue and one brown. It nudged the gate with its nose.

"Him?" Ian asked with skepticism.

"Her," Katie corrected, never looking away from the dog.

Ian grabbed the clipboard attached to the kennel and coughed before squatting down to be more level with the dog.

"Catie."

"Yes?"

"No, that's *her* name." Ian tilted his head towards the dog before glancing up at his Katie. She was smiling, but he could see a few tears brimming.

"Well that settles it."

Ian didn't know if he agreed. In fact, the more he looked between the two, the less inclined he was to adopt the shaggy Catie.

The man from the front desk peeked his head around the corner.

"Find one you're interested in adopting, sir?"

Ian glanced at Katie, and she shook her head firmly. Letting out a long sigh, Ian called out, "I think my wife wants this one."

The employee came closer.

"Oh, Catie is a doll. Most people just don't want to deal with that much fur or her large size. Your wife must not judge books by their cover if you think she will like Catie."

Ian chuckled "She married me, so I try not to judge her taste too harshly."

After all the paperwork had been completed and Ian paid the adoption fee, the couple and their new pet set out to find a groomer. Walking down Main Street with the fall breeze blowing, Ian felt happier than he had in weeks. He found himself whistling. As the trio rounded a corner, Ian spotted his coworker Grimes having lunch with his family at an outside cafe.

"You can't avoid him forever," Katie whispered.

"Forever? Probably not. I can right now though." He ducked between two parked cars to cross the street.

While Catie was getting groomed, the new parents went shopping in the adjacent pet store.

"It's a dog, Katie. Does she really need this much stuff?"

"Haven't you learned I know best?" Katie winked, pointing out another toy. Shopping together had evolved to this routine: Katie pointed at what she wanted, and Ian was in charge of making sure it was added to the basket.

"Let's go to the park before we head home for the day." Katie said bouncing in her seat.

Catie lay in between the couple on the truck bench seat. She looked up, nudging first Ian, then Katie.

"I guess that's a yes from the mini you." Ian laughed.

The groomer had trimmed and bathed the dog and then they had christened her with a bright pink collar. She officially belonged. Their duo was now a trio.

At the park, Ian held the leash while Catie seemed perfectly content to smell every object her nose came in contact with, letting out yips of delight and bounding from one thing to the next.

Katie started snickering and Ian assumed it was because of the dog's antics. Until he heard a familiar voice call out, "Ian! You got a dog?"

Ian didn't need to turn around to know Grimes was headed his way. He didn't want to deal with this now. He had just started feeling semi-happy again. Conversations with Grimes never ended well anymore. At one time, they had been best friends. Now, Ian found himself wanting to move just to avoid the one person he couldn't seem to dodge.

"Good luck, love," Katie whispered.

Ian turned around. "Yeah, I did."

Grimes smiled and came closer with his wife, Meg, and their two-year-old twin boys, Milo and Tucker.

"Hello, stranger." Meg gave Ian a quick hug and then unbuckled the boys from the double stroller.

"When did you get a dog?" Grimes asked while squatting to pet the now sitting Catie.

"Uh, today. The place didn't mention how she was—"

But he never got the chance to finish his warning because Tucker ran and hugged the dog. Milo tottered over to Ian and pulled on his pants leg, smiling up at him with the pale features of his mom but the dark hair of his dad. Ian picked him up. "You want to pet the doggie? She seems to like your brother."

"She's gorgeous. What's her name?" Meg asked, sitting on the ground petting Catie.

This is where things were gonna get awkward. Or he could lie. Lying suited him just fine in this particular moment, but he could feel Katie looking at him. Sure enough, she was leaning against the tree behind him, her eyebrows raised.

Ian rolled his eyes, just like her to expect him to socialize *and* be honest.

"She came with a name, actually."

Grimes squinted at him, and Ian could see the wheels of suspicion turning.

"And?" Grimes asked.

"It's Catie. With a C."

Grimes audibly huffed.

"Katwii Katwii?" Milo asked, looking around for the human Katie he knew and loved. She smiled and waved from her spot. Milo hugged Ian tighter and waved his chubby fingers.

"Can Meg watch the dog for a minute? I would really like to talk." It was a statement more than a question. Ian sat Milo down.

Both men were walking slowly, though Ian had resigned himself to listening to whatever Grimes said without arguing so he could leave sooner.

"Ian, I just want to help. I don't know what to do that will help."

Ian wanted to tell him he didn't need help; he needed to be left alone.

"I'm fine, Grimes."

Grimes stopped walking and turned to face him. "You call *this* fine? I mean a dog would be good for you, so you're not alone all the time but ... why did you get a dog named Catie? That isn't healthy, Ian. I know you miss Katie. Meg and I do too man. But chances are, she's not coming back."

"She's not coming back because she never left, Grimes! I see her every day. She is literally always around. I can't go anywhere without people looking at me and just seeing half of what used to be a whole." Tears were running down Ian's face.

"I can't do life without Katie. I don't *want* to do life without her. I wake up every day wishing she hadn't been out late that night, just wanting her to be five minutes longer in the store so maybe that damn deer wouldn't have been in the road. That's all I want, Grimes—to wake up tomorrow and this all have been the worst nightmare of my life." Ian started pacing. "I want to wake up next to her and tell her how much I love her! How much I love that she makes me do things I hate just to broaden my scope of life. That I love when she wears dresses and twirls in them. I love that she hates shoes and still owns a zillion pairs. I want to tell her I lied; I *do* want to have kids with her, as many as she wants, and I'll name them every stupid idea she throws out there as long as she's happy and promises to never leave us. What I wouldn't do to be able to just breathe like a normal person again. I can't! Because the world is just so empty without her." Ian sucked in air, trying to slow down the panic attack he felt coming. Grimes pulled him into a hug, tears rolling down his face as well.

"I'm so sorry, Ian. So sorry you're suffering like this."

Ian kept sucking in air but felt like none of it was reaching his lungs. Grimes led him to the nearest bench. It felt like an eternity before Ian had finally calmed down and could breathe normally.

"Do you want me to come with you to see her?" Grimes barely said the words loud enough to be audible.

Ian shook his head.

"How about coming to dinner tonight at our place? You can even bring the dog."

"No. I think I should just go home for the night."

Grimes nodded and gave Ian a pat on the back. "I'm always available, anytime, man."

"I know. I appreciate that, Grimes. More than you know."

The two men stood and made their way back to Meg and the twins. Somehow, Meg managed to not only keep her two boys from mischief but also walk the dog.

"Thanks, Meg. I'll take the furry thing home now."

"Milo and Tucker love her! Maybe you can bring her over and stay for dinner tomorrow?" Meg suggested, handing him Catie's leash.

Ian cut his eyes at Grimes, who shrugged. "What can I say? We think on the same wavelength."

"Oh good, you already invited him." Meg smiled while clipping Tucker back in the stroller. Grimes scooped up Milo who hung his head way back trying to see the world upside down.

"Milo, if you and Tucker ask Uncle Ian to come to dinner, he will have to."

Milo straightened up and looked at Ian.

Ian cast a glare at Grimes. "That's messed up."

"Actually, it's in the parent handbook. Ask Meg."

"Right, page 204: children may be used to guilt trip certain suckers into doing whatever you may need/want." Meg laughed.

Grimes set Milo down and he ran to Ian, hugging his legs. He picked up an acorn and threw it at Tucker, making him cry.

"I think that's our cue," Meg said, putting Milo in the stroller.

"So come join the circus tomorrow?" Grimes asked.

"Fine. But only because I'm Uncle Ian. Not because I particularly like seeing you more than five days a week."

Grimes laughed and nodded. The group parted ways, and Ian made his way home. Alone.

Once furry Catie was settled, Ian checked the back porch for human Katie. She was sitting in her usual chair, curled up under a blanket.

"Was the park a success?" she asked, not looking up.

Ian sat in the chair beside her. "I got stuck going to dinner tomorrow. And I might have had a mental breakdown in a public park."

"Sometimes breakdowns are good. They get rid of all our emotions and leave us open for healing."

"Katie ..." Ian looked over at his wife.

She gave him the saddest smile.

"I picked Catie so you wouldn't be alone."

Ian slowly nodded. The doctors had told him weeks ago that she was never going to come back. She was in a medically induced coma after the car accident. They told him it would be ok to let her go. But then this Katie, ghostly Katie, showed up at home.

"I don't want to lose you," Ian whispered.

"I don't want to leave you either! But every day I feel my grip on this world slip a little. I don't think I'm coming back. It feels more like moving forward." Katie looked out into the setting sun. "I just want to know you'll be okay, Ian."

Everything in Ian screamed to tell her he would not be okay. All she had to do was stay. Come back.

"Katie, I will love you till my last day! I'll never be the same without you, but I'll be ok."

Katie nodded, satisfied. "One last dance, my love?"

As the sun set lower, Ian twirled Katie around and pulled her close to his chest.

"You're my forever." Ian kissed her forehead gently.

"You're my always," Katie replied.

One second, she was there. The next, Ian was alone. He stood there long past dark. The moon coming to rest in full glory, surrounded by starry sisters glistening brightly.

THANKS
Sera Amoroso

I think maybe I was meant to suffer; if only my sacrifice weren't made in vain. I longed for the impossible, feeling my wings crushed, my heart shattered. Do dreams come true? Or is it just another tale of blue roses and blood? Maybe I was never meant to love; maybe I was meant to forever be alone. Maybe it was written in the stars that my eternity of pain would never end. Perhaps my story was already set—I was born to be another grain of sand in the hourglass of time.

Yet how I longed for an illusion. I chased after a breath of wind. I was caught in a lucid dream as I danced among the trees. How I wished I was something other than a human. I wished I wasn't so naive. I wanted to drown in words—in alternate timelines where you loved me, but that is so futile because I was out of your reach, and you were out of my league.

I wrote you a letter that day. You won't get it for a few months, or perhaps a few years. I know that because I'm too scared to send it. If I do send my love to you, will you answer? A question, from one dreamer to another, will you care if you understand my message? Will you smile, knowing you have changed my life, or will you ignore it as I get lost in a pile of other words that mean more?

Will I ever get the chance to prove my thanks? There are daisies growing out of my palm, roses wrapping their thorns around my heart. Why does philia hurt so much when I only love you as a friend? Maybe it's just my conscience saying *this is your family, even though they don't know you.* This is the only way to justify my thanks, to sing my gratitude to you.

To the boy with the loveliest eyes I have ever encountered, whose words pierced my soul. To the one who makes flower petals tumble out of my mouth, without even knowing I exist. To you, who has touched millions of people, never realizing what you mean and what you have inspired.

You have a special place in my heart.

They say I will forget you, but I don't think I will. Maybe I will only outgrow you, use your heart as a steppingstone in the ever-growing lake of my life. I will keep that memory tucked in my pocket—a memory of an eternal ache to repay you for your kindness. Color me blue, color me red, color me missing one I have never truly met.

But this letter is still for you, no matter where you are. Whenever I see your eyes, I see the stars. And, maybe, it's better for us never to meet. Fate has an odd way of making us feel complete. You'll never know my name, but I know yours. So from a friend across the sea, remember you are adored.

Sincerely,
a friend you have but will never know

A DANCE AND A DISCLOSURE
AJ Skelly

Tonight was the Winter Gala—the one Magik Prep Academy function I'd been dreaming of for weeks. Tonight was the night Tyler Crawson would notice me.

I'd had a crush on him for ages but lacked the courage to do anything about it. Not tonight. With bravery I didn't feel, I stepped boldly into the great hall.

Music pealed, and lights twinkled. Bright strands of magic floated effortlessly through the air, only to be soaked up by the ancient stone walls now festooned with tinsel and evergreen. More multi-colored strings of magic hovered over the carved rock.

With my best friend, Aida, next to me and her earlier pep talk still ringing in my ears, I gulped, trying to calm my frantic heartbeat.

"You've got this, girl." Aida winked at me. The flashing red and green lights bounced off her caramel-colored skin. Her ebony hair, curled tight as springs, absorbed the lights and shadows alike. I wished it would absorb my anxiety.

"Breathe, Lainey." She looked me over once more and nodded in satisfaction. "That red sequin dress is perfect.

You sparkle like fairy dust." Her plump lips pursued, and she reached behind me, plucking a thread of opalescent magic from the air before swishing it around the hem of my dress. She snatched a golden thread near the bottom of the make-shift bleachers where we stood and wrapped it around my white-blonde hair piled on top of my head. Tucking the end behind the long point of my ear, she smiled. "There. Now you're radiant."

A bronze head bobbed on the other side of the room. My heart seized.

Target acquired.

My knees knocked and sweat ghosted my palms.

"I'm going to go make sure the werewolves haven't spiked the punch." Aida was on the social committee. The werewolves generally liked to party ... alternatively to com-mittee plans. "You never know when they might try to turn a perfectly good school function into some full-moon brawl." She winked and smiled tightly. With a final squeeze to my shoulder, she was off, and I was left staring at Tyler's head as it dipped and weaved throughout the crowd.

The music was loud. Too loud. It vibrated up my legs.

I swept up a handful of my shimmery skirt so my feet wouldn't tangle in the hem. The opalescent string of magic soaked into my dress, straightening my back, and giving me confidence while the golden strand had a calming effect on my poor ragged heart.

I'd only gone a few bodies deep into the crowd when a hand reached out and snatched mine.

"Kieran!" I gasped as my other best friend released me.

"Lainey. Wow. You look ..." he trailed off as his eye-brows rose to his black hairline. He was all dark where I was light. I couldn't tell if it was the red lights or if the points of his ears colored slightly in a flush.

Searching the crowd again, I found Tyler's head. He was only a few yards to my right.

"Looking for Tyler?" Kieran's voice broke in dryly.

"Yes. Tonight, he's finally going to see me as more than the smart girl in math class." I practically hissed the words between my teeth.

Kieran's expression soured. "You don't want him, Lainey. You really don't."

Anger and the sting of unintended betrayal crept into my belly. I glared at Kieran. Wasn't he supposed to be on my side?

"Lainey Rowan? Wow, looking hot, babe!"

The voice froze my blood, and Kieran could probably see the whites all around my green irises.

Plastering a smile on my face that I hoped didn't look deranged, I turned.

"Hey, Tyler." My voice came out higher than it should have. Maybe he didn't notice over the boom of the music.

Without any preamble, Tyler grabbed my hand and put his other low on my waist, swinging me onto the dance floor. Kieran grunted somewhere behind me.

We danced for long glorious moments. I was in ecstasy. The song wasn't particularly slow, but it wasn't fast. We moved together, faster than a slow dance, but no weird gyrating. Which was fine, because it let me savor every second of Tyler's hands on my waist without worrying if I was writhing appropriately to the music.

When the song ended, Tyler's copper-colored eyes gazed into mine. My hand fisted into the lapel of his jacket without my permission. A smile crooked his lips as his eyes roved over my face and one eyebrow rose.

Slowly he leaned down and let his lips caress my cheek. Figurative fireworks blasted out my ears.

"Don't go anywhere," he whispered huskily against my ear. "I'll be back in a few." His hand squeezed my side before his fingers slowly trailed away.

I'm pretty sure I grew roots right there on the parquet floor.

I don't know how long I stood there like an idiot in the middle of the room, but I came to when Kieran tugged on my hand.

"Kieran, did you see?" I sighed. "He's glorious."

Kieran snorted, his dark elf side showing in his pessimism. His forehead furrowed, his heavy black brows hanging low over his eyes as his mouth tugged into a thin line.

"You need to see something," he muttered as he grabbed my hand and pulled me through the throng of students and out the arched doorway into the quiet corridor.

Kieran stopped us beside one of the heavy tapestries that lined the antechambers outside the great hall. A string of purple magic clung to the bottom of my sparkly skirt.

"Look. I ..." he trailed off and ran a hand through his black hair. "I don't want to show you this but consider the truth my gift to you this year."

My eyebrows drew together again as he pulled me down the passageway. We crept to the end where it was deserted. His gaze met mine as he put a long finger against his lips, then motioned with his head for me to look around the corner.

Unsure, I peeked out just enough to get an eyeful.

My hand flew to my silent mouth.

There was the boy who'd kissed me minutes before. Who had looked at me like I was the center of the world. The boy on whom I'd hung my hopes.

He was necking a gorgeous red head. And his hands ... were not appropriately placed. My eyes burned as I turned and fled soundlessly back down the ancient corridor, kicking up a dusting of magic in my wake.

I sagged onto a stone bench in a deserted hallway—far away from the snogging couple—who, for all I knew, were no longer snogging and had moved on to other things. I angrily swiped under one eye. Kieran slowly sat beside me.

"I'm sorry, Lainey. I know you liked him." He rubbed the back of his neck. "He doesn't *see* you. Doesn't know how special you are." He hesitated and swallowed hard. "Maybe you should look at someone who has seen you all along."

The sincerity in his tone jerked my gaze to his. His chocolate brown eyes swam with vulnerability, and my heart lurched painfully in my chest.

Because he *did* see me.

Kieran had always seen me. He'd seen me when I was all awkward limbs and angles. When I won the science award. When I burned my bangs off with a spell gone wrong. When I dropped chocolate frosting all down my shirt. When my gran passed away. He'd seen me.

A heaviness around my heart lifted as I stared at his face, my eyes tracing every line of his messy hair, his pointed ears, his strong jaw, his dark eyes fringed in thick lashes, the tilt of his lips. The intensity and vulnerability in his eyes.

"I see you, Lainey," he whispered roughly.

And for the first time, I saw him, too.

MY DISGUISE
Adella Quick

My heart had a dream, and it was of you
It dreamt someday you'd love me too
A love that time would never undo
But I know this dream will never come true
So, I put on a disguise
You tell me that friends, we'll always be
And that you really care about me
But all I want is for you to see
Me through different eyes

Then one day, you looked me in the eye
You hesitated but then, with a sigh
You said something I thought was a lie
Nevertheless, it made me cry
You saw through my disguise
This love that I had held so dear
Was now being whispered into my ear
As if you'd known what I'd been waiting to hear
I saw myself in your eyes

Then I woke up, and my heart cried out
It knew you were someone I couldn't live without
I tried to remember what my dream was about
But the pain in my heart left no room for doubt
So, I went back to my disguise
Deep inside, I hid my heart away
It would have to cry some other day
I know it waits to be able to say
I see the love in his eyes

Slowly I'm giving up and letting you go
If my heart has yet or not, I don't really know
Although my love for you continues to grow
It changed its form such a long time ago
I no longer need my disguise
Now I'm just happy to have you as a friend
I know on you I can always depend
I know it from morning until the day's end
When you and I both close our eyes

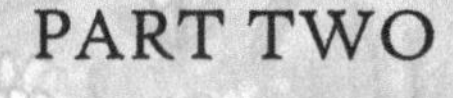

PART TWO

Never Meant to Be

WHERE RAIN MAY FALL
Effie Joe Stock

I hugged the classical books tighter to my chest, trying fruitlessly to shelter them from the sprinkling rain as it sought to soak the already dreary streets. If only God had blessed me with foresight instead of an unquenchable desire for knowledge, I might have brought an umbrella instead of these priceless, rare books.

I jumped over a puddle, feeling the wetness of the road seeping in through my sandals and in between my toes. If I wasn't careful, these shoes would get too slick to walk in and I might fall. I batted my stringy hair out of my face and focused on the uneven cobblestones ahead of me.

A shoulder collided against mine, and I yipped as my precious treasures nearly slipped from my hands. Before I had an unpleasant meet-cute with the wet cobblestones, the stranger's hand reached out to steady me and himself alike.

Our eyes met, and I almost dropped my books again.

Stars.

That's all I could think when I looked into those mysterious eyes. They were like stars, with their black expanses and little gold flecks.

"Are you okay?" His voice was rich and hidden by a thick

accent.

I took too long to snap out of the wonderland his eyes had trapped me in before I answered. "Oh, yes," I whispered blandly, awkwardly making no move to step away from his half embrace and struggling to say much more.

His brows furrowed down before one rose along with the corner of his lips. "Are you okay?" he asked again, and a flutter of embarrassment brought me down from the stars.

"I am." A strange laugh left my lips as I stepped away from him and quickly brushed the wet strands of hair out of my face, realizing I was most likely only making myself look more frightful. "Thank you. For catching me."

He shrugged his broad shoulders good-naturedly. "No need to thank me. *I* bumped into *you* after all."

"Why aren't you using your umbrella?" The question jumped from my lips before I could stop it. I quickly shot an apology after it, but he had already started laughing. I blushed red hot, suddenly feeling warm despite the cold water that trickled down my back.

"If I told you, you would think me strange and laugh." His starry eyes sparkled like the galaxies I loved painting with acrylics back home.

A stab of offense shot through me. "I will not."

His brows raised as I stared a challenge at him before he broke out in that beautiful laughter again.

"I watched a movie once, with a man and woman dancing in the rain. They seemed so happy being wet, like little ducks, that I soon lost interest in using umbrellas."

I wrinkled my nose in amusement.

"You're laughing." He sounded almost wounded, but I quickly shook my head.

"I am not. I find it endearing. Why do you carry one, then, if you've no intention of using it?"

The umbrella twirled in his hands and then opened with a pop before he handed it to me. "In case I meet a woman, and she doesn't want to be wet." His eyes motioned to the books in my hand. "Perhaps you are that woman?"

My heart slammed against my ribs, and I could do nothing but sputter for a moment and dumbly reach for the umbrella as I balanced the books in my other hand. "Thank you," I finally managed when I was safely sheltered under the black, cloth expanse.

"Absolutely." He bowed as they used to in the olden days, and I couldn't help but wonder if he had gotten that from one of his movies as well.

I clutched the umbrella tighter in my hand as he tipped his hat to me, bid me a good day, and strode away.

I watched him go, too dumbstruck to move. It was only after I had watched him weave his way through the crowd and my heart had stopped running that I realized my mistake.

In a world where names meant everything, I hadn't asked for his.

With reckless abandon, I rushed after him. Water splashed up my legs, soaking my chic business suit pants and destroying my sandals. I kept a tight hand on my books and umbrella but had less success keeping my heart and hopes from running themselves to the grave.

I called for him, pushing people aside in my haste, frantically inquiring where he had gone, but he had disappeared.

I stopped running when it became apparent I wasn't doing any more than making a fool of myself, my legs and lungs burning, my face streaked with rain and tears.

His starry eyes and accented voice played over and over in my mind, and my heart did somersaults. My lip quivered as I bit back the overwhelming sense of defeat that had suddenly overcome me. I felt like I had lost everything I had ever wanted, though I didn't know why. I stood under that flickering streetlamp for God knows how long, people and cars passing me by, unfazed by the crying girl in the rain.

Finally, with my heart left to rot in the puddles on the streets, I turned and made my way home. With labor, I trudged up the stairs to my studio apartment, dripping water in a miserable little trail across the light brown carpet.

The door clicked shut behind me, and I set down the books, which had survived my wild goose chase far better than I had hoped and then I myself had fared. With a long sigh, and the weight of knowing I would need new shoes again, I went to close the umbrella when my eyes caught a name engraved on its handle.

My heart lept into my throat, and a gasping sob left my lips. There was only one name, no middle or last, but it was enough.

Jack.

I tore my jacket off, baring my arm.

Jack.

My trembling hand covered my mouth as I sank to the ground, half in horror, and half in awe.

Everyone in my world was born with two names somewhere on their body—one of their soulmate, and the other of the person, or persons, who would kill them.

One of the names on my arm was Elizabeth. The other was Jack.

No one ever knew which name was which. Either Jack or Elizabeth could be my soulmate. But now, as I remembered his starry eyes, his wet hair, and the way he raised his brows, I knew more than anything Jack was my soulmate.

But how would I find him?

I searched the internet, I searched the phone book, I called my friends, my family, my coworkers, but none of them knew anyone named Jack. Not even one.

Finally, exhausted, I sank down onto my couch and turned on the news for white noise as I stared at my cracking popcorn celling. I would need to fix it someday. Perhaps I would paint a mural once it was smooth again. I tried to think of a design, but the only one that came to mind was the great expanse of the universe. And with the promise of stars and dreams came, once again, the crushing weight of reality.

One soulmate. Only one. And they were the only ones we could truly be happy with. I had known many people to try and make relationships work outside of their soulmates but had watched as all of them ended in disaster. I'd waited nearly thirty years for mine, holding out for that one person, knowing they would come, praying they would, that we could be happy together, truly happy. That's all I had ever wanted.

If Jack was my soulmate, and I never saw him again, was I doomed to loneliness? And he too? Was Jack doomed to always search for his girl in the rain? Would we never be able to dance together in the rain?

The news announced an emergency, and I only faintly heard the passing details. Some girl had stepped out into the street at a crossing; a car hydroplaned and almost hit her. Thankfully, a man had pushed her out of the way. She had come out unscathed, but the hero man had been admitted to the hospital in critical condition. His name was ...

I nearly screamed as I stared at the screen, the name ringing in my ears.

Starry eyes stared back at me.

I didn't remember much as I ran from my apartment, forgetting my shoes, my jacket, even Jack's umbrella.

I ran all the way to the hospital, forced my way through security, and made it all the way to his room just as I heard the nurse pronounce him ... deceased.

My blood ran cold. I sank to the floor, my heart tearing itself apart in my chest.

Dead.

Dead.

Dead.

The nurses and security escorted me to the waiting room, comforting me, trying to help me, but I hardly heard them. My soulmate. Of course he had been. He loved old movies. So did I. He was a gentleman, a connoisseur of beauty. A rescuer ... a hero—everything that would've made me happy. Everything I could've loved. Everything I would never have. Never again.

And then, I realized what I must've always known deep down.

A cold calm poured over me like the rain had only hours earlier as I dragged myself from the waiting room and out of the hospital. It had stopped raining, but that didn't cheer me up. In fact, I missed it. It was as if the rain collected in puddles on the streets were the last piece of him I would ever have.

My feet carried me mindlessly down the dark streets, in and out of the streetlights' eerie glow, until I heard the rushing water beneath me.

The iron under my hands was cold as I gripped it.

Dead.

I now knew why the other name on my arm was Elizabeth. I put one foot up on the railing and pulled myself up, balancing on the small metal strip with one hand on the pole next to me.

I would never be fully happy without my soulmate: that was the one cruel truth of this world that everyone knew.

The metal left my fingers as I loosened my grip and let myself fall.

Now, as the raging, cold water rushed up to meet me and darkness consumed me, I knew, truly knew, why the other name on my arm had always been my own.

ENCORE
Nobel Shut Chan

Here's our seat now.
Isn't it amazing? This is her third show!
She's the lead. Do you know
The story—of a young boy
Who falls in love with her and loses her?
They say it's one of the best this season.
Hush, now. The lights are dimming.
Have you ever heard such wonderful music?
I can't believe—oh, there, there,
There she is! Isn't she lovely? She's as
Beautiful as the day I met her. Had
A coat on, pretty thing, shivering in
The gas station buying a bag of chips
With pennies. Dew-drop eyes, I loved her then.
She can act; oh, boy, can she act, when
The second act kicks in, you'll see.
The first act, she plays it nice, sweet,
Loves the boy with tender kisses and shy eyes.
Those kisses ... can you believe they're mine?
I've got to say I'm jealous of that boy. Each night

Trampling the stage and kissing her, kissing her
Hearing her say she loves him. Too good
For a scrimpy boy like that. Who cast him?
I'll have to ask her tonight. Yes, I've asked
Before. But she doesn't like to talk about him.
Plus, she's been out lately, preparing for this,
I haven't had a chance to talk to her. I miss
Her. But after tonight, she'll be back.
The show will be over, and she'll be back
With me. Oh, this is my favorite number!
Watch: it's their love song. She practiced this
At home with me. The first verse by her alone,
Singing how lonely she's been, then I—
Then the boy—tells her she's not alone anymore.
Then the kiss, long, passionate. She's so good,
So good. The way she kisses him, just
The way she kisses me. Longer, even.
That's how you know it's acting. Exaggeration.
I should tell her to dial it down, shouldn't I?
You aren't too cold, I hope. Feels like death in here.
Say, is your wife not coming? Is she ill?
That's too bad. That's too, too bad.
I think I'm going to ask her to marry me.
Tonight. I'll ask her tonight.
Well, that's the first act done. I'm going to find her.
She's usually with that boy somewhere; they
Share a dressing room, she said.
Tell me what you thought before I leave.
Did you see how she looked at him in that final scene?
She can act. My god, she can act.

GOLDEN HOUR
Cassandra Hamm

The tip of my brush dips into the paint and hovers over the canvas propped up on my knees. The bench wood presses against my back as I close one eye and mark the painting with a golden streak.

It was a beautiful hour—an hour I thought would lead into the rest of our lives. But life is strange that way.

Footsteps pound against the concrete. A man jogs along the park pathway, backlit by trees and a cheery blue sky. I turn back to my painting. When his footsteps slow and his ragged breaths quicken, I look up once more.

"Sorry, can I sit here?" His reddened face highlights the pale stubble clinging to his chin, sparse in some areas, thick in others. "I'm dying."

"Don't apologize for dying." I lift my palette to clear room on the bench.

"Sorry," he says again, plopping next to me. The bench rattles. He holds his head between his knees and inhales, exhales, inhales, exhales.

I balance the palette on my lap and resume. Another stroke of gold—another spark of memory imbued in color.

The man lifts his head, unscrews the cap of his orange

water bottle, and guzzles the liquid. Frizzy blond hair curls over his protruding ears.

"Sorry for interrupting your flow." His voice comes out in gasps. "I know it's hard to get into the zone or whatever."

"You don't need to apologize." He's a moment in my head I will eventually capture. But first, I need to portray this golden hour so I can finally let go.

"Whoa." He lets out a low whistle as he leans over to look at my painting. A drop of sweat slides off his face onto the paint, making me flinch, but I don't think he notices. "You're, like, really good. Wait—am I not supposed to look at it before you're finished? I don't know if there's, like, an artist code—"

"There is no code." I lift one shoulder. The scent of paint burns my nostrils. "I try to capture moments, hours, days. It's simple."

"Are you kidding?" His eyes devour the painting. Aaron never looked at my work like that. "This is awesome. You're right; it's like time froze or something. I bet you could do that with any subject you tried. Could you, like, paint me?"

"I could." And I most certainly would if I didn't have this one to finish. Maybe another time—if I ever see this man again. Still, I think he will lodge in my brain. Perhaps I don't need to see him again to depict his flushed, glowing form.

"Yes!" He pumps his fist, then looks away, as though ashamed of his display of excitement. "I mean, if you want to. Eventually. Hey, wait." Now his expression shifts to a pronounced frown. "Why is the sky gold? Aren't you paint-ing"—he gestures in front of him—"you know, *this?*"

"In a way." I gaze across the path to the forest. The trees rise tall and majestic, nearly blotting out the sun. "I am painting a day that is not today."

"Oh." His face smooths out. His chest moves in a slower, steadier rhythm now. "So you're painting something that already happened, right?" He points at the figures, almost touching the wet paint. I stiffen. "Who are they? Is that you?"

"That one, yes." In the painting, I'm leaning my head against Aaron's as we sit in this very bench, staring at the golden sky. I can almost imagine that this man next to me is Aaron—or perhaps I can't. Aaron was smoothness and sophistication; this nameless man is all rough edges and honesty.

"What about the other one?" the man says. "Who's that?"

There shouldn't be a lump in my throat. My heart shouldn't have skipped a beat. "He made the days beautiful." Once. But things change.

"Oh." He swallows hard. "Sorry if I'm bringing up a painful subject or something; I can just go now—"

"No." Painful, yes, but it's a good pain, a pain I need to deal with. "I am celebrating what was beautiful about our relationship."

"Oh." The man coughs. "Um. Is he ... like, is he still ...?"

"Alive? Yes." My lips flatten. "Very much alive."

"But you're not ... together anymore."

"He is engaged now." The words come out with a bite. I exhale, trying to expel the bitterness. *Let go.*

"Oh." The man runs his fingers through his sweat-soaked curls. "Look, I've bothered you long enough—"

"No, stay." I laid my paint-stained hand on his slick arm. "I appreciate the company." I dip my paintbrush in pale gold and bleed streaks of light across the canvas.

"I feel like you should at least know my name since I've been asking all these personal questions." Though his breathing has eased, the words practically spill from his mouth. "I'm Seth."

"Stella," I say. My brush flies across the canvas as I perfect the sky. I swallow hard. Yes, that was exactly how it looked.

That was a slow moment, but it was a good one. Usually, the good ones go by too quickly, a day spanning a breath. But sometimes the slow moments crawl, and you just want them to be over, but you can't fast forward.

"I just don't love you anymore." It's almost as though Aaron is here with me, once more speaking those cruel words.

"Look, I'm sorry, Stella."

Seth's words snap me back to the present. I blink to focus on my current companion.

Seth stands, shifting the weight of the bench. "You're probably totally creeped out that a stranger is asking all these questions about your art and stuff—"

"I always appreciate interest in my work." I lower the brush and smile up at him. "You, Seth, have made my life beautiful for these few minutes." In a different way than Aaron had, yes, but perhaps just as potent.

Seth's eyes widen.

I look back at the painting, my golden hour. Only the backs of our heads show as Aaron and I sit facing the trees. Maybe his smile wasn't really as bright as I remember it being.

Standing, I gather my paints and brushes. My spirit exhales. The memory is etched into art. Now perhaps I can let go.

"Thank you," I say. Then I start down the concrete path. To where, I don't know, but it won't be with Aaron hanging over me.

"Wait, don't you want this?" Seth grabs the canvas from the bench. The sun turns the gold paint into pure light.

I do. I don't. It's a moment where time slowed, expanded, seemed endless.

But there will be more moments like that. I just need to keep walking the path that is placed in front of me.

I shake my head. "It's for anyone who wants it."

"But it's special to you."

"I did not make this to keep it."

"That doesn't make any sense."

It has served its purpose. Now perhaps it can give someone joy instead of pain. I cock my head at him. "Would you like it?"

"I—" His mouth opens, then closes. Then his head bobs, swift and jerky.

I leave the painting in Seth's arms. The sun shoots a ray of gold across the sky.

A LONG EMBRACE, BUT NOT LONG ENOUGH

Jessica Smith

He wrapped his arms around me and held me tight.

My body was stiff at first.

Suddenly, I didn't know what to do.

But then, he stepped closer.

He rested his chin on my head,

And I allowed my cheek to rest against his chest.

"A long embrace," I thought.

He whispered sweet words

Of which I do not remember,

Because his words did not hold as much weight as the sigh
he released—

The sigh that washed over me like gentle ocean waves,

The sigh that drenched my soul in delight,

The sigh that uttered, "Finally, it's been you all along, and I
am home. I am home."

All at once, I fell in love.

For the first time, I fell in love,

And I embraced him with my whole self,

And I was home. I was home.

He wrapped his arms around me but let me go too soon.
He pulled away,
and I was cold.
The distance was cold.
I stood there, drenched in rain,
And told him I'd always be his friend.
I smiled to mask the pain,
As we got into our separate cars and drove away,
Even then, I knew we were unfinished.
He had started to get close—
His sigh had said what words could not.
How was I to know that the thrill of his sigh
Covered his cruel fear underneath?
He could not get close.
There were walls he'd built,
And I knew now he'd do his best to keep me at a distance—
Always at a distance.

He wrapped his arms around me—reunited, at last!
Then, the imaginings of my heart faded
As the reality of sitting alone at a coffee shop hammered every muscle.
I gathered my belongings and rushed to my car,
Knowing the tears would come.
The lowest moment of my life was sitting in my car
In a nearly empty parking lot,
With the shade of night to guard my weeping.

Loneliness swept over me like an angry tide,

And I couldn't breathe. I couldn't breathe.

"A long embrace," I had once thought.

But not long enough.

He left us unfinished, I knew.

His sigh had been like a prisoner

Nearly broken free of the chains holding him back,

But he was both the prisoner and the jailer.

He cared for me—of that, I am certain.

And because my heart longed for that embrace,

I could do nothing but let the tears flow.

He wrapped his arms around me.

"Thank you for the birthday card," he said.

"I'll keep this forever," he promised.

"You better," I said and laughed.

My heart didn't laugh.

He wrapped his arms around me.

We're just friends, I reminded myself.

And I'll always love him as a friend.

Always, always, always.

Yet, as I rested my cheek against the warmth of his neck,

Longing to hear once more the sigh that never came,

I leaned in with my whole self,

And I was home. I was home.

A long embrace,

But not long enough ...

THE FALL OF THE SWANS
Beka Gremikova

When we dance together, it's like no one else exists. Every lift, every twirl—it binds us like the ribbons on my shoes.

"One, two, three," he whispers in my ear, because at times I forget myself and the dance becomes about the feel and not the numbers. The rasp of his voice, heavy with a Russian accent, flows through me like honey.

"One, two, three," I murmur, matching the number to the step and listening to his breaths. Over the years, our synchronism has improved dramatically. Now, I almost believe we *breathe* on the same count.

He draws me closer, pressing me against his chest. His heartbeat is so loud I can feel it in my veins as well as hear it in my ears. I nearly miss a step.

"Relax, Elena," he says softly.

I laugh a little. "I just can't stop thinking about the tour." In only a few short weeks, we'll be travelling with our company: packed ballet houses, hushed, adoring crowds, and dance after dance after dance ...

His eyes flicker away for a moment, then his hands drop to my waist as he prepares for a lift. He heaves me upward, fingers splayed across my stomach, other hand clutching my leg. Carefully, surely, he spins.

He's never dropped me. I don't think he ever will.

He slows, and my hands creep to find his, our fingers interlacing as I slide along his shoulders to reach the ground. We continue across the floor, steps in tune.

"I can't wait to get to Toronto," I whisper. Little old me, from the middle of nowhere, performing in front of thousands ...

"Your dream's finally coming true," he murmurs.

"*Our* dream."

His lips twist, and he doesn't say a word.

My fingers clench around his hand. "Isn't this what you want? To star in *Swan Lake*? To travel the country, see new things?"

My toes drag across the floor, and I realize I must have stopped dancing. Dmitri pulls me along, his eyes cast upward and downward and everywhere but at me. "Sometimes, I think so," he says. "Sometimes, I forget that there is a real world out there."

I flinch. "What are you talking about?" I sweep my hands through the air, gesturing at the lights and the stage and the curtains. "This is real."

"Real for you. But for me ..." He shrugs. "It doesn't feel the same anymore."

My throat goes dry. Heat sweeps through me. "What, just like when *we* didn't feel real anymore?" I hiss.

He stiffens. "How many times must I apologize for that?"

Until you mean it. He must see the words flare in my eyes, because he turns and lopes across the stage to the stairs, hurrying down to the floor. On the other side of the room, a set of doors leads to the changing area.

My fingers clench into fists. Why is he *always, always* walking away from me? We're supposed to be in sync. We should be dancing, *together*!

"Dmitri!" I shout, running across the stage. I stumble as I reach the stairs, and the ground rushes at my face.

Dmitri catches me, arms wrapped around my waist and lips pressed against my hair. Their warmth spreads across my scalp in a hot blush. He's muttering a jumble of Russian and English, and a shiver quivers through me.

*"**What did you** say?" I asked, turning my head. He sat beside me at the cafeteria table, his homework strewn across the cold, hard surface.*

His face was red as beets. "It was Russian."

"For what?"

He swallowed and ran a hand through his thick dark hair. "I love you."

I almost laughed—but then he kissed me, and whatever warnings my mother had offered about falling for my dance partner were forgotten. I leaned into him as he wrapped me, with his words and with his kisses, into his spell.

If I had not thought of him as my Siegfried, perhaps I should have known he would turn out to be Rothbart—the only one with the power to destroy Odette.

"What did you say?" I whisper, my voice hoarse, my fingers curling into his shirt. *I love you. I love you still. I'm sorry.*

"I was asking if you were hurt," he says stiffly.

My stomach clenches. "I'm fine—"

"Dmitri?"

He steps away from me so quickly I stumble. A woman stands near the doors, Dmitri's duffel bag in her arms.

My nostrils flare, but I force myself to nod coolly at her. "Guess you should go," I mutter to him. Because the sight of her reminds me that no matter how much I wish it were true, Dmitri and I are *not* in sync. Perhaps in dance, but not in life.

I knocked on the door and let myself in without waiting for an answer, a bottle of champagne in my arms.

They were on the couch, legs tangled, her head on his chest. A blanket drooped to the floor, and her hair tumbled across his face.

I swallowed the scream building at the back of my throat. Setting the champagne on the counter, I crept out of the room.

Later that night, he called me. "Elena, I'm so—"

"Sorry?" I snapped. "Was this the reason you didn't want to get married?"

His voice was strangled. "It wasn't because of her, honest. I just didn't want—"

"You didn't want to commit yourself to anyone." I gripped the phone so tight my fingers ached. "Right? Because deep down, you're afraid. And she probably doesn't care."

"Elena, listen—"

"I don't want to!" I snapped. "I don't even want to dance with

you anymore!" I slammed down the phone.

Ten days later, heartsick with missing the sound of his voice, I called him.

"Are you ready, Dmitri?" my Odile asks, her voice echoing across the room. She glances at me, the cast-off Odette, and something flickers in her eyes. Pity? I don't want it.

Dmitri snatches his jacket from her, shrugging into it, still not looking at me. "Yeah," he says, "let's go." She ducks out, and he makes to follow. At the threshold, he turns. "After Toronto, Elena ... I'm quitting the company. I can't keep doing this anymore."

"Finally ready to commit?" The words sound worn—perhaps because I feel worn, like a swan plucked of her feathers, battered by howling gales.

He bows his head. "She wants me, Elena. You ... you want a Siegfried. A ballet-partner-turned-lover. I ... I don't dream ballet like you do." He shakes his head, and then he's gone.

I stare at the door, as if I expect him to rush back in, ditch everything, assure me that it's all a lie, that *I'm* his true Odette and that he'll dance with me forever.

He doesn't come. I totter back to the stage, climbing the steps on my hands and knees. Tears blur my vision.

But, heaven help me, I still need to practice. Dmitri might ditch the company, but ... but it's all I have now.

Oh, help me. Someone help me.

Of their own volition, my legs jerk in a drunken dance.

Leap, twirl.

Stagger, fall.

Crash to the stage, ripping skin off my elbows as I skid. Sobs burst out of me. Tears make the world swim, rippling as if I'm underneath a lake.

I lurch back to my feet, blood dripping like crimson feathers. I dance through the pain, as I have so many times before.

The edge of the stage brushes my toes. The dance carries me away from it, away from the danger of broken bones.

I always thought of myself as Odette, the doomed swan princess. But perhaps I'm more like Odile after all, wishing for someone she cannot have.

Without my partner to help keep me in rhythm, my thoughts make me stumble. The stage edge veers close again. My legs give out. Bruised and sore, I fall.

This time, he isn't here to catch me.

FIN

THAT BENCH
Annie Kay

Do you remember
When we were younger,
And you took me to the park,
The place where you first stole my heart?
We walked on the grass,
Took most of the paths
That lead us down to that bench.

We watched the lake and geese.
Your legs, a cushion for my aching feet.
Your smile matched mine.
It was the most perfect time.
I thought my chest would burst
From all the happiness making my heart hurt,
There on that bench.

I know why my heart hurts now.
Even then, I knew I'd lose you somehow.
I didn't expect it to be your decision though.

Your heart that changed and let me go.
Now, I only have the memories you gave me.
They sting and cut like a winter storm raging.
But I always go back to that bench.

Because that's the only place I find it,
Not peace or clarity or longing to change this.
Instead, what I find is broken and brittle.
That's the spot that reminds me it was all real.
What I felt for you,
And the pain you put me through.
I can't let it go, so I return to that bench.

You're gone, oceans away,
But I still go to that park to sit and stay.
I return to that spot and watch the lake sway.
Pretend the geese aren't walking away,
Like you did all those years ago.
It was the darkest place I'll ever know.
But not here, not this bench.

You see, this is happy; this is warm.
This is where I watched joy form.
And I'll never forget the shine in your eyes,
That told me you would forever be mine.
So, I come to this spot and reminisce,
Try to pick out the warnings I always missed.
I only do that here on this bench.

It's a fortress for my pain,
An escape to leave the world away,
And sit forever in this hurt.
I feel it every time your mention is heard.
I went today, to rot in that place,
But someone blocked my way.
She was sitting there on that bench.

I watched a tear roll down her face.
Beside her, fingers rubbed at an empty space.
And there I found it, without being brave—
The answer I didn't know I always craved.
For there was a girl just like me,
Alone in the darkness trying to break free,
Sitting alone on that bench.

That bench, my fortress of pain.
But my joy wasn't the only one it drained.
And there I heard it pound in my ears,
My heart was mending or drowning out fears.
And hers would too, that girl like me.
Her pain would fade like an old memory.
So, I turned and walked away from you and that bench.

And I don't plan on returning.

HEAR THE WILLOWS WEEP

A standalone short story for The Abandoned Crown Series

Cerynn McCain

*M*a*rÿ?" I ran* through the forest, dread urging me faster. "Marÿ!" I heard her screaming out of view, but all the trees looked the same. Dusk fell rapidly, and the once clear path was now obscured in darkness gathered amongst the leaves. I stumbled on, her screams growing louder as I plunged through the underbrush.

"Marÿ!"

Silence fell. My heart wrenched, and I paused mid-stride to listen, but I heard nothing. Nothing but the whispers of wind sweeping through the forest. Panic filled me as I blindly searched for her.

I crashed into a clearing.

Torches flickered around a tree in the center, its branches long and bowed toward the ground as if it were weeping.

My stomach clenched and I fell against the roots of the tree, stroking the bark softly, reverently.

"I tried to save you," I whispered. "I'm so sorry."

I jolted upright, gasping, and squinted at the early morning light.

"You don't need to save me," a sleepy voice giggled beside me. I looked over and my wife smiled up at me from the pillows. She reached out and walked her fingers up my arm before gently tapping my nose with another chuckle. "Was it another vision?"

I nodded, my heart still racing. "They're getting stronger."

"I told you to block them," she sighed. "Look what they've done to me!"

"I'm an Elder; it's my job. You're not even supposed to view them."

"Well, I needed to. The Elders weren't reading them right. But they'll destroy you." She snuggled into the blankets and shut her eyes once more. I sighed and climbed from the bed, wandering into the kitchen just as the morning trumpet sounded over the castle. Normally we would have dressed and hurried down to the dining hall to eat with her people, but the past few cycles we'd chosen to take our meals up in our suite, observed only by the maid. Tucked away where no one would notice the insanity eating her mind. My stomach knotted over thoughts of the day ahead, and I gratefully took the coffee our maid held out to me. The liquid burned as soon as it hit my tongue, but I didn't really notice it; my mind was still trapped in my dream. In my vision.

"Did the Ṙèлïǎ sleep well?" The maid bustled around the kitchen preparing a breakfast we both knew would be wasted. Maŗÿ hardly ate anymore, and I would eat during my meeting.

"Better than most nights," I lied, trying to protect my wife from the rumors flying through the castle. "It was I that was restless."

"Of course, Sir." She didn't believe me.

My wife's … condition … was all the castle talked about these days: the mad Rèлïǎ, who spoke of wars that could never happen. The Elders had advised me to lock her away, to hide her from her people, but the rumors persisted.

"Why don't I get the baby up while you tend to the Rèлïǎ?" The maid suggested as she curtsied and hurried from the room, nervous to even face my wife.

My sweet, harmless wife who instilled so much fear.

My stomach clenched as my visions came to mind again: the desperation of her screams, the pain in her voice, the chill of sudden silence.

It must not happen. My vision must not come to pass.

"Didn't you hear the morning trumpet, Sweetheart?" I returned to our room and bent over the bed, smoothing her curls out of her face. Her eyelids fluttered briefly before she sighed and nestled deeper into the covers. "Marÿ, Love, time to get up." I nudged her shoulder, but she brushed me away and squeezed her eyes shut.

"I am still tired, Pïaṯ. Please let me sleep."

"The Elders have called a meeting. I have to go." I lifted the heavy clock-face off the nightstand and draped the chain around my neck, letting the clock swing against my chest. "I want to get you up and fed before then."

Her eyes finally opened, and she grinned at me. "You treat me like such a child sometimes." She sat up. "I can feed myself. I can dress and bathe myself too, you know."

"Hopefully not in that order," I winked at her, but her smile faded, and that familiar confusion settled in her eyes.

"Why not?"

"So you're not dressed in the bath."

"Would that be a bad thing?"

"Marÿ," I sighed. I hoped I'd get at least a few lucid minutes before the madness snuck back in. "It's a little early for this, Love. Please, please try to be sane a little while longer."

"I do try, Peter." She flung off the sheets and swung her legs over the side of the bed. "It's just not always easy."

"My name isn't Peter," I mumbled, helping her to her feet as she swayed. Her hand gripped mine as I led her to the washroom.

"Not yet." She twisted out of my grip and stumbled toward the bath. "Go. You're late to your meeting. The Elders do not want you there."

"Of course they do, Love. I'm an Elder myself."

"You are?"

"I've been one since before we married. Did you forget?"

"You just ... don't seem like an Elder." She narrowed her eyes as she studied me. "You feel ... lost."

I stared down at my wife as she bent over the tub, drawing the same bath she had a hundred times before, and a pang of sadness filled my heart.

How had this happened?

I fought so hard to protect her, to keep her grounded, sane, but somehow, she'd slipped just out of my reach.

I'd hidden her madness for cycles, but it was no longer something I could conceal.

"I have to go, Love."

"A war is coming," she whispered, but didn't look up as I ducked out of the washroom. The maid met me at the door with my infant daughter, still sleepy from her crib. I took her carefully and thanked the maid before I hurried out into the castle.

She speaks of war." Elder Vaлṯij folded his hands on the table, his eyebrows arched in concentration. As his fingers wove together, a slight breeze rustled through the room, stirred by his powers. "She speaks of death."

"We see none of that." Elder P̈ïlűл's gaze shot over to me, waiting for me to argue. I almost mentioned my vision of the tree but bit my tongue. Most of my visions showed only peace. No war, no death. The humans had been fairly quiet over the cycles. There was no war brewing.

"What does she speak of with you?" Elder Đæл narrowed her eyes on me as she bounced my daughter on her hip, splattering the floor with waves of water from her powers. "Surely you've heard more of her madness than we have. What does she say in private?"

I swallowed hard. I heard plenty of madness, it was true but wanted to share none of it with my peers, desperate as they were for an excuse to dethrone her. "She mostly speaks nonsense, tells me my name doesn't fit, skips meals claiming she's already eaten them." I ducked my head and shook it sadly, unable to face either Element Elder, or my own counterpart as Time Elder. "She apologized to an herbalist and told her that honey would make her sad someday."

A gasp passed through the room and Elder P̈ïlűл straightened, the clocks ticking across his robe stilling as his concern slowed time for just a moment.

"She's spreading it outside the castle?"

"No." I immediately saw my blunder, and horror filled

me. "Just to the herbalist, and Sienna won't tell anyone. I can still control Marÿ. I can still hide this. Please."

"You can't, Elder Pïat." A gentle hand rested on my shoulder; it felt impossibly heavy. "This is uncharted territory. Never before have we lost someone to madness, and we can't know how she'll affect our people! The burden she carries will ruin her, and us as well unless we act."

My heart dropped as I turned to study the sad, understanding face of my friend. "Well ... what do you propose we do about it?"

"Marÿ!" I ran back to her room, screaming her name through the halls just in case she'd wandered out into the castle. "Marÿ!"

"Yes, Dear?" She flung our bedroom door open before I reached it, smiling at me as she twisted her wet hair up into a bun.

"We need to go." I grabbed her arm. "Right now."

"But—"

"They're coming for you!" I tugged at her again, but she planted her feet on the floor.

"I know."

"We need to—" I paused. "You ... you know?"

"Of course I know, Peter. The war is coming; I've been saying so for cycles."

"I'm not talking about war. I'm talking about the Elders!"

"So much death. So many lives lost." Her voice was monotone and distant as she took a few steps forward under my prodding. "But we'll win ... eventually"

"Maṛÿ, snap out of it. This is serious!"

"War is serious, Pïaṯ. I know it is." She wasn't listening. She wasn't running like I urged her to, and I could already hear the Elders on the tower steps. "I think I'll take a walk." She didn't react to my panic, her eyes glazed in the familiar way that told me she was unaware of the world around her. She shook me off and hurried through the castle as the Elders ran toward us.

She didn't even acknowledge them.

Didn't see them.

"Where's she going?" Elder Ðæл panted as she slowed to a stop beside me, a trail of water pooling behind her. "You can't let her loose in the castle; her mind is gone! She'll create chaos."

"She's harmless, Ðæл." I frowned, blocking her from pursuing my wife into the castle. "She won't hurt anyone."

"We don't know that." She handed me my daughter, and I blushed. I'd been so panicked over my wife I'd completely forgotten about her. "Why don't you take the day off, Pïaṯ? Spend it with this little blossom," she suggested as she tickled the baby's toes. "This ... isn't something you should see."

I chilled, clutching the infant to my chest. "Please, Ðæл, don't do this to her."

"Her mind has failed, and the things she knows, the things she's seen ... we can't let them get out. We can't let her spill our secrets."

"You can't kill her."

"Of course we can't." Elder Ðæл touched my arm gently, the water flowing over her, soaking into my shirt. "Don't worry, Pïaṯ, we'll just ... quiet her mind. We still need her powers." she let out a chuckle and gestured around us. "The world needs her power. Without them, everything would fall to disarray. We can't kill her without killing ourselves."

"I can reach her," I insisted. "I just need more time."

"You're out of time." She sighed, her eyes wandering over the halls behind me, searching for my wife.

"I'll take anything! A few days even. I know I can reach her, Ðæл. Let me try."

"Two days." She held up two fingers and took a step back. "That's all I can spare." With one last fearful glance at the spot where Maɼÿ disappeared, the Elder shuddered and returned to her section of the castle.

Two days.

I had two days to find a way to burn the madness out of Maɼÿ's system and convince the Elders to turn a blind eye.

Two days.

I fiddled with the clock around my neck, tempted to use it to slow those days, make them drag on like hundreds of cycles instead of only a few moments. But my power was only bending time and moving through it. I could not stop it like Pïlůл could, and my meager attempt would probably kill me.

All I could do was sit in the garden and watch her play with our daughter.

"Look, Pïaṯ! She's nearly walking now!" Maɼÿ giggled, letting our child wrap her tiny fingers around her mother's thumb to help her balance on wobbly feet. The baby squealed as she shifted through the grass. Maɼÿ hovered over her, holding her up, and she took a shaky step toward me. "Oh, my darling, you're going to love watching her grow up!"

"So will you, Maṛÿ." I chuckled, but confusion clouded her eyes.

"My name isn't Maṛÿ."

My heart stopped. "Oh?" I tried to sound casual, to ignore the hope blooming in my chest.

"Of course not, silly." She laughed as our daughter squatted down into the grass and released her hands. "My name is Ana, you know that."

Ana!

So she was in there! She'd insisted cycles ago that I no longer call her that. She insisted 'Ana' no longer fit her.

"You asked me to call you Maṛÿ," I mumbled, eyeing her, searching for the confusion and distance that had lived in her eyes long before her mind deserted her. But I only saw a clarity and mischievousness that spoke of days long gone.

"Well, that's ridiculous. Why would I proclaim myself a collector? What do I collect, other than these precious moments?" She scooped our daughter up and cradled her close, bouncing slightly as the baby giggled.

"The Elders assumed you meant soldiers." I shrugged, soaking in the glimpse of sanity I got as she played with our child. Over the cycles, I'd been gifted a few moments of clarity with her, but they grew rarer and rarer as time passed.

"I have no need to collect soldiers. There is no war." She twirled in the grass, holding the baby close and I relaxed. I should go find Vaлṭïj or Pïlữл, show them that she was fine, but as she said ... this was a precious moment, and it was ours. The Elders could wait.

Then she stopped suddenly, turning wide, horrified eyes

back to me. My heart sank.

"Don't fight her death, Peter!"

"What?" I suppressed a sigh as grief clawed at my chest. She was gone again.

"Our daughter. You'll fight her death, but you must not!"

"Ana ..." I groaned as tears flooded my eyes. "Please, please hang in there."

"Why do you call me 'Ana'?" She set the baby in the grass, and turned to face the garden, dazed and unsure. "My name is Marÿ."

"Marÿ!" I crashed through the woods. The path was clearer now, lit with torches. There wasn't as much underbrush so I could run to her easily. Her screams haunted me as I ran, though they'd stopped long ago. Still I couldn't find her, but I must be close now. "Marÿ!"

"A *war is coming!*" Her cry jolted me out of my sleep, though her voice sounded far away. I patted the bed beside me, but my wife wasn't there.

"Now, now, Marÿ," Elder Vaлtij's voice followed my wife's fearful cry. "Don't make this any harder than it needs to be."

"Why are you calling me Marÿ!?" Panic seeped into her words, and I hurried out into the house in time to see her dash out of the nursery, clutching our daughter to her chest. She ran to me, her eyes wide. "They tricked me! Made me think the baby was crying but they were waiting for me! Why are they here, Pïat?"

"I don't know." I glared at Elder Đæл as she stepped out of the nursery, frustration evident on her face. Elder Vaлṯij, Pïlúл, and four castle guards followed her, though they wouldn't look at me.

"You weren't supposed to wake." Elder Đæл sighed. "I'd hoped you'd sleep through the whole thing." She stepped up to my wife, holding her hands out for the baby, and Maɼÿ shied away, pressing closer to me.

"Pïaṯ, help." The Elder shot me a helpless glance, and I recoiled.

"Help?" The word felt ridiculous on my lips. "Help you betray her?"

"Fine, Pïlúл then." She snapped her fingers, and he reluctantly stepped forward, though he kept his eyes to the ground. My friend! He gently grabbed the baby as Elder Đæл wrapped her arms around my wife, trying to pull her free. I launched forward, trying to wedge myself between them, and then Elder Vaлṯij's hands rammed into my side and knocked me to the ground. I scrambled back to my feet, but Pïlúл had already ripped my daughter from Maɼÿ's arms. My child screamed, reaching for her mother, and Maɼÿ desperately tried to grab onto her again but Elder Đæл and Elder Vaлṯij dragged her away.

"You said I had two days!" I caught hold of my wife's hand, gripping it as tight as I could, determined never to let it go.

"I lied," Elder Đæл grunted, wrenching her hand out of mine. "We've never had one go mad before. I can't let your bias risk our people."

"Peter!" Maɼÿ clawed the air as the Elders wrestled her towards the door. I surged forward again, but Pïlúл blocked me, holding out my screaming daughter.

"His name isn't Peter, Rèлïǎ," Elder Vaлtïj tried to soothe her, but she still screamed as they dragged her out into the hall. Elder Pïлл pressed my daughter into my arms as two of the guards stepped forward to restrain me.

"Let her go," he whispered. "You can't save her." He nodded to someone over my shoulder and a maid stepped forward, taking her place in front of me as I struggled against the guards. Elder Pïлл followed the others out without another glance.

"Let me go!" I twisted, trying to break their hold, and the maid shook her head sadly and braced her hand on my daughter's back, protecting her while I struggled helplessly against the guards' strength.

"Trust me, Sir, you won't want to see this!"

"I have to, I have to see!" My heart raced in my chest, adrenaline flooding me as Marÿ's cries faded. "She's mine to protect. I have to go! They're going to kill her!"

"You can't! I'm sorry, Elder, but I can't let you." She pressed her sleeve over my mouth and whispered, "Zlat."

My legs gave out and I fell into her arms.

My head pounded as I woke. At my groan, the maid lifted her gaze from my daughter, now sleeping soundly in her arms. Tears stained her cheeks as she stared at me, regret spilling from her eyes.

"The Elders commanded it, Sir. I'm so very, very sorry."

"How long was ...?" I jolted off the floor, my head spinning as I lurched toward the door. She scrambled after me, trying to steady me, but I threw her off.

"Not too long ... but long enough ..." she trailed off and my stomach clenched.

Long enough.

Long enough for the Elders to kill her.

Long enough to keep me from saving her.

"Marÿ," I whispered as I stumbled into the castle halls. The maid trailed behind, rocking my daughter as she stirred and woke. Torches flickered on the walls, lighting the path, but I saw no one. Usually, guards and people mingled throughout the castle no matter the time of day, but it was deserted.

With a flash of cold rage, I understood the story the Elders were trying to paint. No one was around to witness the tragic story of the mad Rèлïä, and the drastic decision forced upon the Elders to protect their people. No one would be able to speak the truth. I, blinded by love, could be easily dismissed, but witnesses could not.

The torches led out to the garden, and through the gate out into the forest.

The forest.

I barely convinced my legs to keep moving forward, and though I wanted to scream for her, her name stopped frozen behind my teeth. The forest. The tree in my vision. I didn't hear her screams in the woods, but they haunted my mind.

Her people lined the forest trail, bowing their heads as I passed. Everyone from the castle was here, in a mourning procession. The Elders hadn't wanted to be rid of witnesses after all. They'd invited all these people to watch their Rèлïä die and no one stepped in to help her.

"Elder Pïa_t_," Elder Ðæл said carefully as she stepped into my path, blocking me from the beautiful tree towering in the clearing. "I know you're angry, but this was the honorable path to take. We gave her a monument; we respected her properly, and now she cannot hurt anyone. Look at the tree we placed her in. It's as proud and strong as she should have been!"

My legs numbed as I followed her finger, studying the tree.

"The tree we placed her in."

Buried alive.

They buried my wife alive, and claimed it honored her?

The laugh that ripped through me belied my grief and outrage. Elder Ðæл took a step back, her eyes narrowing. Perhaps she thought I was mad too. I certainly sounded it right now.

Good. Let her fret.

"A proud tree is no way to remember her." I stumbled forward, anger coloring my words as it drowned my thoughts.

I'd tried so hard to save her. I tried so hard to hide her madness, and for what?

"This is not a proud denouement of your pierced Rèлïà, rejected and humiliated by her own people. Are you proud of this, are you proud of what you've allowed to happen? She loved you all, and what did she get for it? A stupid tree that lies just as well as the Elders." I glared at the people gathered around the monument to my wife and settled my gaze on Elder Ðæл. They chose this. They chose to trap their Rèлïà within the tree so we wouldn't lose her power. Forevermore buried alive, never allowed to be at rest. I pressed my hands into the bark of the tree, a lump rising in my throat. "Xгÿ."

Cracks rent the air as the spindly branches of the tree twisted and bent toward the ground in a hunched, defeated pose. People gasped and stepped back, some fleeing into the assumed safety of the tree line that marked the clearing. Tears fell from my eyes in streams, fusing with the bark and making the tree appear as if it were crying as well, weeping and grieving the betrayal that stole my love's life.

"This is how we will remember her," I declared, squaring my shoulders and fighting her screams echoing in my head. "We will remember her as the distraught, dejected Rèлïä she was, and the pain she experienced because you were too proud to support her and consider that she might be right."

The Elders didn't stop me. They had the good sense to hang their heads, ashamed, as the gathered crowd slipped slowly back into the forest, leaving me alone. As they left, so too did my wrath, until finally, I sagged against the tree, pressing my head against the bark. My daughter toddled up to the tree as I sobbed, pressing her tiny hands against the bark. Her curious little coos tore through me as she raised her hands for me to pick her up.

"Oh, Maŗÿ," I whispered, clutching the tiny baby to my chest as more tears fell. "I am so sorry I couldn't stop them. My love, please forgive me." I trailed my fingers over the cracks of the tree, tracing the patterns of her tears, and a chill ran through me as a vision pressed into my head.

A vision that took the place of the peace I'd seen for cycles, crowding out the happiness our future promised every time I looked.

A vision of blood and fire and anger.

A vision of impending war.

IF I WAS IMPORTANT
Sarah Elliott

If I was important to you,
You would have said it in more than just words.

If I was important to you,
You would have said good morning.

If I was important to you,
I wouldn't see my good mornings next to my good nights.

If I was important to you,
You wouldn't make me feel like this.

If I was important to you,
I wouldn't feel like a plaything—
A doll cherished and then discarded.
Never truly loved.
Forgotten.
Tossed aside.

If I was important to you,
You wouldn't have promised empty promises.

If I was important to you,
You wouldn't have told empty, candle-lit dreams.

If I was important to you,
Tell me I wasn't just manipulated.

If I was important to you,
Tell me you really loved me.
Leaving would be easier,
Knowing we simply grew apart.

If I was important to you,
Would you let me go?

If I was important to you
Why did you always ask for more?

If I was important to you,
You would find the time to talk to me.

If I was important to you,
You would find the time to see me.

If I was important to you,
I wouldn't hear my echo as the only answer back.

If I was important to you,
You would tell me my rose-tinted glasses didn't cover the
red flags.

If I was important to you,
You would read this.

WAITING LIKE I PROMISED
Effie Joe Stock

I'm **waiting. Like** I promised I would be."

My eyes fluttered open before squinting at the light streaming through the window. For a long time, I lay there, unmoving, just staring into the light. It reminded me of that flash of light I had seen so many years ago before everything had faded away.

Slowly, I stretched my arms then my legs before sitting up, the thin blanket falling off me and halfway onto the floor. With a sense of confusion, I looked down at my clothes. I had slept in them. Again. They were the same clothes I remember from the day before, and the day before that—a little yellow suit jacket and a button-up collared shirt tucked into a plain, dark, knee-length skirt. Strange how I couldn't quite seem to remember when I had first donned these clothes or how many days I had gone wearing them and then sleeping in them again. And strange how they weren't wrinkled. In fact, they were as smooth and crisp as if I had just finished ironing them.

The light streaming from the window blinded my vision again as I stared into it and a fog settled over my brain. Faintly, I heard voices. Some of them were familiar, and some of them were not. I strained to hear the ones that stirred something in my heart.

A man's voice became clearer through the softly buzzing air. "I have to go. I have to. But I'll come back. I promise. You wait for me, yeah? Wait for me. Wait for me. Wait for me." The words echoed again and again until I heard the shadow of my own voice whispering back, "I promise I will wait."

The words faded again, leaving me with only the unfamiliar drone of a stranger's words. Drifting from thought to thought, feeling as if I were floating through time, I focused on the voice, trying to grasp something from the hum.

"I swore I had already made my bed today." The voice was of a young girl. I squinted against the bright light. A young girl was standing at the foot of the bed. Or was she? It was too hard to tell. She was more like a shadow, a hallucination, than reality. Perhaps I was still asleep, still dreaming.

Another voice, one I couldn't hear well, answered her, but the young girl's voice interrupted loudly. "No! I swear! It's happened again! It must be a ghost!"

Sternly, the other voice disagreed, causing the child to descend into tears. Faint, echoing footsteps gave me the impression the second stranger had left the room, if they had even been here in the first place.

The disturbing sobbing grew softer, and with the quiet that followed, the brightness of the light faded as well. My tired eyes scanned the room. It was dark. Too dark. But no ... there was still light. It wasn't a dark room. Rather, there was no color. I glanced at my jacket. The yellow of it was disturbingly bright against the grey tones of the room. I frowned, but it was almost all too strange to think much of.

Toys filled the room. Dolls, paper clothes, tops, and little building blocks. I noticed the bed I was sitting on was much too small for my own size. So it wasn't my bed, and neither was it my room. But if none of it was mine, then why was I here? I looked to the window again. I knew that window— knew the trim that cut little squares across the glass, and the hinges the windowpanes swung open on had those same gouges where we had once tried to pry them off to replace them.

We. Who was *we*? A face flashed before me, a laugh filled the air, a smile brightened the room. "Wait for me," he whispered again.

The little girl's voice drew my attention back to her. She had knelt down at the foot of the bed. A doll now rested in her hands. Her mouth was moving, and I strained to hear her words.

"... long time ago, mommy says ten years, during the war, a man was drafted to go fight ... promised he would come home to his new wife. And so he did. But he came home to find his wife dead ... bottom part of the house caught fire ... couldn't escape ... smoke killed her."

A restlessness rose in me at those words. It was disturbing enough that a child would speak so freely of death and sorrow but even more so was the itching, no, the burning that had kindled in my limbs and the way my breath caught in my throat, heavy in my chest as if I couldn't breathe.

The girl leaned down to the doll, placing her chubby red lips to the porcelain ear. "It was this house, Sue. This very one! ... This was the room they found her in—the wife I mean." Her small round eyes looked up and pierced into mine. My breath caught in my throat.

A fury of emotion and memory flooded through me. I remembered our wedding: the ridiculously silky and lacy white gown I had worn and the funny little top hat he had worn. I remembered buying this house, and then the war starting, and then the letter proclaiming my new husband had been drafted. Then I remembered screaming. So much screaming. And the house growing hot and filling with smoke, filling my lungs, and the burning, burning pain before that blinding flash of light.

Tears streamed down my face as I turned back to the light streaming through the window. "I'm waiting. Like I promised I would be," I whispered. But I knew I could wait no longer. I had nothing else to wait for. Time had moved on without me. A new family lived in my own. Perhaps my widower husband was widowed no longer, having found a new wife.

I stepped up onto the bed and placed my feet in the window frame. Looking out, I saw not the ground beneath me, or the neighborhood I had remembered, but only, shining, blinding light reached for me, called to me. I took a deep breath, released the lingering phantom of smoke in my ghostly lungs, and felt no fear. Then I let go.

UNTITLED
Piper l. White

I wish I'd seen through
every translucent interaction.
You threw at me over the stove
when you looked into my eyes
and stole bits of me throughout the night,
leaving me plucked like daisy petals
to be drowned by rainfall.

The rain pitter-pattered on your window
(the one with the trinkets on the sill)
and my heart raced until it settled
to a steady beat in your arms.
It was lovely, wasn't it?

But I walked alone after that,
with your silent symphony
driving me crazy
because I thought I did something wrong.
It wasn't my fault.

You tore through me like wind
sharp enough to cut shutters in half.
You muddled my heart and grinded me down
to ashes, ones I scattered all the places you graced,
including my fingertips, my hair, my waist.

Our footprints lace together on the concrete,
invisible, but the imagery is too much to bear.
I don't know if I can go back there.
But I have to.

I'll wade the shallowness of your words
once more, when I walk through the door
and sit in the same spot I felt my heart rip,
biting it back and shoving it down
to look you in the eye one more time.

It tore me apart to swallow my pride,
but I did it for me, never you.
You don't deserve a title—
you never gave one to me.

SILENT ANGELS
Mariella Taylor

I loved the way
you silenced my thoughts
because I miss the silence now.

I long for the way
the quiet resounded through me
because it won't come again.

I miss the way
you brought out the best in me
because all I have are black-hearted jokes.

I need the way
you drew out my angels
because now I'm only dancing with my demons.

THE RED UMBRELLA
Anne J. Hill

If only it hadn't rained that morning, she might have lived.

Slumping on the edge of her broken-down loveseat, Ms. Digger checked and rechecked that her gun was clean, loaded, safety off, and a bullet in the chamber. If she were lucky—no, if she did her job well—this would only take two shots.

She screwed the silencer onto the end of the barrel with swift, practiced turns, then slipped the firearm into her purse. There were some things old age couldn't rob her of.

She stepped out onto her front porch, rain pelting down on the roof of her old ranch-style home and looked up at the sound of a door creaking open. Mr. Johnston, the man across the street, was exiting his house. He held a steaming cup of coffee in his right hand and a red umbrella in his left. His slippered feet shuffled across his puddle-laden driveway, and his night robe flapped in the piercing breeze. Reaching the end of the drive, he bent down and scooped up his newspaper. "Morning, Digger!" he called.

"Morning, Johnston."

He blew on his drink, making some of it splash onto his slippers. He scowled down at the mess then asked, "Going to work?"

"Sure am."

Johnston sipped his scorching coffee and spat it onto the gravel, making a pained face. "Have a good day."

Ms. Digger chuckled, shaking her head. "Never did have patience to let your coffee cool, did you?"

"No, ma'am! See you tonight?" he asked, his voice rising at the end.

Digger bit her lip in pause, then nodded slowly. "Tonight."

Johnston's eyes lit up like those of a man born no later than the Great Depression, and he shuffled back inside, scolding his coffee.

Every morning, he asked to see her that night. She always said yes, but she never showed up, and he never remembered.

This time, she intended to show. She'd finally let him in. No one wanted to die alone.

But first, she had work to do.

She drove to the nearby city, reminding herself that this would be her last job and then she could finally live. At the age of seventy-five, she would begin her life. Better late than never.

She parked on the street, windshield wipers plowing away the rain. Just in front of her was a couple around her age. Instead of holding hands, they held onto the black umbrella they shared, fingers overlapping. The man leaned over and kissed his lover's cheek. She glanced back and beamed like it was their honeymoon.

Digger's thumbs tapped against her steering wheel. *That will be us tonight.* She smiled at the thought then got out of the car.

Every building was white or cream except for the building with the green door. She trailed quietly behind the couple, watching the green door get closer as she walked.

She wondered what her targets did to deserve the bullet this time. Murder? Theft? Spying? Could be anything.

The man glanced back at her and offered a smile. She nodded. No one ever suspected an old lady. She had that going for her. Shoot, then fade into the street as a granny looking for her lost cat. Worked every time.

When the man looked away, Digger picked up her pace until she was inches behind them. No one else was on the streets. Most people were still sleeping. Just how she liked it.

The couple stopped in front of the green door. The woman looked back at her this time. "Are you lost, dear?"

"Not me. Lost my cat. Name's Charlie. White fluffy thing. You seen him?"

The lady frowned. "Can't say I have. We'll keep an eye out for you."

"'Preciate it." Ms. Digger gave her a toothy smile. Then she shot the woman through the back and put a round through the old man before he had a chance to react. The silencer-muffled concussions disappeared into the wind like a couple of innocent sneezes.

Two limp, once-happy bodies lay at Ms. Digger's feet. She locked eyes with the lady's forever-unblinking gaze and shook her head, then knocked on the green door and walked away, calling, "Charlie! Here, kitty kitty!"

The door creaked open behind her, and the sound of dragging bodies grumbled amongst the pattering rain. The blood would wash off the sidewalk soon enough. Easy. Clean. Done.

She never knew what they did with the bodies, but she didn't really care. She knew she'd have a wad of cash in her mailbox when she got home, and frankly, that's all she needed to know.

Digger smiled up at the rain, feeling angels' tears plummet down on her face. She was a free woman. She'd pulled her last trigger and would be rewarded with true love.

If only it hadn't rained that morning, she might have lived.

She looked back down to the street and froze. A man stood in front of her under a red umbrella, coffee thermos in hand, mouth gaping.

"Johnston?" Digger could have sworn the street had been empty.

"Saw you leave the house without an umbrella, so I came to walk you to work so you wouldn't get wet." His face was ghostly white like he'd seen, well, everything.

She glanced to his right. He must have turned down the alley behind her just as she'd pulled the trigger. If only it hadn't been raining. If only Johnston hadn't been so sweet to bring her an umbrella.

If only ...

If only Digger hadn't inclined her firearm toward Johnston out of habit. If only Johnston didn't carry his old World War 2 pistol and a strong sense of self-preservation. Then she might have walked down the street under his umbrella to a happily ever after. Instead, she now lay in a pool of her own blood with a hole between her eyes.

Nobody likes to die alone.

LOSS
Betsy Smith

It's when I see your smile brighten across the room,
And my heart aches at what could have been.
Your laugh is my destruction and salvation.
I lost you, but you were never mine.

I had been alone in those dark, dark days
And you had lifted me up into the light.
(Did you even know that? Do you know how much you did
for me?)
I lost you, but you were never mine.

(Have you a clue at all, how many nights I longed for you?
When I cried myself to sleep?
All I wanted was to be in your embrace.)
To you, I was a good friend,
But to me, you were my everything.
I lost you, but you were never mine.

There are times when I wonder if you ever knew,

If you saw the truth behind my eyes
When I joked with you.
Maybe you did know how much you meant to me.
Perhaps I wasn't as good at pretending as I thought.
(But I know the truth: I know how well it was hidden,
None of them ever knew, nor did you,
That I was in love with you.)
I lost you, but you were never mine.

(Why did it have to be him?)

(It could have been anyone else.)

She tried to help, too.
Even though she didn't know the truth,
She still helped.
She put us together so many times, alone, too close.
You two are so cute! she'd say. *You should be together!*
He looks at me expectantly (and I know it's all in my head,
But he looks hopeful. Almost as if he feels the same.)
And we both laugh. (He's so beautiful when he smiles.)
"Well?"

I've said it in my head a thousand times, so why can't I speak?
It's only a few words.
(I love you, I love you, I love you!)
"Ew, why would I like him?!"
Exactly! He echoes, pushing me away.

(I hate myself.)

Now I see you laughing with another girl,
Charming her as you charmed me.
(It's not his fault; he didn't know.
It was me, my fault, mine alone.
If only I had confessed! If only I could have spoken.
Too late for me, for us.)
I lost you, but you were never mine.

She's so beautiful, you know.
The girl I never was, the better girl.
I want you to be happy. Of course, I do!
You're my best friend! (But why can't it be me?)
Nothing is wrong! (Everything is wrong.)
You two are perfect! (But not as perfect as we could be.)

Now I know how it feels to lose someone.
(But why do I care? We were never together anyways,
You were never mine.
But why can't I sleep anymore?
Why does my heart die when I see you now?)
Sadness returns as my light fades.

And now, I'm watching you from afar.
And you seem to be doing fine without me.
(I should have expected it.)
You seem happier. (You never cared.)

I miss talking to you.

(I still love you.)

I lost you, but you were never mine.

LIGHTNING
Beka Gremikova

From the corner of the classroom, I watch them. He leans back in his chair, quiet, thoughtful, chewing the end of his pencil. The girl beside him mutters something, and he snorts, shaking his head.

Someone tosses a paper airplane at him, and it bounces harmlessly off his shoulder, drifting to the floor like wilted petals.

"You're quiet today," the girl says.

He scuffs his tennis shoe across the floor. "Got a lot to think about."

"Her?" she asks quietly.

He bows his head.

My heart aches as though it's been pounding against itself for too long, and the question I often ask about other people returns: Why do I torture myself like this? I sigh, but nobody notices. Of course they don't.

"You need a distraction, Liam?" She wraps an arm around his shoulder. "We could go to a movie, or watch some shows at your house—"

He glances up at her, his brow creased. He adjusts his glasses and blinks, as if she's shaken him awake. "I—I think

I'd just like to be alone today after classes."

She nods, though her eyes flick to the floor and I can tell from her drooping shoulders that she wishes he'd rely on her more. I understand the feeling. Liam's one of those guys who loves to help you—and hates letting you help him.

The teacher walks into the room, and they turn to pay attention. I spend all of class studying Liam's back: the tenseness in his shoulders, the deep wrinkles in his oversized sweater, the greasy sheen of his thick black curls.

When the bell rings, he shuffles out the door. The girl lingers with his other friends, shooting a worried glance after him.

"It's all right," I whisper to them as I pass by. "I'll watch him."

They don't respond. They never do, but it makes me feel more real to speak anyways.

I trail Liam through the school's cold, narrow halls, making a few lights flicker as I go.

The students milling around me glance up at the ceiling. "You think the power's gonna go out?" one asks.

"It *is* supposed to storm today," another answers, slamming her locker door shut.

I fight a grin. I always loved a good storm.

Liam pushes out the front doors, hurtling down the steps.

Overhead, storm clouds fester while a cold, mournful wind blows, scattering my hair across my shoulders and singing the song of ghosts. Tree branches click and clatter like bones dancing. I laugh, the adrenaline of a thousand thunderclaps coursing through me, giving me new life. I run, daring the encroaching storm to fight me, to nip my cheeks red, to whip my hair from its ponytail.

I feel alive.

The residential neighborhood fades into tattered, tumble-down shacks with brown, dead grass and peeling fences. At the end of the street, the graveyard gate swings open, clattering against the surrounding stone wall.

Liam walks straight through, hunched now against the screaming wind. I stroll after him, hands stuffed into the pockets of my old jeans. He marches straight to the back of the cemetery, careful not to trod on any graves, winding around pots of flowers left by other mourners.

He stops at a small gravestone and stares down at its smooth, marbled surface.

I peer over his shoulder.

The cross is small, yet elegant, adorned with flowing script:

Miranda Low—beloved daughter of Tom and Lydia

Lover of laughter, the Lakers, and lightning.

Liam's body quivers. He tilts his head to the sky, blinking rapidly. "Hey, babe," he murmurs.

A shiver curls through me. I flit to hover in front of him, wishing his soft eyes could actually meet my gaze. I reach out as if to touch him, even though I can't. My hands merely sweep through him like he's the one made out of air, not me.

His thick black brows furrow. He continues, sniffling slightly, "Miss you lots. You'd probably laugh if you knew—it's about to storm."

I follow his gaze up to the tightly coiling clouds. My breath catches at the memories of walking with him in the rain, lightning flashing around us. The way I'd laugh and dart about, splashing in puddles. All the while, he'd shake his head at me and try to coax me indoors to cuddle and watch movies.

"You always acted like you were high or something when the storms came." He coughs out a laugh, and I frown. He sounds hoarse and raspy. He better not have started smoking ... "You were nuts. But I miss watching you ..." His voice chokes.

It starts to rain. Within moments, he's drenched, his curls sticking to his skin, droplets streaming down his face to drip off the edge of his nose. He's beautiful.

With a sound like singing, lightning flashes, illuminating the clearing. In that second, I swear he sees me; his eyes widen, and he staggers backwards, gasping. "*Miranda?*"

Then the light flicks out again, plunging us back into a dreary grey world.

He passes his fingers through his hair, shivering with cold, and shakes his head at himself. He leaves, shutting the graveyard gate behind him.

The rain continues to fall. I reach out, feeling its driving cold wetness without its effect. Lightning flashes again, bright and bold. Puddles form on the ground. I wish Liam had stayed; I wish he could see me; I wish he knew that, right now, I'm jumping from puddle to puddle, giggling like a madwoman as the storm rages above our heads.

HALF OF MY HEART
Cassandra Hamm

Half of my heart lies
in scarlet shards on the floor,
glittering like drops of blood
I keep forgetting to clean up.

But I'm fine, really.
I'm okay.

Maybe I can believe this lie
and pretend I don't need to heal
from the wound you unknowingly inflicted.
You just love to let things go

but sometimes you forget that
when you let something go, it falls,
and sometimes there is no one to catch it.

No one caught my heart.

Half of my heart, that is.
I gave you half of my heart
without your knowing, thinking
maybe you'd realize how blind you'd been.

You did.
You told me it was like
your eyes were opened to see
what had been there the whole time.

But you weren't talking about me.

How quickly you turned.
How easily you dropped me,
along with the rest of your past,
and half of my glass heart
hurtled toward unforgiving ground
and I couldn't breathe—

Then you sent the first love poem.
Not directed at me, of course—
written about her.

My glass heart impacted the earth and
shattered, flinging shards across the ground,
and there it lay, discarded
along with my misconceptions.

Who could want this half-shattered heart?

THE LONELY SAILOR
Ariel Choate

The smell of earth and rock brought me back from the sea salt air as the boat coasted up to the dock. I've always felt whole out there. That was where I belonged, out at sea, exploring lagoons and reefs.

While Dad was a fisherman, I had always been more interested in studying the creatures we caught. See how different each one of them is and how special they can be in their natural home. To explore the unknown reaches of the depths below. What creatures live down there, and what can they show us?

A splash rained small droplets of saltwater against my cheek, and I smiled, my mind drifting to my future. I'll get my own boat, set it out, and travel the globe. It'll be a sailboat, smaller in size but big enough for me to be safe and explore the seven seas.

I can't wait for that day. I'll be free from land and its heavy ways of life. Free from anything that tied me down. Free to explore and never look back!

Seems awfully lonely.

A lump formed in my throat as I tied the rope to the dock.

Alone.

I would be alone. My dad couldn't go with me forever. He was getting on in years, and he'd need to stay back on land where it's safe.

I looked out over the port side at the sunlight dancing across the waves. They sparkled like the eyes of my best friend when she laughed at my jokes.

"Luke!" Olivia called from where she was sitting on the dock. "Did you catch anything for me?"

I smiled up at her. "I got loads!" Several shiny silver fish wriggled in the red bucket at my feet as I began lifting it from the deck, spraying droplets of seawater onto my face. "Caught them all by myself!" I sat it down beside her, sending a new splash up by her feet.

"Geez." She stared down into it. "You got a lot."

"'Course I did! I'm the son of a master fisherman. 'Course, I'd be an expert at catching fish!" I laughed, hopping up next to her.

"Momma is going to make a feast for us. We have to pay you for this."

"No, it's my gift to you guys." I towered over her small stature, wiping sea salt from my hands on my shorts. "It's in exchange for those pies you make dad and me."

Olivia smiled up at me, brushing some of the curls from her face. "Okay fine." She laughed. "Then you're coming over for dinner." She smirked and spun on her heels, not giving me a chance to respond before she walked away.

"Hey! Wait up!" I picked the bucket up and held it on my shoulder. "I'm the one carrying the dinner!"

She turned her head, laughter escaping her perfect smile. I found myself laughing along with her as we walked. We talked about school starting soon, how we're going to graduate this year, and I started to notice how carefree she walked. The way her face lit up as she got excited for her senior trip before school, the passion that filled her voice ... I couldn't help but just watch in awe.

I went to the house and cleaned myself up as Olivia's mom made us dinner, all the while glancing at my best friend as if I were seeing her for the first time. How come I only just now realized how beautiful she really was? How perfect she was ... Every part of her I saw in a new light, from the freckles across her skin to the golden flecks in her eyes. They were so beautiful.

"Luke?"

My heart skipped a beat when she called my name. "Yeah?"

"Do you want another slice of pie?"

"Of course," I responded with a nod, never refusing another slice of apple pie. But when her eyes met mine as she served me, my cheeks grew hot. Why was I so suddenly overcome with this feeling? Why now? Was this falling in love?

Our eyes stayed locked between us, seemingly forever. Was she seeing what I was feeling? Could she see how I felt so much more between us now? If she did, she didn't say anything, breaking eye contact with me to converse with her mother.

I looked down at my pie, my heart thumping. What should I do? Tell her how I feel? Ask her if she felt the same?

My chest ached. Was I now uncomfortable in my second home?

"Luke?" I looked back up into Olivia's hazel eyes. "Everything okay?"

"I'm fine, just tired," I lied, not wanting her to worry. "I think I should head home. Dad and I have another long day tomorrow." That part was true. We did. Another all-day fishing trip out to sea. But that wasn't why I was leaving. I just had to get out of there.

"Oh." Her expression fell, and that made my chest hurt even more. *Please ... don't make this harder.*

"I'll come over again sometime this week," I promised, reaching over and touching her hand. From the touch of her skin, I felt like lightning shot through my arm and heart and then into my stomach. It flip-flopped, and I pulled back, my heart racing. Such a simple gesture caused that?

I stood up, trying to keep myself composed while internally my body was electrified. "Thank you so much for dinner." The small tremble at the end of my words left me nervous for Olivia to find out. "Have a great evening." I turned and went towards the door, hoping not to hear her tiny footsteps behind me.

That night, I spent my time on the boat, laying in the hammock close to the water as I stared up at the starry sky. The rhythmic sounds of the waves lapping against the boat brought a sense of calm to me. This was my home. My place of comfort. A place I could rely on. Honestly, my dad raised me on his boat, and he was certain I was more comfortable out at sea than on land. I think he was right.

She returned to my mind, and I felt that sense of longing. Longing to be with her. Longing to be beside her, to hold her hand, to hug her, to kiss her.

That's when it hit me.

I was utterly in love with my best friend.

"No." I quickly shook my head. "We're friends. Best

friends."

My thoughts failed to be reigned in as my mind drifted to what it would feel like if I were to kiss her. Soft? Gentle? Would her kiss be passionate? Or just a small peck? To pull her in close, hold her waist, and brush my fingers through her hair—

Stop it!

I sat up in my hammock and nearly lost my balance as I shook my head, pushing my hands through my hair. "Stop thinking. Stop it."

Small breaths escaped me as I tried to calm myself, my heart beating faster.

"Stop." Imaginative pictures crashed into my mind in waves, showing me and her together on dates, engaged, the wedding day, the wedding night, and then holding our first child as we sailed into the sunset.

My heart pounded against my chest, and tears welled in my eyes. It was so beautiful. So perfect ... I never realized how much I wanted that. Wanted her.

All the years we'd been best friends, I had never seen her any differently. She was my partner in crime, my biggest supporter, closer to me than my own father. Now that all changed.

I love her.

That thought rang throughout my head like the horn of a large freighter ship. Such a small phrase said repeatedly between us so many times, now had so much more meaning to me. I loved her. I think I always did. I just didn't realize it until then.

Did she love me? She'd been my friend all those years; she had loved me. Maybe even more than just as a friend. She had to. All those late-night conversations, all the secrets we shared, the memories we had together. They weren't meaningless, right?

Exhaling a breath, I laid back down in my hammock, arm over my face. *I really need to stop thinking about this.* I could already feel knots forming in my stomach. Exhaustion was swarming my body, but my brain wouldn't shut up.

Be quiet. I begged for rest and sleep to overcome me so I could just stop thinking about her. About us. Should I even tell her? What would happen if I did? She might not feel the same, and then our friendship would be ruined. I didn't think I could ever see her the same way as I did yesterday.

Maybe the time would be soon, just not yet. I'd wait for her. Wait till we were' out of high school then I could ask her.

With the lap of waves against the boat, gently rocking the ship side to side, I felt my body finally succumb to the rest I so desperately needed. My brain followed suit with the decision I had made.

I would wait for her.

Senior year flew by with me being busier with school and working for my dad. I barely saw her except on the days she would pick up her order. But every time she came, I would be there waiting, smiling up at her from the boat and handing her the bucket of fish, just like we always had been. Although, every time she smiled back at me, my cheeks would pink. I struggled to hide it, but she never took notice.

Graduation day came along faster than we could think, and we walked the stage, grabbed our diplomas and shook our teachers' hands.

Her eyes met mine as I smiled to the crowd, beaming

with pride. We did it. We finished school. We were graduates.

We met afterward, taking pictures and chatting with our teachers before leaving to celebrate together. We had a shared small gathering with just a few friends and family, too busy greeting everyone or saying goodbye at the door to even talk with each other.

By the end, we were exhausted. Nothing sounded better to me than getting away after we cleaned up from our party. And that's where I was going to do it. I was going to tell her. If not now, then when? I had to do it.

"Let's meet at the docks. For old times' sake?" I asked her, helping lift the final folding chairs into her mom's truck.

She closed the liftgate, brushing her hands off before looking to me with a tired smile, "That sounds really nice."

"Perfect!" I smiled back, grinning "I'll be waiting."
We parted paths and met at my dad's boat a few hours later, staring out at the open sea.

"What are you going to do?" Olivia asked. "Now that we've graduated?" She stepped onto my dad's boat, walking towards the bow.

"Oh, you know, travel the world ..." I drew out that last word, smirking at her. "On my own boat!" I laughed, smiling proudly.

"What? No way!" She gaped at me. "You really are?"

I gave a slight nod. "I found one that my dad's friend was going to retire. He said that if I fix it back up, it's all mine." I leaned against the starboard railing, staring up at the mast. "Altogether, the parts for fixing her up should be covered by all the graduation checks people sent me. And I'll even have some left over to get food for the journey."

I looked over at her smiling at me, seawater reflecting onto her eyes and face. "That's so awesome!" She hopped up onto the railing, sitting a few inches from me. "I'm proud of you." She shoved my arm, her touch sending butterflies throughout my stomach.

I felt heat rush to my cheeks, and I looked at the old wooden floorboards near my shoes. "Thanks." I couldn't help but smile. She was proud of me, and that made my heart soar.

After a beat, I glanced back up at her, the breeze blowing her curls from her face as she stared out to the sea. "What about you?"

She drew in a breath. "Well, I'm also going to travel."

This caught me off guard. "What? I thought you were going to art school?"

She kicked her feet a little, swinging her red converse back and forth as she stared down at them. "Yeah, I was."

"What changed that?" I turned my body towards her, giving her my full attention. "Your dream is to go to art school and become a painter. You're not giving that up, are you?" I saw a faint frown appear on her face, and I paled, worried. What was wrong with her? "Ollie?"

She sighed softly and looked back at me, her expression somber. "Well, I met a guy."

My heart dropped. "You ... met a ... a guy?"

She nodded a little. "I did."

I couldn't believe this was happening. Surely this wasn't true; she had to be playing a joke or something. "Where?"

"Remember when I was gone for a week?"

I remembered her senior trip. "Yes ..."

She looked back at her shoes. "At the art class trip where

we went to visit the Institute of Art." She paused, taking a breath. "I met a guy."

Her words hung in the air, heavy on my heart as I processed everything.

She met a guy. But that doesn't mean they're dating, right?

She just ... she just met someone.

It wasn't anything—just a new friend.

"Oh, okay." I tried to relax, playing it off. "That's cool. That's totally cool." My voice was tight. "So cool. Very, very cool." I laughed a small breath, trying to ease the tension growing in my chest as I wiped my sweaty palms on my shorts.

Her gaze fell on me. "We started dating."

And just like that, those words made me want to toss myself overboard. My heart plummeted from the floor it had landed on and sank deeper and deeper into the ocean's depths. I might as well have been stabbed with a fishing spear. The pain in my chest didn't seem real; I struggled to catch my breath. All I could do was look up to her as my insides shattered.

"We're going on a trip together," she continued, hazel eyes looking down at me, having once sparkled, bringing me joy, but now crushing my soul. "He's taking me to visit his uncle in France. Normandy Beach. His uncle is a tour guide for the World War II historical sites there. And he wanted us to experience it."

"You ..." My voice broke. I tried to meet her eyes as mine misted over. I sucked in a small breath, barely able to keep myself upright as she hopped down from the railing and stepped closer to me. Every step, every inch she got closer seemed to hurt even more—wave upon wave crashing down on me.

"Luke …" She looked up into my face, gently reaching up to touch my cheek, brushing a single tear away that had escaped my eyes. "I waited. I waited so long." Her hand cupped my cheek. "I waited too long. And … I moved on."

A tsunami landed on me. Engulfing me in pain as my breath was taken from me, drowning me.

She had waited.

She had waited for me when I thought I had been waiting for her.

My hands trembled, and I clutched the side railing. This was my fault. I didn't act soon enough. I should've been faster. I should've—

"Luke." Her voice brought me back from the depths of my sorrow, and I looked at her. "I'm sorry," she breathed, her own eyes tearing a little. "I couldn't wait any longer for you. I just …" She drew in a breath. "… He pursued me. He knew what he wanted. And he acted on it."

Her words pushed me back under the waves of my mind. I hadn't acted fast enough. I didn't pursue her like I should've. I was too worried about our friendship to even attempt anything further. I was too scared of losing her. And because of that, I had lost her anyway.

Closing my eyes, I let a few more tears fall down my face and onto the ocean-soaked boards. My head hung as I broke my gaze with her to wipe my cheeks. "You … you deserve …" I drew in a short breath and looked back into her face. "You deserve someone much stronger and courageous than me." She deserved the world. She deserved the world and more than I could ever give her.

She smiled sadly and leaned up on her tiptoes, planting a small delicate kiss on my cheek, pulling away slowly. "I'll always be your best friend, Luke ..." she whispered, her soft breath warming my cheek. "I always will."

Her kiss, that small sign of affection across my cheek seemed to calm the torrential waters within me, partially healing the brokenness of my heart. She would still be my friend. Even if that meant we could never be more.

I grasped her hand lightly, my large, weathered palms holding her small delicate ones. "Always ... and ... and forever." I smiled the best I could for her, even with the tear stains on my cheeks. "You'll always be my friend, and I'll always be yours." It seemed silly, repeating something we once promised to each other when we were children, but now, that promise was the only thing I could say.

I held out my pinky finger to her, a sad smile on my face as she interlocked it with hers. "Forever," she said, smiling up at me with a single tear rolling down her cheek.

We stood there, just standing across from one another and holding each other's pinkies as the sun began to set. Olivia broke her hold and looked out to the fading sunlight. "I have to go. Jayden is taking me up to his place for dinner." She smiled and stepped back, heading towards the ladder up to the dock.

I watched her climb up the old ladder and then the stand on top of the dock, looking back at me. "I'll see you around?"

I nodded. "Yeah. Maybe we'll see each other on the beach in France."

"I'll hold you to that." She smiled and then waved at me. "Good luck on your boat. Safe travels."

"To you as well!"

She gave one final wave and then walked away down the dock till her footsteps were gone, leaving me with my father's boat and a broken heart.

It's better this way, I tried to convince myself as I stepped out to the bow and leaned against its railing, resting my chin across my folded arms. *She'll be fine without me being her boyfriend.*

Did it hurt? Of course it did. That whole interaction tore me apart and then tried to put me back together with boat lines and duct tape. Nothing could fix this hole inside me. The missing piece had been torn away all due to my failure to act. And it hurt. The wound couldn't be fixed with any amount of care.

Not only had I missed my chance to act on my opportunity to ask her to be mine, but I had also lost her. Yes, she would still be my friend, but now, there was a new person in her life—someone I wanted to be but couldn't. My closeness with Olivia would never be the same again.

I threw myself into my work of maintaining my boat and pursued my dream of traveling the oceans. I saw things I had never seen before, experiencing every new discovery aboard my new home, The Oleander, named after Olivia's favorite flower.

But no matter what I did, I couldn't get my mind off of her. I couldn't move on. No matter where I went, where I traveled, I couldn't heal from my heart break.

Forever and always, we had said. I still think my heart holds onto that. Onto her, never letting her go and never letting anyone in. It was safer not to experience that pain again. I couldn't take it. I'd rather be a lonely sailor than a broken one again.

FOLD
Piper l. White

I've pierced my skin
with calligraphy,
the pens you used
to write your poetry.

You shared stories with me once.
I thought they were brilliant.
Your careless canine teeth
begged to differ.

I wore the strings to your guitar
as chokers, and watched
them brand my fragility,
my feet across your lap.

You were quicksand, I struggled.
I scratched my fingers across
your skin and little fires lit
to scorch you.

I never listen to my intelligence
and I thirsted for your negligence
when I submitted under your
dissembling hands.

I ate fools gold like candy.
You were sweet to me,
but my coffee tasted bitter
that last day at the Café.

I left the smell of you
underneath my perfume
to elude the truth,
but I was losing.

You played snake eyes
our last meeting, pleading
weaseling, fingers crossed
behind your back.

I left with a lump in my throat,
hands empty save for scars
from your hair fisted in them,
pine shampoo sickeningly haunting.

I fold.

BUOY
Annie Kay

You are a buoy.
I wish I could say that it's me, not you,
But I can't.
I know that makes you sound incompetent,
And me, arrogant,
But it's the truth.

I wish I could say I didn't see a future with you,
But I did.
I saw the predictability and the gradual stagnancy of a dull
life.
I saw empty fights leading to empty sheets leading to empty
souls.
Yes, I saw a future with you.
I just didn't want it.

You are a buoy.

I am a ship and

You are a buoy that keeps me safely tethered.
Not the wind beneath my sails
That carries me off into the unknown.
Not the waves rocking against my sides,
Giving me a challenge to follow through.

No, you are a buoy.
You are safe, stationary, and constant.
It's not your fault,
But it's not mine either.
Sometimes these things don't work out.
In fact, most of the time they don't.
So, I'm not going to apologize for
Understanding that I'm not your one.

I am not your boat.
You are not my buoy.
I need a wave, a wind, a something …
I haven't found it yet.
You need a bird searching for a place to land,
Or a ship that has lost its way.
But that is not me.

One day, someone will come along,
And you will be the buoy they have been waiting for.
And you will forget about
The little ship that came,
stayed a moment,
and left.

GOLDEN CHILD
Beka Gremikova

Halfway up the drive of his sprawling estate, Master Oros encountered the first silver statues. Sunlight slid over them in a soft yellow hue, matching the shimmering, golden tips of his own fingers.

The front gate guards stood motionless, bent over, hands clasped to their knees, as though gasping for breath. As if they'd been running from someone who had caught up to them. Someone who had merely reached out a finger and left them stone-still.

Someone with a gift similar to Oros's ability to turn things to gold. Things ... and people.

His heart thundered. He started running.

Every time I think I have one up on you, Silvis, you counter. As a youth, Oros had asked the gods to give him the Gold-Touch first, forcing Silvis to settle for silver instead. In turn, Silvis had made friends with the right merchants, and eventually, silver's value soared.

Then Oros discovered his own daughter, his golden child Zlata, had fallen in love with Silvis's son and heir, Vasil. To think of Zlata marrying that *boy-child!* Oros hated to consider it.

So, a few hours ago, Oros had infiltrated the Silvis estate, leaving Vasil and his servants as golden statues in his wake. He couldn't give Zlata up to a Silvis. The Oros family—and Zlata herself—deserved so much better.

But now he faced a line of silver statues, and nothing stirred within his glimmering, golden mansion.

Oros tore through the gardens, past more statues, and burst into the house. Maids gaped at him, now the same sheen as the silverware they once polished. The wallpaper, once bright gold from the brush of his fingers, gleamed silver, mocking him.

"Zlata?"

No answer. He raced to his council chamber, where he'd left his daughter puzzling over what to ask for her generational gods-gift.

You should ask for the Gold-Touch, like I did, he'd said.

She'd shook her head, her soft yellow hair bouncing. *That's your gift, Papa. That's not what I want.*

He'd changed the subject, guessing exactly *who* she *did* want.

Oros slammed open the council chamber door.

His golden child sat motionless, a silver statue, unable to rise from her favorite chair. Behind her, glinting on the mantel, sat the Oros coat of arms—a golden dragon setting fire to a hoard of silver coins.

Silvis stood before her, his chin set, his fingertips glazed with silver.

An agonized screech ripped from Oros's lips. Silvis stiffened, whirled, and crouched, gripping the hilt of the dagger at his waist.

Oros wished they could use their abilities on each other—how he'd love the satisfaction of watching gold creep across Silvis's limbs. His fingers slid to his own sword, grasping the pommel. But, as he stared at his gleaming child, strength seeped out of him. He braced himself against the doorframe, unable to move.

Suddenly, he understood why Vasil hadn't fought him earlier that day—why he'd faced his Gold-Death with such conviction ...

Oros's attempt to *ambush Vasil hadn't gone as planned. Now the tall, handsome youth crouched in a defensive stance, making no move to draw the sword at his waist. A tunic of the Oros family's sacred yellow—Zlata's color—hung from his shoulders, and Oros's stomach turned.*

Vasil dashed for the door. Oros lunged, his fingers snagging Vasil's tunic. He yanked the boy toward him, but Vasil threw the weight of his golden clothes sideways, toppling to the floor.

"Why don't you fight me, boy?" Oros demanded.

Vasil gasped, "You're her father! I won't harm someone she loves." He looked Oros in the eye. "Would you?"

Oros's hackles rose. "How dare you." He knelt, grasping Vasil's pant leg as the boy tried to crawl away. Oros reached toward Vasil's face.

"Will you mar the Oros family color?" Vasil shouted.

Oros's finger stopped a breath from Vasil's forehead.

Vasil continued, his eyes wide, "If you kill me, Zlata will never associate with you again. She'll never even want to look at gold."

He panted. "This color should be something she can wear proudly."

"Our family's honor isn't something a Silvis could ever understand," Oros snapped. He jabbed his golden fingertip into Vasil's forehead.

Vasil sighed deeply, his lips trembling as his limbs slowly stiffened. "Zlata," he breathed, and then went still—a gleaming, golden statue.

Oros covered his mouth with a quivering hand.

"I did it for Vasil!" Silvis croaked. "I couldn't lose him to an *Oros!*" He drew his dagger. "Vasil *will* thank me one day."

Oros bowed his head, his throat closing. So their timing was coincidental; Silvis didn't yet realize ... He sucked in a breath.

Crouching forward, Silvis frowned. "Why don't you fight me?" he snapped.

Oros shook his head. "There's nothing left to fight for," he whispered, holding up his gold-tipped fingers, yet to return to their usual dark brown.

"No." Silvis's face paled. "Vasil is ..."

Oros swallowed. "Gold."

"My son." Silvis clutched his chest, glancing behind him at Zlata's statue. "My son ... and ... your daughter." He slid to the floor, burying his face in his arms, his shoulders shaking.

Oros tilted his head to the ceiling, its golden gleam blinding him. Emptiness felt colder than the press of coins against flesh. "We've destroyed ourselves." He stared toward Zlata with her eyes half-closed, her silver lips parted in a long-suffering sigh. She'd warned him against continuing family grievances, had tried to show him a better path ...

But he hadn't wanted to lose her to a Silvis. He'd wanted control, not sacrifice.

And now he had nothing.

Oros reached out, brushing a finger against his child's cool, unmoving cheek, turning her gold instead of silver.

My golden child. Zlata ... His gaze drifted to Silvis.

Zlata had come to love someone she was told to see as an enemy. Perhaps he could follow her example.

He extended his hand to Silvis. "Let us make peace, Master Silvis. We cannot do this any longer."

Silvis rubbed his eyes, tears trickling down his cheeks. Then he reached out and clasped Oros's gold-tipped fingers.

BROKEN PROMISES
Levi Mitchell

It was an eerie, frozen feeling day. Like watching new paint dry on an old wall, endless longing for something foreseen but inescapable. It was on that bleak day, in the last weeks of February just before spring, when I got my answer—a confirmation that would deter me from trying any further to save what we had.

I had been struggling for a while because your thirst for more seductive fame and knowledge had gotten the best of you before I could understand how to help. It was for that, I felt betrayed, not only in the sense of love but also in all notes and texts, that day you sat there cold and lifeless, stiff and solemn. That day I realized I would never be enough. When you pursued your next desire—a desire that had slowly replaced me.

You cried when I confronted you about your treason against me and my love. But, "Fine," was a lie all those times you said it. "Fine," was a lie when I comforted you, and all the times I drove home in the early hours. It was all lies when I asked if you still loved me.

And then when we decided the past was gone, and it was time to move on, I sat in silence with rage. I wondered why

I let you abuse my love and time for so long. I was silent, and that terrified you, but you said nothing. You knew you had no way back into controlling or needing me. You knew nothing could change my rage and the choice I had made in my heart.

You had said you would never leave or betray me, and you did both. They were promises broken within a matter of seconds, tarnishing memories for the rest of time.

I made my decision and left you in the past where you belong. Your broken promises can never be recovered.

PART THREE
A Crime to Love

CORRUPT FOR YOU
Effie Joe Stock

Doors banged open as a haggard soldier stumbled into the throne hall, clutching his bloody sword in shaking fingers. "She is here, milord."

My eyes snapped open as I leaned forward in my stolen throne. "Finally." Clapping my hands, I called my guards and soldiers to me. They were all faces I recognized, men and women I knew, some who had been with me from the beginning. Each and every one of them held a special place in my heart, but none of them held a candle to the castle I had built for *her* there.

"Rally to me!" My voice, once so small and tender all those years ago, now chilled blood and stirred the hand of death through the mask which it leaks. "She runs in like a fool and will fall today. This is our territory. We will hold it until we die!"

Their battle cries filled the hall, a prelude to their blood that would fill it later.

Doors slammed shut and were barricaded from the inside. One last, final stand before our fall.

They were no match for her.

Nothing was.

I had made sure of it.

The screams and clash of metal on metal bore upon us, closer and closer until the enemy was just outside my once glorious throne room.

Bang. Bang. Bang.

In moments, she had broken through the makeshift barricades. Wood splintered and hinges crumbled as the doors were blasted from their hangings, killing a few soldiers in their wake.

And there she stood.

My heart skipped a few beats. Warm pride filled me as I gazed deeply into her blazing purple eyes.

She was magnificent.

"Welcome, Melian." I reached my hand out to her, my voice so cold and sickly. "I feared you'd never come home."

With a ragged scream, she easily cut down the first row of soldiers as they rushed her. Their blood slickened the floor, but she glided over it with ease, the blood moving from beneath her feet, obeying her very whim.

"Do not speak to me of home, masked devil."

Her voice struck with such passion. Something stirred inside of me. A bit of regret perhaps? It had been cruel, yes, to destroy her family, all those she loved, banish her from her home, and claim it as my own. But by everything holy, look at what it had done to her! And the way the blood obeyed her ... she was so much more powerful than I remembered. She had grown so much.

I could feel the sting of tears in my eyes but had to bite them back. My façade was not over yet. She had to pass this final test.

"I shall speak to you how I wish." My voice was cold, merciless, powerful, as was everything about me. I was unrecognizable to her now. "You are only a subject of my kingdom, a petty pawn I have manipulated for my own gain. You come before my throne, but you are alone, tired, and weak. Do you dare throw yourself against my soldiers?"

Golden hair, speckled with blood, glowed as it cascaded down her shoulders. A hiss escaped her dark lips. "I would throw myself into Hell for the rest of my life if it meant bringing justice to my people."

"Then you won't have a very long life, I fear."

With a passionate battle cry, she threw herself against my soldiers. Masterfully, her skills with her *kyoketsu-shoge*, combined with her breathtaking power, cut down warrior after warrior. The only fatigue that showed was deep in her eyes, the kind of fatigue that settles and never leaves, the kind I saw in my own eyes sometimes.

I sank back into my throne, exuding an air of superiority, as if this were all just a show to me, something to amuse me before my next reign of terror. Something like a smirk and grimace decorated my face beneath the mask. I suppose it was a show, though I didn't have anything planned after this. This was my great finale, the end of all destruction and the birth of a new era. In the fires of my destruction, Melian would rise like a phoenix: brave, bold, beautiful, and burning.

Gods! Look at her! For she *was* on fire, truly; her hair shone with all her magnificent power. Her knives had been lost in the battle, but she needed them not. Her gold and purple magic was enough.

With titillating shock, I watched as she clenched her hand into a fist and the soldier in front of her clutched at his chest; his face turned blue as he staggered before he fell, his body twitching in the throes of death.

I stood again, my mouth hanging open in shock. I was thankful for the mask or else I knew the pride on my expression would be overwhelmingly obvious.

A man's arm twisted and broke on its own accord, and then his leg did the same, leaving him writhing on the ground. Another's neck snapped, another's heart stopped, and even another bled out in a matter of seconds from a small wound on his face.

My throne room was slick with blood. The last few moans of the wounded and dying softened and quieted as she pressed the air from their lungs with her magic.

Now everything was silent.

She was kneeling, the blood spreading away from her, pushed back by her magic. Her face, which only moments before was covered in blood, was now clean.

She was more than a healer. She could manipulate flesh.

My heart raced in my chest. She had caused that too, but not with her magic. No, she had always had control over my heart. It had always been hers. Now more than ever, she held it still, snug in the palm of her hand, hers until the end, even as she stood in the wreckage she had caused of the empire I built, her own army laying ravish to my castle and followers.

"Beautiful." I couldn't stop the word from escaping my lips, and she looked up, her eyes wide with surprise before furrowing into a glare.

"You know nothing of beauty." She took to her feet, her shoulders pushed back and proud, her gold and purple magic swirling around her hands, ready to stop my heart. I wondered why she hesitated. Maybe we all hesitate when faced with our goals and dreams coming true.

"Oh, you are so wrong, though." My voice was tender now. It was not easy keeping up my cold façade. It had been years since I had seen her face to face. The first time, she had come to me, thinking she was strong enough to beat me, I had destroyed her, humiliated her, sent her crawling back to her people with no friends, no family, and only a sliver of hope and burning sense of revenge. Now, as she stood before me, a full-grown woman, shining in the beauty of her power, I was unable to mask my throbbing love and admiration. I didn't know how anyone couldn't. She was mesmerizing ... irresistible.

Step after step I took, closer and closer to her until we were only a few feet away.

Without thinking, I reached my hand to her, pausing just before my fingers met her skin.

She flinched.

My heart lurched, and I lowered my hand. Her skin was not mine to touch. It was too pure, too perfect. It was everything I made, but like a weary artist next to his masterpiece, I was ugly compared to her majesty.

"No, you are so wrong, Melian. Because I know what I see before me is beautiful. It is heaven on earth, an oasis in the desert, stars against the black—" I couldn't stop the words from pouring out of my mouth, but she stopped them for me.

"Shut up, devil." Repulse on her face, she stepped back. "Your words make me ill."

A pang shot through my heart. No, no, no. Couldn't she see that these were the tender words of a lover? Could she not hear in my voice that I loved her more than anyone else would? I scoffed, wishing I could slap myself. Of course she couldn't. That was the sacrifice I had made. Never would she feel my touch as warm, long to hear my voice, or feel comfort in my arms. That was the price I had paid. I needed more self-control.

"I am no match for your magic, dearest. Why have you not killed me yet?" I opened my arms to her. I had no magic; I held no weapon, so I bared myself to her, showing her I was hers and hers alone to do with as she wished.

I hoped she wished me dead.

She raised her hand and held out her palm to me. My heart raced from her magic, and I knew in an instant she could clench her slender, soft fingers and I would feel no more. I closed my eyes, a smile spreading my lips.

This would be the end. The finale to everything I had built. I was her final test, the last stair she needed to ascend to the gods themselves.

The harsh thumping in my chest slowed, and I felt her power recede from me.

"Open your eyes, masked devil."

I obeyed her in an instant. I would do anything she asked. Anything for her.

"Fight me equally. I have already won. My army is annihilating yours, and within the hour, my land will be my own again. This, I do for my revenge."

A twisted laugh escaped my lips. "That's my girl." I chuckled just low enough so she wouldn't hear.

Turning, I pulled two identical swords from the clenched, cold hands of my soldiers, handing one to her. Where our hands met on the hilt, I felt a tremor run through my body, my skin burning as if on fire. I knew, had I not been wearing my mask, the effect her perfect touch had on me would be written all over my face.

I glanced into her eyes to see if she felt the same, but if she did, she had learned to hide it much better than myself.

So be it.

Bowing low, I waited until she did the same. The blood that had covered her blade slid off, and I knew she would have a better grip than I. Sly girl.

"Fair fight, eh?" I nodded to her sword, and she grimaced before the blood on my own slid off, leaving me with a clean sword. "Incredible."

Before I could marvel much more at her power and generosity, her blade was streaking toward me. As our blades met with a resounding clang and a shower of sparks, our deadly dance began.

I held nothing back.

Over and over, I pushed her to the defense, knowing full well she could kill me with the will of her mind, but also knowing that she was fighting for all those she loved, for all those my armies and assassins had slaughtered mercilessly: her mother, her father, her two brothers—the younger and the older—her best friend, and that old man she always loved caring for. Though it drove me mad knowing the pain it would cause her, I sent the orders out nonetheless—the orders to tear her loved ones from her just to see her overcome her grief again and again, becoming stronger for it.

Some said I never remembered the faces and names of those I killed, thinking they were no better than insects. And that was true, except for those she loved. I remembered each and every one of *them*. And every night before I slept, I prayed to them, remembering their faces and names, thanking them for being a step my love could ascend upon to become this goddess that fought me now, and whispering forgiveness that I hadn't the strength to take their lives myself, that their end must come from another beneath me.

But little did she know, she was also fighting for me.

So I couldn't hold back on her, even if she had fought through hundreds of guards to get here. As much as I wanted to make this easy for her, I couldn't deny her this. She was strong enough to beat me now. She wouldn't leave here broken. She would leave with my blood and head, and I would make sure she had earned it.

Now my blade nicked her skin once then twice. I growled in frustration. *Come on, love. You're stronger than this*, I chanted silently to her over and over, wishing she could hear me, wishing she could hear it from my own lips.

A craze had entered her eyes. She knew she was losing. She was failing everyone she loved. She was failing *me*, the one she had first fought for so many, many years ago.

No.

No.

No!

As if she heard me, as if she heard my soul pleading with her to step into her strength, her eyes met mine, burning through the dark holes of my mask, and a determination set in her soul.

Yes.

With a cry like a caged animal, she threw herself on me, unleashing an incredible dance of death. It was masterful, entrancing, beautiful. Where our skin grazed, my soul lit aflame, and when her blade pierced my skin, I shed tears of joy.

Yes. This is you. This is your strength. Yes. Yes. Yes. My love, my everything. Finish the game. Finish your journey. Finish me.

I fell to my knees. My blade had been thrown from me. My hands stretched before me, not asking for mercy, but asking for the end. Quiet tears poured down my cheeks, and I wondered if she could see them drip off my chin.

I waited for the final blow, waiting in perfect peace, knowing I had done everything I could to make her the very best she could be. My time was done and so was my mission.

"Take it off."

My brows dipped. "What?" My voice was tripped over confusion.

"Take it off." The tip of her sword tapped the edge of my mask, and my blood ran cold.

"Please." I tried to shake the tremor from my tone. "Do not gaze upon me, the devil. It is enough that you have beat me. Kill me and let me pass in peace."

"Take. It. Off." She wasn't asking. She was demanding.

For the first time since that day, I died to myself and sold myself to this life of evil all those years ago, I felt fear, true fear. But I knew I couldn't disobey. My goddess asked this of me.

Slowly, I lifted my hands to my mask. I felt as if I couldn't breathe, but it had nothing to do with her power. I locked my eyes on hers, trying to draw strength from her, from the love that rotted in my chest for her.

In one quick stroke, as if I were beheading myself, I slid the mask off, my eyes never leaving hers.

How can I describe or understand what went through her eyes, across her face in that moment? It was everything.

Horror, repulsion, terror, shock, exhilaration, realization.

A strangled croak left her lips as she staggered back, her knees giving out as she fell to the ground, her hand hovering over her mouth. She couldn't tear her eyes away from me, but I knew she wished to unsee everything she saw before her.

My façade was over. The game was over. Everything was real again, and it was as if we were back where we started, or perhaps where we had ended, that day we died to ourselves.

"Melian ..." I didn't know what to say. I stood, my hands extended, offering a place of solace, but how could I comfort her when I was the terror?

She stifled a scream and scrambled away from me, forgetting her power, and slipping in the blood.

"Please, Melian. Finish this. Finish this."

Golden hair swept around her shoulders as she violently shook her head. Something like words came from her mouth, but they turned into another scream as she sobbed, trying to get away but unable to force her body to obey.

I sank to my hands and knees, my shoulders sagging. This wasn't how anything was supposed to end. This was supposed to be triumphant for her. She should be marching from the throne room, my masked face a trophy to those who had finally won peace.

The seconds stretched into minutes, and her hysterical sobs quieted until she simply sat still and numb, rocking back and forth.

Everything in my heart broke. She was sitting so broken in front of me. She was just a girl again. Where had that goddess gone? But she was still mine, all mine, even if she wasn't my masterpiece anymore. And like an artist does with a broken sculpture, I longed to collect her broken pieces and put her back together again. But I couldn't, not now that my secret was revealed. So instead, I crawled toward her carefully, afraid I would startle her away.

She didn't move.

"Melian?" She didn't look at me. "Melian, please look at me. Please."

Slowly, her head rose, and her purple eyes met mine. I knew the expression on my face, and she did too.

With a mix of repulsion and bestial need, she threw herself on me, bloody hands grasping my hair, her hot tears on my neck.

I gasped in surprise, my heart racing against my ribs. Finally, I wrapped my arms around her, unsure of her touch. But once I held her, I didn't want to let her go. As her hands tightened around me and she pressed her body against mine, I realized with disbelief that she didn't want to either.

But her heart quivered in her chest against mine, and her nails dug harshly and sharply into my skin. A growl of hate rumbled against my throat, and I could feel my own heart tighten. She didn't love me. She loathed me. Loathed what I had become.

Desperation filled me.

I had to make her understand.

My game was still in motion, but it must end.

This could not last.

We had only minutes before someone came looking for her, to see if she had won the great fight against the murdering masked devil. If they came in now and saw her in my arms, she would be ruined and everything I had worked for, that we had *both* worked for, would be destroyed. She had to understand, and she had to be strong to do what she must.

"Melian, look at me."

She shook her head. I knew this was devastating to her. It was impossible for her to understand, to wrap her mind and heart around, but she had to.

"Melian, look. At. Me." I used all the strength and power I had gained over the years from leading armies and forced it into my voice.

She obeyed.

Her red, swollen eyes searched my face, her expression going from disbelief to awe to hate within seconds, and I knew she was trying to reconcile in her soul who I was.

The masked devil.

The murderer who cut down everyone she loved.

The destroyer who desolated her kingdom and drove her people out of their homes.

And her beloved.

The boy she had grown up with. The boy who taught her to sing, to ride horses, and who used to stay up all night with her watching the stars and making new constellations. The boy she had ridden to their first battle with. The boy she had watched be captured and tortured. The boy she had believed died. The boy whose death had driven her to revenge and strive to lead her own army so she could bring justice.

The boy who survived.

"They forced you." Her voice was strong, ragged, as if she were making herself believe what she was saying.

"Melian ..."

Crazed eyes met mine as she violently shook her head, spit slick on her lips as she licked them. "They must've tortured you, blackmailed you, threatened you. You would never … not on your own …"

"But I did—"

"No!" She thrashed against me, her nails ripped my skin to red ribbons. "You wouldn't!"

"But I did!" My voice boomed through the room, too loud. I didn't want to yell, never wanted to yell, to hurt her, but how else would I get her attention?

She saw it then, the truth in my eyes, and all hope in her deflated as her shoulders sank. Her mouth hung open as if she were going to vomit on me. I tried not to flinch away. This was my game, what I had made.

"Why?"

I barely heard her when she spoke.

I was the one searching her face now. "Do you remember the last time we saw each other?"

Her eyes teared up, and she opened her mouth before realizing she couldn't find the words; she nodded instead.

I closed my eyes and took a deep breath. She smelled like sunlight and jasmine; it was delightful. "Remember with me."

"I don't want to."

"I didn't ask."

She said nothing more.

"A boy and girl, in love, desperate to be known. The girl was a healer of the rarest kind. She could mend flesh with the wave of her hand. Gold, her magic was, gold and pure. She healed sick animals and wounded animals. She healed the King! He praised her, but soon, she was forgotten. Our kingdom was thriving, we had nothing more to do than sit around and wish we were more than peasants. The boy couldn't offer her anything except for his silly antics and the hollow promise that love provides for all. She wanted to be a well-known healer, but who was there to heal? They became soldiers, just so they could prove something to someone, so they could make a name for themselves. They fought side by side. He maimed and she healed."

"Please stop," she sobbed, but I couldn't. She had to understand.

"They were sent to battle. A little skirmish against some rebels. Their first battle. Their first chance to become *something,* to be *someone.* He was just like every other soldier, fighting, sweating, cursing, and spilling blood, but *her* ... oh gods ..." I cursed as I remembered.

My eyes opened and locked onto hers. Fierce pride exuded from me as I gripped her hands in mine, remembering that day clearly.

"*She* was *magnificent.* No soldier near her would fall. Their wounds stitched themselves together, and it seemed even their lost blood jumped back into their bodies."

I thought my heart would burst thinking of how she had been that day, truly in her element, truly realizing the power she held and what it felt like to wield it.

"You remember," I whispered, and she nodded. The corners of her mouth twitched up even though they were held down by her tears, by what came next.

"The enemy figured it out. They singled out the healer. They came for her." I tucked a lock of her hair behind her ears, ignoring how she flinched from my touch.

"The boy was so brave, so brave. He was cut down, but she healed him, over and over again. He should have died, but she didn't let him. She couldn't let him. Because she loved him."

Skin so soft, I cupped my hand on her cheek and brushed her tears away with my thumb. Sighing heavily as if against her better judgement, she sagged into my touch, her eyes blinking slowly as if she were going to sleep.

"But she couldn't last forever. Just before the reinforcements came, they took the boy, dragging him away, torn and broken, almost shredded to bits. But just before he was consumed by the darkness, he saw *her*.

"Like a goddess, she had become. Her magic twisted with purple, and two men fell just by her touch. She wielded such power! Such control! In that moment, when everything she loved was dying, was being snuffed out, she became the best she could be. But she wasn't strong enough. She wasn't ready. She collapsed, and the rebels took the boy away. She never saw him again, thought he was dead, swore she would avenge him, and so began her journey."

Silence encompassed us.

"Do you understand now?"

She was staring at her clenched hands, her teeth urging blood from her lips as she chewed them.

Please understand. I don't have much time. We don't have much time. We never had any time.

"No. Why did you kill—" A strangled sob left her lips as she turned away, unable to face me, unable to believe it really was me.

"Because I had to see you succeed. You wanted to *be* someone, Melian. So did I. We both did. We wanted to do something great. But we couldn't. Not in a world of peace. What good can a healer do when everything is whole?

"When I saw who you became on that battlefield, I knew what I had to do, *who* I had to become so you could be who you wanted to be." I took a deep breath. "I had to be the *villain*. I became corrupt for *you*. For love."

Realization dawned on her face, but not acceptance. She couldn't understand that I was alive, that boy she loved. She couldn't understand that he had started a plague for her, killed the king and queen for her, ordered the death of her family and friends for her, burned her city for her. For love. It didn't make sense.

"I don't understand. I don't understand." She tried to say something more, but she couldn't find the words. "No, no, no. This is all so wrong, so wrong! This isn't love. I don't understand." Hysteria crept into her voice, along with the horror that had been there previously.

"But it is, love. Because I loved you more than anything else. I burned everything else for you, Melian. I destroyed everything for you, sacrificed everything for you. Nothing matters but *you*."

My hands were gripping her shoulders, shaking her gently, trying to make her understand, but she didn't stop shaking her head.

"No! Why would you do that?" Her voice rose to a frenzied pitch, and I could see that hate in her eyes again. She couldn't understand this was love.

She would never understand. I loved her far too deeply, so deeply only I could understand it. Our time was up. Acceptance flooded through me. It was time for me to be strong, to sacrifice one last time for her, for love.

I could hear the army cheering outside the throne room. I could hear the thundering feet up the stairs. The finale had come.

Reaching towards the nearest body, I pulled one of her knives from his chest, the coagulated blood sliding off it onto my thigh. Taking her hand in mine, I placed the hilt in her palm and wrapped her soft fingers around it, placing the tip at my heart.

Her eyes widened in horror, moving from the tip of the knife to my face, back to the knife.

"Be the hero. Be who you wanted to be."

"No." She pulled the knife away, but I snatched her hand in my iron grip.

"You have to, Melian. This is what I've done for you, this is who I have helped you to be, this is who you must be. This is what must happen."

"I can't!" She was screaming again, but even her screams couldn't drown the sounds of the nearing soldiers.

I had to save her before they saw her. I had to be the hero before she became the villain.

"Here they come! They have come for you, Melian!" I grabbed the mask and shoved it back down onto my face. "Look at my mask, this is me! Think of how much you hate this creature, this masked devil."

She threw herself onto me, sobbing, shaking her head. "No, no, no! This is all wrong. This is all wrong!" Hungry, shaking fingers clawed at the mask, trying to rip it from my face, but I wouldn't let her.

Maybe it was, but this was the game I had made and played, and now it was time to wake up again.

"Stop! It will make it all easier."

Her hands fell limp to her sides, and her shoulders sagged.

"Darling," I hushed softly, suddenly tender. I brushed a lock of her silky hair from her face, a smile shining through my tears. "It's okay. It's okay."

I took her hand in mine and raised the knife between her fingers to my chest.

She screamed and shoved against me, but I held her fast. She had to succeed. She had to win. She had to make this one, last step. I looked over her face, memorizing every little spot, every golden hair of her lashes, the flecks of gold in her purple eyes, the rose in her cheeks.

"Darling, Melian, they come for their hero. Be the one I made you to be. And remember, my love, I was only corrupt for you."

"No ..." she groaned. Her eyes clung to the knife as if she wanted to rip it away, to free me from this looming death, but her hand didn't move against mine, because as her eyes roved over my mask, she remembered her hate for me. This was still what she wanted—revenge.

"Think of all those I killed. Think of what your father said to you before my assassin tore his throat from him. Think of what your mother whispered as she choked on her blood when I left her to die in your hands ..."

Her gripped tightened on the handle. A snarl formed on her lips.

"But I don't want you to die too," she hissed softly, her whole body shaking. "Not again." Tears dripped to my face, but I knew she was lying as the blade slid forward.

A rough gasp parted my lips as my hand fell from the handle. The rest of the knife buried into my chest. By her hand. And hers alone.

A ravishing craze hung in her eyes, a thirst for blood, a

hate so strong, I thought it was love.

My heart ached to see that hate, or maybe it ached because it quivered around cold steel.

I couldn't move to hold her, to wrap my arms around her as my body failed to obey me, failed to strive for one more breath.

But, oh, were those tears in her eyes? Her mouth parted in horror as she gazed down to her hand wrapped around the blade. The tears escaped her eyes and raced down her cheeks. The hate faded, and I saw clearly what the hate had covered—love.

She screamed. A horrible, gut-wrenching cry as if she had been the one stabbed and not me.

A smile spread my lips as I sagged to the floor. My vision darkened, and warm liquid filled my lungs. Wretched anguish spilled from her as she cradled my dying body to her chest. Oh, the pain she felt for me. How magnificent ... how inspiring ...

I only hoped she felt the same from me.

I only hoped she felt my love. Even if it was corrupt and twisted.

I heard the doors open.

I heard the people cheer.

And I knew my game was over.

I had won.

And, even if she didn't know it now, even if she couldn't see it through all the loss I had given her, she had won too.

CHAOTIC LOVE
Anna Augustine

I stare into my crystal ball, steepled fingers tapping a steady beat as I watch her. She's sleeping with her brown hair cascading across the pillow like a chocolate river.

Running my hands through my jet-black hair, I sigh. Deep, dark regret spears me as a couple enters the edge of the picture. Golden clothes glitter in the light of the candle as they bend over the young woman, pressing kisses to her temple. Jealousy churns in me, and I look away.

The coldness of my tower presses down on me, stifling any hope that has dared to bloom within its dark depths. Water drips from the ceiling and it pools across the stone floor. I tug my cloak closer. What woman would want this?

Yet I turn back to the ball once more. To the vision sleeping among velvet pillows and warm blankets. That all too familiar pinch stings in my chest and I swear.

"Why do I torture myself?" I say aloud to my empty chambers. "Why are you all I dare to think of?"

She stirs as if hearing me, her deep brown eyes fluttering open. I swallow, stepping back until I bump into one of the many pillars that support the roof.

The young woman sits up, her eyes darting around. "Is

someone there?"

This should not be possible. She should not be able to hear me.

I step back to my crystal ball, an invisible string pulling me forward. My hand caresses it. My muse leans her head to the side, and I feel her soft skin beneath my fingers. A strand of silky hair brushes the back of my hand.

"What is this?" Her voice is breathless. Her eyes gleam in the faint light of the moon, and I am at a complete loss for words.

She reaches up, her small, tapered fingers sliding against my cold hand.

I clear my throat. "I don't know how this is possible."

"Who are you?"

I wince. This is the thing I've been dreading, the moment she learns of my true nature, my true self. I open my mouth to tell her the truth but what slips out is far from honest.

"I am your one true love."

She cocks her head to the side, her brows narrowing. "You do not sound like Rafe."

Grinding my teeth, I manage to say, "Rafe is not your love."

"We are engaged. I love him." Her brows lower and she pulls away from me. I fist my hand lightly against the ball, a million words of destruction on the tip of my tongue. But if she truly loves Rafe, I cannot kill him. That would simply hurt her. But an accident could be arranged if it came to that.

"I am Eira, first princess of Onan." She draws her legs up to her chest, resting her chin on her knees. She looks so innocent, so kind. So different from myself. "What is your name?"

"You do not wish to know me. I am not a thing to toy with, Eira." Her name sends warmth to my core.

"Yet you toy with me."

"You're my muse, my inspiration, my reason for living."

Why on earth had I said *that*?

"Then the least I deserve is your name."

"What do I get in return?" I cradle my chin in my palm, the other hand tapping against the smooth surface of the ball.

"You may ask me anything and I shall answer honestly."

My interest is piqued. "You swear it?"

"I vow on my family name, I will answer."

Her family name. Ditechra, the high ruling family of Onan. They reign over all the land that stretches from the Flectic sea in the north to the sparkling sands of the desert of Tikra in the south. They are sickeningly good and just. A vow on their name will hold true.

I hesitate for a long moment, my heart beating hard enough to ache. Then, with a painful swallow, I whisper, "My name is Ophir of the North Isle."

She starts, her brown eyes growing wide. Her gaze sweeps around the room before her shoulders relax, and she nods once. "Very good."

"That's all you have to say? 'Very good'?"

"Is there something else I should say?"

"I—Do you not know who I am?"

"I do, but I also know that rumors may only hold a shard of truth. You are not only what rumors say. You are who you choose to be."

"And what if I am what the rumors say? What if I am

evil, cruel, and vengeful?"

I do not know why this answer means so much to me, but it does. One word from her, and I will be reduced to ash, just as my name implies.

"Then I find you intriguing."

"Truly?"

"I do not lie." She smiles, soft and sweet, and the ice that has encased my heart for ages upon ages begins to slowly thaw.

We spend many evenings together. Though she cannot see me as we always meet through the crystal ball, Eira asks questions about the North Isle, about me, about what living as an exile is like. With each meeting, our knowledge of each other grows as does our bond. We connect as I have never connected to another in all my years. I am blissfully happy, though a small part of me fears that it is all too beautiful to remain intact. Like a thin piece of colored glass, the slightest pressure will have us cracking, breaking, shattering into pieces.

Tonight, I stare into the ball as Eira tells me about her childhood.

"I was orphaned when I was a babe. King Robert adopted me, and I became princess of Onan."

"What was it like growing up in the palace?" I ask.

"The Ditechra monarchy could not have children. I was always told I was a blessing. Living here is the only memory I have, honestly." She reclines on the bed. I trail my fingers over the ball, making her shiver as they move across her cheek in a wake of cold. "I remember Mama reading to me, Father teaching me to ride, baking cookies with the cook in the kitchen, and picking flowers in the garden. It was a good childhood. Happy. And yet,"—she rubs her hands together, a distant look in her eyes—"I have always felt as if something is missing."

I blink, rub my eyes, and blink again. A hazy glow dances around her fingers. A thrill shoots through me. It's not possible. Yet my eyes have never lied to me before.

"You know nothing of your past? Of your village?" I ask.

"Do you not believe me?" she snaps, and my mouth falls open. She's never been cross with me, never raised her voice. Something here is very wrong.

"I believe you, my dear." I caress the ball again. "I would never doubt a word you speak. I simply want to know everything about you."

Eira relaxes again. "Of course, I'm sorry for my reaction. Our connection is such a strange one, and I am learning more about myself through it."

"Are you?"

"Yes. It's ... magical." She smiles, wagging her brows as she giggles.

I smile back, the motion making my cheeks ache. It's been a very long time since I've smiled. And with that smile, something stirs within me. Something akin to hope.

A few months later, I trail my fingers along the crystal ball. Eira is lying on her bed, listening as I tell her the story of my banishment again.

Abruptly, she asks, "What is it like being a sorcerer?"

I stiffen. "You should not ask such things, my dear."

"Why not?"

"It is better for both of us if we do not dwell on it."

"Why?"

"Because curiosity can breed dissatisfaction," I growl. She jerks back, and I clear my throat. "Truly, Eira. This has been a marvelous three months. Let's not ruin it with talk of my magic."

At the mention of it, the faint, blue-grey light of my power flares. It dances around my hand as I struggle to pull it back into me. I gasp and Eira's brows lower.

"Your magic is a part of you, Ophir. Hiding it is criminal."

"It is the evil side of me. You don't understand how it begs for release, Eira. But I do want you to understand this: my magic is not good in any way. All it is capable of is destruction. It has burned kingdoms to ashes."

"Some kingdoms deserve such."

I blink at her blunt statement.

At my silence she laughs, and there is a low, menacing quality to it that I have never heard before.

"Eira, no kingdom deserves to be reduced to ash. Even ones committing horrible acts. There are always innocents in those places."

She waves aside my concerns. "I am merely jesting, Ophir. Since when have you been so serious?" She stands, moving to her vanity. "You should come to the wedding next month. Rafe and I would love to have you there."

"I highly doubt that your fiancé would love to have the exiled sorcerer of Onan at his wedding. Especially considering our ... special bond."

She smiles, running her fingers through her luscious hair.

I lay my hand against the ball once more, feeling the smooth skin of her face.

"He may not," she whispers, "but I want you there, Ophir. Please, come?"

Her plea melts more of my ice. The sweetness of her touch and the heat that pulses through my frosty veins at her voice is a heady drug. One of passion and longing that I can never satisfy.

"If I come, I cannot promise the outcome," I say.

"Meaning?"

"I may swoop in and steal Princess Eira Ditechra of Onan and make her my bride instead."

She laughs and something wild and dangerous gleams in her eye. "I would not oppose that. After all, you are my true love. I would do anything to be with you."

The day of the wedding is here. I stir the potion that will transport me beyond the barrier to Onan and the royal palace as dread presses down on me. It has been years since I've touched my pestle and grinding the bat bones makes me gag.

When did I change? Why do I despise the very thing that had given me meaning for years?

When you fell in love with the good girl.

I blanch, closing my eyes. I love her. I love Eira, the daughter of the Onan rulers. Dare I take her with me to my isle? Lock her in a prison and call it love?

I finish crushing the bones and dump them into the cauldron. It hisses, steam rising to the rafters along with the putrid odor of rotten apples and coppery blood. I wave my hand over it, a single droplet of my magic falling into the concoction. As it hits my potion, the door I must step through swirls to life. Blue and grey blend and pulse and I find myself frozen in place, indecision warring in me.

Do it. Go to your love.

But is it love if it's stolen?

You crave it. You need it to survive, so you must take it!

With that thought echoing in my mind, I step into the portal. Cold shards of ice pelt me. They rip at my hair and exposed skin, bringing tears to my eyes. All at once, I'm within the cathedral of Onan. The pop of the magic echoes across the vaulted ceiling as it dissipates and the people that line the pews turn at the sound of my boots against the stone aisle.

"King Robert of Ditechra!" I call out with a sweeping bow of mockery. "I have come to claim what was given to me freely."

The king leaps to his feet. He is a great deal older than I remember, though I have barely aged a day. His grey beard quivers and his dark brown eyes spark with rage. "How dare you show your face here, Ophir! After the catastrophes you brought on Onan, you know what your punishment should be."

"Yes, yes. Death and all that." I smirk, waving a hand to dismiss the king's threats. My stomach clenches when I lay sight on Eira. Her white dress cascades over her skin like a snowy river and her smile is enough to make the strongest man melt into a puddle. I stride over to her, ignoring the tall blond man at her side. "I claim Eira as my bride."

A gasp ripples through the crowd. King Robert shakes harder, his skin molting red as Queen Victoria grabs his hand, her face paling.

"You cannot take her!" Even the king's voice wobbles.

"I can and I will." I wrap my arm around Eira's waist.

"I wish to go with him," Eira states, leaning closer as a sly smile curves her lips. "He is my true love, Father."

"What utter nonsense!" The blond man grabs for Eira, but she pulls us both back from his grasp. "He's bewitched you, my dear."

I shake my head. "I swear I did not! What love is there in magic and spells? No, Rafe. Until today, I have not touched magic in years."

"Then how does she know you? And you her?" Rafe points between us, murder in the set of his shoulders and jaw.

"Magical devices are not the same as magic itself." I glance over my shoulder to the king and roll my eyes. "Even some of your own people use magic. In fact, Eira here has some magic of her own, I do believe."

"What?" Eira leans back, but only enough to look at me.

"That is the only way you could have sensed and heard me through the crystal ball."

She looks at her hand, but Rafe decides to step forward at that moment, clasping Eira's outstretched palm. "You're coming with me. You are marrying me!"

Eira's lips curl, a flare of purple growing at her fingertips. "I will not. Unhand me, Rafe."

"You are engaged to me."

King Robert wrenches my arm off of Eira's waist. Leaning in close, he threatens, "You will never have my daughter, Ophir. You are the reason we adopted her. You destroyed her life once; you won't do it again."

His voice is loud enough, however, for Eira turns to me. Stepping back and toward Rafe. Betrayal makes her shoulders hunch. "You destroyed my village all those years ago?"

My rage ignites and I turn on the king. "You know full well it was an accident. I was only coming into my magic; I was learning its strength and limitations. But I still don't know the full extent of it, since that day was when I learned I had to hide it."

"You turned them all to ash!" Spittle flies off Robert's lips. "You deserve worse than banishment. I should have killed you that day!"

"No!" Eira reacts before any of us can blink. Purple magic flares, wrapping around Rafe's throat. His eyes widen, rolling back into his head. He exhales, purple tinting the air as he turns a disturbing shade of gray.

Eria turns, wrapping her arms around my neck. With a smile, she whispers, "Take us away."

No one moves as I snap, the magic of my spell engulfing us. We are whisked away to my tower. My brain catches up to my actions as we stumble into the tower's great room.

I shake my head as Eira stumbles, her hands sliding across the rough stones. Her shoulders shake as she cradles them under her chin.

"You killed him," I say. "You killed Rafe with your magic."

I kneel beside her but am shocked to hear laughter slipping off her lips rather than tears. I step away, my eyes widening as she tips her head back. Blood from her scrapped hands streaks across her face. Sheer madness gleams in her eyes.

"That was fun, my love. Let's do it again."

My hands trembling as I stare at her. "What are you talking about?"

"Killing Rafe. Let's do it again."

"He's already dead."

"Then let's kill someone else."

Purple magic swirls around her and I curse my own stupidity. Purple magic. The strongest, most unstable magic there is. My grandmother had that magic. For years she refused to use it, but one day, it was unleashed and the only way to stop her was to slay her.

"Eira, you must fight this," I plead.

"Why?" She sashays forward, a small smile on her lips. "Think about it. We could rule Onan. We could rise up and take it from the Ditechra line. Isn't that what you always wanted, Ophir? Power?"

I ignore the question. "You are part of that royal line already."

"You heard my *father*." She spits the word as though it is bitter on her tongue. "I am no daughter of his. I was saved as a child merely because you failed to kill me."

"I didn't want to raze villages. That was an accident."

"The first one was. But what about the second, the fifteenth, the twentieth?" She shakes her head. "You slaughtered millions, Ophir. Why?"

"Anger." I swallow, looking away from her. "Bitterness, guilt. I was already labeled the villain of the Ditechras and Onan as a whole, so that's what I became. But you changed that. You made me want to be good."

"And you showed me how very good it can be to be bad." She smiles, the blood twisting the beauty of her face. "Let's be wicked together, hm?"

Before I can think, she grabs my shirt and pulls me close. Her lips close over mine. She kisses me with reckless abandon, and for one fleeting moment, I wonder what it would be like to let go, to be what she's asking me to be.

Wild, wicked, free.

But I wouldn't have the Eira I fell for. The good girl with the golden heart is gone.

Did I destroy her too?

Yet in my heart there is something new, a seed of hope that I can redeem the wrong I've done. I may have destroyed the woman before me, but she has been my saving grace.

I push her away, my lips tingling and heart thundering. With a shake of my head, I say, "Eira, this is wrong."

"How can you say that? You took me from my wedding. You claimed me as yours. I killed a man to be with you, and now you want to walk away from me?"

"No, not walking away." I step back, my fingers snapping as the little magic left from the spell creates a portal. "I'm preparing to fight you."

She lunges, but I am already through the portal, the magic closing around me like a suffocating cloak of failure.

The cathedral is in upheaval. Guards run back and forth, three stationed by the still body of Rafe. His eyes stare up unseeingly at the roof, horror on his face. Guilt stabs at me. My magic swirls once again and I hide my hands in my cloak. Catching sight of the king, who sits with his elbows on his knees, I step up to him.

"If you say a word to your guards, I will kill you," I whisper.

He stiffens. "Come to gloat?"

"Quite the opposite, actually. I want to help you stop her, Robert."

"Why should I trust a word you say? You created that monster."

I squeeze my hands into fists. "She changed me as much as I changed her. She taught me to hope again. I know I have made mistakes, horrible ones I'll never be able to atone for. But if I can stop Eira, maybe I'll be a little closer."

"What is wrong with my daughter? How could she kill her childhood friend so carelessly?"

"She's a death mage." I shudder. "My grandmother was one. The only way to stop them is by killing them."

"Kill?" He leaps to his feet, the eyes of his guards following him as he slams me up against a wall. I feel the cold steel of a dagger beneath my ribs. His brown eyes meet mine, and I don't look away. "You want to kill my only daughter? My heir?"

"She will kill you, Victoria, Onan as a whole. Trust me, Robert. Just this once let me help you."

His eyes flick between mine. "You were once my closest friend."

"I know. I'm sorry for the pain I have caused all these years."

"Can I trust you, Ophir?"

"Can you afford not to?"

He steps back, waving the dagger in my face. "When this

is over, you're back to your isle."

"Of course." I smooth my hands over my vest. "It's best for me to be alone."

Forever alone.

I steeple my fingers, resting them on my knees as I stare into the fireplace. Dying embers glow back at me, ripples of heat dancing across the ash.

I hear her. Ever closer the heels of her boots tap. Eira, coming for her father and mother. She's enjoying the hunt.

I have turned the golden into decay. The city to rubble. The trees to ash.

I stand, turning silently as the door ghosts open and the small form steps through. Purple gleams about her hands, illuminating her face. My throat pinches. I freeze as she steps to the bed, sick pleasure in her gaze as purple magic wraps around the slumbering forms there.

"Eira. Let them be."

The magic—the death—vanishes and she turns her cold gaze on me.

"You left me."

"Yes. But I am here now."

She juts out her chin. "Why should that matter?"

"Because my dear. You still love me." I step forward, weaving my fingers with hers and leaning closer. She smells like my tower, musty with damp and decay.

The light in Eira's eyes is cold. She turns her face up to me, her lips stained redder than normal. "I do. But not as much as I did."

Her hands land on my chest and I feel her magic tightening around it. My magic flares protectively from within, blocking her magic from touching me. The more we war, the wilder Eira becomes. I clamp my hand around her neck, and she stiffens. Her back arches, pressing her into me as my burning magic shreds her skin.

"Ophir. Please?"

A tear drips down my cheek. I want to stop. I want to save her. If there were any other way to protect Onan—to stop her—I would go to the ends of the earth to do it. But there isn't. My veins warm, my chest aching more from loss than from her magic tightening around it. "This is your mercy."

"My ... mercy?"

"Yes, my dear. The only way to stop you." I lean my forehead against hers. "I'm so sorry for what you've become. It's all my fault."

Eira tries to pull away, but when my grip holds fast, she presses her lips against mine. I don't relent, even as she deepens her kiss, her arms pulling me closer. I hate that I enjoy it, savor it though it is a desperate attempt to escape her fate.

Eira pulls away, gasping in pain. Her eyes clear as the blue and grey of my magic reaches her face. "You never loved me, Ophir."

I step back as she crumbles, vanishing into a pile of ash.

"You're wrong," I whisper. "I loved you far too much."

The decoy king and queen quickly leave and report to the king what had happened. I scrape the dust into a pouch, pocketing it as King Robert strides into the room. He nods once at me, not even a thank you on his lips before he turns and walks away. I swirl the portal to life and step through.

My tower is far lonelier than it was a mere three months before. Guilt gnaws at me, flaring my magic ever brighter.

"Hold it together."

I hurry to my table and grab up my book of spells. Flipping through it wildly, I find the incantation I need:

Recite to bring the dead to life.

WARNING: a mage may only use this spell once in his life. Choose wisely.

Opening the pouch, I stare at the ash, then the spell, then back at the pouch.

Slowly, I pull the ties closed. I finger the lump of ash beneath the canvas before I pocket it and let the spell book close with a dull thump.

Someday, I think, patting my pocket. *Someday. But not today.*

For now, I shall live with the guilt that my love—my wild, reckless, all-consuming love—reduced Eira to ash.

EXPENSIVE LOVE
Effie Joe Stock

Why is it that love is never enough?
It's not the love we crave,
That feeling of devotion,
Of care,
Of loyalty,
Of adoration.
It's everything that comes with,
Everything that's expected with.

The late nights.
The slow kisses.
The hands—or bodies—entwined.
The fancy dinners,
The nights at home.
The little surprises.
The hours alone.
The matching jewelry and clothes.
The next greatest feeling.
The next burning desire.

Love itself is never enough,
And neither is the way we love.
You want what I can't give.
I want what you can't give.

We love, but we compromise.
Too much, too much!
I compromised my love,
To love,
To love you more.

Love expressed,
Love misunderstood.

I give, and you take.
You take, and you take.
And it's never enough,
Never enough to simply love.

Love is expensive,
And not all of us are rich.

STATUES
Cassandra Hamm

The icy curve of Gwyneth's cheek was as pale as it had been in life.

Eirwen's thumb lingered on her half-sister's face as she gazed into the blank eyes of the ice statue. "Good day, Gwynni," she murmured.

Gwyneth didn't answer, of course. But if Eirwen stared hard enough, she could almost imagine breath on Gwyneth's lips, a breeze stirring her hair, a twitch in her forever-outstretched hand.

Eirwen blinked to ward off the tears that would never come. Turning away from Gwyneth, she fastened a glare on the other two statues at the edge of the snow-white throne room. "Hello, Father, Stepmother."

Father's frozen lips were stretched wide in a never-ending scream. Stepmother's were curled in a sneer, her eyebrows arched with disdain.

"I can touch you now." Eirwen dragged her nails across her stepmother's frigid form. "You cannot stop me, you cold-hearted—"

"Your Majesty."

Eirwen jerked her hands away from the statue. "Idris,

my love!" Her silken dress spun around her as she faced the arched entrance.

Idris' smile warmed her almost to the core. He bowed deeply. "Eirwen, my queen."

She moved toward him, but he matched it with a step backward. Her stomach twisted.

"You seem upset." His red hair was slicked against his head, practically begging her to muss it. "Were you talking to your family again?"

Eirwen forced herself to relax. It was *Idris*. He wouldn't judge her for her private, nonsensical musings to the dead.

"Yes." She lowered herself onto her icy throne, barely noticing the chill that seeped through the fabric of her dress. Low temperatures didn't affect her, not since her heart froze ten years ago. "Do you have any news for me, Idris?"

He moved toward her, leaving a man's-length between them—closer than most, but the distance was still far too much for her thirsty heart. "The people wish you would leave your palace more. They think you are ... unsympathetic to their plight."

Their plight? What of *her* plight? At least they could hold the people they loved.

She could barely remember what it felt like to touch a warm-blooded human. The only brief touches she'd experienced in the past ten years were tainted with intense emotion and grief, skewing her memory.

But she held her tongue, instead letting her eyes trace his angular cheekbones, his almond-shaped eyes, his full lips. Oh, those beautiful lips.

"Please don't look at me like that, Eirwen." His throat bobbed up and down—how she wanted to trace the hollow there. "It makes me want to kiss you."

"Then kiss me."

His eyes darted toward the statues.

A pang shot through her at his continued rejection. If anything could break her curse, it was love. Why couldn't he see that? Why couldn't he trust her?

"You know why I can't," he said.

But she *wouldn't* turn him to ice. The thought had been building in her mind, the surety that Idris was the key to her freedom. That theirs was a love so potent and powerful, nothing could withstand its warmth, not even her frozen heart.

Still, what if she *did?* What if he ended up like Gwynni?

Eirwen couldn't take that chance. She couldn't risk Idris. If it failed, she would truly be alone.

But she wasn't alone, was she? She would always have her family with her, even if they were ice.

"You're not upset with me, are you?" Idris asked.

"Why would I be upset?"

He didn't look convinced. She couldn't blame him, not when she didn't believe it herself.

Idris looked at the ground, then at Eirwen. "Do you miss your sister?"

The change of subject startled her—and it stung, too. Gwynni may have followed Stepmother's edict, but her little kindnesses revealed her love where touch could not. Not even when Stepmother froze and Father turned against his bastard child had Gwyneth treated Eirwen like a monster. She'd even released Eirwen from prison, her first act as queen after Father died.

She'd believed in Eirwen when no one else had. She'd sought to break the curse when everyone else had given up. *And then the curse claimed her too.*

"How can you ask me that?" Eirwen's voice was barely a whisper.

Instead of apologizing, Idris said, "Some say you murdered Gwyneth to get the throne." His face seemed paler than normal, accentuating his freckles.

"But you don't believe that."

He didn't answer.

Her chest constricted. "Of course I didn't murder Gwynni! I never wanted this throne!"

Gwyneth had touched *her*, not the other way around. Even the statue showed that—Gwynni forever reaching out. Still, a thought pushed into Eirwen's mind—*did I touch her first?* The details blurred in her mind, just like the memories of her family's faces. Ice could only capture so much.

"Don't you?" Idris said.

"Why would you ask such a thing?" She fought to keep the hurt from her voice. Did he really think she enjoyed being hated by her people, judged for a curse her stepmother brought upon her? Did he know her so little?

"Then why do you still sit upon it?"

"Because I must! I have a duty to my people, to my family!" She stood, fists clenched. "Is it because of my heart?"

"Eirwen ..."

"Stepmother made me what I am." Eirwen's voice rose. "She kept me from being touched, from being loved. She is the reason my heart froze. She deserved the fate that befell her." Father had, too, once he had started hating her for her newfound powers. But Gwyneth ...

If only Gwyneth's husband and newborn baby had lived. Then perhaps she wouldn't have reached toward Eirwen in her darkest moment. She would still be queen.

Or ... was I the one who touched her, who gave her relief from the pain of losing her husband and child? Did she leave me, or did I send her away?

"I'm sorry, Eirwen. I didn't mean ... I know you loved Gwyneth."

Her eyes found her half-sister's dead, cold ones across the room. Her throat tightened.

"I will be the last of my line, you know," Eirwen said softly. "My family is dead, and Gwyneth's child did not survive. I cannot bear any children. There is no one for me to pass the throne to. But ... perhaps that can change."

Idris waited.

"I love you," she said. "Surely that counts for something. It could break my curse." When she took a step toward him, he stumbled backward, boots skidding on the ice. She flinched. "Or am I really so repulsive to you?"

"Of course not!"

His hesitation was any icy dagger to her fragile soul. Could it be that he did not find her beautiful? Perhaps he stayed with her out of obligation—because she was a powerful woman whom he could not refuse. "How can I truly know you love me if you cannot bear to touch me?"

"My love, you know why I don't—"

"I *need* you, Idris!"

"Don't ask me to do this." His voice broke. "I want to, Eirwen. You must understand that. But I can't."

"Please, Idris. I'm so ..." Her chest felt hollow, though she knew her heart still resided inside. It simply could not function the way it needed to. Each breath felt wrong, as though she were missing something, grasping at air. Sometimes when she stared at Gwyneth's statue, her heart seemed to flicker—to awaken—just for a moment, but it never lasted. "So ... lonely."

His hand stretched toward her. Her breath caught. Then, he jerked back as though he'd been about to touch a flame. "But you have me, my queen."

"It isn't enough." The words burst from her lips, drawn from a place deep within her soul, a desperation that grew with every passing year of watching and wanting and being rejected. *No one cares about me, not truly. Only Gwyneth did, and now she's gone.*

Pain flashed across his face. "Then I am not enough."

He turned to exit the throne room. Eirwen's pulse thumped against her throat. "Idris, wait! Don't leave."

Idris paused, facing her once more. Shadows darkened the skin underneath his eyes. He would leave her, despite everything they had endured together, despite her devotion to him.

Does he really care about me? Has he ever cared?

"I'm sorry." Eirwen forced a light tone. "I know the limitations of my ... condition. They simply frustrate me at times."

His shoulders relaxed. "They frustrate me too," he said with an awkward laugh.

"I know that we cannot be together—not the way I want us to."

"I want it," he said quickly. "Please don't misunderstand

me, Eirwen. But it just can't work."

"I know." She paused. He would stay, at least for now.

How long would that last? Even Gwyneth had tired of a world with Eirwen in it.

"At least be near me, Idris," Eirwen said. "I want to feel you."

Uncertainty played across his face. "You won't ... touch me?"

"No." She let her eyes soften, her shoulders relax. "I just want you to be with me."

"As you wish, my queen." Now he was only a few steps away, closer than anyone had ever voluntarily been since Gwynni's death. Only because she had asked him to. Otherwise, he would've left—just like everyone else did.

The warmth of his breath stirred the air between them. "I'm here, Eirwen."

She memorized the sharpness of his eyes, the vibrancy of his hair, the gentle rise and fall of his strong chest. "Idris," she whispered.

He moved closer, as though spellbound.

She kissed him. His warm, full lips covered hers, sending a shiver down her spine, before hardening. Ice crackled across his body, freezing first his face, then spreading down his spine and through his limbs.

Eirwen pulled back, her lips cold, her body numb. Idris stood before her, his lips forever puckered, his body stiff, never to breathe again.

Icy horror spread through her, from her frozen heart to the tips of her fingers. *What have I done?* She cradled his face in her palm and traced his brittle eyelashes, the curve of his beautiful lips. A whimper escaped her, and she leaned her face against his, tearless sobs shaking her shoulders.

Stepmother she had not meant to freeze. Father had grown violent in his fear. Gwyneth had lost all hope for the world. But Idris had not needed to die. Now her life was empty.

Never again would he call upon her just to see if he could make her laugh. Never again would his smile melt her heart. Now she truly was irreparable. The ice had gone too deep.

He would have tired of me eventually, she reminded herself. *And then I would have been all alone.*

Now he was perfect. The Idris before her would never reject her, never hurt her, never leave her.

Perhaps her life was not so empty. He was still here, after all.

Eirwen slid the statue along the slick floor and let it rest beside her family. "Hello, dear Idris," she murmured, staring into his blank eyes. "Now you will be with me always."

NO REGRETS
Nathaniel Luscombe

I hung from a girder, the straps of the harness digging into my shoulders, and tried not to think too deeply about what I was doing. Who was I kidding? I'd been consumed by the thought of my actions for years, knowing it would eventually come to this.

By now, I was too desperate to consider turning back.

Each time I moved, I felt bruises forming beneath the harness. I was going to be sore tomorrow. I reached to my belt and pulled out the last bomb. I held it carefully between my fingers, marveling at the fact that one of these could do so much damage.

"How's it going?" Alice asked through my earpiece.

"Good. I'm almost done." I glanced at the time. I was running just a few minutes behind schedule. Soon, the shifts would change and people would fill the floor below me. Large machines towered around me. They were loud, drowning out any of the sounds I made. I pressed the bomb to the metal and engaged the magnetics. I carefully moved my hand away, ready to catch it if it fell.

It stayed ... the final piece of our escape plan.

"Be safe." Her voice was tight with nerves. "Don't do

anything to draw attention to yourself."

"I won't," I promised. I felt the tension too. While we'd been planning this for a while, actually carrying it out was hard. We'd gotten the bombs through one of the supply ships. As long as we had money to pay them, they didn't ask questions. It wouldn't take many of these to cripple the station, and by the time it was fixed, we'd be far out of reach.

I grabbed onto the metal and pulled myself up. The straps were too tight, and I winced as they cut off circulation around my legs. I wrapped them around the girder and rolled on top of it, hugging the cold metal as small bells went off.

An alarm rang. The floor filled with people. I watched them from above, careful not to let them see me. Their movements were so calculated. Like insects, they scurried across pre-planned paths, filling their roles perfectly. Just one more night. One more night of tradition and pain before I was finally free of this cage.

The first time I saw the station as a cage was the night my mother took her own life.

She was a good woman, sacrificing herself again and again for the wants of my father. All she wanted in return was love.

So she sang songs when he wasn't around, and spoke of the universe beyond our small station. I couldn't believe that millions of people lived beyond our walls, their ways of life so different from ours. My father was the leader of the station. It was his visions that had brought us out here. He called the people of the universe blight, said they were against us, seeking to destroy everything we'd built.

In reality, most of them didn't even know the station existed.

I always knew that my mother would leave one day. I just didn't know that death would be her way out. She gave herself to the cold hands of space through one of the station's airlocks. I hated to imagine her body floating in space, but it also gave her a sense of freedom. She was out there. That's what she truly wanted.

That night was also the first night I kissed Alice. It was before I heard, of course, but based on the recorded time of my mother's death, I think we were both seeking some form of freedom at the same time. It was then that I knew I had to leave before life on the station brought me or Alice to that same fate.

Alice waited by the door. "Come out," she said, her voice speaking right in my ear.

I opened the door and slipped out. The door closed with a hiss, and a small crowd of people turned the corner. I let out a sigh of relief. Alice leaned against the wall, her back to me.

I took a few steps away from her, choosing to focus on the small pieces of glass that were fitted into the wall. Beyond them, the pinpointed stars glimmered. When the people had walked between us, we turned to look at each other. We didn't have much time alone.

"It's done, then?" Alice asked softly.

I nodded. Her eyes didn't leave mine. I watched as pain flickered through them, followed by a cold, steeled look. She was as conflicted as I was, but at this point, we were too far in to stop.

Right now, I just wanted to hold her in my arms. I never felt more at home than when we were together, working through the issues that made our lives a living hell. I stepped forward, then stepped back.

It was too risky. Anyone could come at any time.

"We should head back up," I said hesitantly.

Her shoulders fell. "We should."

But we didn't. She went back to leaning against the wall, and I turned to the windows. There wasn't much to see through them. Only a few places on the station had a good view of the universe.

"I love you," Alice whispered through the earpiece. I smiled to myself.

"I love you too," I said. There was a long pause before we headed toward the elevator. When we got on, she stood on one side and I stood on the other. To the public, we had to look like nothing more than casual friends. I smiled at her politely, and she blushed and looked at the ground. The doors closed, and we shot up toward the mid-levels where the people lived.

The doors opened and we were thrown into the general hubbub of life. The workday was almost over. There was a ceremony tonight, so people were in a rush to get home. I let Alice walk out of the elevator first. She looked back at me, her red hair perfectly framing her face. I caught a glimpse of the same red hair in the crowd and inwardly groaned.

"Alice!" Her mother's shrill voice cut through the noise. Alice turned away from me. Though a lot of people filed through the hall, her mother always managed to make herself seen and heard. She pushed through the people and brought herself up to Alice's side. She saw me in the elevator and grinned slyly. "I didn't realize you were with Jasper."

I almost snorted. Though it would be frowned upon for Alice and I to be alone together, it was clear that her mother would be overjoyed if we ended up pairing together. I think it had less to do with her liking me and more to do with the fact that I was the station's future leader.

Alice filled her role perfectly, pretending I was nothing more than a coincidence. "I just bumped into him."

Her mother scanned the hallway to make sure people were noticing that her daughter was esteemed enough to be noticed by the son of the leader. I shuddered. Alice's mother was a leech waiting for power to latch onto.

"You shouldn't be running off on your own. You have to tell me when you're heading out. Especially if you're going to be alone with other people." By people, she meant boys Alice's age. She placed a protective hand on Alice's arm. I almost laughed.

"Don't worry. Nothing happened and I'm going to head home with you." Alice cast me a look. I saw the annoyance, anger, and confidence that filled her. Alice was a girl of many hidden emotions.

"We'll see you later." Alice's mother said to me. "Maybe one of these days, your father would like to come to a meal at my house. I'm sure that it has been a while since he's had a nice home cooked meal."

"I'll pass the invitation along."

"Good." She lingered, as if waiting to see if I would say anything more. "Well, there is much to do before the ceremony tonight. I'm sure you have duties yourself."

"I do. I will see you and Alice there." I nodded politely once more before turning and mixing into the crowd. The station held close to two thousand people. It was bigger now than it had been when my mother was around. More people came in, seeking the safety and fulfillment my father promised them. It turned out there were many people who were willing to live under the control of someone else if it meant they could live a simple life.

I didn't go straight home. There was a place I wanted to visit first—a place I considered my haven. It would be the last time I saw it before I left. In a little nook, there was a maintenance tunnel with a secret door along the wall. It opened to a place my mother had called the outer deck. My father had it designed for her when they were still in love, and when he stopped caring for her she made it our space. After she died, I showed it to Alice and made it special again. This space was designed for love. It was the only place on the station my father had stopped caring about.

I stepped into the small space, glass wrapping around the walls and up across the ceiling. The universe greeted me like an old friend. I walked forward and placed my hand against the thick glass. Just inches of it between me and the world that now held my mother.

"You mustn't tell your father I've shown you this," Mother said, holding my hand tightly as we approached the glass. She shook. I thought it was from excitement, but looking back it was probably from nerves. I looked out at the universe and something filled me. It was a longing for more than what the station offered me.

"There are so many stars." I sighed, leaning against the glass. I saw the dim shape of my reflection staring back at me. The eyes held so much wonder.

"These aren't just stars. They're stories. Warnings for the ones that walk through them." She settled on the ground and started pointing them out to me. I leaned against her, her soothing voice pushing me toward sleep. Eventually, her words muddled together and filled my dreams with the majestic creatures she saw among the stars.

They weren't really there, but they were her hope. For if they could live among the stars, so could she.

"Where have you been?" the voice chastised me immediately. I turned from the door, letting it close before answering.

"I was helping on a shift in the control room."

He stood by the far wall, dressed in his ceremonial robe. It was black and draped down his entire body, hanging just above the floor. Two single lines of golden thread adorned the collar. Not too much adornment, but enough to show off his status.

"You don't have to involve yourself in that stuff. You should've already been dressed. The ceremony starts soon." His voice held no patience. It was clipped, the type of voice that expected to be obeyed without question. "Go on."

I walked past him, going further into the house that held the best and worst of my memories. I couldn't stay within these walls anymore. It was like living with a ghost. My emotions never got to rest.

None of my mother's belongings remained within our walls. All the paintings she hung and the shelves she filled were long gone, transported off the station right after her death. Father hadn't been able to control her death, but he could try to control the way I felt a deep, digging sorrow in the absolute absence of her.

I think he enjoyed it for a time, knowing that I missed her more than he did. He just missed having someone to keep the house up to his standards.

I entered my room. It was pretty empty, just a bed on one side and a chest of drawers on the other side. I opened one of the drawers and pulled out the loose black pants and black shirt that went with them. They slid over my skin, whispering memories of all the ceremonies past.

When I'd fastened them, I took a quick look in the mirror. I was still playing the same role I'd always played, the role of a perfect son. I ran fingers through my hair to flatten some of the rougher parts. It was enough for tonight.

He waited silently by the door. I pulled on my shoes, and we set off for the great hall. It sat at the top of the station, the only room with a vaulted ceiling; it took up the space three floors could've filled. The unusual design was supposed to give the mind space to be free.

Almost everyone was inside the hall. They stood in five rows, signifying the five universal currents my father claimed to be in tune with. I joined the middle row, and my father continued to the front of the room on his own.

A palpable excitement clung to the air. This moment only happened twice a year. When planning the time that we wanted to escape, Alice said her last wish was to experience one final ceremony with our people. Though I wasn't as attached to the ceremonies as she was, it was hard not to get swept into the emotions that worked through the crowd. Unified, they moved like the ocean, their voices resonating across the ceiling as my father stood at the front.

It was now that my father would share what he'd heard from the stars lately. He opened his mouth, ready to speak the first proclamation. The people leaned forward. His mouth opened wider, and he let out a scream. It was so full of rage that it jolted through the room, echoing in the wide chamber.

Every part of me froze. He locked eyes with me, and I saw unspeakable rage simmering. It took all my willpower to hold his gaze. When he moved his eyes, I didn't feel any relief.

I knew something was wrong the moment I set eyes on Mother. She leaned against the wall, her head in her hands. I thought she was crying, but she turned to me and I saw the black bruise hiding beneath her fist. She was abused and broken by the man that she'd tried to love. And I, the statement of their love, could do nothing.

When she spoke, I had to concentrate in order to understand what she was saying. The quiet words came between sobs. "Your father is not a good man, Jasper." She closed her mouth as if scared of the words she was saying. I felt the emptiness in the house and knew it was just the two of us here. We were alone, if just for a moment. She came closer, the dark bruise already yellowing around the edges. She brushed the back of her knuckles across my cheek. "He thinks the universe is telling him things. If only it would reveal his own stupidity to him. If he ever hurts you, you will tell me. You understand?"

I nodded. I didn't know what I was supposed to do, too young to understand how my father had manipulated an entire station of people to worship him. I believed him when he said the universe spoke through him. It never crossed my mind that the universe could be as cold to him as it was to everyone else.

We waited in a trembling silence. My father held his hands up, the wide sleeves rolling down his arms, and stared at us. I dared to glance at Alice. She was already looking at me, her face pale.

"The universe has spoken of many things of late," he stated. His words were so sure. "Most importantly, that the blight continues to spread within this station. We are to turn ourselves away from the world outside. It is a sick world, one run by greed and desire. The blight entered my wife, who killed herself because of the guilt she bore. She could not be who she was meant to be. It has carried on in her absence, taking root within all of you who think of a life beyond these walls. It has even carried on through my son, who I foolishly left alone with my wife while she was infected." He locked eyes with me. "The blight is tearing through my crop. Sometimes, the only way to stop blight is fire. Fire can take many forms."

His thread hung heavy in the air. I couldn't breath, completely paralyzed beneath his words. Throughout the room, a unified hum rose. I opened my mouth and joined in the familiar tune. As it grew louder, we started to move with it, the currents dipping in and out of each other. I joined in, all the while aware of my father's hate-filled eyes following my every move.

She had only been dead for a month when my father first confronted me. He pinned me against a wall, sweat dripping down his face, and asked me who I thought I was. I didn't know what answer he wanted. I spoke his name, then Mother's, and said that I was both of them. Their child.

He held my head between his hands and shook it slightly. "You are not part of her. Though she bore you, you will turn out to be like me. She did not deserve a child. She was an infection."

I cried then, not for the first time. He let go of me and retreated deeper into the house. I was scared to move. Scared to remind him that I was still here. When I knew he was distracted, I ran out of the house.

Alice was at our meeting place. We didn't always get to meet, but it was nice to escape here ... even if the other couldn't come. She didn't notice me at first. I stood and watched her, the glass wall of the outer deck shining its stars upon her.

I cleared my throat, and she looked up. She always knew when things were wrong. Her eyes searched my face then looked for any marks on my exposed skin. She stood up and opened her arms. I stepped into them, and the station seemed to correct itself for a second.

"Did he hurt you?" she asked, as she always did.

I nodded.

"Then we will hurt him. Maybe not today. Maybe not for a couple years, but we will hurt him." She leaned back, her promise still on her lips. She reached up to her ear and pulled out one of her earrings. "Come." She led me to the glass wall.

The universe scared me. Somewhere, in the currents that my father so firmly believed in, was the body of the one I had called Mother.

Alice took my hand in hers. She took out her earring and pierced our thumbs, drawing out a single drop of glistening blood. She turned our hands to the glass and smeared the blood on it. It felt like a sacred act.

"This is our promise that we will escape."

This was the moment we were bound in our need to leave the station. I stared at the blood, stared at the stars through its red film, and knew we would escape or die trying.

I knew my father was angry at me, but I hadn't expected him to admit it in front of everyone. At this moment, my body trembling with rage and fear, I knew I was doing the right thing. I dared to glance at him mid-dance. He was no longer focusing on me. I followed his gaze and landed on Alice.

I went against the flow of the current. She noticed me coming and matched her movements to mine, the two of us meeting in the middle of chaos. She'd cut her hair. It barely brushed against her shoulders. When she tilted her head to meet my eyes, her hair framed her face so beautifully.

"Your father is going to notice us," she hissed. Then she smiled. "We'd better make this worth it."

I laughed. "We promised to tear him apart. This is part of the rebellion." I took her hand and started dancing with her. People around us noticed, and the flow of the current was disrupted. I pulled her in and spun her out. A circle opened up around us, the humming slowing as people broke from their trances. The current was not a place to dance. We were supposed to be connecting with the universe, aligning our souls with something greater than ourselves.

Alice was greater than me. I wanted to hold her forever. I spun her again, and our footsteps matched as we danced across the room, leaving shocked faces in our wake. I risked a glance towards my father and knew he would only stand still for so long. His face was white with rage. We'd disrupted the current and broken his moment of control.

I grabbed Alice tighter. I wouldn't let him hurt either of us. I would tear him apart with my hands before letting him touch Alice. We were close to the entrance. I turned and pulled her with me. We spilled out into the hall, tripping and almost falling to the ground. The door thudded closed behind us.

She stared at me, breathless. "What did we just do?"

"What we promised to do." I hadn't realized how hard it would be to catch my breath. I was more afraid than I'd ever been in my life. "We have to go now. If we stay, he's going to do something terrible to us."

There was no one to stop us. Everyone attended the ceremony, leaving the entire station unmanned. The ships were easily accessible because they were all built with a tracker and a command for the station to override the controls and bring the ship back in. Once we destroyed the control center, there'd be no way for them to get our ship back.

We were almost free.

We took off. Who knew how many people my father would send after us? Our quick footsteps echoed in the empty halls. Dim lights led us toward the bay. I looked around for the last time, taking in the small windows, the bits of the universe, the eerie emptiness.

We stepped into the elevator. I pressed the button for the bay, which was on the bottom of the station, and closed the doors. The elevator led us through the entirety of our home. I shivered, thinking of everything these walls held in. The thought of leaving was sickening and exhilarating. It was the scariest thing I'd ever decided to do.

"Do you feel ready?" I asked Alice.

She pulled me closer and kissed me. "I don't, but I know we'll be okay if we can just get out."

We stood close together for the rest of the ride down. If I had the time, I would've gone to the outer deck one last time. I was going to miss that space my mother had given to me.

"We don't have time for regrets," Alice said, her careful eyes picking up on my tension.

"I could never regret doing this with you."

The elevator doors opened. The world snapped back into view. We didn't have much time. We hadn't been able to grab any of our things, but going back now would mean never getting out. We stepped out into the bay, a place we had been just days ago smuggling bombs in through various packages, and ran for the ship we'd chosen.

It was one of the newer models, not as large as a transport but big enough for us to be comfortable during our time in space. I slammed the entry point on the outside, and it opened. Alice clambered in

"We have to open the bay doors before they get here," she said breathlessly. I cursed. If there were people in the bay, the doors wouldn't open. I didn't know if there was anyone chasing us. If they were, the elevator would be opening at any second.

I settled into the front seat and looked at the controls. Alice reached over my shoulder and placed her palm on the screen. The ship lit up and rose into the air.

"Here"—I slid off the seat—"take over."

She did. Her hands moved quickly across the controls. The large bay doors cracked open

That was a comforting thought.

"Are you ready?" Alice looked over at me.

"I couldn't be more ready. Thank you for helping me do all of this." The relief coursing through me was intoxicating.

"Of course, lover boy." She chuckled. She guided the ship forward. The doors were open enough for us to get out, but as we neared, they jerked to a stop.

"What the—"

DOOR LOCK INITIATED, the automated voice of the ship announced.

The radio opened, crackling until my father's bitter voice filled the ship. "Come back and I'll forgive you. The station can cleanse those who try to run."

Neither of us responded. Alice pushed on the accelerator, and the ship shot forward, barely fitting between the closing doors. We were out in space, beyond the reach of my father.

"You can't be stupid enough to think you've won," he

growled. "The ship is going to shut down and return. When it does, you'll both be public examples of what happens to those who reject the currents."

Alice wasn't even paying attention. Her head was bent over a screen as she typed rapidly. The ship was already out of our control, slowing down in anticipation of being brought back in.

"What are you waiting for?" I looked at the screen frantically.

Alice looked out at the station. "I'm just giving your father the satisfaction of thinking he's won."

My father's breathing still filled the ship. He was listening to everything she said.

Alice pushed her finger into the screen. There was a brief moment where I wondered if anything had happened, then parts of the station tore open, gusts of oxygen shooting out. It was thrown to an angle by the force of the explosions.

The controls came back online. Alice turned the ship and sped it up. "We have to get out of range. The pieces of the station could become deadly projectiles."

She steered us away and I kept looking back. The station got smaller and smaller, so insignificant in the grand scope of the universe. When it was nothing more than a speck, I turned and sank into the seat. From here on out, it was just me and Alice against the universe. The pain of loss would come, but we would get through it together.

No regrets.

DELANO
H. A. Pruitt

"**I won't let** them take you."

The memory of his words pummeled his skull as his horse's hooves thundered through the mud. Dark splatters flew across his boots. Twisted branches hidden by night clawed at his arms and cheeks. Cold winter wind lashed his face.

Delano sensed none of it. His hands, eyes, and mind were burning with his last memory of her.

The white skin that his fingers had never touched, dark orange locks that billowed around her face, and that red birthmark swirling over her right cheek and spraying around her amber eye all solidified in Delano's mind just as he had viewed them hours ago in her cottage in the woods.

He burst in the door, and Lucy swirled around, terror gripping her face. When her golden eyes met his, she had gathered her flowing white skirt and ran to him. Lucy halted just inches away as she so often did. Her insistence to draw so close yet never touch drove his desire to a maddening, intoxicating hunger.

"I'm sorry," she breathed and put another inch between them.

Delano forced himself to shake his head. Restraining the urge to slide a curl off her cheek and behind her ear then graze the porcelain skin on her neck, he let his gaze entwine with hers. "Don't ever be sorry. It's important to you."

Lucy's God held her heart. Although she had told Delano that she yearned to give herself to him just as he wanted, she also had voiced her fear that if she gave even just one touch, she would hold back nothing. That uninhibited love of Lucy's stirred his desire for her, and the challenge of making her all his kept him chained to her. He didn't see the importance of her God, who caged her passion for him, but he would say anything to bring her closer.

"Thank you." Lucy clasped her hands over her skirt. Her fingers squeezed.

"I came as swiftly as I could," Delano announced, watching the stress also crease her face. "What is it?"

Her eyes broke from his. "What I fear. What happened in the last village. Why ... why do they think such things? I know I'm—"

His hand had caught her dipping chin.

Her face snapped up, and Lucy's own fingers brushed his before they jerked apart.

"You're not." A shaky breath, swollen with rage from the stories and evidence of her pain, heaved in then out of his nose. "You are not what they say. You're beautiful."

Her fingers floated to the birthmark. "My—"

"Every bit of you."

Her shoulders slumped. "You're almost the only one who believes it."

"Does anyone else matter?"

A sigh escaped her, and she turned to the fireplace. From that angle, with only her right side showing and the shadows from the flames sliding through the creases and contrasts of her birthmark, Delano did see why the people of village after village called her unnatural. But while they saw a repulsive, demonic mark, all he could see was unique, entrancing beauty. They called her devil and witch, but he called her a rose and a phoenix. They had shunned and tried to kill her, but he had sworn to protect her as his own. Lucy had risen from destroyed homes and besmeared reputations so many times, he almost believed her God had created her as some kind of mystical creature meant to uproot the villages' skewed idea of wickedness. He didn't know what she was, but Delano dreamed that when his lips finally touched hers, her full mystery would unfold.

"They just can't see it." Once again, he suppressed his urge to reach out to her. "You are the most beautiful woman I've ever met, and your heart ... it's golden. Like your eyes. So full of love and never giving in to their slurs. Or even me forgetting to keep away."

Her light laugh eased out like a bird's song. Lucy slid him a smile. "I don't know which is harder to forgive."

"I don't want to be forgiven for wanting you as mine." Realizing his words after he voiced them, Delano shoved his focus back to his reason for coming. "And I can't understand how you can forgive them. I wish you'd let me break every jaw that ever cursed you."

She turned back to him. "Thank you for wanting to defend me, but forgiving them is the only way to truly escape. I can't change their hearts—only God can do that—but I can let go and ... and keep ..."

"It's wrong what they do." Anger flooded through his body. This girl who willingly shouldered and tried to shrug off so much undo derision did not deserve to keep running. She deserved a different kind of freedom. He could give it to her—he could cut them all down if she would just let him—but Lucy insisted that her God gave real freedom and killing couldn't.

"I–I don't need everyone to like me. I don't need everyone to understand me."

An urge ran through him to slam a fist on the nearby table, but his outbursts had shaken her too much in the past for him to repeat it. "It's more than that, and you know it. Lucy, they're evil! They're sick and twisted in how they treat you! And running away isn't changing anything. You can't keep running from village to village—you shouldn't have to just to stay alive."

"I–I'm not running away." She backed several steps then floated over to a chair and squeezed its back. Now her left side faced him. The purity of her desire to love every creature, no matter how despicable, glowed from this view. Her frustrating yet stalwart faith in her God of love always remained in this angle of Lucy. Delano ached for that unfailing dedication to be redirected to him—only him.

It enraged and melted him. "Lucy."

She didn't look at him.

"Will you tell me what's going on?"

"Will you hurt them?"

"I won't let them take you."

After that declaration, he had swirled around and stormed out into the long shadows of evening. Delano had set his mind on protecting her better than her God—the God that seemed to do nothing for her and yet get all of her love. Pulling his black stallion to Lucy's garden shed, he resolved that if they came for her, he would not let them live.

He had failed.

In the present, Delano snapped the reins and growled. Despite all his throbbing determination and malice, he had fallen asleep. When he had stirred awake, Lucy's door was swinging on its hinges, her chairs were toppled, and she was gone.

A snarl contorted his face. He would keep his promise. He would give her real freedom.

Only seconds passed before sounds leaked through the trees. Then flashes of fire blinked into sight. His fists tightened. At the right moment, they pulled, and his mount slid to a halt. Delano tied the rope to a branch, flipped up his hood, and gripped his cloak shut so he was nothing but another quivering shadow among the trees.

Noiselessly, he wove his way to a house at the edge of the village. Slinking around to the front, he heard a door, and instinct seized him. In another moment his sword slid out of a man, and the body thudded onto the cold ground.

Delano fled.

Never had he murdered anyone, but fire was boiling in his veins, and red was veiling his vision. He had killed once, and he would do it again and again until he set Lucy free.

His feet snuck, then rushed, then recklessly ran as man after man met his blade. Shouts blurred into a seething fog. More flames ignited. More bodies fell. A crowd drew up before him, and Delano's rage screamed that they held Lucy in their midst.

A yell burst from them. "Monster!"

"*You're* the monsters!" he roared back.

Someone rushed him, and Delano sliced and thrust as he ran for the heart of the mob. This was only another cage, and he would set her free. When he did save her, he would take her as his and shield her from this bloodlust that stained every village. She would finally see that the restraint and forgiveness of her God only kept her bogged down in the danger of hatred. He could see it, and now at last she would too. The horde slunk in and out of focus as he envisioned her face just a breath from his. Her golden eyes mingled with the torches stinging his eyes, but his blade never slowed. Blindly, he cut down one after another.

"Dela—"

The voice froze and shattered the overpowering rage.

His eyes focused. They flicked to his red and brown spotted fist, along his stained blade, and to the white dress it had pierced.

Delano's hand recoiled as if his hilt scalded it. His sword remained in Lucy.

"Delano," she gasped. "I told you ... this wasn't the way."

His mind numbed.

"Love saves," Lucy struggled to say as the men restraining her shifted to support her. "Jealousy of a love ... that can never be yours ... kills."

They let her fall.

"No!" His bellow still echoed in the air as one villager ran Delano's own sword through him.

They burned them.

Right where the two demons had fallen, the villagers turned them to ashes. Some whispered that leaving the remains would lure more. Others asserted that leaving them would serve as a warning and repellant. None noticed the wind scattered one pile but didn't touch the other.

On the first night the snow fell that winter, the forgotten ash pile trembled at the kiss of the icy, pure flakes. Once a thin coating of white ensconced it, a red bird shook its head free. It cocked its amber eyes to the sky, trilled a soft lament, then spread its wings and left the village, free.

NOTHING MORE THAN DEATH

Beka Gremikova

The sickroom is in a state of disarray. Chamber pots line the side of Prince Seth-Jairin's bed for the moments his bowels lose control. Master Oro-kor, the lead physician of the royal family, directs the servants to remove the full chamber pots and bring fresh ones in. Prince Seth-Jairin lies still on the bed, choking on each breath, wheezing like a cat with its ribs kicked in.

One maid stands to the side, her only duty to clutch the traditional death shroud of Bevrin in her arms as they all await the final moments. The soft blue silk is meant to reflect the colorful serenity of the Second World. As soon as the prince breathes his last, she will lay the shroud over his chest, leaving his face bare to respect his rank. It is meant to be an honor, but the maid looks ill.

At the head of the bed, Queen Deme-tra and her husband lean over their son. The queen strokes his forehead while King Thral-kor smooths the wrinkles in his son's blanket and tucks it around his legs. Opposite the royals, Life herself holds the prince's hand, unseen by the humans but for Prince Seth-Jairin and the physician.

"My sister Fate says you're to be mine." She clasps his fingers. Her vibrant golden glow reflects in his skin as his body fights the illness. She wishes the king and queen could see her, could know that their son will make it through. Life settles on the bedsheet, reaching out to caress the prince's cheek.

He does not stir at her touch, does not even blink. Life puffs out her lips, nerves gnawing at her stomach. This cannot mean—

She hears distant, echoing screams and stiffens as a familiar presence approaches behind her. With a half-turn, she faces Death. Death, the youngest of the many Universal Sisters, wears the same soft sky blue as the Bevrin shroud, but there is no peace to be seen in the fabric. Each fold holds a dream broken by her presence, and every decorative silver bead reflects a life cut short by her hand. The awful voices of lost souls scream out from the cloth.

Life presses her hands to her ears, casting her sister a narrowed look. Master Oro-kor flinches, tugging at the collar of his tunic.

Death gives a slight cough, and the wails, though not cut off, lower to a less noticeable pitch. "I do not have the power to silence them. I can only remind them that they cannot be found, so why scream so loudly?"

At Death's words, Seth-Jairin stirs, his eyes creaking open. A sticky-looking glaze crusts the corners of his sockets, while the same substance coats his lips. As he locks eyes with Death, Life feels her sway over him trickle away.

Death feels the moment Seth-Jairin's gaze falls on her. His breath hitches and his dark brown skin breaks out in bumps. As he sinks back into his pillows, his breathing laboured, his mother snatches his hand. Frantic murmurs course through the servants.

"What happens if His Highness dies?" The maid holding the shroud inches closer to Master Oro-Kor, as though his authority can relieve her trepidation. "Will there be civil war if the king and queen can't have another child? It was bad enough when poor Al-yen died—"

"Hush," Master Oro-Kor snaps. "There are steps to take in finding another to inherit the crown," he adds in a more reassuring tone when the maid's eyes fill with tears. But his eyes dart to the king and queen. The queen is looking at him.

"What has happened?" Usually, it would come out as a sharp demand, but grief has pummeled the hardness from her voice. When Queen Deme-tra was yet a princess and just twenty-five, her mother followed Death into the Second World. The queen had lost much of her sharpness then, too, and the only thing that brought any of it back was her marriage and queenship. Death wonders if this loss will break Prince Seth-Jairin's mother entirely.

"Do you need me to tell you?" Master Oro-kor asks. His rigid shoulders tell all—he does not want to have to say it.

"Death is here," the queen murmurs. She has lain herself out beside her son, and her breaths come in deep, choking gulps. "Seth-Jairin," she whispers.

"*Malyin*," he croaks. It is a pet name, the name a child calls his mother. Queen Deme-tra presses her cheek against his skin.

"Oh, my *yin-mal*." She uses the Bevrin term for an unborn child, one still protected by his mother's womb.

"There is nothing more we can do." Master Oro-kor glances at the king, who nods.

"You cannot protect him anymore, Deme-tra." King Thral-kor grips his wife's shoulder. "And you cannot wait any longer. I don't wish you to see—" His voice hitches.

The last breath.

Death averts her gaze, meeting the eyes of her sister across the bed.

Life's golden glow flares in rage. "Why are you here?"

Death inclines her head toward the prince. "Fate has told me I'm to take Seth-Jairin," she murmurs. She wishes she could speak mind to mind with her Sister, but they are not allowed to hide or embellish the truth from those they serve. Fate, as the eldest, rarely speaks to mortals at all.

Despite her attempt to lower her voice, Seth-Jairin hears.

A shudder courses through him, and an agonized cry escapes his lips. His mother throws her arms around him, drawing him close, sobbing into his neck. His father sways.

"Out," Master Oro-kor snaps. "All of us. Say your good-byes. Now." The servants all but dash out the door.

The queen collects herself enough to press a kiss to Seth-Jairin's forehead.

"Though Death approaches, may Life yet prevail," King Thral-kor murmurs to his son, a final blessing and a desperate wish.

Both king and queen drag their steps as Master Oro-Kor ushers them away. Even they cannot disobey an order from the physician, who, in cases of illness and death, has been given ultimate authority in Bevrin.

"How can Fate be so fickle?" Life explodes.

Death shrugs. "Did you have such brilliant plans for his future?" As soon as Death utters the words, she wishes she could bite her tongue. Life does not appreciate sarcasm, and the last thing Death wants is to have Life as an enemy. Though natural rivals, they often must work beside each other on the Bevrin battlefields: Life reviving, Death revolving lives into the Second World. "I apologize," she says as Life's chin quivers.

Life bends over the prince. "Remember your parents. Remember how your aunt and uncle mourned the loss of Al-yen. Remember your kingdom, the wars you must win for them."

At that, Seth-Jairin flinches.

Life lifts his chin and presses her lips to one of his cheeks, then his forehead, and then his other cheek, completing the circle of blessing of Unersa, the far eastern empire she has been trying to reclaim from its death and disease for centuries. "Fate may yet change her mind, oh prince. If she does, I'll be waiting to rescue you." She straightens and hurries to the door, casting Death a withering glance as she passes.

Death replaces Life beside the prince, standing by the bed. She realizes with a slight start that time has flickered past with its usual speed, leaving her impressions twisted. She remembers Seth-Jairin last as a laughing boy of thirteen who fell off his horse and nearly died from his injuries.

Now his skin is hardened with fine lines of both laughter and sorrow. The plump cheeks of the boy have sharpened into the ragged contours of the man. The man who should have become a king.

"Hello," she says softly. She brushes her fingers against

his cheek. He leans into her touch, his eyelashes fluttering.

"This should be a warrior's death," he croaks out, struggling to sit up. "I don't want you to see me wasting away." He leans closer, his lips thinning and drying out as the inches decrease between them. His breath stirs against her eyelashes as he lifts a hand to stroke her face. She flinches at his touch, which, despite his illness, is still so warm, so full of life and vigor.

"This *is* a warrior's death," she says. "To live day after day, suffering ... it is not 'the easy way.' And to watch it unfold takes a warrior's heart." She nods to his mother, who lingers in the doorway, gripping the frame. Queen Demetra's eyes blaze with grief and a fierce, grief-defying love—a love that keeps watching for any signs of life and hopes even when her heart cannot bear to witness that last breath.

The queen's shoulders quiver. Death knows she's thinking of watching her own mother die, wasting away with a quickness that took their family by surprise. Deme-tra had been old enough that people assumed she no longer needed a mother—but Death knew it was just when she'd lost her that the queen needed her mother more than ever.

"Not you too," the queen whispers. "I'm not ready—I need you. My baby. *Malyin!*" She cries out for her own mother, sinking to her knees. "Why did I have to lose you, and now I must lose my son?" She wraps her arms around herself, weeping, just as she did that day twenty-five years ago. Then, she'd been alone in her chambers sobbing into her pillows. Now she weeps openly, unashamed of her grief, challenging the husband and physician trying to coax her out of the room.

As her mourning sinks into the souls of those around her,

nobody can say a word. Her husband kneels beside her, his arms circling her shoulders. He presses his face into her neck. Tears stream down her cheeks. Even as she leans into him, her eyes seem to stare right at Death, glazed and vulnerable.

"Would you have him die a warrior's death?" Death murmurs to Queen Deme-tra, even though the prince's mother cannot hear her. She glances down at Seth-Jairin. He meets her gaze, his own frightened yet assured. "Do you want to be torn to pieces on a battlefield?"

He flinches. "I ... never wanted that," he says, the truth slipping out of him.

"Of course not," Death says. "A man's best shield is his bravado." She perches on the edge of the bed, peering over her shoulder. To her relief, Life stands between the king and queen, exuding comfort. From where she stands, Death can feel it—a sensation like an invisible embrace and soft, murmured words weaving through her hair. She watches as the king and queen waver in Life's presence and allow Master Oro-kor to finally lead them away from the sickroom. *Even when your heart is dying,* Death thinks, *life drags you on whether you want it to or not.*

She is grateful to her Sister. Death hates having an audience for her work. The stress and sorrow of the atmosphere is straining and distracting. It is difficult to woo with so many people watching.

Silence falls but for Seth-Jairin's gasping and the drip of rain through the cracks in the ceiling.

She realizes Seth-Jairin's hand is still on her face, and his eyes, though glazed, are steady on hers. "I was dying," he says. "And you came. You let me go. Twice, when I was younger."

"I cannot take credit for that. My Sister Fate decreed it. I would not have let you go if I could help it."

"And now I must go with you?" he asks.

She nods. "Are you ready?"

He bites out a laugh. "Is anyone ever ready?"

"Some are," she says.

"Like Al-yen," he murmurs. His fingers flicker from her face to her hair, burying themselves amongst the strands. "I found her smiling. You were kind to her."

"Kindness is not a word that applies to death," she says. "It is a mortal construct."

"Dung," he retorts. "Most of us wouldn't know kindness if it hit us in the face."

"Fine. Kindness is a requirement for me."

"Dung again." He juts out his chin. "I've seen criminals suffer horrid deaths. You don't soothe them. But you care for children, for those like Al-yen."

Al-yen. Death tilts her head back, remembering. A child with the brown curls and wide smile of the prince. She had wondered about their relation. Al-yen had been an easy steal; she'd followed Death's whispers with a satisfied sigh. She had not feared the Second World. "You are very much like her."

"Thank you," he wheezes. "It helps." He pauses. "If I must die, may I ask one request?"

"Of course," Death says. Final requests have become quite popular amongst Bevrin nobility in recent years, as though they might prolong the inevitable until Death gives up on them and releases them from her clutches. "A final request is usually given, if I'm able to fulfill it."

"This is mine," he says, and takes her hand to pull her toward him until she rests against his chest. He snakes one arm around her waist while his other hand cups her neck, forcing her head to angle. She realizes what he's about to do and sighs inwardly. He is hardly the first, and he certainly won't be the last man who falls for his own demise. How many young men, though full of life, have still written about the arms of Death encircling them in some poetic romance? How many of them have dreamed darkly of her, using her as an escape from life?

His nose brushes against her cheek, and his eyelashes flutter as he sighs. His mouth is but a breath from hers when his gaze shifts to the door. His eyes glaze and his lips twist. The prince sits back with a huff, a deep frown digging into his brow.

Released, Death steps away as quickly and subtly as she can. "You're confused," she says.

"My parents." His voice falters. "I can't just leave my mother."

Death shakes her head. "You have no choice. Fate has decreed it."

"Do *you* ever get a choice?"

She smiles. "I don't know if you will understand," she says, "but my will is different from that of humans. You think of it as something you alone can own. My will is communal—it must be in harmony with both Life and Fate in order to keep History going and appeased. We do not always agree with or like our decisions, but we all know these decisions must be seen through."

"You aren't human?" He straightens, piercing her with his glance.

"Are you upset?"

He twists his bedsheets in his hands. Then, catching notice of the shroud, he kicks it off the bed. "I suppose you've had your share of princes falling for you."

"Some. Though not as many as you might think," Death says. "Most princes try to run the other way." She chuckles before adding, "You must not love me before the proper time and out of the proper manner. There is a saying like that in the Holy Bevrin Annunciations, is there not?"

He bows his head, abashed. "Indeed," he murmurs.

"I do not say this out of spite. But to love Death more than one ought ... it does not bode well for one's mind. Healthy respect is necessary, but do not feed your yearnings."

He tilts his head. "But what if I love you not because you're Death, but because I want you to stay. To be more. To be—" He breaks off.

"Human?" she says.

"Why can't you? Can't you love?"

About to settle back on the edge of the bed, she thinks better of it and remains standing. She grips the clasps of her cloak in her fingers, the cool metal giving her purpose to fight his wheedling. She has found humans attractive before, and this will not be the last time. "I am part of a cosmological order," she says, "just as you are. It's not so much that I do not have desires to leave my lot—but that I physically cannot. I am *nothing more* than death." She points to her eyes, the bright, marbled yellow-green of the precious gems mined in the Bevrin deserts. "Every part of me that appears human is merely that—*appearance.* I appear human because I am a *reflection* of humanity, which is the pinnacle of the Creator's order. I am kind to children and full of judgement for criminals because those are *reflections*, however imperfect, of the One who rules above all the Universal Sisters. My love is that of the sun withering the grass so new growth can replace it. For me, romantic love can exist only in this realm, for it does not belong in the Second World." She grasps his reaching hand tightly, not sure if she should crush his fingers like a soldier or enfold them like a beloved. She settles for the firmness of a friend. "Now, as Fate has decreed, Seth-Jairin of Bevrin, follow me into ..."

She tenses, realizing that the rain no longer drips from the ceiling.

Sunshine filters through the gauzy curtains of the prince's sick room, even though it is the middle of the night. A glowing presence approaches, vibrant and humming a victory tune. The scuff of skipping steps echoes in the far hallway of the palace.

Death's knees buckle, and she swallows the urge to gag. "It—it appears I have been hasty. Or that I was meant only to visit you briefly. It seems that Life is the one who will win you this time."

"You're leaving?" Seth-Jairin's eyes widen in alarm. He tries to tug her closer, but she resists.

"You should be relieved," she says sharply and leans over to slap his cheek.

His hand rises to his face. "Relieved that I can die a horrid death on a battlefield?" he snaps.

"You have been very blessed by the Creator thus far. Haven't many of your enemies died in the battlefield?" She says this to assure herself as much as him. For all the man's silly notions, he has valor and a deep love for his parents that she cannot help but admire. She does not wish to see him butchered like a pig, surrounded by mud and blood—

Enough. Fate's voice, ringing with the authority given her by the Creator, pushes the images from Death's mind. *Sister, I have called you back. You cannot save him from a gruesome death on the battlefield if it is Decreed.*

I will come, Death says. *Why is it so unfair?*

This entire world is unfair, dear sister. It is not what it once was—but take comfort that we know our purpose and our plan. Not all humans can say so. You are Death, I am Fate, and neither of us can change that. You have purpose, and so does the prince. Now, tell him to be ready for Life. Fate's voice fades from Death's mind.

"Why can't you live, stay—" Seth-Jairin is saying.

"Good-bye, my prince," she says heavily. She bends over to brush her lips against his forehead. His hand splays across her neck, his palm rough with callouses. He murmurs, "I didn't get my final request."

"You're going to live. Men who live don't get final requests. But this isn't good-bye, Seth-Jairin," she says. "This is 'until we meet again.'"

"Then I'd like to say that for myself." His tone is pleading.

She sighs. "You may, then."

His mouth finds hers, and her fingers curl into his tunic. The life throbbing in his veins consumes her with sensations of salt and light, the warmth in his skin battling the coldness of death in her fingers until her limbs begin to weaken.

His hands drop to her wrists, his thumbs pressing against her skin to feel for a pulse. Laughter tickles her stomach at his desperation to make her seem human, but her body plays along, arms wrapping around his neck. He kisses her again, a needy kiss that begs her to stay with him forever.

Her yearning to stay has been steadily increasing, and with it her annoyance. "I am Death. Death cannot Live, even if a prince orders her to," she reminds him.

Seth-Jairin merely smiles and kisses her again. Her eyes flutter closed, but then a tugging sensation snags her attention. His fingers are on the clasps of her cloak, as though by casting the garment from her shoulders he will free her from her own existence. For a moment, she contemplates letting him do so, letting him guide her footsteps and her whims.

His knuckles brush against her collarbone, and the warmth that flares out is too much for her. *You are part of an order,* she tells herself. *Your place, your existence, is far greater than one man's desire and your own temptation. Temptation has nothing to give you but a brief escape from truth.*

She slaps his hands away and sits back. "Even if a king declares it," she says sharply, "Death cannot Live. And you will make a wonderful king."

She rubs her tingling collarbone as the sensation slowly dies away. "You have much living left to do. There are others who need someone familiar with grief and death. Do you understand?"

After a moment of wide-eyed shock, consideration returns to the prince's gaze, and he nods.

"There is more to life than death, Seth-Jairin," she says. "And there is more to death than trying to reassure yourself it won't hurt too much by thinking you're in love with me. You and I shall meet again soon enough but cherish Life." She licks her lips. "Be kind to her. Though it doesn't always seem like it, she is your ally as much as I."

"Then why is she so difficult?" His eyes glint.

"You're asking why Life is difficult?" Death asks. She grins despite herself. "I shall have to remember to ask Fate to offer your lot on a silver platter."

He glares at her, but it's lost as the door opens and Master Oro-Kor pokes his head in. His lips are thinned, his eyes glistening. When he sees Seth-Jairin, propped up in bed, still breathing, he steps fully into the room.

Life sweeps past him, her face radiant as she wraps her arms around Seth-Jairin's neck. Health glows in the prince's cheeks. The physician approaches, his gaze darting between Life and Death, as though uncertain which one to believe. He grasps the prince's arm to check his pulse.

Death stands and inclines her head toward the door, indicating that she is about to leave. She crosses her arms in front of her chest, the silent sign that she will not be returning in this battle.

The physician's lips part, and a croak of joy escapes. The pain and weariness of his job falls from him. He turns and almost bursts out of the room.

"As difficult as Life can be," Death says, with a teasing glance at her Sister before becoming somber again, "it has its moments of grace to ease the grief. Look, Seth-Jairin, your mother is coming."

Once more the door opens and the queen flies in, her skirts tangling around her legs. She collapses beside Seth-Jairin. The prince's breath catches, and Death knows he's forgotten all about Life and Death and Fate as he wraps his mother in his arms. She cries into his neck.

"I'll survive," he whispers, rubbing soothing patterns against her back. "I'll survive, *Malyin*." Determination settles in his eyes, and they almost seem to sparkle in the light of the candles. He glances at Death. "I may have fallen for Death," he says, his voice tight. His gaze slides to Life on the other side. "But that doesn't mean I cannot appreciate Life for her friendship and all the chances found therein." Relief flits across his features. Death can see that whatever feelings he may have for her, and whatever her love for him might look like, he is glad he doesn't have to die.

Queen Deme-tra pulls back from him, cupping his face in her hands. She cannot speak, so she simply stares at her son and weeps.

Death smiles as Life stretches between the queen and her son. Her Sister's eyes shine. Instead of defeat, Death merely feels anticipation—she is the most patient amongst her Sisters.

"I leave him to you," she says to Life. "Treat him well, sister."

"I will treat him as well I can," Life says. "As long as Fate decrees."

Death nods.

Life picks up the shroud from the floor and gives it to Death. "Take this with you. Burn it for me."

"No," Death says, her voice thoughtful. "I think I shall keep it awhile. It would make a lovely cloak." She catches Master Oro-Kor's eye as he returns with the king. She lifts the shroud with a questioning raise of her eyebrow. The physician confers with the king, and then he nods at her.

"It is a gift of thanks," Life says. "They think you had some sort of choice in the matter."

Death sighs. "Sometimes, I wish I did." But at other times, she admits, she feels oddly glad she is merely following orders. She glances down once more at Seth-Jairin, and then she is gone, the silk shroud wrapped around her shoulders.

Life shrugs out of her golden cloak and drapes it across Seth-Jairin's chest as his mother bids him to sleep. He passes out quickly, his brow clear of the furrows of illness. His mother joins his father and together they leave, their whispers low and full—not the broken, uncertain mutters of grief.

This victory belongs to Life, if only for a time. Then, it will be Death's turn, until the Third World comes, all begins anew, and Death is no longer needed.

I will take care of him, Sister, Life says softly. Although physically her sister is gone, she can feel her lingering. *And one day, he'll be all yours for a while.*

Seth-Jairin sighs in his sleep.

I will be waiting, Death answers.

DO MONSTERS MAKE WAR, OR DOES WAR MAKE MONSTERS?

Sera Amoroso

We've never really cared about tomorrow. Our only thoughts were the drunken dark ones as you slung your arm across my waist and let your fire lick my hand like a pet.

We were never monsters, not in the way that *they* were. No, they tore each other apart just for the thrill of stabbing each other in the back. We were monsters only in name.

And as the story reaches its peak, and I hold onto you for the last time, I am once again reminded, that we are not the problem. Why are heroes praised for murder?

Ask me why I'm the monster? Because you took everything I ever loved, when we didn't even fight you.

Killed an innocent and called it victory.

Everyone's a monster in someone else's story. But at least the blood under my fingernails is called revenge. And when my head is displayed on a stake in your city, put yourself in my place.

What would you have done if it was your soulmate dead on the floor? Lifeless because of a misunderstanding?

CAN'T HAVE
WHAT YOU WANT
Katrina Nappi

A knock on the door makes me jump from where I'm sitting on my bed.

I was really hoping that knock wouldn't come; I'm not ready for what I have to do tonight.

If he hadn't come, I could've put this off for longer.

If I had been lucky enough, I could've done it over the phone tomorrow when he realizes that I'm gone.

As shitty of a thing that is.

But I'm not strong enough to do this face to face.

It's not even something that I *want* to do. It's something I've never even dreamed of doing.

I don't want to break up with Kayden.

But worst of all, I don't want to break up with him because someone else is forcing me to do so. Someone else who thinks Kayden's reputation is more important than his happiness.

He knocks again. I stay where I am and hug my knees to my chest.

"Casey," a soft voice comes through the closed door. Maybe if I stay quiet enough, he'll think I'm asleep and go away. That would make things easier, if only postponing the inevitable.

"Kayden. Hi honey!" My mother's voice drifts through the cracks in my hotel room door.

Everything else is too muffled for me to hear but I can tell that Kayden and my mother start a conversation.

And then the door to my hotel room is swinging open, my mother holding the handle and the extra key to my room in her hands. Kayden is next to her, dressed in an oversized gray sweatshirt and a pair of baggy black shorts.

If I had known that my mom was going to let him in, I would've tried to fake sleep to deter Kayden from staying after the door was opened.

A cold feeling develops in my chest, right where my heart is. Well, where it should be if I had one, because no one with one could do what I'm about to—have to—do.

Have to do. I *have* to do this; it doesn't matter what I want. I have to do this so Kayden's secret doesn't come out, because there is no coming back if that secret comes out because Kayden's reputation will be ruined.

"Oh, you're awake." A small pout forms on Kayden's lips. "I knocked." He points to the door—which my mom is now closing—and walks slowly towards me and the bed. He looks so cute tonight but slightly put out with his hands in his sweatshirt pocket, his hood up, and his damp hair hanging in his eyes. He must've rushed through a shower and getting dressed to come to my room as fast as he could. He wants to know why I wasn't watching him tonight.

But how am I supposed to watch him play his heart out

and bear his soul for the crowd, knowing that I have to break him tonight?

I can't be thinking like this right now; it'll only make things harder. Averting my eyes, I mentally put up a wall against Kayden, everything I feel about him, and any single thought that involves him.

Why does this hurt so much?

"Hey, hey. Casey, are you ok? What's wrong?" Kayden is on the bed in an instant, cupping my face in his hands, his thumbs rubbing right below my eyes, his hands wet. "Why are you crying"

No, no, no, no. I don't want to be crying right now. I can't cry; I have to do this. It has to be done tonight.

"Baby, what happened?" Kayden says in the softest voice I've ever heard which contradicts the fierce look in his eyes; he wants to help me through what's wrong. To protect me.

How can he help if the problem is with us? He can't protect me from protecting him.

He won't even want to look at me after tonight.

"I swear to God, what did Carter say to you—"

I cut him off with a tilt of my head to make our lips meet gently.

"Kayden—Kayden I—" sobs in my throat are cutting my words off. I can't do this. I don't *want* to do this. But I have to. So, I will.

Kayden stops my choked words by kissing me and pulling me closer, squeezing my knees between our chests. I deepen the kiss by grabbing the sides of his face under his hood and pulling him even closer to me. Kayden's tongue brushes against my lips and I let him in, his tongue soft on mine.

He pulls back just enough that only our foreheads are touching. "Come on, baby. Tell me what's wrong."

I keep my eyes closed.

The ice in my chest is spreading, reaching down to my abdomen where the butterflies usually wreak havoc. Now they lay frozen and dead as weights in my stomach.

Finally, after a few moments of silence, I open my eyes to Kayden's piercing green eyes staring deep into mine. I don't want to do this.

Why can't we both just be normal people? I wish we could go back to when we were just Casey and Kayden—back before Kayden was famous with fans screaming his name and a reputation that doesn't involve a girlfriend.

His intensive, caring stare-down is putting chips in the walls I built. Instead of pulling him in for another kiss like I want to, I lurch forward and wrap my arms around his neck, pulling his hood off in the process. I drop my knees so that I'm sitting in his lap and hugging him. Kayden follows suit and wraps his arms around my waist, pulling me impossibly closer.

With my head in the crook of Kayden's neck, I breathe in his familiar scent, although he mostly just smells like the hotel soap from his recent shower. Tears free-fall from my face and onto his sweatshirt. That's all I give myself.

My tears stop and I harden my face into nothingness.

My walls are back up and stronger than before; now there's no breaking them. I need to do what I have to in order to protect Kayden, no matter how much it hurts both of us.

The emotionless mask I'm so familiar with comes back. I've gone most of my life wearing this mask. It's easy to bring back. It's easy to make it convincing.

"I can't do this anymore. I can't do *us,* anymore." The ice finally hardens my whole body; my sorry excuse for a heart turns to dust. "I don't think we should see each other anymore." The words fall out of my mouth just as I had rehearsed in my head.

Kayden's entire body stiffens, his arms slacking in their grip around me. "Cass, what do you mean, you're done with *us?*" His voice is steady enough, but I've known him long enough that I can hear him wanting to break. The false confidence is only skin deep—it's not how he really feels. "Is this why you weren't at the show tonight? Because you were planning on breaking up with me?" I nod against his neck.

In quick movements, Kayden has me off his lap so he can see my face. I wish he didn't do that. There's so much pain visible on his face, and he isn't trying to hide it like I am. Kayden in pain isn't something I like to see.

"Is it because of the media attention and the fans? Because I told you I didn't post that photo." He's talking so fast trying to rush out everything he wants to say. "I don't know how it got posted, but Casey—" He grabs ahold of my hands and hugs them to his chest as he searches my eyes for any type of answer. He won't find any. I keep my head turned away from him. His gaze is trying to burn through me to find the real reason behind why I'm doing this. "I can't lose you and I don't want to." His voice cracks as he chokes on his words. I swallow the hard feeling in my throat. "Whatever it is, we can work through it Cass, because you're my girlfriend and my best friend and my person, and ... and ... I ca ... I love you."

I love you.

Three simple words.

I can't break.

Don't break.

I won't break.

My head falls against his heaving chest; he's trying not to cry.

"I love you so much, Casey." A choked sound escapes him.

A frozen butterfly breaks a hole in my stomach and falls, spreading the cold even faster.

"That's the problem, Kayden." I finally meet his eyes again. I was expecting anger, but all I see is hurt. That's what's going to haunt me. I wish he *was* angry, furious even. It would make this easier. My mask holds its indifference. "We weren't supposed to catch feelings."

There's the anger I wanted. His eyes harden and his face blanks of any and all emotions. He looks just like me now.

Kayden flings my hands away from him as if they have burned him. And, for all I know, they could've. Everything is so numb from the cold inside of me I can't feel anything, not even his body underneath me.

"We were just screwing around, a summer fling, or a tour fling. *You weren't* supposed to catch feelings." I roll my eyes to further my point and when I look back at him, I can see rage simmering just below the surface. This is good. This'll make him hate me more. Hate is what I need right now, not love. I don't want the thing that I've been yearning to hear him say. Maybe if I can convince myself to believe I never wanted him to say those things, it'll make this easier. "We only started the whole 'dating thing,'" —I roll my eyes in what I hope is an annoyed way— "because we were outed and had to play the part."

Since the start of our friendship all those years ago, Kayden has always been able to read my mind. Why can't he this time? I've never wanted someone to break apart this mask I put on and call me out on why it's there in the first place more than I have right now. Why can't he just see that? Why can't he see that all I want is him? All I want is for him to come back to me, to hold me close and to tell me that we'll figure it out.

Kayden says nothing, just stares at me. His eyes are searching mine and my mask. What is he looking for? The lie? Regret? Heartbreak? He won't find any of it; I've perfected this mask. It's too perfect, life ruining perfect. Upon finding absolutely no hint of any emotion, Kayden jumps off the bed and storms to the door but doesn't move to open it yet.

"Are we ... we—are we still friends?" Kayden's voice completely breaks, desolate sounding, just how my insides feel. Maybe even colder. Kayden has had just as long to perfect his mask.

"I'm leaving tomorrow to go home." The nail in the coffin. Kayden and I could've found a way to make being 'just friends' work, but I'm leaving him, like a coward.

This will be the last time I see Kayden, at least for a while, and he won't even look at me. Kayden doesn't give me a second glance, just slams the door behind him and leaves.

"I lo—I love you too." I say to no one.

EPITOME
Annie Kay

I used to shake when I was near you.
The mere thought of your voice sent shivers down my spine,
But not the good kind.
No, these shivers were a result of
A crushed spirit,
A ruined heart,
And a bruised soul.

I replayed the memory of your touch
Over and over like waves kissing the sand.
Your eyes were my sun that rose every day.
I never had to doubt their presence would find their way back
into my mind.
You were the epitome of my sadness,
My demise.
You fanned my flame until your older one sparked again.

I wanted to love you,
but you left before I could get the words out.

And you were gone.
And I was alone.
And our flame was out.

You were gone,
And it was dark,
And all I could feel was the chaos you left inside me.

Time moved on but you were still gone.
And that chaos grew louder and louder.

My heart was like a house.
Your essence tainted the windows.
Your presence bolted the doors.
Your existence built the walls.
Your friendship filled the rooms.

It took some time, but slowly the chaos faded.
The lights came back on,
And I was out of the darkness.

I still don't want to be near you in fear I'll shake.
It's best that I don't hear your voice,
Your eyes still bring a smile to my face,
Though I try not to think of them often.

MOTHS AT BAY
Jessika Grewe Glover

Somewhere at the end of a private street which seemed to have run out of funds to sentry the guardhouse was a chain-link fence. Half obscured by a mangrove and outcropping of Florida holly, sat jagged evidence of where someone took bolt cutters to the wire and pried open space just wide enough for a crouched human to crawl. Seb burned his fingers on the cigarette butt he'd been holding when Hazel emerged from the fence.

He was lost in the fantasy world he often created in his mind, flushing out words for the next great novel. As a young twenty something, Seb's debut had been on the best sellers' list for a solid year and the subsequent eight, he'd spent chasing the follow up. Two more were published and didn't catch on as well. After that, his agent met an untimely end in a cocaine fueled car wreck on the Garden State Parkway. Seb pondered his shortcomings, while tossing the swords and magic in his mind as Hazel's freckled arms clawed through the fence.

The cigarette flipped and blistered the webbing between his fingers and disappeared under the shallow brackish water of Biscayne Bay. Year after year, he'd been sitting in that spot and never seen another soul. Yet, out of the tetanus threat of an opening, climbed a girl. He scrambled back over the slick rock on which he perched, just as Hazel saw him and squealed, knocking her own head on the ragged metal links. Seb reached out, forgetting he had nearly wet himself a few seconds prior. Her fingers pulled away from her scalp with a smear of blood. He liked how she swore a little too colorfully yet still crawled out of the fence and sat on the rock neighboring his like they had planned this rendezvous—as though they had known each other for years. It was nearing two in the morning and neither had any real business being out there, likely trespassing, on the edge of the bay. He offered her a cigarette which she waved off as she popped open a can of sparkling water.

"That's boujie," Seb said, pointing to the can. She slid her eyes to him and drank before responding.

"It's far less expensive than that shit you're inhaling," she shot back. He smiled at her, wide and amused, forgetting the cigarettes altogether. If he were being honest with himself, the cigarettes were a sort of boredom filler. Some people liked reality tv, others snuck out to hidden mangroves to smoke.

"Seb," he said, holding out his hand, painfully aware that the fingers of his right hand stunk of nicotine. She tapped the hand with her can of cucumber mint sparkling water and winked.

"Hazel."

They sat in a comfortable silence for ages, watching lights flicker on the quiet bay in front of them. It didn't surprise him when she straightened and spoke, interrupting the splash of water and chirp of cicadas.

"I've seen you before," she said. "At Greenstreet Café a couple weeks ago. You were bent over a laptop, and I kept watching the way your lips read out whatever you had typed."

He cringed hearing that, thinking he'd left that particular habit back in his youth. It wasn't a humiliating statement though, he realized. She was offering him something. A rope to climb, linking them.

She talked into the dead hours after midnight and well before dawn. He could read the things about her she refused to say out loud. Pictures of her formed in his mind and shouted their truths to him in a roll tide of connection.

Seb always had the affinity for understanding people. An empathy which sent him into bouts of depression and the sort of anxiety which hissed at the light of day. He read her like he read others, but with Hazel, even on that very first night they met between the mangroves, he found someone whose inner most thoughts laced fingers with his ability—curled those laced fingers into his curse.

Read me, they seemed to say. And he did. The more she spoke, the closer he leaned in, smelling the jasmine of her perfume under the salt air layer on her golden skin. She looked at him a moment, and it was as though he was seeing what she saw. She took in his large, dark eyes, which were all but black in the night. He was close to her, and though she'd been leery of getting close to anyone lately, Seb felt his nearness calm a manic thrashing in her. He felt her shift like the first sip of liquor, coaxing and inviting.

"Do you mind this?" he asked her without preamble. He saw the flash of alarm in her eyes and knew she was afraid of getting close to anyone again. He knew it as well as he knew in that moment, she would let him in. Still, he asked. And, as she ran a freckled hand across the sharp angles of his face, she gave him a cocky, confident smile that made him laugh. "All right then, princess." He sat back, bracing his dark hands on the rock.

Nights later, the two met again on the barnacled rocks at the end of the private street. They hadn't exchanged numbers, nor planned to see one another again because Seb foresaw, as though he'd read it in a prophecy, Hazel would find him again near the bay. What's more, Seb understood she needed a few days to process their meeting. In that process, he knew she would feel magnetized to him in a way she hadn't felt before. He'd left the half empty pack of cigarettes on the table by the front door to his apartment, which he only regretted as he sat trying to not reach and touch the side of her neck where a vein pulsed with the rhythm of her heartbeat.

"Is it Sebastian? Or just Seb?"

"It was Sebastian once," he answered, earning an eye roll. He sighed and blew out an imaginary stream of smoke. "Sebastian was the name of a child born to be someone else. He was an idea—an ideal I could never live up to."

Hazel laid the side of her head on her forearm, blinking her eyes for him to continue. With anyone else, Seb would have felt that would have been enough of an answer. A shut down. He was aloof on a good day. An asshole on the others. His curt answer was pretentious and forced. He knew with Hazel, just as he knew it was the opening of gates he might never be able to close, that it was not answer enough for her.

"Why not choose a different name then?" she asked, pulling a rogue blade of crab grass from the base of the rock, an act Seb briefly thought merciless given what the grass must have endured to grow there on the mangled edge of land and sea.

"I am who I am," he said, a sneer escaping and catching her off guard. He mentally kicked himself, not wanting that part of himself to show too fast. He wasn't ready to watch her run. Not yet, anyway. "I mean that my parents expected things of me I was never interested in pursuing. Sebastian was the good son. Seb is just ... the offspring." It wasn't a lie. Though he didn't feel that way. Not really. But it was easier than the physics-defying knots of complication of which the truth was made. He shoved a hand through his dark hair thinking he might have needed a haircut. Hazel reached her free hand to him and brushed the errant strands away from his sun bronzed forehead. That brush of her fingertips sent his nerves on a path of sure destruction. When he looked at her, he saw that her elongated eyes were a smoked over moss, matching her name appropriately. Behind that gaze he saw a little bit of what she wanted from him. And he froze.

"We aren't there yet," he growled, standing from the rock and brushing off the black joggers he wore. She didn't move. Her freckled brown face stayed pressed onto her forearm, the rise of goosebumps on her despite the heady summer evening her only movement. He stood there a moment, holding onto an undue string of anger her touch elicited. His skin tingled under the rising heat, inching him toward a faster ending to this thing they'd started. Seb looked out at the sailboats anchored for the evening and tried to focus on the orange buoy hopping over white caps.

Hazel didn't know why he'd reacted that way when everything he had said, every smile he had given her felt like encouragement. That confusion was watermarked across her features. Like he could see inside her and know she wanted him, though really, they'd just met. His rush of temper caused an automatic regression of the openness she'd experienced with him. She was back in a place of fear, and that apprehension heated her blood in the weakness she felt. Her tiny incisor worried at her bottom lip, pulling the skin from pink to white. He looked down at her in that moment and sensed her fear. Her self-hatred. Her disappointment. It was as if he had lived every year of her short, desecrated life. With that, the hesitation of moments before evaporated into the humid night air. So, Seb squatted beside Hazel, hiking his trouser legs up. She refused to look at him, one hand clenched, nails biting the flesh of her palms. It was a ridiculous thing she had felt. A silly, childish giddiness which propelled her from the moment she met Seb, to thinking they had become something so quickly. He knew she was thinking that. He had the same thoughts.

"Can I show you something?" he asked her, his voice far softer than the snarl which had ripped from him. He watched her mossy green eyes which reminded him of ferns and forest glens in the books he wrote. Her face stayed where it lay on her arm, but her eyes locked onto his consuming dark ones. He pushed up the sleeves of his jacket. The same one he'd worn the first night and it had been one of the first impressions of him she had-—that he'd worn a jacket and joggers in the ninety-degree night. She remarked on it at the time, and he refused to comment.

Under the sleeves of his jacket was a pattern of ink that reminded Hazel of lacework. Delicate lines took shape on his arms like a pen and ink sketch of a butterfly. What made her finally lift her head and look closer, her jasmine and wind scent assaulting him, was that the intricacies of the lacework were moving. He inhaled and upturned his palms. There was always enough light in this alcove by the bay, but the swell of darkness in his palms somehow dimmed the atmosphere around them and sparked a cloud of void. He held the void aloft, allowing her to peer from all angles. He pulled his hands apart, extending the darkness like taffy. It swelled and shifted like a fetal kick in a pregnant belly.

"What is it?" she asked, though she knew the answer, just like he knew she did. "It's you. The parts of you that can't be Sebastian."

He nodded, beginning to sweat, knowing he had never shown this to anyone before. Hazel stood, acknowledging his discomfort, and put her arms around him from behind, resting her chin on his shoulder, watching the void. Watching the shadowed parts of himself. The negative space he hated, and his parents had hated. The negative spaces which left room for the way he could read people and understand Hazel but also made him the sort of demon who never really belonged. Hazel reached around his waist and ran her hands down his arms, shivering when the lattice ink danced beneath her touch. His throat moved, more of gasp than swallow.

"Tell me when to stop," she whispered. His chest heaved like he was drinking in something heavy and sweet, while disbelief took hold in his gut like a cancer. When he didn't stop her, she smoothed further down his arms, skating over the bumps of muscle in his forearms, and the place where he had a constant ache from perching his hands over his keyboard. All the while, the ink played with the movements, following her fingers and making her smile, the cheek pressed against his, lifting. Strands of black levitated from his brown arms, wrapping around her fingertips, ducking over and under in a disembodied game of cat's cradle. She wasn't running. He wasn't telling her to stop, and both those things set them on a collision course with a reckless union.

At his wrists, she stopped and circled the bones with a maddening touch, drawing a line around him like manacles, then slipped her hands under his. The void pulsed, the heart of the thing mimicking Seb's erratic breath. Hazel pressed in closer to him, lining herself up with his back. He wasn't much taller than her and she found it comforting to not feel overwhelmed by the size of someone. To not feel outgunned. Her fingers threaded through his, and he felt the void plunge into her. Together they pulled it toward them, and Seb held back at the last minute, his head falling against her.

"I won't hurt you, Hazel," he said, turning so that his words touched the corners of her mouth.

"I know," she said in a shifty breath. "I won't hurt you either."

He let a chuckle escape and said, "Yes, you will. You won't mean to, though."

He knew she had no idea how to take that, so all she did was move around him like a planet in orbit, until she stood in the midst of his darkness and leaned forward. Seb held out. For a few counts, his hands clutched her hips like he hadn't been with a woman in ages when really, it had been little over a week. Though that had meant nothing. Too much whisky and too little to write. This, though...this girl leaning into him here in this private enclave of muddy rocks hidden between mangroves... this was everything.

This was the undoing of Seb.

He stepped away from her and unzipped his jacket, pulling it off along with a t-shirt. Swarms of the same ink buzzed over his entire torso. Wonder shone on Hazel's face. Not shock, disgust, or worry. The instant that her thoughts settled in him, a lock clicking open. He knew when it was okay to move closer to her, and she placed both hands on his chest. Her head tipped up, lips finding his and holding him there, until he responded in kind.

I'm broken. He screamed in his mind. *You don't want this.* And curiously, she smiled against his mouth.

"I *do* want this," she said with a hand over his heart. The thoughts in her mind fluttered at him like sheets in the wind, reminding her of how little she had been told she was worth. Of how she believed anyone in his right mind would tire of her. Of just how much work she thought she was as a partner. Hazel rested her forehead against his collarbone. Through that ripped open fence portal, they left the abandoned piece of waterfront property which no one seemed to want or maintain, and started months of waking beside one another, cocooned in Seb's enmeshing of night. It was the beginning of a union he had sworn to never attempt.

"I know that it's part of you," Hazel said in the early hours of one of their dawns. His apartment was still mostly swathed in night, though the sun was rising outside. She tickled the inside of their bubble, running a toe along it. In whatever capacity he had to create, Seb was able to cast a sort of shield around them in sleep. It dissipated once he was fully awake, but Hazel slept better within it than she ever had before. It was their own isolation chamber. "But what made it? Why you?"

Seb's sleep doused eyes blinked. Most days he was still in awe of waking with her golden body aligned with his. She turned to him,

"I made it. My anger. My alienation. My desire to be more." A half-truth, buried in the tucks and folds of what caused the first swirl of onyx on him.

"Many people are angry and misunderstood, Seb," she countered. "No one else manifests a dark tempest of tattoos." Said tattoos shifted in a wave at her mention, moving over him in a current, towards her. The void around them dropped. Sounds infiltrated their room then. Traffic and the hideous shrieks of sirens in the predawn hours, complimenting his rapid temper.

"I never said I was like anyone else. I said I *think* I made it. Or that it formed because of me," Seb snapped at her, his teeth grinding together. "Maybe a cat jumped across the grave of my former life or my mother ate something dodgy when she was pregnant with me," he lied, sensing she either didn't recognize the deception, or didn't care. "Maybe I'm a changeling. Not a child of my parents, but something other, displaced from whence it came."

"Whence it came?" she teased, nipping at the skin under his heart. A place she found made him hold her tighter. Made him smile at her longer. He knew. Like a self-fulfilling prophecy. Knew when she needed more. More of him. So, he held her tighter, kissed her longer. This aberration of a man wrapped his arms around her, so nothing veiled them from one another. Just as Seb had no trouble reading Hazel, he saw that she felt at a loss for what he needed from her. Hazel couldn't figure out how he truly felt for her. Her hints and probing of him led her nowhere. Seb evaded well, feigning indifference or downright refusing to acknowledge the question, and Hazel backed down from confrontation. Cowering in corners fit her brand of operations. He recognized it in her the moment they met in the haze of summer heat. The demon in him gravitated toward it. Her vulnerability was a siren's song to the black maelstrom in his soul.

Regardless of what Seb knew she wanted, he kept her at arm's length. What he could never see, however, was what she *needed* from him. Beyond the small physical gestures, Seb was no more blind to Hazel than anyone else he'd been with. He could make out her every desire and urge. He knew when she began to crave him. They always craved him, but he never wanted that from Hazel. And so, it was a fissure. A mounting threat in the structure they had built. He was so used to reading people, reading her even, however, he was blind to her needing more of him.

Each day, she woke tracing the latticework of moth black ink on him—each time she allowed the swell and dance of the markings to pull her under like the most consumptive drug, she fought it. Fought the onslaught of what was happening when she slipped into the fog of his chemical pull. Yet, not once had she been able to resist. Twenty-six years of trauma eroded to silt while Hazel moved within the vacuum of Seb's spell. It was those early mornings when Seb wasn't fully awake to stop it from happening that he would wake, the girl he may have loved—if he believed he could feel such things—drowning in the essence of his curse. She never told him of her past and he never shared his. It was an unspoken détente between them.

He never could tell why she felt she needed to be pulled under, and he was never coherent enough to stop her. His demon was lucid even when he was not. As they slipped through the trip wires of each other's battered soul, tearing for purchase on what it would take to truly know one another, she would trace him. Trace anywhere the line and plaits wrote their ancient portentous poems on his flesh. He would claw her fingers free of his skin, his demon and all of hers in protest. He swallowed her desire and consumed her ache for deliverance. Seb never let her know what it felt like to be touched by her. For her willing fingertips to move like blown bubbles over him, the way she fed his curse a rising tide in him, clearing the mess of his mind and soul. She never knew it fed him, and he tried—he always tried to keep her away.

Seb hung his feet from the rock at the bay's edge, turning the cigarette between his fingers, making notes for his newest manuscript. His spidery script moved across the grid of a bullet journal with his initials embossed on the outer edge. A gift from his mother so many years ago. Her own shaky hand had penned *My Sebastian* on the inside cover, plucking his memories every time he read it, a ghostly refrain, teasing a nearly vacant conscience. His non dominant, yet oddly ambidextrous hand wrote on the linen paper. The words flowed as they hadn't in years, fueled by what fed him lately. Or, rather, who fed him lately, and the extent of pull he felt for her as well.

It had been a slow bargain he made all those years ago— to be someone stronger than the parents who never saw his worth. A bargain made with an amorphous entity Seb had manifested in the late hours of wandering he tended toward. By morning, the day after his bargain, the tattoos began to appear. First on his core, climbing like passion-soaked hands rising from his waist. The markings tip toed up his ribs with skeletal ambiguity.

With every touch of another's fingers, he became stronger, his writing clearer. The higher the energy and emotion from another, the deeper his necromantic inhalation. With every ounce of strength he gained, the tattoos grew. Years later, they covered his body, from his ankles to his neck, leaving glimpses of caramel brown skin Hazel was able to find and trace. She laid beside him, promising to not touch the black lace designs. She would instead run the pointed tip of her nail in every negative space of his skin. He fought time and again against feeding from her nearness. A begrudged détente with his demon, and a knowledge that Hazel's exploration of his negative space was a sickly honest analogy for their coexistence. That knowledge left an oil slick on his rotting soul. Every last scrap of his humanity hid inside of his feelings for Hazel, making a final stand against the battalion of his curse.

On that bayside hideaway where they had first met, Seb then finished notes for a new draft. A manuscript which was guaranteed to place him back on the list of relevant writers. He felt that promise as surely as he felt that spectral sludge biding its time. Summer heat made him pull his long sleeves off, leaving him shirtless in the swamp thick Miami night. Four days he had been gone from Hazel. Four nights of staying in a shady motel on U.S. 1, trying to put some space between him and the girl he was slowly killing. Seaweed caught on a discarded can of hard sparkling water in the spot Seb felt more a church to him than the services his parents dragged him to his whole damned life. He lifted the can from the bay water and muttered about it being the shit people drink when they want to pretend to be healthy. *Like a salad with fried chicken strips,* he thought to himself, moving the can to the crushed crab grass behind his rock. Pinpricks of light from vessels on the bay winked in a smudged array against the swollen clouds of an offshore storm. Even in the gunmetal sky of late evening, hard lines of the approaching swell were visible, making Seb's eyes water when he tried to focus on the horizon.

Metallic rattling had him snap attention to the gaping maw of the chain link fence. Hazel's dark head popped through, her honey-colored skin alighting when she saw him. He discerned each emotion, turning her face into a palimpsest of her wants and needs bleeding through parchment. Hungry eyes took in his naked torso, following the drips of sweat slithering down the tucks of his muscle and bone, hopping over repellent ink. He knew it wasn't him she was craving then. The small human part of him thrashed at that. The wicked parasite he had mostly become puffed its chest. She loved him. He knew that. He had devoured that knowledge early on, allowing it to spiral from awe to anger. The way she looked at him then, in the strange way the city lights reflected on Biscayne Bay, though, that was the callous need of an addict.

In that moment, he knew she would touch him; he saw it like a film reel. He also knew that he must be incapable of this thing called love. Because he would not fight her touch. Because he craved her as much as she craved him. Hazel didn't take her fern glen eyes off his while she walked across the pine needle blanketed sand. As she sat beside him, knees pressed to his, on that slick rock where they first met, he brought his lips to hers, a near meeting of skin. And when she plummeted to the place they all went when he was touched, skin to ink, he kissed her lips. Kissed her cheeks. Her eyelids. Her nose.

He knew from that first day she would indeed hurt him. It did not take long. He held on as long as possible, her warm lips pressed to his. He held on, letting her have this last comfort. She kept tracing his striations, following the smoke trail lines and patterns, marking this insatiable history on his person. Each brushstroke of marking over him told a whispered tale of his bargain. Beyond the orchid trees and holly bushes, stood the tenebrous deity with whom Seb's bargain was made. Only a slash of pitch between the foliage marked its place. But Seb could see it. He would recognize it anywhere. The immortal who gave him back his life, his success—and claimed every part of it in turn. Seb's eyes looked over Hazel's shoulder, his hand fisted in her curls. Had there been eyes with which he could have locked, Seb's would have bored into those of the dark deity. His stare would have stripped the being of its power over him, a last attempt to save this girl in his lap. There were no eyes. There was no soul to plead. What remained was the fact that Seb wanted what he had been dealt. Each absorption of life he stole from another fueled his craft. In this covenant with his god, the simple fact that the girl in his arms had fallen in love with him, imbued more power to that which she fed him.

As her eyelashes fluttered along his cheekbones, his arms locked in cages around her slight form, he imbibed. His throat worked, drinking her essence as he ran lips over her, and she touched the configurations which mapped his fate. Her fate.

"It's okay," she whispered causing his breath to catch, staggering in his chest. "It's okay." Her arms twined together behind his head, holding him in place. *She had known,* he thought to himself, revolted with his mercenary ways. Her wet cheeks dampened his jawline while she pressed salt-edged kisses to his heated skin, telling him over and over it was going to be fine. Pockets of night crowded the two, converging around them, as though questioning Seb's true intent, monitoring his resolve.

This borrowed time had run out. Nebulous fog enveloped what was left of the storm promised night. Hazel's namesake eyes shot to his, a flash of apprehension dawning for the first time. His must have told the inevitable. The girl's dark shoulders fell, a balmy cry escaping her. Even Seb's chest clenched in the suppressive cloud around them. Her body slipped from his lap. She released from his grip, dissolving into the lacework of his arms, his face, his chest. All of Hazel diffused into him, his body a sieve, pulling her through into the depths of his blight. Arms which had been warm around her, were assaulted with needles of her becoming one with his body. The curls of her hair became whorls of ink around his heart, coiling in a calligraphy of their story, infinite and keening. Stroke after stroke of Hazel's departure dug trenches through his skin, a process he had never before felt. A portion of his soul, his last remaining shred of humanity, fell to the clutches of those trenches. A barrage of heavy fire held him down. Under that mortar of fate, he thought he might like to dissolve along with her. Become the ink dripped upon skin, slowly decaying in a plot underground. If only he could die.

CIRCUS OF MACHINES
Effie Joe Stock

I searched for my muse in the crowd, adjusting the goggles on my face. *Vivian.* I had spent so many years crafting a persona from her likes and dislikes. Maybe that night the façade would finally be perfect enough to trick her into loving the creature I had become.

But first came my circus—the magic I, the Ringmaster, had made for her. To awe her. To draw her in.

I crouched, perched on the metal grid overhanging the stage, taking in the bustling crowds, the warm smell of peanuts and popped corn, the screeching of metal against metal, the sound of turning cogs, the hum of anticipation—it was thrilling. But though my show was minutes from beginning, nothing could tear me from searching for the woman more beautiful than any doll I'd ever fashioned.

Box five was empty. The box I always reserved for her. A stab of vexation stirred me; she must be speaking with another guest. Perhaps another man ... I took several breaths to calm the storm within me. It was no matter if she was. My annoyance faded to confidence. After tonight, she would never have need to desire another.

I cocked my head, humming through the gold beaked

mask over my nose and mouth, peering through my multi-lensed goggles. Small knobs on the side of the lenses allowed me to see the distance with clarity but I couldn't find her in the crowd either. I would have to wait.

I swung down a level of the metal rungs and pattered across a plank, my boots making more noise than I would ever allow if we were performing. Up here, in the gridiron, I was a god. I crouched and studied her empty box, waiting for her to emerge. From this angle, I could better see box five. She had to be alone tonight, or else it would befoul my plans. I would've liked to accompany her this evening, as I often did, but I needed to appear in my circus sometimes.

She finally stepped into her box, adjusting her lovely, ruf-fled blue skirts—my favorites. She brushed aside the ringlets around her face, the rest having been swept into a braided knot at the base of her neck. The design reminded me of the machines that had made my life magical. Her eyes were blue like the moon shining through the thick haze that hung over our overbuilt, industrial city. I once thought that haze was a curse, a testimony to the horrors that machines had brought us, but now I knew differently. Science was but another form of magic, and machines were the creatures that brought it to life.

A smirk lifted my lips. *Sweet, clueless Vivian.* Did she know that only a half hour before, I had been the young man with the braided hair, tall striped hat, and ridiculously bright clothes with a red mask who checked her ticket and directed her through the maze of spectators? It was almost impossible for me to restrain the cackle of vibrant laughter that bubbled up in my throat.

A gong boomed, and the crowd quieted. My heart pounded in anticipation, the same thrum that hummed like a purring engine through the room.

They were ready, and so was I.

Let the show begin.

The butterflies raged in my stomach as I jumped to my feet and climbed through the bars—like a creature of the night.

The second gong sounded as I swung down the last rung and slipped. Barely was I able to catch hold of a rung to halt my descent. And there I hung, dangling over the whole arena as if trapped, as if I had accidentally fallen, and not planned this as my introduction.

The crowd gasped, then fell silent. I tried not to smile, tried not to think of how these people were so easily fooled.

Machines, magic, and mystery.

I let go of the rung.

Screams echoed through the arena as my body twisted.

The whirring of machines filled the air.

In a shower of sparks, wings spread out beside me and caught a draft.

My foot brushed the sandy floor before I shot upwards in a spray of gold sparks and wind.

The crowd went wild.

My performers dove off their platforms, their silver wings spreading and carrying them into the tall, vaulted arena—the grandest circus arena of the Metal World.

I made it myself.

I made it for *her*.

My eyes darted to her dazzling blue eyes. She was standing and clapping. Her lips were parted in a smile. No matter how the silver wings around me darted and danced, falling and then shooting to the beautiful tapestry of clouds and stars above, her eyes never left me. I felt them on me like the hot metal against my back.

Everything went according to plan. How could it not? It was *my* circus—a whirlwind of chaos and trickery. My long dark hair fell traitorously into my eyes as I weaved through the machines, pretending to assemble entire creatures with my nimble fingers and quick tool work. To the audience, I was a genius, though it was all a hoax. No one could create an elephant in a few minutes.

Of course, if it weren't for my role as Ringmaster, the crowds would never identify me. They recognized my talents, not my face. It was magic I brought them, not my voice or my clothes.

Every show was different. Every machine and face, new, even my own. Last time, I had short blonde hair; the time before, I had dark skin. Once, I even had four life-like arms.

From the biggest machine to the smallest card trick, everything I had created was for Vivian—my first unwitting audience. It had been her face which lit up in wonder at the shapeshifting machine I made to dance to a violin; my first creation had drawn her smile.

That was back before I truly understood the power of illusion, of how you could trick the spectators not only into believing in magic but also anything else you wanted ... even love.

If only she knew ...

The night flew by in a blur. The show came to its finale. A shower of gold sparks landed on the sand with me, my wings creaking at my sides.

"Ladies and Gentlemen! It is time for my finale! One of you shall scale the skies with me and my wings. Who is brave enough to scale the ether? Daring enough to sore the heavens?" Hands flew up, everyone desperate to prove their dauntlessness, to be close to the illusive Ringmaster.

But I only had eyes for one.

Vivian rose her hand, and I smirked. I knew her audacious spirit wouldn't let her deny this opportunity. "You!" I pointed, and our eyes locked. "In box five, lady in the blue skirts."

Elation lit up her face as she stood still in shock before running down the steps and through the crowd, hundreds of strangers' hands reaching out to touch her—the girl special enough to be chosen.

I couldn't look away from her as she drew closer and closer. *So close.* I was only minutes away from seeing if I had become the man she wanted. We had met a thousand times before, but I had never been perfect. She wanted something real, something she could touch and rely on. She didn't understand I was the most real thing she could have in this world.

She was standing in front of me now, appearing almost fake against the illusion of the arena.

I bowed low, a chuckle escaping my lips, sounding mystical through the mask and voice changer. "I'm surprised a lady like yourself would dare to scale the heights of the sky."

Her face lit up in indignation, the fiery spirit I admired so much in her. Reminded me of an engine who loathed to stop its roaring movement.

She planted her hands on her steel bone corset around her waist. It was old with tattered edges fringing rusted buckles and decorative cogs. "And why not?" she snapped.

Rusted cogs, her voice was more beautiful than any music box I had fashioned. Was there a way I could trap her voice into something forever? Perhaps I could put it in a doll. Would she like that?

"You are so delicate ..." I lightly brushed my fingers through her hair, watching as she shivered against my touch. "So fragile. The wind might blow you away."

She shook herself and narrowed her eyes. "Not as much as you think."

I could hardly drag my eyes from her lips. Roughly, I pulled her to me, one hand on her waist, the other cupping the back of her neck.

Surprise lit up her face. She could change faces as well as me ... almost.

"Then you must prove it, *mon cheri*." I brushed the beak of my mask against her ear, hearing her gasp lightly before I twirled her around, sparks entwining around us and making us like gods to the audience. Another illusion, of course, but in that moment, even I thought I could believe it too.

Somewhere, the announcer declared this the finale, the grand resolution. I could nearly feel the raging envy hanging in the air. Every woman wanted to be *her*, in the arms of the illusive Machine Master who could be anyone or anything you could dream of.

The wings spread behind me, and with quick fingers, I pulled her back to my chest and strapped the protective leather around her, binding her body to mine; then weightless, we rose into the expanse above the sand.

It was enough excitement for the cheering audience to see a mere citizen fly with the Ringmaster, but tonight, for

Vivian, I had so much more planned.

The panels of the ceiling slid back on massive tracks with a shuttering groan, exposing the open night to us.

The crowd gasped with Vivian when they realized what I was doing.

"What's going on?" She struggled against me, against the straps holding her in.

"I'm taking you for a flight." I was grateful her back was to me so she couldn't see the smirk that decorated my lips.

"But only in the arena!"

"Oh really? I don't remember specifying."

"Let me go!"

I pressed my mask to her ear, and she stilled. "Do you really want me to do that?"

Her wide gaze shifted to the sand far below her, and then to the open night sky above us.

"Trust me ..." My gloved fingers slid across her chin, down her throat, and she shuddered with a light gasp and quick nod.

The wings pushed against the drafts, carrying us quickly out of the dome, away from the frenzied crowd who thought a girl was kidnapped and the announcers who convinced them otherwise.

Her heart raced against me. Her breath caught in her throat as she looked down at our city.

My heart, usually a well-trained machine, betrayed me by mimicking hers.

"Where do you want to go?" I spared a quick glance down to her wide eyes. It seemed she couldn't take enough of the view in.

We were gliding now, the straps from the machine tight around her body, holding her steady against me.

"To the beach."

I wanted to tell her I already knew she wanted to go there, that we were already on our way, but I only nodded solemnly as if it were a great surprise. "A lovely choice."

She tried to look back at me. Her blue eyes shone in the night, but the little ringlets around her face kept flying into her gaze. What I wouldn't give to brush them out of her way. But I couldn't. Not as the Ringmaster. Not yet.

Then we were flying over the lake, big enough that our city called it the ocean. After all, few ever left the great Metal City. Most of us would die before seeing the true sea, before seeing anything other than this lonely stretch of sand on water. Of course, they could see the ocean if they came to my performances, to my circus. I could make the ocean itself. I could make the waves spray on their faces, and they would be able to taste the salt and hear the gulls.

I could make all their dreams come true.

Just as I had with *her*.

Our feet touched the sand, and, in moments, I released her from the straps that held her to me.

She lingered a moment longer before slipping away. I could feel the wonder from her. It was the same emotion I always felt when others were in my presence.

Not respect. Not fear. Not familiarity.

Pure wonder.

And I never tired of it.

I saw the yearning she held in her eyes for the magic that lifted me from the ground as I danced from foot to foot.

"You have a great deal of audacity, Ringmaster." The harsh tone of her scolding was not lost on me as she brushed the hair from her face and trained her narrow gaze on me. "My father will have your head for kidnapping."

I tried not to chuckle, tried not to diminish her suppressed annoyance and the way her eyes flashed with spark. I spread my hands before me, as if offering my innocence. "Taking a willing passenger on a midnight flight is hardly a kidnapping. And I haven't refused to take you home."

She raised her chin in a challenge, crossing her arms. "Then do so at once."

I let my shoulders sag slightly, my feet dragging the ground, just enough to trigger some guilt. "*Mon ange.* Shall we really end this night on such a sour note? I have not harmed you, and I do not intend to do so. Do you not trust me?"

Her eyes narrowed and she shifted her stance, turning slightly to face me as I hovered on the wings. "Most certainly I do not, but if I am to stay, I must be permitted answers to my questions."

I licked my lips, my heart racing in anticipation. Such spirit, she had. "Very well, what is it you desire to know?"

"How do you do it?"

I landed in front of her, my hand extended. She took it after a long moment of hesitation. "Magic, *mon cheri.*"

She laughed and shook her head, some of her hair falling from the braided knot and spilling over her shoulders. "Please, *monsieur.* I know it's not magic." She was lowering her defenses, I realized with triumph.

I clutched my heart as if wounded. "You don't believe me? You don't believe that this—" I extended my hand and twirled it a few times, swirls of gold shooting up to the sky like campfire sparks, "—is magic?"

The gold reflected in her eyes, and I knew in that moment, despite what she said, that she believed, truly believed it was.

"It's all a trick," she whispered, but she couldn't tear her eyes from the sparks, from the heavy wonder in the air that begged her to believe differently.

"Isn't everything just a trick?"

Her eyes turned back on me, and she said the last thing I ever thought she would.

"Love isn't."

If I had been a machine, I'm sure her words would have been a wrench stuck in one of my gears. *Love isn't.*

"Oh, but it is. Everything is."

Did she know even this lake was metal?

Not the water, of course, but everything it rested on. The basin was a metal tub, like a sink in one's kitchen. Even under the sand, we stood on a metal sheet.

"Everything in this city is a trick, a lie, an illusion." I didn't realize I'd said it out loud until she crossed her arms, a strange look on her face.

"Does that make people only a trick?"

I didn't miss a beat and merely shrugged. "Of course. They're always lying, saying one thing and meaning another, making promises and breaking them. The only true reality is the one we make for ourselves. Nothing else is real."

For a long moment, neither of us said anything, simply staring at each other as if waiting to see who would break the silence first.

She stood taller than me in her heels, I noticed. Did she

like that? I knew of ways to make my legs longer if she didn't …

Finally, she turned from me, her gaze wandering over the strange lake that stretched on for miles, held in by never-ending metal.

"This is my favorite spot."

"I know."

She turned to me, darkness shrouding her face. Her voice didn't hold the wonder it had a few minutes before. Something like suspicion had replaced it. "How did you know?"

Because you've told me so many times. Because you've brought me here before. I bit my tongue and drawled confidently instead, "I just guessed."

She tilted her head as if she didn't quite believe me. "Some sort of magic again?"

"A magician never reveals his secrets."

"Even to those he loves?"

This time I didn't stop the laughter that bubbled up. Thankfully the voice changer made it sound humorous. "Especially to those he loves."

"Why?"

"Because love is magic, and magic is only beautiful with mystery."

"So that is why you and your shows are so beautiful." A strange little smile lifted her lips. "The mystery."

I hummed in agreement. "Of course. It would be no good if you knew all the tricks."

"Then how do you have any fun? Knowing all the tricks, I mean."

I shook my head and chuckled. What a silly question.

"Because *mon cheri*, I *am* the mystery. I am everything I want to be and anything I can dream of being."

Her little mouth furrowed in ponder. "Then why do you do it?"

My eyebrows rose with surprise before my lips curled in a pleased smirk. No one before her had ever cared to ask. "I want everyone who ever lost sight of beauty to find it again. I want to show people that once upon a time, before all the machines, the steam, the clocks and cogs and gears, before all the blue haze, there was a world of majesty and magic. That a world of color and smells and tastes, of creatures you couldn't even imagine had existed. That even if you lived a hundred years, you would never tire of your reality ..." I gazed hesitantly at her, unsure of where these words were coming from. Perhaps they came from that boy who had started this dream all those countless years ago the moment he saw the awe in a young girl's eyes. "I do it because I want people to be awed."

Suddenly, she was standing close to me. Much too close. I could smell her perfume—strong, intoxicating. It was a new scent; why had she changed it?

"I want to be awed." Her breath was warm on my face, warm in contrast to the cold winter air, calling me back to reality, or perhaps back to my imagination.

"And you haven't been already?" I raised an eyebrow at her, wishing I were taller than her right now so I could look down into her eyes. My fingers fiddled with the small nobs at my hips, and I felt the whirring in my legs. In a second, I was looking down at her, suddenly inches taller.

The surprise on her face was delectable. Oh to kiss her in that moment to see what this surprise and awe tasted like.

But to do that, I would have to take my mask off. Unthinkable.

"H–how, wh—" she stuttered over her words, completely unable to fathom what she had just seen.

"Magic, *mon amour*. I thought I told you?"

"Impossible ..." she whispered breathlessly, but her eyes told me she believed. She was fooled, just like everyone else.

"Or perhaps you want a different kind of magic? Perhaps you want me to read your mind? I'm sure I could know you better than any devoted lover."

Her eyes widened, and she took a step back. "You can't."

"Oh, but I can, Vivian."

She took in a sharp breath at her name, taking a few steps back when I took a few forward.

Feet sinking in the sand, I stepped around her, circling her. The façade of the Ringmaster was gone. I was the creature of the night now, teetering on loving this creature of light and fighting her. She was so tempting, so close to making me bare my secrets before her, but she was also so sweet to fool, so willing to believe anything I served her, and I never wanted that to change. She was my little fool, and I was her trickster. And if she could accept who–what–I was, then she would learn I could be so much more.

Taking a deep breath, I closed my eyes and hummed a light, airy tune. In a moment of her distraction, I switched the knob on my neck, changing my voice from the soft, higher pitch to a low, hypnotic tone.

"You like lower voices in men."

She gasped at the change and whirled to face me. Realization dawned in her eyes, but denial quickly clouded them.

"You like them to be more muscular." I dug my nails into my palms, three times with my right-hand ring finger, four with the left. The metal in my limbs shifted and changed, bulking. The change was painful, but it never showed on my face. This was magic now, not science, and while magic was frightening, it could never appear painful.

Her lace gloved hands tightened around her little top hat decorated in gears and clocks—a hat I had made her behind the face of an infatuated hat maker.

"You wear the blue dress—" I nodded to her skirts under her brown corset "—to your favorite occasions and red to ones where there will be eligible young men." Her dark painted lips dropped open, but I didn't pause for a moment.

"You've changed your perfume. You used to wear Joice's Autumn, but I believe ..." I drew close to her and gently breathed in her scent, just by her shoulder. She stiffened, though she didn't move away. "This is a more flowery mixture, perhaps because the winter makes you long for warmer, greener days?" I didn't wait for her to answer.

Now, I was standing in front of her, our eyes locked, though I knew she wouldn't be able to see them well through the goggles. I, however, could see every fleck of brown in her bright eyes. I knew every freckle on her face, every little scar from when she used to play with machines as a child, even though she tried to conceal the marks under makeup. Like how she tried to hide from her father that she decorated her walls with cuckoo clocks and her hats and corsets with gears and old miniatures of someone else's grandmother.

"How do you know? How do you know all this about me?" The shock on her face was more like horror.

"Magic," I whispered in her ear.

She moved before I could stop her, and in one swift movement, my illusion was shattered.

Suddenly, my features were bare to the world, to her, to anyone who wanted to see; my mask was held tightly between her fingers.

For a moment, I could do nothing but stare into her eyes with my own, without the goggles or mask between us.

Dismay and the weight of failure slowly leaked onto my face, but I knew she wouldn't be able to see the emotions hidden behind the metal.

Her eyes widened as her eyes roamed over my face.

"You—you're ..."

I waited for the words "hideous," "disfigured," "mutated," "broken." But they never came.

Her hand reached out slowly, hesitantly as if she were afraid I would flee. But how could I? I felt nothing more than dread as I waited to see how this would end. Only numbness in knowing that my muse might turn from me and leave, just as everyone else had before I became the greatest Circus Master in the Metal City, before I had made a million new faces for myself, before I had become something, *someone*, people actually wanted.

Her skin met mine, and I leaned into her touch, feeling her fingers trace over the half of my face that was metal, the half that didn't have a scar running over the little flesh that remained.

"You're—"

"An illusion," I finished for her.

She didn't have anything to say. I could see a war raging in her mind. If her mind were cogs, they would be spinning out of control.

"This ... this is how you do it?"

I stepped back from her. "Yes. This is how I make magic." I held out my hands, and sparks tumbled from my fingertips. Not magic, just sparks from the mechanics that made up my body, or at least the parts I had improved upon myself, the parts the doctor hadn't been able to save from the gas explosion in the factory I was raised in.

Tears collected in her eyes, but I couldn't make out the emotion that drove them. "But, how do you know?"

"How do I know all those things about you?"

She nodded slowly.

A lazy grin spread across my face. "Because I am anything I want to be. An illusion, a reality ... a lover ... or a hundred lovers."

She studied my eyes, the only things that never changed, their dark green always remaining the same.

Realization finally dawned on her face.

"You—"

I didn't let her finish and instead pressed my lips against hers. They were so soft, so sweet, so delicious ... So this is what her surprise tasted like. I knew then, and I wondered if she did too, that in the space where her flesh touched my metal, where our lips moved against each other, my hands on her waist, her hands pressing my chest, *that* was reality.

She pushed against me, whimpered against the coaxing of my lips; I could taste the salt of her tears, but for a moment longer, I held her tighter, stealing the warmth I desired. *You are mine. My muse. You belong to me!*

I pulled away only for a moment, only long enough to whisper, "I am metal in a metal world. Everything else is a trick, remember? I am the only real thing you've ever seen, and so is my circus. I am everything you ever loved and everything you will ever love. You will never escape from me, your creature in the night."

Then, ignoring her breathless curses, I kissed her unyielding lips once more—a promise.

"I best be getting back, *mon ange*," My lips wandered from her lips to her neck as I brushed my fingers through her hair.

She flinched from their cold.

Grasping her chin, I forced her eyes to meet mine. I searched them for love, for anything warm she might hold for this frozen, metal monster.

"Don't you realize?" My breath came heavy, my words, desperate. "I can be anything, *anyone* you want me to be. You only need to say the word and I will conform to your desires."

Her teeth worried her bottom lip, tears sparkled in her eyes. When her gaze met mine, I saw only rejection. "I would rather be alone."

Her words stabbed like a cold knife. I stepped back, narrowing my eyes down at her. "They'll be missing me at my circus." I let my golden wings unfurl from my back, never moving my eyes from hers, which burned through pained tears. "I will see you from behind another face." The wings hummed to life and lifted me from the sand. And I pondered, as I rose, what she would think now. Would she forever wonder if any man she met now or in the future would be real?

Bitterness and resentment ate at the cogs in my heart. If she couldn't accept my love, or metal body, then I would secretly consume her mind with my magic instead. Eventually, she would abandon her defenses, and she would be *mine*.

CAGE OF PROMISES
Cassandra Hamm

He built the walls around her piece by piece,
not enough to alarm, just a bar at a time.
A sense of disquiet, swiftly ignored because
he is so good to her.

Now the walls curve over her head,
pressing in on her so
she can barely breathe.
It's a lovely cage made of promises,
but as she stares at the iron bars,
her chest heaves,
and her eyes burn.
She can barely stretch her wings,
barely taste the sweetness of the air.

The door hasn't quite shut yet, but
she stays where she is.
It really isn't so bad—
He's a good guy.

She's making a big deal out of nothing.
Still, the glimpse of open sky
taunts her, reminding her of
when she was free.
When she could be herself without fear
and answered to none but God.

She edges toward the door, heart pounding,
and lets her foot slide through, just an inch.
The sensation buzzes through her,
hot and fierce, tantalizing and terrifying,
burning her throat, filling her chest,
bubbling forth in giddy laughter,
and she starts to spread her wings—

His desperate pleas cut into the air,
slicing into her skin, spilling her heart's blood.
He'll hurt himself
without her to keep him grounded.
His life is nothing
without her in it.

Perhaps the cage is a
symbol of his love, a sign of
just how much he wants her—
how no one else can have her.
She should be flattered
at his desire, his need, his dependence.
No one else could ever want her

like he does.
She is lucky to have him.

So she draws back and closes the door,
letting the lock click in place, and settles
into his arms, ignoring the way
they tighten like chains.

VOXSTEIN'S MONSTER
Kaitlyn Emery

My **bloodshot eyes** rove over Lavenza's body stretched out on the table, silver scalpels arrayed alongside her. Her pale, cold skin pulses with the harsh fluorescent bulbs overhead. An entangled mass of bubbling hoses pump life-preserving fluids through her arteries.

The weight of the engagement ring in my pocket preys on me. If this doesn't work—I don't want my last memories to be like this, but I have to try.

I hesitate, then roll up my sleeve, exposing the veins that run beneath the surface of my skin. I know she would object to what I'm about to do, but I must make amends. In saving her, I pray I'll save my own soul.

I ease the needle through my skin. It makes a sickening pop when it breaks through, then the tubes turn red as my blood flows directly into Lavenza's veins. I take deep breaths, waiting for the monitors to signal completion.

She saw where we were going.

The future would be bright. That was the promise we made to the hopeful masses. Instead, it brought overpopulated cities, invasive body modifications, and an ever-widening gap between the privileged and those who lived in the toxic alleyways beneath the shadow of endless factories.

The future awoke amidst neon lights, and humans became the minority. And I, Doctor Victor Voxstein, had helped to create it all. I had added my voice and talents to the creation of this age—The New Evolution, we called it—only to regret everything when it was too late. Assassinators were created, slowly removing the *nonessentials* of the human race.

Lavenza was one of those innocents gunned down by the very progress we had created. An orphan, she was of no value to those few who dwelt in the capitol's glass towers. Even though my mother had taken her in as a companion, like a gem plucked from the garbage, her connection to my family wasn't enough to save her.

So now here I was, forced to act without the reassurance of guaranteed success. My situation was unendurable. It was my fault she died. My lust for science, progress, and my inability to see when we had gone too far, just as Lavenza had warned.

What I did, I did for science and the improvement of humanity.

What I do now, I must do for us. I cannot live in this guilt and loneliness that is consuming me. All the lovers who have come before are nothing compared to Lavenza. She was passion and adventure, ridiculous in her hope for others, and all-consuming compassion.

I miss the closeness I felt with her, the bond of growing up in that big old mansion, and the mutual sharing of ideals. But what I miss most right now—what I *need* most right now—is her goodness. Lavenza was goodness personified. And I need that quality to save the monster I have become.

The ghost of failure haunts my thoughts as I remove the

transfusion needle and start hooking up the electrodes. Science gave us the means to eradicate population pressure, but now it will give me our salvation, I know it will. In the end, science will prevail.

With a sense of finality, I conclude my preparations. There is nowhere to go but forward.

I pull the switch.

Lightning arcs between electrodes attached to Lavenza's chest. Her muscles spasm, firing randomly. The thick leather restraints dig into her flesh. It is as if a demon has possessed her.

The tubes writhe, forcing chemicals into her body. A green pallor begins to creep over her porcelain complexion. Blue veins thrust from her skin, crawling across her face and down her arms. The hideous alterations make me shiver, but I press on. We're so close.

To my relief, the monitors flash. Optimum levels reached. I cut the power and turn off the chest pumps, willing her heart to accept the stimulants.

Her chest heaves. I stumble back as her eyes flicker open.

"I've done it!" I cry, the realization of my accomplishment crashing in upon me. I, Dr. Voxstein, have led The New Evolution out of the darkness and into a time when we will be conquerors over the grave!

With Lavenza at my side, I can atone for my mistakes. I can become the man she wanted me to be. The man she believed I could be when she begged me to abandon my pursuits and run away with her.

An animalistic scream tears from Lavenza's mouth, cutting my jubilation short.

"I'm sorry, darling, I didn't mean to scare you. I'm sure

this must be a shock." I surge forward to comfort her, but an angry growl vibrates in her throat, halting my steps. "Dearest, it's me." I reach my hand towards her.

The restraints snap like rotten twine. Lavenza leaps from the table, knocks me into the monitors, and pins me to the ground. Her eyes flash rage as she claws at the tubing in her chest—all that restrains her.

"Please, Lavenza! You mustn't!"

Gnashing her teeth, she stretches her hands over my throat and down on my windpipe. I fight back and kick her off before rushing toward the emergency button on the other side of the glass partition. My fingers reach it, sealing off the lab seconds before she begins beating and clawing on the glass.

Something is terribly wrong. With the protective barrier between us, I can look into her eyes. I see the absence of a soul. That same absence I see in my mirror every morning ...

This is not the woman whose love can save me. Her passion for life is gone, just like my will to live.

I have failed.

My mind shuts down. I reach for the fatal green switches below the emergency seal button and flip them. The pumps begin to hiss, feeding odorless poison into both the lab and the sealed chamber where I slump to my knees.

I created a monster. But not the one gulping for air, frightened and alone on the other side of the barrier.

Now no one is left to save this monster.

I breathe deeply, filling my lungs with toxins, unable to watch her suffer any longer.

All hail The New Evolution—

My legacy.

My curse.

My monster.

I'D DO ANYTHING
Lorelei Jensen

Julianna Volsaire, the most sought-after woman in all aristocratic society, sat on the settee in her dearest companion's private study. Lukas called for her earlier that week, but with running the duchy in her father's place, Julianna could only slip away for a couple of hours.

An oak desk sat in front of large bay windows, and bookshelves filled with documents and literature lined the walls. The plush red settee Julianna sat on was placed across from a comfortable chair she had spent many hours in, helping Lukas with paperwork and comforting him when things went wrong at his home.

A maid brought in tea and sweets, curtseying before she poured the wonderful smelling drink into a beautifully rose painted cup. Milk followed. The black tea swirled into a warm brown. Many small cakes complemented the tea. Julianna sighed happily.

Lukas walked over and sat across from her. Her heart fluttered when his stormy grey eyes met with her black ones. She carefully tucked her black curls behind her ear before placing her hands around the teacup in order to hide how badly her hands shook. A little tea splashed onto her gloves.

His excitement made her nervous.

"I wanted to tell you the news in person," Lukas purred in his rich melodic voice.

Julianna smiled. "What a pleasure."

Brushing his brown hair from out of his face, Lukas pulled out a fancy letter, most likely an invitation. Julianna's heart plummeted as he handed her the paper. The white stationary was decorated with silver and red flowers.

"I'm getting married," he said excitedly.

Julianna stiffened. Her posture remained perfect despite her desire to whither up like the dying flower of society that she was. Each already broken sliver of her heart sank into the pit of her stomach. Her smile blossomed even more beautifully than before. She clasped her hands together.

"Congratulations, Lukas." Her voice sounded too cheery, even to her own ears. "She must be very lovely. Would you give me the honor of knowing her name?"

"It is Baron Lumos's daughter, Lady Marie."

Anger fluttered around the broken pieces. Lady Marie, a sweet and gentle-looking young lady, had gotten into the habit of trying to take what belonged to Julianna. First, the position of the flower of society was threatened when Marie attacked Julianna for speaking to someone with a fiancé. The man was Count Lagran's son, Julianna's aide. The second incident was when Marie tried to make Julianna step down from society by spreading unrealistic rumors about her. They were easily disproved but high society held onto rumors for as long as they could. Finally, Marie stole the love of her life.

How Marie found out was beyond Julianna, but it stung. She loved Lukas more than anything in the world. Everything she did was for him. She took over the position of heir of the duchy so he could live comfortably. Her information business helped him with work from the royal family while she set all trends with the clothing store her family ran.

Julianna looked at the ornate grandfather clock. She arranged her schedule so that she could stay for another hour and be able to finish the last bit of work for today, but her broken heart said otherwise. She smiled, tilting her head to make it look apologetic. "I must go back. Thank you for telling me the news. Congratulations on your engagement. I wish you all the happiness in the world."

Julianna got up before Lukas could say a word. She let herself out, hoping Lukas would come after her. Her guard helped her into her carriage. Lukas waved at her from the door but didn't follow. His grin brightened when she raised her hand.

"Send Louis to my office when we arrive," Julianna commanded with her cheerful facade crumbling into something much darker.

Marie was right when she tried to defame Julianna by calling her villain; there were few people she acted kind to, Lukas being one of them. All the nobles were wrapped around her finger. Her information guild could and would bring destruction to any family name.

The servants called Julianna the "Queen of the Night" for a reason. Behind her beautiful exterior laid a monster, or so they said. Julianna got what she wanted when she wanted, and if it was impossible for her to get what she wanted, she would ruin it for anyone else.

The hour ride home shook all her servants. TVolsaire acted like a villain. He was the second most powerful man in the kingdom. Even the crown prince had to listen to her father.

"Young Earl Bolvaille must have disappointed you," he pointed out.

Julianna smiled. The servants shivered at the cruelty and wickedness in her eyes. All of them knew she would never harm them or their families, but fear struck their souls regardless. The elderly butler, Louis, offered the future duchess his arm.

"You called for me?"

"Ready my men."

Julianna sat on her throne in her dungeon. Marie huddled on the cold cobble floor. Water ran between the grout of each stone. The only light was the flickering of a single torch, barely illuminating the room. Julianna wore her hair down. Her red dress brought out the darkness in her eyes. She gently pulled Marie's chin.

"You disappointed me, Lady Marie. I expected more from you. Stealing what belongs to me is very low," Julianna whispered. "Especially when you already have the crown prince."

Marie stared at her with disgust. Her blue eyes shone with determination. Julianna patted her cheek endearingly.

"Did you like the gifts I sent you?" Julianna dropped papers on the floor and Marie read them. Julianna imagined her paling at the words. "It would be a tragedy if the villain got a hold of your son, or if the crown prince found out that his lover hid their child from him. Didn't he kill the last woman who birthed his heir?"

"You wouldn't dare," Marie spat. "The Crown Prince would have you executed too. You don't even know where the child is."

Julianna laughed. "You think I wouldn't know where someone was? On top of all that, you believe the crown prince can touch me. What a fool. I'll teach you some history. At the founding of the nation, my family had a pact made with the royal family: their mistake. The magic that binds the royal family and the Volsaire lineage is everlasting. Elvish magic, I believe. Your son is bound to me, and his father is my slave. Abandoning your child was really your own fault. There were better ways to keep him safe, you know? Sending him where you cannot keep track of his movements was a bad move.

Julianna gestured to one of her men. The captain of her guard carried a small child into the dungeon. As soon as the boy saw Julianna, he ran to her and buried his face in her skirts. Despite being the spitting image of Marie, little Owen loved his mother, Julianna.

"Mama, who is this lady?" Owen asked.

Julianna smirked. "No one important. Now, why is my dearest child still awake?"

"I wanted to sleep in your room," he said shyly.

Julianna picked him up and kissed his cheek, staring at Maria as she did so. Amusement twinkled in Julianna's eyes as Marie gawked at her. "Let me finish my work."

The guard took Owen away as Julianna sat back on her throne. "Now do what I say, and you and my child will be safe."

Marie whimpered. The life died in her eyes and Julianna filled with satisfaction. Marie nodded slowly so Julianna snapped her fingers. One of her employees handed her a paper.

"Now if you'll sign here."

Julianna sat on the settee in her dearest companion's private study. Owen climbed in her lap as she worked on paperwork for Lukas. A month had passed since Marie suddenly went missing. One letter explaining she had to leave and wanted to break off their engagement arrived at Lukas's home.

Lukas cried in Julianna's shoulder for quite a while after he read the letter. She pitied him, but Marie was not for him. There was only one person good enough for Lukas, only one who loved him more than anything.

Julianna smiled. Soon, Lukas would become hers and hers alone. After all, she had removed all the pests in his life.

KEROS
D. A. Randall

When she first arrived at Angelino's Italian Grille, Vicki Edgerton sat tall in her chair, eagerly awaiting her husband's arrival. The lit candle danced in the center of the table while their gold-etched dinner plates gleamed, reflecting the roaring blaze from the brick fireplace embedded in the far wall. Through the full-length picture window, she could see the black waves of the lake outside twinkling beneath the moonlight. Heart-shaped decorations, flowers, and lace curtains framed the window and the corners of the room, along with the hum of whispered conversations from lovers, enjoying their Valentine's Day dinner.

Vicki wore a red satin dress she had trouble breathing in, along with her cherished sapphire necklace. From the moment Mal had given it to her, she knew she had found her soulmate. So she gave no thought to applying the perfect amount of rouge and eyeshadow and getting her hair done that afternoon. She used to consider such things an extravagant waste. But love makes a person feel alive and full of energy, to do whatever it takes to sustain that love. Not that Mal ever needed much encouragement.

Though lately, he seemed less eager to kiss her the instant

he came home, and more forgetful of their plans together. Thankfully, it would all be different tonight, on this night when everyone celebrated their burning love.

If only he would call or text. It had been over an hour.

Whatever the reason, it had to be important. She only hoped he was all right. And that once he finally glimpsed her crushing dress and brilliant necklace, he would be more than satisfied.

She sipped her water, then set it beside the untouched wine glass. All around her, women leaned close to their men, smiling, laughing, sharing whispered conversations. She took another sip.

She thought she saw Mal enter across the room. But it was a much taller man, whose well-cut navy suit contained a beefy chest and broad shoulders, topped by a full head of striking blond hair. How could she have mistaken him, even at a glance, for her five-foot husband's dark complexion and hunching shoulders?

She found herself staring at the blond man. His strong cheeks. His piercing eyes.

Vicki put a hand over her mouth. What on earth was she thinking? She was married to the most wonderful, most attractive man in the universe. And here she sat gawking like a schoolgirl.

And yet ...

She imagined herself seizing the blond stranger and kissing him full on the lips. Pictured him striding to her table to lift her into his powerful arms and whisk her away for a weekend in Venice, or perhaps Sweden.

Stop it, she ordered herself. Though she couldn't resist a final glance at the statuesque figure. She had never seen anyone so beautiful, with such brilliant blue eyes.

Which turned to stare directly at her.

Vicki glanced down, ashamed.

When she looked back, he was still staring, with a powerful gaze that seemed to speak to her. Telling her something she desperately needed to hear with his commanding eyes.

Vicki shuddered, forcing herself to turn away. What was wrong with her? She hadn't even looked at another man for six years. After being swept up in her whirlwind romance and wedding to Mal, she had never needed another man. And she never would.

Until this hypnotic stranger.

She straightened, folding her hands on the table. Mal would show up any moment. She would devote her attention to him and him alone. As soon as he arrived.

Mal entered at a brisk pace and Vicki nearly gasped with relief as he marched toward her.

The blond stranger stepped right up to Mal, who stopped mid-stride and gaped as if he had met the Grim Reaper.

The blond man addressed him with hostile eyes, clenching his large fists. Mal shook his head and raised his hands as the man loomed over him. Vicki wondered if she should call the manager, or the police.

Mal indicated Vicki's table and started toward her again. The blond man followed. Vicki watched the two men approach, her heartbeat and temperature rising.

"Hey, sorry I'm late," Mal greeted, stepping around the table to kiss her cheek. "Got tied up at work. Uh, this is Kyle, a friend of mine."

She stood and smiled, extending a quivering hand. As if

she had not been eyeing the man at all. "Hello, Kyle. I'm Vicki."

He took her hand, meeting her gaze in a way that seemed both harsh and compassionate. "Pleased to meet you, Victoria."

Feeling her hand tremble in his, she withdrew it. "People usually just call me Vicki. Mal used to call me Victoria, but he hasn't for a while."

The stranger kept staring.

"Kyle and I had business a while back," Mal explained. "But we made arrangements, and everything was settled. So there's nothing more to talk about."

"There will be, if you proceed," the man said, his voice a slow rumble of thunder. This stranger could command legions, without even shouting.

"Look," Mal said. "Vicki and I need to talk in private, if you don't mind."

"I do," the man pressed.

"Mal?" Vicki asked, her voice rising. "What's going on?"

The towering man focused his stare on Mal. "Tell her your intentions," he ordered.

Vicki trembled at the imposing stranger. What business did this man have with Mal?

Mal lowered his head, his lips tightening. "Listen, Vicki. I kinda need that necklace back."

The blood drained from her cheeks. "... What?"

"The necklace you're wearing. I need it back."

She clutched the sapphire to her chest. "But ... this was a gift. You said this represented the two of us. That we were meant to be together forever."

"Yeah, that's just it. We're not."

She felt her insides turn to ice. "We're not ... what?"

"Meant to be together. Look, I've found someone. Her name's Laticia. She's just ... she's the one for me, that's all. We met a few months ago and started talking, and I realized she's who I'm meant to be with."

"You mean she's the one you have now chosen," the blond man corrected, forcing his way into their conversation.

"Whatever," Mal said. "Look, Vicki, I know this is hard. But once you give me the necklace, you'll see things differently, believe me."

Vicki gaped at him, trying to understand. He seemed like a foreigner speaking an unintelligible language. "What are you talking about? You expect me to turn over the symbol of our love for the past six years? So you can, what? Give it to some woman you met a few months ago?"

"Yeah, that's why I need it," Mal said matter-of-factly. As if he expected her to simply accept it.

She cringed as she stared at him. The man she had loved, suddenly transforming into some hideous insect with no remorse, no conscience. "No," she said, hoping to make her disgust clear. "You can't give my necklace to someone else."

"But you don't need it anymore." Mal reached across the table as if he meant to claw at her throat. "You said yourself, it's a symbol of our love. And that's gone. Why keep that painful reminder? I can give it to somebody who can use it."

She shoved her chair back in horror. She felt herself quivering as tears started. "If this is what you really want, then give her some other bauble. Something cheap, to symbolize *your* love! Why do you need my necklace?"

"Because it's not yours, or his," the blond man said with

inappropriate calm. "It belongs to me."

Vicki looked up, blinking through tears. "What?"

"Ignore him, Vicki. He's trying to keep me on the hook for something that no longer concerns him."

The man leaned into Mal's face. "It concerns me more than you know, Malcolm. You insisted Victoria was the one you desired above all others, and I gave her to you. Then you dare to choose another!" He seized Mal by his shirt lapels and yanked him from his chair, lifting him to his enraged face. Mal hung there like a frightened puppy before a scolding master.

Vicki jumped from her chair. "Stop! Put him down! Or I'll—Wait." She stared at the two men. At her beloved Mal, dangling in the grip of this strange Adonis. "You—*gave* me to him?"

"Yes," the man said, his eyes burning into Mal's.

"Put him down," she said quietly.

The blond man turned to Vicki, and his temper seemed to cool slightly. He set Mal back down, to slump into his chair.

"My name is Keros," the man said, sneering at Mal. "Not 'Kyle.' Long ago, Malcolm fell in love with you, but you took no notice of him."

"Not at first," she admitted. "But when he gave me this necklace, I realized how much he cared for me. That he was sincere and devoted, exactly the sort of man I had been waiting for my entire life."

"That is what you were meant to believe," Keros said bluntly. "The sapphire in that necklace contains part of my essence. My passion. The passion you now feel for your husband."

Mal nearly lunged across the table, waving off the man's words with a smile. "Vicki, don't listen to this guy. Let's you and me go somewhere private and hash this whole thing out."

"Silence, liar!" Keros ordered him. Mal raised his hands over his head, as if shielding himself from a vicious blow. Keros returned his attention to Vicki. "Like you, I believed Malcolm's desires to be sincere. Perhaps they were. But his desires have now changed."

Vicki fondled the gem in the heart of her necklace. "You're telling me this sapphire ... makes me love him?"

Keros shook his head. "Love cannot be forced. The sapphire simply gives full vent to your passion, allowing you to see Malcolm's best qualities, ignoring all other traits. So you could easily choose to love him."

Vicki felt her cheek twitching. She fumbled for the glass of water and downed the rest of it, then reached for the pitcher to pour out more. She stared at Mal, nervous and hunching. And suddenly believed it. She had grown to love him, yes. But what could have drawn her to him at first? Or made her idolize him for the past six years, as if he could do no wrong? To fall so deeply for a man who could casually shun her for another woman—she had to have been under some kind of spell.

Which had just been broken.

"All these years ..." she hissed quietly. She narrowed her eyes at the blond man. "How? Who are you?"

"As I said, I am Keros. Your lore refers to me as 'Cupid'."

Vicki blinked, trying to process what he was saying. "Cupid," she repeated dully. "Our entire marriage, I've been struck by Cupid's arrow."

Keros soured. "A fanciful way that your race describes it, but yes. I ignited your passion for Mal, and you kept it alive all these years, focusing on all that attracts you while downplaying his faults."

Vicki nodded slowly. "Which is what love does, doesn't it?"

"I did not infuse you with love," Keros said, like a teacher correcting a student. "I infused you with passion. A fire lit from a spark of attraction. Love is the hearth that surrounds that fire. Passion drew you to Malcolm, but the love is your own."

"Look, we had a deal," Mal broke in. "You said you'd help me find the woman I love. I thought it was Vicki, but now I realize it's someone else."

Keros whirled on him, his face flaring with rage. "You act as if you have reached the end of a quest and found genuine treasure. You are merely wandering, groping in the darkness for something you can never have, because you cannot appreciate what you have already received. Love is not a mindless quest, discovered by random chance. It is a decision to devote yourself to one person for life. Vicki offered you her passion, but you spurned her love for that of a stranger."

"Hey, I'm not spurning anything. It just grew old, you know? So I need to—"

Vicki tossed the contents of her glass onto Mal's face. She watched him squeeze his eyes shut at the cold water dousing his thinning hair. "Get out," she ordered him. "Shut up and get out."

Mal collected himself for a moment, as water dripped off his sharp nose. Women from the surrounding crowd gasped, as all eyes turned toward the shocking scene. Mal rose slowly and faced Keros. "You can see it's over, right? You want something to do? Try helping her. I mean, she's free to choose another now, too, right?"

He turned without another word or a glance back, as he strode out of the restaurant and out of sight.

Vicki watched him leave, anger sizzling through her pores and her hollowed heart. Six years, reduced to ashes in under five minutes.

Happy Valentine's Day.

She returned the stares of onlookers, observing the collapse of her marriage, like people watching an airplane full of passengers explode. Vicki stared down at the provocative satin dress she had worn, just for Mal. The man who had longed for her affection so desperately that he imprisoned her mind and soul, until tonight. Now she was free.

Free to choose another.

She wrinkled her nose and looked up. "What did Mal say? I'm free to choose another?"

"Yes," Keros said in a mournful tone of sympathy. "Your necklace holds the same power for you that it held for Malcolm. When you are ready, you can instill that passion in someone else. Someone you can truly love, if that is your desire."

Vicki mulled over his words. Like a person busying herself with funeral arrangements while trying to make sense of her tragic loss. Her marriage had dissolved into nothing, and this handsome stranger was suggesting she plan out her next move. "I can't think about any of that now. I just want to go home."

Keros folded his hands in front of him. "I understand. I am grieved by what Malcolm did to you."

She stared up at him, wondering whether to appreciate his kindness or loathe him for enabling her husband's deception. "Why did you come tonight? Have you been checking up on him—on me—all this time?"

Keros shook his head. "I am connected to each part of me that has been shared throughout your world. I felt something amiss, something hollow, in the sapphire you bear. So I sought it out. On this annual celebration of love that you mortals have created, I spied Malcolm, bestowing his affections on another woman."

Victoria swallowed hard. Then wrinkled her brow. "How did you know it wasn't me?"

He lowered his eyes, then glanced away. "I remembered you from before. It was clear that Malcolm had abused my gift."

"A gift," Vicki sneered. "I was like a new puppy, complete with a leash and collar."

His eyes popped, his nostrils flaring like a bull's. "Do not belittle yourself. You are a woman full of passion, to be shared with a man who deserves you. Malcolm's love was short-lived. Your passion for him, however, was steadfast. Had he remained faithful, both of your desires would have been fulfilled for your entire lives. That is not slavery. That is devotion."

Vicki wanted to argue, to tell him he had violated her and robbed her of her choice. But he was right. She had loved Malcolm. Still loved him, after everything he had done. Her shoulders seized up and began to tremble. She felt herself collapsing inward as she doubled over with wrenching sobs.

Keros was instantly beside her on one knee, his large arms surrounding her and pulling her close. "I am so sorry,

Victoria. No creature should be treated this way."

She clung to his arm, feeling his mighty strength, his warmth. "What are you? Where did you get this power?"

"From the one who empowers all things and gives life to all on this planet. I was sent to instill passion, to stir the flames of desire for deep love between humans. I am allowed to choose those on whom I bestow it." He ground his teeth, his muscles tensing. "I made a foolish choice with Malcolm, but I am no longer bound to assist him. I will now act as his enemy."

Vicki jerked upright. "There's no need for that."

He studied her. "You still care for him."

She couldn't deny it. "I shouldn't, but I do. I did love him. But I don't even know who he is now. Like you said— he's made plans with someone else." She stared into his brilliant blue eyes, stunned by how beautiful he was. Stunned by everything she had lost in a matter of minutes. "Keros. Would you please take me home?"

The blond man stared at her.

"I got a ride here," she said. "But I'm hoping you have a car?"

His stare finally relented. "I do." He stood and stretched his hand toward her, like a fireman's ladder extending into a burning building. She took it and let him help her to her feet, latching onto his arm as he escorted her from the restaurant and the crowd of nosy spectators. Away from the blistered, smoking remains of her abandoned marriage.

And out into the cool night air. They had gathered her matching satin shawl from the coat room, and she drew it closer about her shoulders as the light wind tickled her cheeks. The street was still damp from the afternoon rain. Vicki examined her reflection in a puddle below the sidewalk curb. A pretty woman in a fiery scarlet dress and shawl, framed in a distorted puddle of muddy water. Until fifteen minutes ago, she had seen her marriage as a beautiful jewel to treasure. Now she saw nothing but shame and ugliness.

Keros led her across the street. He slowed his pace behind a bright red Maserati, its waxed frame glistening beneath a streetlamp. Vicki froze, awestruck.

Keros strode to the passenger door and opened it for her. She tugged her shawl closer around her shoulders and eased herself in. The seat was soft and warm, the interior roomy and luxurious, set at the perfect temperature. She had never felt so relaxed in a car, like she could rest here for hours.

Keros sat behind the wheel and cast those hypnotic eyes on her. "Are you comfortable?"

She almost laughed. "Very. I've never been in a car like this before. It's perfect."

"I'm glad it pleases you."

The engine purred to life, and they were soon cruising past the city lights reflected on the lake, in the smoothest ride Vicki had ever experienced.

"You probably know I've always dreamed of riding in a car like this. I suppose every girl dreams of a beautiful sports car, but this is exactly what I've always wished for."

He remained stoic as he drove. "Every woman has different longings. But I am familiar with yours. Delights such as peppermint bark."

Vicki blinked in surprise. "I love peppermint bark. You can never find any after Christmas, but I—"

"You may take some from the glove compartment."

Her throat went dry. Then began to salivate with anticipation, though she wondered if he was joking. She yanked open the glove compartment.

Inside were about twenty small candies in red-and-white striped wrappers. Vicki took one and examined it. Peppermint bark. As promised.

She peeled it open and the minty fragrance filled her nostrils. She bit into the candy, letting the chocolate and peppermint flavors shoot into her mouth. It was the most magnificent peppermint bark she had ever tasted. "This is fantastic," she said, immediately embarrassed by her silly understatement. "How did you do that?"

"What a person can do is less important than why he does it," Keros said.

Vicki thought about that. Mal had controlled her like a puppet, while he remained free to switch his own feelings on and off. The more she thought about it, the more it steamed her. Even if he had brainwashed her, they could have loved one another forever. If only he had stayed.

A minute later, the angled incline brought Vicki out of her private rage as the Maserati climbed into her driveway. She stared up at the house she still shared with Mal. A house that was no longer a home. "Would you come inside for a few minutes?" she asked.

His eyes locked on hers. "That might not be prudent."

Vicki stiffened her chin. "My husband of six years is leaving me for someone else, after forcing me to love him and him alone. Something you helped him do. All I'm asking you to do is keep me company for a few more minutes. Please."

He kept studying her as they sat in silence. "All right," he said at last. He switched off the ignition and climbed out.

Instead of moving, Vicki waited for him to open the door for her. Knowing he would treat her like a princess, even if it was only for a short while. As he opened the door, she settled her hand into his, letting him help her up once more. "Thank you," she said.

She unlocked the front door and led him into the kitchen, turning on lights as she went. She took a filtration pitcher from the refrigerator. "Would you like some water?"

"Thank you, yes," he said quickly.

She jerked. It was the first thing he had accepted from her without hesitation. She poured two glasses full and handed him one, before putting the pitcher away. He sipped his water quickly and closed his eyes. Was Keros ... nervous around her?

He opened his eyes and met her gaze. She began to study him, the way he had studied her. "So you're the god of love," she said, feeling strangely lighthearted. "I always pictured you as a fat little cherub with a bow and arrow, flying around in a toga."

Keros frowned. "That is all very amusing on a greeting card, but it is not what I look like."

"And I'm glad." Vicki relaxed against the counter as though she had enjoyed a few glasses of wine. "Though you wouldn't look bad in a toga."

He paused a moment. Then took a slow sip of water.

Vicki blinked. What was happening to her? She was actually flirting with this man! Yet she felt no real shame in it. Why should she, after what Mal had done, taking that sapphire of passion from Keros and—

Of course. The sapphire stirred up her passion for Mal, but it was part of Keros himself. His own deep passion, here in her kitchen, was now stirring up her feelings for him. And yet ... she didn't mind at all.

Keros stared into his glass. "I am a Mosai. What you have come to know as a Muse. We infuse passion into your species. And we seek those we can entrust to direct that passion toward beautiful pursuits. Malcolm burned with desire for you, eager to claim you as his own, and to care for you all his days. I believed him. Especially when I saw you for myself. How could any man fail to fall in love with you?"

Vicki's mouth parted. Keros glanced up, then stepped away with his back to her. "I helped him as I have helped other humans, so that they could create families of peace, enjoying the one they loved and the children they bore. To cease envying their neighbors or other nations and find contentment." He turned to face her. "I truly believed Malcolm would love you forever."

Vicki stepped closer, trying to peer into his soul. Into the centuries that he had lived through. "You said I'm free to choose another. How would I do that?"

He stared into his glass, frowning. "Are you so eager to secure another lover?"

"Perhaps."

Keros sighed. "The necklace can be molded into anything you wish. A ring or a watch, to give to the man you desire. If I trust your passion to be sincere, and there is potential for that man to return your love, the sapphire will ensure that he burns with passion for you."

Vicki clutched her necklace. It had been such a part of her for six years. Yet it was no longer a cherished object, or even a fond memory. It had become a mere tool to secure her future. She lifted it from her neck and held it out for him. "Make this into a medallion. Something a man would be proud to wear."

He soured. "Always so temporary," he said, stepping toward her to lift the sapphire in his hands, as if admiring it. Perhaps recalling how he first fashioned it for her to wear, at Mal's request. He pursed his thick lips with distaste, then closed his fist around the sapphire. Within his palm, the sapphire glowed with a fiery light. Keros set it on the counter and removed his hand to reveal a sparkling ruby medallion. He shook his head. "You humans flit from one companion to another, as if you were birds. Only you never wish to nest."

Vicki shook her head, taking the medallion. "You're talking about Mal, not me. I want a relationship that will last."

"I speak of the human race. Fickle, ungrateful and immature. Are you even seeking love, or merely revenge?"

Vicki met his cold gaze with a firm resolve. "I admit, I'm angry and hurt. But I deserve something—and someone—far better than Mal."

"Yes, you do. But like Malcolm, you now rush after something you hope to see or feel or otherwise imagine, deceiving yourself into believing you love someone. Love is not a fleeting emotion, woman. It is a decision. Once made, nothing can truly break it. Your vows are as meaningless as his, whether or not you confess it."

Vicki chewed her lip. There was no convincing this man. Fortunately, she didn't need to. "Will this medallion work on anyone?"

Keros heaved another disappointed sigh. "Yes."

Vicki whetted her lips and met his eyes, that sea of commanding blue. "Then ... I choose you."

Keros held her gaze a moment longer, with widening eyes. All his majestic beauty, all his fierce passion, seemed ready to explode. "Do not be rash, woman. You do not know me."

"What more do I need to know? You're the embodiment of love and passion. You want the best for all people, and for me." She stepped closer to him, noticing with pleasure that he took a half step back. She continued to advance on him as he finally stood in place, nearly backed against the wall. "You want so much for us. To help us find peace and true love. But you have no outlet for your own passion. You must get lonely." She took his enormous hand in hers. "I'm attractive, aren't I? I'm no goddess. But I could persuade you to love me. Couldn't I?" She stood directly before him, her toes touching his.

She watched him slowly lift his head. Taking in her long legs and full curves that pressed against the tight satin dress. Admiring the auburn hair that spilled in waves over her shoulders. His lips parted. "Yes," he admitted, as if releasing a tremendous weight. "I could easily be ... persuaded."

"Then we could satisfy one another, you and I."

"Take care, woman," he warned. "Unrestrained passion is dangerous. I am no mortal. And once you have chosen—"

"I've already chosen," she said. "I'm going to possess the most handsome, most powerful, most passionate man in the universe. Someone who can provide for me, and who will never grow tired of me, thanks to this little medallion you'll be wearing."

She stood on her tiptoes and strung the pendant over his feathery blond head, as Keros shut his eyes to receive it. He stood in tense silence, as if fighting a fierce inner struggle.

Perhaps he could not accept this love, that someone would truly want him. Not only for his beauty, but for everything that he was. His kindness and compassion. The embodiment of love itself. She wasn't being rash. She had found what she had been seeking her entire life, and she had found it in a single evening.

"Whoa, what's this about?" Mal snarled as he stepped into the kitchen. Vicki hadn't even heard the front door open. Mal's eyes flashed on Keros, like a mouse challenging a lion. "I said you could help her find somebody, not steal that necklace. I told you I need that back. Now give it!"

Mal grabbed at the medallion on the towering man's neck.

Keros seized his wrist. Then glared at him, his eyes glowing with wild light. The light became a fire that roared to life and spewed twin flames directly at Mal. Vicki screamed in horror as Mal gasped, the fire encircling his entire body to lick up his skin and bones. Popping and sizzling and smoking with sickening intensity, until the blaze devoured him whole, leaving a pile of ash where Vicki's devious husband had been.

Keros lifted her into his massive arms, his eyes aflame with passion, as her heart beat madly with terror. The last flickers from Mal's smoldering ashes reflected brilliantly in the golden pendant hanging from Keros' broad neck.

He smiled at her. "Alone at last, my love."

ACKNOWLEDGEMENTS

Who best to start the acknowledgements with other than the authors themselves?

What. An. Incredible. Cast. How was I so lucky that so many amazingly talented authors wanted to be a part of this publication? Not only are their stories rich, complex, and full of the emotion I was looking for, but they're each wonderful individuals I've had the pleasure of getting to know a bit better. Special thanks to each and every one of you. Of course, this anthology couldn't have gone anywhere without you, and *with* you, it will go amazing places. Thank you!

Thank you to Nathaniel Lucombe and R.C. Lloyd for being my two biggest hype-men while releasing this second edition of Aphotic Love! This anthology has been an incredible journey all the way from step one, and they've done so much to support me. I couldn't be more grateful for having them in my corner.

Of course, I have to thank YOU the reader for even picking this book up and reading it. No book would be anything without its audience and those who read it and hold it dear to their hearts. I hope you have enjoyed this collection and walked away with a deeper comprehension of what romantic love can be.

—*Effie Joe Stock*

Authors

Effie Joe Stock

Effie Joe Stock is the author of The Shadows of Light series, creator of the world Rasa, and head of Dragon Bone Publishing. When she's not slaving away in front of her computer, you can find her playing music, studying psychology, theology, or philosophy, playing fantasy RPG video games, riding motorcycles, or hanging out with her farm animals. Her publishing journey only just beginning, Stock looks forward to the release of the rest of her fantasy series along with other Dragon Bone titles.

Website: www.effiejoestock.com
Instagram: @effie.joe.stock.author
YouTube: Effie Joe Stock

AJ Skelly

AJ Skelly is an author, bookish business owner, and lover of all things fantasy, medieval, and fairy-tale-romance. And werewolves. She has a serious soft spot for them. You can read all about them in The Wolves of Rock Falls series. As an avid life-long reader and a former high school English teacher, she's always been fascinated with the written word. She lives with her husband, children, and many imaginary friends who often find their way into her stories. They all drink copious amounts of tea together and stay up reading far later than they should.

Instagram: @a.j.skelly & @books.and.whimsy
Facebook: AJ Skelly
Website: www.ajskelly.com

Anna Augustine

Anna Augustine has always loved to tell stories that share the love of God through them. When her mom forced her to write a short story for English one year, she discovered how fun the written word can be and has been writing ever since. She lives with her family of eight in a small, midwestern town with two dogs and a whole lot of crazy.

She is the author of "When You Found Me" a collection of three novellas about three princes and the women they fall in love with. She has also had a flash fiction piece published with Go Havok.

When she's not writing, Anna is either working as a teacher's aide in her local elementary school, going to school to someday be a kindergarten teacher, taking photos for her bookstagram, or trying to put a dent in her never ending to be read pile.

Follow Anna on Instagram: @anna_augustine_author

Adella Quick

Adella Quick is an aspiring author from southern Ontario and is currently working on her first novel. Her love for writing poetry began in high school and she is thrilled to have a poem from her early writing days included in this anthology. In her spare time, other than writing, Adella can be found crocheting, sewing or reading. She also loves spending time with her husband and daughters, being active, and cuddling her cats.

Anne J. Hill

Anne J. Hill is an author who enjoys writing fantasy for all ages. Her love of words has also led to her career as a freelance writer and editor. She spends her days dreaming up fantastical realms, talking out loud to the characters in her head, and rearranging her personal library, which has been affectionately dubbed the "Book Dungeon."

Where to find Anne:
www.annejhill.com or
@anne.j.hill.editing on Instagram

Annie Kay

Annie is an aspiring author and accidental poet. She began writing poetry as an outlet, which quickly became a passion. She wishes to become a middle school English teacher after graduating in May. During her free time, you can catch Annie reading, bullet journaling, embroidering, and playing with her beloved cat, Louis.

You can find her on Instagram at @anniekay.reads

Beka Gremikova

Beka Gremikova writes folkloric fantasy from her little nook in the Ottawa Valley, Ontario, Canada. Her flash fiction can be found on Havok Publishing's website and in several of their anthologies (*Bingeworthy*, *Sensational*, and *Prismatic*). She has also been featured in the collections *Whitstead Harvestide*, *Moonlight and Claws*, *What Darkness Fears*, *A Kind of Death*, and *Faces to the Sun*. When she's not travelling, playing video games, or sketching, she's often curled up in a corner with a mystery novel. Currently, she's plotting a plethora of fairy tale retellings and planning to release her dark fantasy thriller short, "Perchance to Dream," in March 2022.

Newsletter/ Website: https://bekagremikova.com/
Instagram: https://www.instagram.com/beka.gremikova/
Facebook: https://www.facebook.com/bekagremikova/
Twitter: https://twitter.com/DreamofWriting

Betsy Smith

Betsy Smith has been hopelessly obsessed with fantasy and magic for many years and spends her time daydreaming about other worlds that will never exist. She is an aspiring poet and author, who will one day get around to finishing her trilogy (eventually). Betsy loves romance and fantasy and can frequently be found losing her mind over a book couple in the corner of a room. She also, regrettably, enjoys breaking her own heart through writing about tragic lovers and twisted destinies.

Instagram: @betsy.k.smith

Cassandra Hamm

Cassandra Hamm is a psychology nerd, art collector, jigsaw puzzler, and hopeless romantic who spends most of her time lost in another world. She is passionately anti-abuse and writes about toxic relationships both to show people that they aren't alone and to reveal the factors that keep people trapped in unhealthy situations. Her work appears in various anthologies, including several of Havok Publishing's collections, *Warriors Against the Storm*, *When Your Beauty is the Beast*, *The Depths We'll Go To*, and *Aphotic Love*.

Website: https://cassandrahamm.com/

Instagram: https://www.instagram.com/cassandrahammwrites/

Facebook: https://www.facebook.com/CassandraHammAuthor

Cerynn McCain

Cerynn McCain has been writing since she was a child, weaving as many stories as she can from the tales her imaginary friends tell her. She grew up curled in a nest of art supplies and yarn, and has always found a creative answer to every challenge thrown at her. Right now she lives on the beautiful Lake Chelan with her husband and two cat babies, writing her stories and moonlighting as a librarian in her spare time. Her love of creative arts follows her through every aspect of her life, and her husband constantly has to pull her back to earth when her daydreams take over. And, when all is said and done, she'd have it no other way.

D.A. Randall

D.A. Randall is the fantasy and paranormal thriller pen name of Randall Allen Dunn, who was raised on a steady diet of Star Trek and The Twilight Zone before pursuing his studies of Buffy, the Vampire Slayer, *Harry Potter, The Lunar Chronicles*, Richard Matheson, H.G. Wells, Edgar Allan Poe, and Doctor Who.

He has taught writing, acting, and storytelling techniques to teens and adults. He now writes fantasy and paranormal thrillers that read like blockbuster movies. Action-packed, fast-paced & fun, with larger-than-life heroes wrestling with moral dilemmas and diabolical villains. He publishes Character Entertainment stories that build character through fiction, demonstrating courage, friendship, acceptance, faith, and self-sacrifice.

You can find his books online, and subscribe to his newsletter for upcoming releases at www.RandallAllenDunn.com.

Emily Anne

Emily Anne is an avid reader who has always loved telling stories as much as reading them. On any given day you can find her with a snack and her nose in a book. She is an animal lover , and is trying to convince her family she needs a horse . When she is not reading or writing , she is often crocheting, cuddling her fur babies, or watching black and white movies. Emily is currently trying to collect enough books to make her bedroom a library.

You can connect with her on Instagram @emilyannecreates

Everly Haywood

Everly Haywood imagines herself to be a shieldmaiden of great prowess ... but you're more likely to find her in a dusty library than on the battlefield slaying monsters from the underworld. She seeks to combine dark fantasy worlds with clean, sweet romance. She loves strong but sweet leading ladies and smoldering, tragic heroes. She lives in the country with her husband, two daughters and their protective dog nanny.

H. A. Pruitt

H. A. Pruitt is the Christian fantasy author of Anelthalien who lives with a rowdy herd of guinea pigs and her sarcastic husband. H. A. Pruitt never intended to be an author, but God started giving her the story of Anelthalien, and now her mission in all she does and writes is to listen to, obey, and glorify God.

To learn more about H. A. Pruitt and Anelthalien:
Website: www.hapruitt.com
Instagram: @hapruitt
YouTube channel: HAPruitt Anelthalien
Facebook page: Anelthalien HAPruitt
Goodreads: HAPruitt or Anelthalien

Hannah Carter

Hannah Carter is just a girl who wakes up every day hoping it will be the day she discovers she's secretly a mermaid. Her work has been included in several anthologies: *Whispers From Before, The Depths We'll Go To,* and Havok's *Prismatic.* Her short story, "Lara," won a competition, and she has two published novellas, *Amir and the Moon* and *Seashells.* In addition to fiction, she also has had over a dozen devotionals published in various magazines, as well as three devotions published in *Finding God in Anime.* Connect with Hannah through social media at @introvertedmermaid3!

You can connect with Hannah using her Linktree:

https://linktr.ee/theintrovertedmermaid3

Jessica Smith

Jessica Christine Smith is a writer of YA epic Christian fantasy and Bible study devotionals. She is working toward publishing her Christian fantasy Evergreen and the Silver Tree, the first in a series, and her devotional for women called Instruments of Hope: God's Mercy Bestowed to Women of Faith. When she isn't traveling to other realms through writing her stories, she's either scrapbooking, singing with her church family, equipping others for the work of ministry as the Bible Study Administrator at First Baptist Fort Smith, performing at Fort Smith Little Theatre, or sharing pieces of her journey through blogs and poetry at www.christinessmithereens.wordpress.com.

Follow her on Instagram: @author.jcsmithereens

Subscribe to her YouTube channel: youtube.com/JessicaChristine0875

Follow her page on Facebook: Author Jessica Christine Smith

Jessika Grewe Glover

Growing up in Miami, Jessika always dreamed of fantastical places and started writing to escape. She is a University of Miami graduate with a degree in both English: Creative Writing and International Studies: Intelligence and Foreign Policy, though has yet to use her degree. She is the author of the Another Beast's Skin adult fantasy series.

Currently, she works as a personal trainer in the Los Angeles area, having Saturday night singalongs with her husband, two kids, and the world's fastest bulldog. In her free time she make dragons out of chocolate.

Joanna White

Joanna White is a Christian Author and fangirl. Hunter and Shifter are the first two books in her debut series, called the Valiant Series. In December 2019, one of her short stories was featured in Once Upon A Yuletide. Dark Magi, a prequel in the Republic Chronicles came out in November 2019. Glimpses of Time and Magic, also featured one of her stories. She graduated from Full Sail University with a BFA in Creative Writing for Entertainment. Ever since she was ten years old, she's been writing stories and has a deep passion for writing and creating stories, worlds, characters, and plots that readers can immerse themselves in. In 2020, she reached her personal goal of writing a million words in a year. Most of all, Joanna loves God, her family, staying at home, and being a total nerd.

Visit her website at: authorjoannawhite.com.
Facebook Page: https://www.facebook.com/authorjoannawhite
Instagram: https://www.instagram.com/authorjoannawhite

Julia Skinner

Julia Skinner is a modern day hobbit with a love for good stories, and chocolate ice cream. Abiding in South Texas with her parents, and six siblings, she spends her days juggling college, writing, family adventures, and random entrepreneurial dreams. She is a sinner saved by Jesus, and she wouldn't be the person she is today without her Savior, Jesus Christ. When Julia isn't typing furiously away on her laptop, she can be found playing video games, reading aloud to her little siblings, riding roller-coasters, convincing people to read Brandon Sanderson's books, and hanging out with her two Miniature Australian Shepherds. Even though she has yet to publish one of her many fantasy novels, her flash fiction has been published in a number of anthologies, including: *Prismatic*, *Aphotic Love*, *The Willow Tree Swing*, and *Fool's Honor*.

Instagram: @litaflameblog

Kaitlyn Emery

Kaitlyn Emery was obsessed with dragons and fantasy at a young age. When she grew up, she learned reality was darker than anything she read in a book. Through writing, she learned to cope with the world around her and find a voice in fiction. Kaitlyn has written short stories for various magazines, Flash Fiction for Havok Publishing, and been published in several anthologies including Rebirth, Sensational, Prismatic, When Your Beauty is the Beast, Moonlight and Claws, and The Depths We'll Go To. You can learn more about her writing and other creative endeavors at her website Kaitlyn-Emery.com

Facebook: Kaitlyn Emery | Facebook
Instagram: @kaitlyn_scribbling

Katie Marie

Katie Marie is a young author located in Arkansas. She has always enjoyed reading and making up stories, and when she was ten she decided she wanted to be a published author. Katie never stopped pursuing her dream, and now, years later, her debut novel, *Saving Zora*, is out for the world to see.

Instagram: @author.katiemarie

Katrina Nappi

My name is Katrina Nappi, and I am a 21 year old aspiring writer. I've been writing since I was 11 years old, and it's always been my dream to publish a book for other people to read. I started by posting fanfics and other stories on Wattpad and now I'm moving up to share my writing with more people!

I love to read and write, fantasy, science fiction, and romance are my favorite genres.

Instagram: @treesboooks

Levi Mitchell

Levi Mitchell is a parttime poet, using words to express things harder said than written, and a full time LOTR fan. Most often you'll find him at the archery range or crafting cosplay armor, 3D models, leather work, or tinkering with any other project that might interest him.

Lorelei Jensen

From a young age, Lorelei R. Jensen has adored books. Reading with a flashlight late into the night wasn't uncommon for her at all. She wrote off and on during elementary school, but it wasn't until she got hold of her first self-published book that she decided she wanted to be an author. Currently, she lives with her parents and younger sister in the hot and dry desert of Arizona.

Instagram: @reading_instead_of_sleeping

Mariella Taylor

Mariella Taylor was raised on fairy lit paths somewhere between the backstreet alleys of Jackson, Mississippi and the jazz infested avenues of New Orleans. She spends her days juggling armfuls of books while trying to reach the top shelves in all the local libraries and spends her nights grumbling at her uncooperative characters. Her writing can be found in Twisted Grimms: Fairy Tales Retold, Whispers From Before: Tales of Myth and Legend, Aphotic Love, Fool's Honor, and other collections

Instagram: https://www.instagram.com/mariellataylor-author/ Facebook: https://www.facebook.com/profile.php?id=100069398805415 Goodreads: https://www.goodreads.com/user/show/136400154-mariella-taylor
Pinterest: https://www.pinterest.com/thefoldedworld/_saved/
Email: thefoldedworld@gmail.com

Moriah Jestus

Moriah Jestus is an 18 year-old writer from Oklahoma. Writing has been a passion of hers since it was introduced to her through her classical education and anything with literature or writing were her favorite subjects. Her other interests include reading, painting, anything artistic, and musical theatre. She hopes to one day be a set designer for theatre and continue writing for any other opportunities that may arise.

Instagram- @mjestus
Facebook- @Moriah Jestus

Nathaniel Luscombe

Nathaniel Luscombe is an author and publisher from Ontario, Canada. He's known for his existential writing, mash-ups of speculative genres, and making everything cozy (even horror). He is known for *Moon Soul, Human Scars on Planet Skin,* and *When One World Ends, Another Begins.* When he's not writing, he's busy co-running Dragon Bone Publishing and Dragon Heart Press.

Instagram: @nathaniel.luscombe

Nobel Shut Chan

My name is Nobel and I'm currently a junior at Boston University, studying English and Deaf Studies. Hailing from Hong Kong, I love reading, writing, and musical theatre. My work has been published in Burn, The Beacon, and Applause magazine. I hope to continue writing poetry and short stories in the future.

You can find some samples of my work at https://nobel-chan203.wixsite.com/nobel-chan

Piper L. White

Piper L. White is a self published author of two novels titled Flicker and Flare. Her work has been featured in Atlantis magazine, Grimsy lit mag, Roadrunner Review, Press Pause Press and Girls Right The World.

Her work can be accessed on her website, piperwhitewrites. com or through her Instagram @piperlwhite

Sarah Elliott

Sarah Elliott lives near Indianapolis Indiana, she has been writing as a pass time since her Eragon fanfic at age 11. She has won National Novel Writing Month seven times(though is still editing those works!), and spends most of her free time creating art, reading and writing, cooking and thrift store shopping. Sarah loves pinà coladas and getting caught in rain. You will most likely find her at the midnight showing of the next Marvel movie.

Instagram: @sarah_sponda_anne

Savannah Jezowski

Savannah Jezowski lives in a drafty farmhouse in southern Michigan with her Knight in Shining Armor and two wee warrior princesses. She studied Commercial Writing/English in college and eventually founded Dragonpen Press, a small publishing house that offers author services such as cover design, developmental edits, and interior formatting. Savannah specializes in fantasy and Christian fiction with colorful and dimensional characters and likes to deal with emotional themes. She is also featured in many different anthologies such as Five Enchanted Roses, A Kind of Death and What Darkness Fears. When she isn't writing, Savannah likes to read books, watch BBC miniseries and play with cover designs. She also enjoys having tea with her imaginary friends.

Instagram handle: @savannahjezowskiauthor

Sera Amoroso

Sera Amoroso discovered her love for writing at a young age. Inspired by books like Ender's Game and Eragon, as well as authors such as J.R.R. Tolkien and Eoin Colfer, she decided to write her own books. She published her debut novel Torsion in May of 2021, right before her birthday. Now, Sera writes sci-fi and fantasy books while pursuing a degree in Applied Linguistics.

Instagram: @seraamoroso

Zimri A.Z. Zoran

Zimri A.Z. Zoran. Tea Drinker. Cat Collector. Introvert bordering on absolute hermitude. When he's not partaking in the standard authorial clichés, he's drowning his stories in sarcastic satire and metaphor with a healthy serving of adventure and sometimes a dash of romance. Or simply drowning in anime and video games. Still a mysterious stranger to the world of published work, he's currently scheming his inevitable conquest. You can keep up with his world domination and his animal minions on Facebook or at @zimriazz on Instagram and Twitter.

Instagram: https://www.instagram.com/zimriazz/
Twitter: https://twitter.com/zimriazz
Facebook: https://www.facebook.com/Zimri-A-Z-Zoran-169658293954123
YouTube: https://www.youtube.com/channel/UCv3eTG-GUV7OSKo2uZ4tS6Dw

Continue the Experimental Exploration of Love Through Aphotic Love's Sister Anthology,

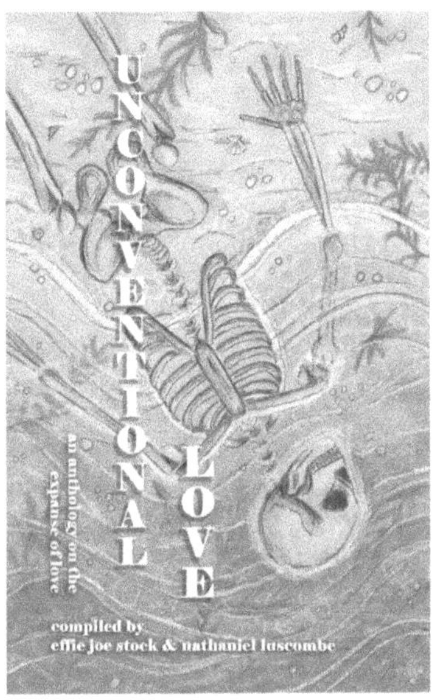

UNCONVENTIONAL LOVE

An Anthology on the Expanse of Love

Familial. Romantic. Platonic.

Love is but one word struggling to encompass a wide variety of emotions, connections, relationships. This anthology seeks to sail the vastness of love's expanse and discover all the many ways humans love and are loved.

From loving your partner as a worm, to a love letter from a daughter to mother, to faun and mergirl lovers separated by culture, to a telepathic friendship nearly cast away, Unconventional Love is a collection like no other, bringing together hearts and emotions scattered across a universe so vast and an even greater love.

9 781962 337205